PRAISE FOR *THE SWEET TRADE*

"Garrett vividly re-creates the eighteenth-century outlaw world of Nassau and the high seas. This is a colorful, true-life novel about fighting, love, death, and, above all else, friendship."   —*Booklist*

"An absorbing blend of action, historical events and emotional drama."   —*Publishers Weekly*

"Prepare to be boarded and held captive by this fascinating and meticulously researched look at life among those favorite anti-establishment rogues of literature and film, the pirates. This novel offers the unglamorized ring of truth along with the ring of steel as it explores issues of courage and freedom and the intriguing psychological terrain of those rare but persistent women in history who risked their lives by choosing to live a lie as men at arms rather than accept the strictures forced on conventional women of their times."

> —Carole Nelson Douglas, bestselling author of *Fair Wind, Fiery Star* and the Midnight Louie mystery series

"I loved the book. It is most surely a non-put-down read. . . . With a sure narrative touch and impressive insight into the conflicts and passions of the early eighteenth century, this newest chronicler of seafaring women breathes life, warmth, and veracity into this story of the two most famous female buccaneers."

> —Joan Druett, author of *She Captains: Heroines and Hellions of the Sea*

"If you love pirate stories, as I do, you'll love this. An exciting era vividly recreated."

> —Fred Mustard Stewart, bestselling author of *Ellis Island* and *The Magnificent Savages*

The Sweet Trade

Elizabeth Garrett

TOR®

A TOM DOHERTY ASSOCIATES BOOK
NEW YORK

This is a work of fiction. All the characters and events portrayed in this book are either products of the author's imagination or are used fictitiously.

THE SWEET TRADE

A Tor Book
Published by Tom Doherty Associates, LLC
175 Fifth Avenue
New York, NY 10010

www.tor.com

Tor® is a registered trademark of Tom Doherty Associates, LLC.

ISBN: 0-812-57851-1
Library of Congress Catalog Card Number: 00-048450

First edition: April 2001
First mass market edition: April 2002

Printed in the United States of America

0 9 8 7 6 5 4 3 2 1

To L. M. N.
The pirate who first told me about Anne and Mary
and then plundered my heart

Acknowledgments

Thanks go out to so many for their help in this project. Thanks to Dirk Bes for the Dutch and Veronica Hanna for the Spanish. Any linguistic mistakes are entirely my own. Dolores Carbanneau gave invaluable assistance with birthing, both real and fictional. Thanks to Ken Kinkor, pirate scholar, for answering my questions and to my early readers, Lola Furber, Melissa Sparks, and Elizabeth Page.

My deepest appreciation goes out to Nat Sobel for his efforts on behalf of this book, and to Stephanie Lane at Forge for believing in Anne, Mary, and Jack.

Prologue

THE BELLS RANG OUT FROM THE WHITEWASHED TOWERS of St. Jago de la Vega on Jamaica's north shore. Their deep bass tone filled the narrow cobbled streets, the cool, stucco homes, glanced off the red-tiled roofs of the government buildings, so like those of Old Spain on which they were modeled. Pealing, pealing . . . *Today the court sits in session. Today is a trial of pirates. Today will be tales of the sweet trade, of murders and crimes most notorious, villainy on the high seas.*

The ringing found its way into Mary Read's cell, where she sat on the stone bench—an outcropping of the cell wall, really—and traced with her eyes the lines of dark mold that snaked along the mortared crevices between whitewashed bricks.

A pretty sound, she thought. She had been hearing the bells for five minutes, but she was just now listening. *Pretty, for a death knell.*

A shaft of morning light came in through the single window, divided into five equal parts by the iron bars. The light looked like a solid thing as it passed through the ubiquitous dust, as if Mary could reach out and break off a piece and hold it in her hands.

At least it is warm, she thought, *warm and dry.* There were times enough in her life when she would have gladly traded freedom for a prison cell, if it meant being warm and dry. In fact, she mused, that was just what she had done, and she still reckoned she had ended up with the best of the bargain.

She shifted uncomfortably, looked up at the arched ceiling. It was stone, whitewashed like the rest of the cell, like all the buildings of those Spanish colonial towns. Now that the British were the masters of Jamaica, it was a wonder to Mary that they did not paint everything brown, or some such dreary tone, as the British were wont to do.

But no, the West Indies would not allow that. It affected people, it got inside them, and before the English could remake the West Indies into a drab replica of London, the West Indies had remade them in her own bright image. Mary had seen it happen time and again, to Englishmen on Nassau and Jamaica and Bermuda. It had happened to her, and that was why she loved the West Indies so.

She stood up at last, paced the few steps forward and then back again. Her body still ached from countless bruises, some overlapping one another, purple and ugly. Her skin was hard and tight where a dozen lacerations were just now healing.

She paused, stretched, idly scratched herself. Realized what she was doing and stopped, thinking, *I have been too long in the company of men.*

She was wearing a dress of sorts, no more than a crude homespun wool sack with sleeves. It hung like a monk's rope and itched intolerably, and caught in the sharp places of her half-healed wounds. It was difficult to get any relief from the scratching fabric and the vermin that were starting to plague her.

Mary Read was no stranger to itchy clothes and vermin, but familiarity in this instance did not bring comfort.

The cell, her home for the past few weeks, was not a closed room, with four solid walls and a single, impenetrable door. Rather, the front of it was all bars, floor to ceiling and side to side, an entire wall of bars. It made Mary feel like a circus animal, there on display for the amusement of others, and she hated that.

Anne's cell was directly across the narrow stone alleyway that ran down the length of the cellblock. They had unimpeded communication across that five feet of space, and that alone kept Mary from going mad. Confinement was something new to her, and it did not sit well.

She paced again to the front of the cell, thrust her hands through the bars, rested her forearms on a crosspiece, laced her fingers together. She arched her back, flexed her legs, groaned slightly as she worked out the kinks that came with sleeping on a bed of matted straw. *Not bloody seventeen anymore,* she thought.

Mary looked across the alley into Anne's cell. It was on the west side of the building and did not get the morning sun and was still mostly lost in shadow. Near the back wall, on a straw bed like hers, she could make out the hump of rumpled homespun that was Anne's sleeping figure.

The ringing stopped. Mary looked up, cocked her ear, listened for . . . something. Anything. But there was only silence in the wake of the bells.

Mary looked back into the darkness of Anne's cell. Anyone who did not know Anne would have to believe she was feigning sleep, or was too bitter and despondent to rise. How could anyone actually sleep on such a morning? But Mary knew her friend well, and knew she was genuinely asleep, slumbering untroubled.

Anne Bonny was twenty years old, seven years Mary's junior. She still had the sense of indestructibility that accompanies youth, and she had not a fraction of Mary's experience with violence and death.

For a few minutes Mary watched Anne sleep and involuntarily she smiled and shook her head. Even if Annie lived to see old age—an unlikely prospect—she probably would grow no wiser. Anne was not one for lessons. Her passions burned like a pyre and she was ruled by them, and Mary loved her for that.

"Annie! Annie! Stir yourself!" she called across the alleyway. She saw Anne move a bit, heard her mumble something incoherent. "Come on, Anne! They can't hang you lying down like that, you know."

At the far end of the cell, all but lost in shadow, Mary saw Anne sitting up, heard her spit a bit of straw from her mouth.

"Oh, sod it," she heard Anne mutter. Anne was not given to springing cheerfully from bed, not even in the best of times.

At last she stood up and staggered toward the front of

her cell. Her thick, reddish blond hair was askew, falling in great disorganized piles over her shoulders and hanging half over her face. Bits of straw clung to it, nearly the same color as her wild locks. She paused, arched her back, ran her fingers through her hair, forcing it into some kind of order. "Sod it," she said again.

Mary waited silently while Anne stretched and scratched and came a bit more awake. It was pointless to try and talk to her now.

Finally Anne yawned, wide, like a lion, flashing flawless white teeth. Mary had to marvel again at what a beauty she was, even in those unfavorable conditions. It was no wonder that men had died for her, that more would die before her story was told.

"Mary, dear, did I hear bells?" Anne asked at last.

"You did. They are a signal that a Court of Admiralty will sit today."

"A Court of Admiralty? Whoever is to be tried?"

"Pirates, as I hear it. Notorious cutthroats and piccaroons."

"Detestable people. I wish they would hang them all."

Mary smiled and Anne smiled back. "They may yet, Annie, my dear."

"Indeed. Well, I must now go and express my opinion of all Courts of Admiralty and prosecutors and judges and such," Anne said, and with that she retreated to the back of her cell and made use of the night jar there.

When she was done she returned to the bars that fronted her cell and said, "Do you reckon they will give us a shift of clothes? Or a hairbrush, at all?"

Mary shook her head. "The prosecutor will find it more convenient to prove us pirates and sluts if we look like pirates and sluts. I do not think they will give us leave to look otherwise."

Anne nodded. "Would they but give me back my cutlass and a brace of pistols, I would show them what a pirate and slut I truly am."

At the far end of the alleyway a key rattled in a lock, loud in the still morning. Neither woman made an effort to look. They knew who it was, why they were coming.

Their eyes met and Mary gave Anne a half smile and Anne gave Mary a slight cock of the eyebrows, and then the heavy door at the end of the walk swung open and the footfalls on the stone floor echoed around the cells.

Quite a lot of footfalls. The thickset jailor in his homespun coat, wool stockings over thick calves, worn shoes, battered cocked hat over thinning hair. Beside him the bailiff in the more elegant dress of the court: silk coat and waistcoat down to midthigh, breeches to match, silk stockings, silver buckles on his shoes. A guard of four soldiers trailed behind.

"Look how many they have sent," Anne said. "One would think these men afraid of us, weak and helpless women though we be. Sure we are not a threat to great brutes such as yourselves?"

"Shut yer gob," the jailor growled, though he did not sound as fierce as he might have wished.

For all of Anne's sharp tongue, the jailor and his assistants had treated them well. Mary had all but assumed they would be raped in prison, but in fact they had not been molested at all. It was one reason to be thankful they had been captured by the British, and not the Spaniards.

The fact that they would be hung, and not burned alive, was another.

The jailor opened Mary's cell door first, with the guards arrayed in such a manner that she could not step out as the bailiff stepped in, manacles jangling in his hand.

"This one becomes a sword," Mary said, nodding toward the bailiff. "Do you reckon he knows the use of it?"

"Shut it, you bitch, or by God I'll see you gagged!" The bailiff was not the kind soul that the jailor was.

"It won't answer, Mary, dear, caressing that one," Anne said. "I don't think he likes women. Perhaps if you dressed as a boy again, he'd fancy you more."

The bailiff scowled, flushed red. Mary held out her hands, made no effort to resist. There might be the chance yet for an escape, or a clean death while making the attempt, but this was not it.

The bailiff put the heavy iron shackles around her wrists, slid the bar through them, and fixed the pin in the end that would hold the manacles in place. She let her hands fall across her belly.

"Now you look a right villain," Anne called from behind the bars of her cell. "I should convict you sure, were I on the jury."

"Then I am pleased you will be on the same side of the bar as me," Mary said. The bailiff took her by the arm, half guided and half pushed her out of the cell and up against the wall. Two of the soldiers who made up the guard stepped off, faced her, the stiletto points of their bayonets a foot from her chest.

The other men turned to Anne's cell, opened it and secured her in the same fashion, and then she, too, was moved roughly into the alleyway. Two soldiers ahead of the women, two behind, with the jailor and the bailiff last of all, they marched down the narrow space between cells, like a tiny parade, toward the door at the far end.

It was the first time the women had left their cages in a fortnight, the first time since the long sail around from Negril Point, locked down below aboard Barnet's sloop. Mary could not resist glancing into the other cells as she passed by, but as she suspected, she and Anne were the only residents of that block.

They stepped out the door at the far end and into the big room that Mary recalled from the one other time she had seen it, on the way into the prison block. The rough stones of the prison floor gave way to polished Spanish tile. The walls were a smooth stucco, white, of course, but without the streaks of mold that found their way into the humid cells.

The bailiff and the jailor led them through the big door and into the courtyard around which were clustered the jail and His Majesty's court and sundry government offices.

It had been dark when last they had passed that way, the courtyard ringed with torches. But now it was lit brilliant by the morning sun and Mary had to turn her eyes from the brightest spots, blinking tears from her streaming eyes.

Great irregular pieces of flagstone covered the open ground. The ubiquitous whitewashed buildings made up three sides of the courtyard, and the fourth was a row of columns, connected along their tops. Beyond the columns Mary could see the red roofs and the white homes of St. Jago de la Vega, and a quarter mile beyond that, the sea. A fresh breeze blew unchecked across the open space.

Mary breathed deep, glanced around, took it in the way a woman dying of thirst might gulp water. The sea. It glinted in the sunlight, sharp diamond slivers on the aqua-blue surface, right up to where it made a straight, sharp line on the horizon.

Mary sucked the clean ocean air into her lungs. She lapped it up, swallowed it, devoured as much of the sensation as she could in the time it took their escort to hustle them across the courtyard and through the door at the far end.

And then the ocean was lost from sight and they were in a small room with benches on either side, another door beyond, a soldier posted guard. The bailiff stopped.

A few men lounged on the benches in the bored attitude of government officials, but they sat up, their interest piqued, at the sight of Mary Read and Anne Bonny.

"Take a good look, boys, it's the best you'll get," said Anne, her head up, her eyes fixed forward at some distant point.

The bailiff nodded; the soldier at the door stepped aside, pulled the door open.

Through the door, the courtroom. A big, airy space, the ceiling thirty feet overhead, rows of polished benches like pews in a church. It was crowded with spectators for this event, after a month of mounting anticipation. They filled the benches, stood at the back of the room and along the walls. The Members of the Council off to the one side, a long table with a row of clerks, already scribbling with their quills. And over it all the judge's bench rose like a cliff.

Their little parade stepped out, down between the row of benches, and Mary could not help but think how like a wedding it was. Past the gawking faces, she and Anne kept their heads back, eyes forward, looking at a spot just above the judge's bench.

They have taken everything, Mary thought. *Everything but our lives, and soon they will have those too, but they cannot take our dignity if we do not yield it.*

To her left, standing in chains, were her former shipmates, the pirate band, the hapless sea robbers taken down at Negril Point. They were pushed off to one side, waiting for their chance to be set at the bar, to plead guilty or not, as if it would make a difference.

The men were not center stage. Mary knew that that spot was reserved for her and Anne, because they were the chief attraction that morning. Mere pirates were commonplace, but female pirates were something else altogether. The prosecutor knew his business, knew how a spectacle should be staged.

Anne was led to a place just left of center of the judge's bench, Mary right beside her. Their hair was wild, their hands manacled, and they were clothed in prison garb. It seemed impossible that any juror could look on them and think them innocent.

Mary glanced to her left, quick, looking for Jacob, not letting her eyes linger. She did not want anyone to notice the particular interest she took in that one individual. But in any event he was not there.

"All rise!" the bailiff's voice rang out. The great mass of sound that rose from the muttered conversations of the hundreds of spectators dropped off, and in its place came the sound of the people getting to their feet.

"This Wednesday, November the sixteenth, year of our Lord 1720, a Court of Admiralty to be held before His Excellency Sir Nicholas Lawes, His Majesty's Captain General and Governor in Chief in and over His Majesty's Island of Jamaica and other territories thereon depending in America, Chancellor and Vice Admiral of the same, President!"

A soldier opened the door off to the side of the judge's bench and Sir Nicholas, the bearer of those weighty titles, stepped out. His black robe hung down to his feet; his massive wig stood out against it in sharp relief. He did not look up, did not acknowledge the presence of the vast audience as he stepped up to his bench.

He sat, arranged some papers before him, scowled down at them, left the rest of the courtroom standing. Finally he looked up, and still scowling, he said, "You may be seated."

Mary studied the judge's face, trying to read in his visage what kind of man he was. Pink, jowly, heavyset, British to the core, he would not be seduced by the easy ways of the Caribbean. Neither did he look to be a man of great sympathy.

The buzz of the spectators grew again, like an approaching swarm, and Sir Nicholas said, "Bailiff, you will order silence."

"The court will be silent!" the bailiff cried, and dutifully the noise fell away.

"Let us proceed with the reading of the King's Commission," said Lawes. He nodded to the secretary, who stood, a great sheet of paper in his hand, cleared his throat, and began.

"George, by the grace of God, of Great Britain, France, and Ireland, King, defender of the faith, et cetera. To our truly and well-beloved Sir Nicholas Lawes, Knight, our Captain General and Governor in Chief in and over . . ." The secretary's voice settled into an easy monotone, no more intrusive or interesting than the hum of the spectators whom the bailiff had silenced, as steady and mesmerizing as the surf lapping the beach.

The words moved in and out of Mary's ears, swirled without meaning around her head. On and on the secretary droned, five minutes, ten minutes; she was ready to plead guilty just to shut him up.

"Sweet Jesus!" Mary heard the voice of George Fetherston. She glanced sideways at the big man standing in irons with his fellows. "Hang us if you will, but don't bloody bore us to death!"

Sir Nicholas scowled, slammed his gavel down, demanding order. It was the only sound in the vast chamber. No one had dared laugh.

Mary wanted to, she wanted to laugh out loud, but she did not even smile. She had learned long ago how to keep emotion from her face.

"Silence!" Lawes ordered. "One more word from the prisoners and you all shall be gagged!"

The pirates fell silent. The secretary continued on.

Mary's eyes wandered to the seven Members of the Council who sat as jury in the Court of Admiralty—some tanned, some pink faced—wealthy Englishmen all, with their long white wigs draped over rich silk coats, ample midriffs.

She heard the secretary read, ". . . to call and assemble any other persons on shipboard or upon the land, to make up the number seven. And it is thereby also provided that no persons, but such are known as merchants, factors, or planters, or such as were captains, lieutenants, or warrant officers in any of His said late Majesty's ships of war, or captains, masters, or mates of some English ship, should be capable of being so called . . ."

Bloody marvelous. None could be called to sit in judgment save for merchants, planters, naval officers, officers of merchant vessels—just the men to have no compassion for the men (or women) of the sweet trade, just the ones who would have suffered the most by the depredations of the pirates.

No, she thought, *"suffer" is not the word.*

They might lose ships to the pirates, they might be plundered of a cargo or two, lose some slaves, and come out the poorer for their investment, but they did not suffer. She did not think these men sitting as Members of the Council knew what it was to suffer, and she wished she could teach them, as she herself had been taught.

At last the secretary stopped and set the King's prolix Commission down on the table. Sir Nicholas publicly opened the court, took the oath that the act had directed him to take, then administered it to the Commissioners.

It was all so formal, all so silly. *Just bloody hang us, you'll do it in the end in any event.*

When the oaths were done the prisoners were ordered set at the bar. Rough hands grabbed Mary's arm, pushed her forward, right up against the low wooden rail, Anne at her side. Off to their left, the men were brought forward as well.

The Register now stood, ready to read the articles brought against the prisoners, but President of the Court Sir Nicholas held up his hand.

"Hold a moment, Mr. Norris," he growled. "Mr. Nedham." He turned to the Chief Justice, who looked up in a great wave of white wig. "It is your intention to try for any piracies, felonies, or robberies committed upon the sea—" he looked at one of the papers, as if he could not recall the name "—one John Rackam, et al, late of New Providence?"

"Yes, Sir Nicholas," said William Nedham.

Sir Nicholas looked up from his papers, still scowling, swept the court with his eyes, as if just now noticing it.

"Do you intend to try these—" he nodded toward Anne and Mary but did not look at them "—these women along with the others?"

"Yes, Your Excellency."

"No, no, this won't answer. These women stand accused of adultery and fornication along with piracy. Do you mean to charge the men with adultery and fornication?"

That brought a laugh to the courtroom, and when it died the prosecutor said, "No, Your Excellency."

"Very well, then, we shall proceed with the charges against Rackam and the others, and them we shall try separate. Bailiff, you may return them to their cell."

So that is it, Mary thought, *so ends our day in court, after waiting for better than a month.*

She could hear the guards assembling to march them back and she took that last chance to glance around once more. She cocked her head, looked to her left, where the others were standing in their chains.

In the center of the group, and two steps in front, Captain John Rackam. Calico Jack.

God, but he looks a pathetic sight.

His coat and breeches were filthy and torn, and his stockings hung baggy around his shins. His enviable hair, long, brown, and curly, was matted and tangled. His face was dirty, his long mustache twisted, a week's growth of beard on his cheeks. He seemed physically smaller, as if he had collapsed into himself.

His fine bright clothing, once the mark of the flamboyant buccaneer—the calico of Calico Jack—now seemed to mock him.

He glanced over, as if sensing that he was being watched. Anne kept her eyes straight ahead, would not look at him. But Mary caught his eye and they looked at one another for a second—less than a second—and then Jack quickly looked away.

Mary Read, Anne Bonny, and Calico Jack Rackam.

How many coincidences and accidents needed occur, that we three should find ourselves in this place? Mary wondered. *How very odd that our three lives should this way intersect.*

She heard the bailiff step up behind them and mutter a gruff order for them to follow.

But it was not an accident at all, that their three lives should come together as they had. Mary understood that. There was no other way that it could have turned out.

They had been born to it. It was their fate.

BOOK I

FATE INEXORABLE

Chapter 1

FATE HAD INTERCEDED TWO YEARS BEFORE, IN CHARLES Town, in the colony of South Carolina.

Then, a young couple stood before a minister. They held hands. The church was cool and dark in the autumn evening, lit with a half dozen candles that illuminated only the altar area, leaving the rest in deep shadow.

The girl was jubilant, charged, her heart pumping with the recklessness of their act. The young man was sullen, bitter, silently cursing the unfairness of it all.

"If there be any here know why this couple should not be joined in holy matrimony, let them speak now or forever hold their piece . . ."

There were only three people in the church, besides the couple. Just the minister and his wife and a servant to act as witness.

God, but she wished her father were there! How he would have been provoked by this. Big Bill Cormac, trying to bend his daughter to his will. Her life had been filled with petty defiances, minor assertions of independence. Each time her father pushed her down, she came back, stronger, more eager to be free.

And now this.

William Cormac, Esquire, would have come up with some reasons why they should not be joined, all right, couched in his lawyer's language, edged with a father's anger. But he was not there, and no one else spoke.

"Do you, Anne Cormac, take this man to be your lawfully wedded husband, to have and to hold, for richer, for poorer . . ."

Poorer indeed, she thought.

Anne Cormac had known only wealth, at least from the

time she was old enough to recall. Now she was eighteen years old, beautiful, her body taut and voluptuous, her hair thick, cascading down her back, reddish in winter, yellow in the summer. Her face might have been that of an angel, but for the look in her blue eyes, that flash of something deeper than mere mischief.

Anne Cormac could have married any of the bright and wealthy young men in the colony, fellows that had one thousand pounds a year and kept coaches and had been sent to England for their schooling. They came around like dogs to a bitch in heat. Over them all she had chosen this penniless sailor, and her father was not well pleased.

". . . in sickness and in health . . ."

It had been no small task, convincing the minister to perform the ceremony.

The minister knew her, knew Billy Cormac. He did not wish to get in the middle, to stand at the point where the irresistible force meets the immovable object. He had only agreed when Anne told him that she was with child, that she wished for the baby to be legitimate, not a bastard like herself, the result of her father's liaison with the lovely and willing young Peg Brennan.

Fiery, lusty Peg had been the family's maid in Cork. The scandal had ruined William's law practice. He had fled to the New World with his illegitimate family. Passed Peg off as his wife, mistress of their home. He loved Anne and spoiled her as much as any father ever had a daughter.

". . . until death do you part?"

So the minister had agreed to marry them, for the sake of the unborn child, who did not exist. The sailor had not enjoyed Anne's favors, not to that degree.

Not because of Anne's sense of chastity—she had her mother's inclinations in that regard, and they were none too strict—but because she knew men and she knew that there was little chance she would get what she wanted once her man's desire had been sated.

At thirteen years of age she had come to understand the powerful force of lust, predictable as the tide and just as unstoppable. She learned to work a man's desire the way some could handle a horse, or work rudder and sails to move ships.

Hard lessons, but others paid for them more dearly than she.

The first was a brash young buck from the outlying plantations, a young man she had taken as suitor when she was fifteen years old.

Evenings they would walk together in her father's well-tended garden and indulge their soft, murmured talk of love. She yielded to his tight embrace, let him kiss her deep, standing in the orchard under a full moon. Her thigh pressed against his cock, throbbing under his breeches. She allowed his hand to grope her breast for a few beats before she pushed it away. She loved the wickedness of it all.

Then one night, panting and groping, hot breath on cool skin, sighs deep in their throats, she said, "No . . ." but he was far beyond listening to "no." Hands on her breasts, pulling her bodice down, hands under her shift, reaching up, fingers looking to violate her.

Anne Cormac was not afraid. She was not sorry or repentant or guilt ridden. Her mind was wiped clean by a red-hot rage. She had been angry before, but now as the boy's big hands tugged at her petticoats, his tongue forced its way down her throat, she was swept up in a violent passion she had not even known was in her.

She thrust a knee straight up into his groin and he gasped, bent over, tried to curse her. She raked his face with her nails, leaving four bright red gleaming lines across his cheek.

Knee up into his face and he was down and she was kicking him in the groin, over and over, and he could do nothing but lie there and hold his hands over his crotch. And when she was done with that she leapt on him and pounded on his head and slashed at him with fingernails, screaming like a banshee, like one of the legendary spirits of her native Ireland.

She felt big hands on her shoulders, then more on her arms, and her father and one of the servants lifted her off the boy, and as they pulled her away all she could do was kick and claw at the moaning figure in hopes of wounding him one last time.

Anne learned a great deal that night, about herself, about her power over others, and about her own potential. She was amazed and frightened and intrigued, all at once, by this demon she had discovered within her.

The young man who footed the bill for that lesson spent the next two weeks recovering in bed.

"I do," she said.

Her rage was legendary. In Charles Town it was taken as fact that she had slashed a servant girl with a clasp knife, and there was no point in her denying it, though it wasn't true. The little bitch had been too fast, had leapt back from Anne's attack, fled out the door and away before Anne could plunge the blade into her.

At least Anne had managed to cure the girl of her habit of stealing perfume.

"And do you, James Bonny, take this woman to be your lawfully wedded wife, to have and to hold, for richer, for poorer, in sickness and in health, till death do you part?"

Anne watched her bridegroom as he listened to the words. His face was in profile and she noticed for the first time how weak his chin looked, as if he had no chin at all. Why hadn't she noticed that? There was stubble in patches where whiskers grew between weekly shaves, but it was clear from the pattern that James Bonny would never grow a real beard. His Adam's apple bobbed up and down in his long neck. His hand was clammy and wet in hers.

He was dressed in a sailor's blue jacket, loose trousers, wool stockings, battered shoes. The clothes were old, patched, tar stained, but of his two suits, this was the better.

"I do," he muttered, as if he did not really wish to, but was too afraid to decline.

"Then I pronounce you man and wife." The minister did not sound any more pleased about it than did James Bonny. "You may kiss the bride."

James Bonny turned to her and they faced one another, eye to eye. James was less than half an inch taller than

Anne. He kissed her, with the same grudging cooperation
with which he had married her.

Anne kissed him back, put her arms around him,
squeezed him tight. He was thin, girlishly thin, and though
he was strong and agile in the way of topmast sailors, he
was limp now and unresponsive. But Anne did not care.
She was delirious with joy, with excitement.

She was married, and she was free.

Her father had kicked her out of the house for her in-
sisting that she would marry the broke and homeless sailor
James Bonny. And now, because of that, William Cormac
had no hold on her at all.

She was Anne Bonny now, and the entire world was
opened up to her.

And at her side, a man who had sailed half the oceans
of the world, a man who was not tied down to a grand
family and a plantation in South Carolina, but someone
unfettered, ready to wander with her, wherever their ad-
venturous spirits might lead.

Anne liked James Bonny, seaman. But she was deeply
in love with the idea of him: a young sailor, a footloose
and wild companion, one who had roamed the world before
her and would take her along now.

They thanked the minister, took their certificate from his
wife, then turned and walked from the light of the altar
through the shadows of the church and out the big front
door. They stepped down the granite steps to the street.
Anne held James's arm, squeezed it in her excitement, but
it elicited no response from her husband.

The cobbled street was lined on either side by the brick
homes of the Charles Town elite. It was dark, and a cool,
wet breeze wafted in off the ocean. There was a rustle of
something, a door closed, a burst of laughter from far off.
They took a few steps down the street, then stopped. They
had nowhere to go.

"Anne, it ain't right, a girl and her father, fighting like
that . . ." James turned to Anne. "Now that we done it . . .
got married, I mean, don't you reckon the thing for it is to

go back and tell your father you're sorry and ask won't he bless our union?"

"James, James, my beloved James! We are free now, don't you see that? The whole world is out there for us to conquer!" But James Bonny, who, at twenty-two years of age, had been free with the whole world before him and not a groat in his pocket for the past eleven years, was not swept away with the romance of the thing. He turned and spit on the street.

"Anne, you are a silly girl, a goddamned silly girl. You don't have a buggering notion what you're about."

Anne felt the anger flash in her head, but she was silent and let it pass. Then she stepped closer to James, put her arms around his neck, pressed her body against his, rubbed against him just a bit, and whispered, "I've enough money for a room, at least, for a couple of nights. It's time you had what you've been wanting for so long, my darling husband."

"What dross have you?"

"I have some money, don't you worry about it." Anne had seen this moment coming and had stolen a decent dowry from her father's desk. William Cormac owed her that much at least, even if he did not believe it. "Now come along, my darling."

But James Bonny was not distracted from his unhappiness. Raw desire did not sweep away every other consideration, as Anne had thought it would, as it always had with every other man, and she did not find that a hopeful sign.

He scoffed, a soft sound in his throat. "And then what, Anne? Then what? Once it's gone I'll need to find a ship and leave you behind, and you without enough money to set up housekeeping. No place even for you to live." James Bonny had thought to ease his burden in life by making a good marriage, but instead he had doubled it.

Anne pressed her hands flat against his chest, pushed away until she was looking in his eyes. She had been thinking about this moment for some time, this point when her dock lines were slipped, when she was floating free. Staying in Charles Town to "set up housekeeping" was not an option she had ever entertained.

Her mother had died seven years before, and from that point until now she had run her father's house. She was done with housekeeping.

"James . . . I won't have you run off alone. I love you, I can't be parted from you. We must go together."

"Together?" James shook his head, incredulous at his new bride's foolishness and naïveté. "Anne, you ain't thought this through. Where are we going to go together?"

"Nassau," she said without a pause, because in fact she had thought it through, had thought it through quite thoroughly.

"Nassau? Nassau's a wicked place. Ain't a thing to be found but pirates and whores and all manner of villains in Nassau."

"I know," said Anne. She felt herself shiver. The thought of such wickedness thrilled her, right down to the core of her being.

Chapter 2

FLANDERS. THE SUMMER CAMPAIGNING SEASON OF THE Grand Alliance. A full nine years before Mary Read would stand at the bar in St. Jago de la Vega in Jamaica and half a world away. The year, 1711. Mary's eighteenth.

She stood at the top of a small rise, on an evening like so many before, one hand on her horse's neck, the other on her hip, looking out through the mist and fine rain at the small town of Rijsbergen.

She was a horse trooper, a corporal in a light cavalry unit. She was not Mary Read then, of course. Mary Read was someone locked away deep in her memories, a fragile doll to be pulled out and examined once in a while, a thing for her to marvel at, and then put away, unseen.

Rather, she was Michael Read, Corporal Michael Read, of the second platoon of E Company of Walpole's Regiment of Light Cavalry. A young man making a military career, fighting for his country, and no one knew or suspected anything different.

Walpole's was one of those elite squads formed in England by some well-heeled gentleman with a thought toward soldiering and money enough for a commission and for equipping his recruits. Once formed, the regiment of light horse had been sent to the killing fields of Flanders to do battle with the French and stop the alliance of the Bourbon household in Spain.

Mary gazed at the rooftops and spires of the little Flemish hamlet. Cobbled streets, invisible from her hilltop, cut fissures through blocks of buildings where they ran between them. Columns of smoke rose from a hundred comforting fires, lifting above roofs of thatch and slate and split shingle. Just the sight of a roof like that filled Mary with longing.

There was a warm, comforting quality to Rijsbergen, like all of those small fairy-tale places in Flanders. She yearned to get on her horse and ride down there, to sit by one of those fires, smell the bread baking in the big brick oven. Pull her long boots off and prop her feet up before the flames.

It was June, but a cold, steady drizzle had been falling all day, transforming the dry ground into an ugly mire of mud. The rain, thankfully, had not been energetic enough to work its way through Mary's heavy tow shirt and forage cap, and her thigh boots, since she had repaired them, were leaking only the smallest bit. She was still nearly dry underneath her clothing, and that was something to be thankful for.

She patted her horse on the neck and checked Frederick's over one last time.

All of the mounts for Walpole's Regiment of Light Cavalry were staked out on that rise, a place where the grass had not yet been decimated by all the horses that moved with the army. Cavalry mounts and dragoon mounts, the great draft animals used by the artillery companies to drag their three-ton field cannon, the horses of the munitions train and the baggage train and sutlers, the number of animals attached to the army was staggering.

And this, this force encamped near the town of Rijsbergen, Flanders, was but a small part of the Army of the Grand Alliance, a sliver, so small that it was no longer even a part of the real fight, the great history-making engagements in the War of the Spanish Succession.

She turned to go. At the bottom of the rise, between herself and the town, was the encampment, tent after tent in perfect lines, standing like gray soldiers on parade. In the fading light Mary could not see the clothing hung out here and there, the discarded refuse, the broken equipment piled up between tents, the detritus of an army that has been long in one place. In the blue-gray misty evening it all looked neat and orderly.

In the middle of that field of tents stood the general's pavilion, a tall, round canvas affair, which rose above the others. Already there were torches burning around the perimeter, illuminating the ground over which one would have to cross to get to the officers. There was a fire inside as well, lighting the pavilion up with an internal glow.

Corporal Read had been in that pavilion once, briefly, receiving a personal congratulations from the general. She had committed a foolhardy act during a surprise raid on the French camp, but it happened to all come out in her favor, with the result being a dozen more dead Frenchmen than there might have otherwise been, and so Walpole himself had asked the general to single her out for special notice. She had received the general's kind words with pleasure, and a guinea as well, which was always welcome.

But more to the point, Frederick was unharmed, whereas if she had not charged in when she had, he would certainly have been dead.

The pavilion seemed like something from a storybook: the polished walnut table and writing desk and sideboard, the four-poster bed draped with rich velvet awnings, the plentiful fresh food, the silver service glinting in the lantern light, the array of wine bottles, the paintings hung on the poles supporting the canvas walls. It surpassed even the captain's great cabin in the sixty-four-gun ship of the line aboard which she had once served.

She had stood in the pavilion at parade rest, saying, "Thank you, sir, thank you, sir," to whatever nonsense the general was saying, and taking in as much of the place as she could. It was more luxury than any of her fellow troopers would ever know. For the general, it represented the arduous deprivations of field campaigning.

Now she shook her head at the thought of it, headed down the gentle slope, across the thick, wet grass. Sometimes she saw the world as a pyramid. At the top was Queen Anne, all alone. Below her, a row of a few nobles, then, holding up those few nobles, the more minor aristocrats and then the generals and the rich merchants and the country squires.

And at the bottom, part of the wide, wide base that supported the whole structure, that held it aloft so that Queen Anne might perch on its summit, Corporal Mary Read and all of her hundreds of thousands of fellows.

Near the edge of the encampment, the firm grass yielded to muddy tracks where men and horses had torn the ground up with a month of heavy traffic. As late as next summer, Mary knew, the scars of their stay would still be visible on the field: the muddy trails between the rows of tents, the deep gouges where the latrines had been dug, the rows of graves and wooden markers where they had buried men who had died of camp fever or bloody flux or festering wounds or the surgeons' botched ministrations.

She saw her own tent at the end of the row, and the sight of it lifted her spirits a bit. She had rigged up a fly over the front so that she and Frederick might have a dry patch just outside their little canvas home. She could see that her tentmate had built a fire already and it was blazing, warm and bright.

The mud tugged at her thigh boots as she walked and it made the going tiresome. Frederick was sitting on a low

stool beside the fire, studiously cleaning his own boots.
Like her, and most of the regiment of light cavalry, he was
dressed in his camp clothes, a heavy tow-cloth shirt and
forage cap and trousers. He did not hear her approach.

She ducked under the fly, stooping slightly to keep her
head from bumping the canvas. It felt good, this shelter
from the light rain. The warmth from the fire encircled her.

"Just like home, Frederick," she said.

He looked up, smiled, his teeth white, his face, his lovely
face, pleased and disingenuous. Boyish. His hair was a
thick, dark mop, most of it contained by a black ribbon,
tied back in a long queue. "Ah, Michael, there you are. I
did not hear you approach."

"A good thing I was not coming to cut your throat."

"Now, who would wish such a thing?"

"Who indeed?"

Who indeed? No one. No one save the enemy would
wish to hurt Frederick. Frederick Heesch was as kind and
unassuming a young man as one might hope to find anywhere, a great anomaly in the rude world of the army.

He was Flemish. Like so many of his countrymen, he
chose to fight with the English army, which promised more
action than the forces of his native land. His heart and spirit
were set on warfare, and he was eager for combat. But he
was a thoughtful person, good-natured, with a ready wit.
Mary did not think he possessed the soul of a warrior.

His fellow soldiers liked him, after the fashion of a silly
younger brother. Mary Read loved him, deeply, profoundly.

Mary pulled her pipe from her haversack, stuffed it with
tobacco, and lit it with the burning end of a stick from the
fire. She puffed the embers into life. "You must be more
careful in placing the blanket under your saddle," she said
to Frederick. "Your horse has developed a welt, where the
saddle is chafing. If it hurts him too much, he will get
skittish."

Frederick looked up from his boot polishing. "There is
a welt now? What should I do about it?"

"Poultice."

Frederick nodded. "I am not familiar with that. Will you help me make one up?"

Mary puffed her pipe. "Already have. I put it on him this afternoon. But you'll need to give it a care, especially in this rain."

Frederick smiled. It warmed Mary more than the fire, more than a dozen fires might. There was little she would not do to elicit that smile.

"I would be lost without you," he said.

Mary smiled back at him. "You would be dead without me."

"Many times over. Thank you, Michael."

Mary nodded and drew on her pipe.

Michael. To Frederick Heesch she was Michael Read. He did not know the truth, no one did, and if they had, she would have been tossed out of the regiment within the hour.

Regardless of all the notable actions, the duty above and beyond the call, all the dead Frenchmen she had left in her wake, it would be, at best, her sword broken over the captain's knee, the red coat stripped from her back, and an escort to the edge of the camp.

At the worst, they would hang her.

Not that she felt in any danger of discovery. She had played the man long enough that that fear no longer nagged at her. Her body was not so feminine that the bulky clothes of the soldier would not hide her womanhood.

Her voice was naturally deep for a woman, average for a young man. And more to the point, she knew how to speak a man's language, could joke and curse and sing coarse songs like the seasoned trooper she was.

No, discovery did not worry Mary Read. It was a possibility she had lived with most of her life. But as long as Frederick did not know the truth of her sex, then she could never be more to him than tentmate, comrade at arms, protector.

From him, she hoped for more.

Frederick gave his boot a final flourish and tossed it aside. "For all your help, I have a special treat," he said, then ducked into the tent. A second later he was out again, in his hand a long skewer, and impaled on the skewer, two chickens, dressed, plucked, ready for roasting.

Mary felt her mouth water at the sight of them, pale and scrawny though they were. "Frederick, wherever did you get those? Did you charm them from some poor love-struck farm girl?"

Frederick grinned, and set the skewer in the forked rods that stood on either side of the fire. "There are better ways to forage, you know, than sending hundreds of armed men out to scour the countryside."

"Um-hm," Mary said. She puffed on her pipe, pictured some buxom young country girl, giggling, lying in the hay in Frederick's arms. She felt her stomach convulse with jealousy. This could not go on.

They were silent as they went about their evening routine, Mary cleaning her carbine and pistols, Frederick tending to the chickens that crackled and grew golden brown over the fire. The smell of the fresh meat swirled around the tent until Mary thought she would go mad if she did not tear into one of the birds immediately. The army had been so long in that place that there was little fresh meat to be had.

At last Frederick lifted the skewer and slid the birds off onto their wooden plates. He handed one to Mary. She pulled at a leg and it came off easy, the meat nearly falling from the bone. The chicken burned her fingertips and her lips, but she ate anyway. She could wait no longer.

When half her chicken was gone she said, "Body of me! This is fit for the general himself. Whatever did you do?"

"I rubbed the birds first with butter, salt, and basil. Brings out the taste, I think."

Mary shook her head. "Was ever one so lucky in getting a tentmate as me? You see, Frederick, you take good care of me just as I take care of you."

"Of course I do. But soon, I think, they will give you a commission and then we will be parted."

Mary chuckled. "They will not give me a commission. Commissions are sold for great sums of money, they are not given to poor troopers such as me."

"It is not unknown that a trooper is given a commission for valor. I have heard the captain speaking with Walpole himself about you. I think they mean to make you an officer."

Mary pulled a strip of meat from the breast, put it in her mouth, chewed contemplatively. "I think not," she said at last.

"But did you not tell me that you left the regiment of foot and joined with the light horse because you understood you would not get a commission as an infantry soldier?"

"Yes, that's true. I had hoped once for a commission, but I soon learned it would not happen. But I didn't join the light horse hoping it would be any different. I just reckoned if I was destined to be a trooper my whole life, better in a regiment of horse than a regiment of foot."

Frederick nodded. "Well, I would not want to lose you, in any event."

They continued on in silence, and when they were done with their supper Frederick fetched out his sabre, the standard edged weapon of the cavalry, and began to run a stone clumsily along the edge. He had never mastered the technique of sharpening the blade, and it grieved Mary to watch him try.

After a moment of that he looked up at her and grinned, a sheepish grin. She held out her hand and he passed her the weapon and the stone and she began to undo the damage he had done, and to bring the sword to razor sharpness. There was no need for either to speak.

Mary honed one edge of the sword to her satisfaction, flipped the blade over, and began on the other. "This war will not go on forever, Frederick," she said. "What do you think you might do when it ends?"

"I have been thinking of that," he said. "I would like to open an inn, I think. Have a kitchen where I could make food, have rooms, a public house. Travelers coming and going, and I would be there to welcome them. Have a place where people wished to gather, where they would feel welcome. It would be a fine thing."

Mary nodded as he spoke. How many men in that army

would have harbored such a dream? Most would dream of their own tavern, where they could become insensibly drunk for free. But Frederick wanted to cook and to see to the comfort of others.

She pictured the inn, a huge fire burning in the front room, servants bustling about, Frederick greeting guests, supervising in the big kitchen. A warm, well-lit space, the glow of the fire illuminating the painted plaster walls, the rich tapestries.

And she put herself in the image as well, her long hair hanging free down her back and shoulders, not bound in a soldier's queue, wearing fine silk dresses and a cotton mob-cap, frilly petticoats. Perfume. Taking her ease in a big copper bathtub. Frederick putting his arms around her, kissing her cheek, telling her how much he loved her.

"It would be a fine thing indeed," she said. She ran the stone along the blade, turned it a fraction of an inch so the steel gleamed as it reflected the fire, and then she felt an uneasy suspicion rise up in her breast. "Frederick, why are you so worried about the edge of your sword this evening?"

Her tentmate smiled, another of his disarming, abashed smiles, as if he had been caught in a small lie. "First platoon has been ordered out on the morrow. We are staging a surprise raid on a grand forage that the French are undertaking around Brecht. I didn't tell you. Sometimes I think you worry about me."

Mary nodded but kept her eyes on the sword, did not trust herself to look at Frederick. His platoon had been ordered on this raid, but hers had not. That was not unusual at all. But it frightened her, the thought of Frederick in combat, all alone, without her there.

She did not let that fear show. Such feelings were too feminine by half. Instead she shrugged. "I worry about all of our regiment. I would not be much of a fellow trooper if I did not. And I expect them to worry after my sorry arse as well."

Mary slept fitfully that night. Well before dawn she was awake, lying under her blanket, pretending to sleep, listening to Frederick fumbling about, pulling on his boots, strapping on his sword belt, locating his carbine.

God help us if the French ever stage a surprise raid, she thought. *Poor Frederick will be run though as he tries to find his feet.*

At last Frederick stepped out into the predawn black. Mary heard him grunt as he hefted his saddle up on his shoulder. She sat up, listened to the sound of his boots in the mud as he made his way to the rise where the horses were staked out. She remained in her bed for ten minutes more, against the likelihood that Frederick would return for something he had forgotten.

When, after that time, he did not, she threw off the blanket and stood up. Her hands fell without thinking on her breeches, her boots, her shirt, her sword belt, her carbine, her long red regimental coat, and her three-cornered hat. She dressed quickly, efficiently, and three minutes later she stepped out into the cool morning air, fully prepared for battle.

The camp was quiet, but in the distance she could hear the familiar sound of the raiding party saddling their mounts and getting into riding order, ready to head off for their fight.

This would not be a grand fight, a history-making battle. It would not be a Donauwörth or a Blenheim or a Ramillies. The real fighting had moved south, into France and Spain, and only vestiges of the armies were now left in Flanders, to snipe at one another and stage small-scale battles and raids on one another's foraging parties.

But that did not matter to Corporal Read. She had seen enough of real warfare to know that it was not somehow more glorious to die in the midst of an epoch-making fight. She knew death in all its guises, knew the twisted, broken bodies, the dull eyes staring toward heaven, the flies swarming around gaping wounds, knew it was just as horrid in a foraging raid as it was in a battle between the great armies of nations. It was not for her, and she would see it would not happen to Frederick. She could not allow so perfect a man to end up a mangled and bloody corpse.

She swung her own saddle onto her shoulder and headed out, moving fast through the rows of tents to the latrines at the edge of camp. She always tried to do her business in the dark hours and thus avoid having to find some excuse to disappear into the woods for a few moments.

She had never come close to being discovered, had never been suspected. She was clever, circumspect, good at playing her role. And more to the point, the very idea that she could be a woman was too incredible to ever even occur to her fellow soldiers.

When she was done at the latrine she skirted the edge of the camp and made her way up the rise to where she had left her horse staked out. Frederick's horse was gone, as were half of those belonging to Walpole's regiment. She could see them down by the road, just visible in the little light that was available, mounting up, maneuvering their horses, the sergeants and lieutenants calling out orders in sharp, hushed voices.

Mary said a few soft words to her horse, then tossed the blanket over its back and flipped the saddle on over that. Her hands moved by rote, reaching under the horse's belly and grabbing the girth, threading it through the buckle and cinching it tight.

The raiding party had not yet left and she did not want to join them until they were well gone from the camp, so she pulled her carbine from the holster on the saddle and loaded the weapon and primed the pan. It was too dark for her to see much, but she did not need to see at all to perform that task. Eyes opened or closed, there was no difference.

She loaded her brace of pistols as well and clipped them to her sword belt, then pulled her bayonet from its sheath and examined it in the dim light. Perfect. Her weapons were always in perfect order. To let them be otherwise was to create additional and unnecessary risk in battle. She could never get Frederick to understand that.

At last a shouted order from the road below and Mary could see the detached units of light cavalry head out, their dozens of horses trotting together so that the sound of no one individual animal could be heard.

Mary stuck her foot in the stirrup, swung herself up onto her horse. A flick of the reigns, a touch of the spurs, and she was off down the rise, off in the wake of the raiding party.

She reached the road and turned her horse south, matching the speed of the other riders and following two hundred yards behind.

They were on a mission, all of them, all the mounted troops along that road. Ostensibly it was the same mission, to deprive the enemy of whatever food they might glean from the countryside, and to kill as many Frenchmen as they could.

But it was more than that. For the officers the real mission was to carry out their orders in such a way as to bring credit to themselves, to put themselves in the way of commendation, possible promotion.

For the troopers the mission was to fight well and to come back unhurt, with the latter being foremost on their minds.

And for Corporal Mary Read, who could have still been safe in her bed at that hour, the only mission was to see that her beloved Frederick was not cut down. Her only thought was to see that he would not have to plunge into the bloody work of that day without her at his side, protecting him, shielding him from harm.

Chapter 3

JOHN RACKAM CAME INTO HIS ASCENDANCY AS PIRATE captain in the usual manner; through bluff and betrayal, treachery, opportunities recognized and exploited.

That final epoch of his career began in darkness and fire,

July 24, 1718. It began with a show of spectacular defiance staged by Captain Charles Vane, and ended with Calico Jack in command.

Jack Rackam awoke that morning, his head fogged, his arms around a young, pretty trollop lying in the bed beside him. He did not know what had disturbed his sleep. He was not even certain where he was.

He rubbed his eyes and looked around the room. Rough-cut beams holding up the low ceiling, adze marks like fish scales deep in the wood. Plaster walls, troweled on quick and whitewashed. A washbasin with a broken leg that had been repaired with two pieces of wood lashed along either side. The work of a sailor, no doubt, but they were all sailors in Nassau, save for the small shore-bound population of merchants and publicans and prostitutes, the lamprey, there to feed off the pirates.

Jack began to remember. The room was above the Ship Tavern, one of several that lined Bay Street, and his personal favorite. Like most buildings on the island, it was wood-built, a shoddy structure that looked as if it might fall over in a brisk wind. But in the near-perfect climate of New Providence, with as undemanding a clientele as the pirates, there was little need for buildings of great substance. Just four walls and a roof under which to drink and carouse and fornicate.

A torn piece of canvas hung in front of the only window, and around the edges of the canvas the brilliant morning sun glowed bright, too bright for Jack to view directly. It had to be well past dawn. He closed his eyes and listened.

There was something happening in the streets, some commotion, but that was hardly unusual. Since an earthquake had swallowed up Port Royal, Jamaica, back in '92, Nassau had become the home of the pirates, the safe haven from those who might try to end the bacchanalia that was life on the account. There were near two thousand pirates living in Nassau, drinking, fighting, whoring, spending their booty as fast as ever they could, then taking their ships to sea again, prowling the sea lanes once it was gone and they were in need of more.

Disturbances were not uncommon.

But this was different. There was an urgency about the muted voices that Rackam could not place—not a fight or a murder, those things did not command much urgency at all, but something else.

He had no notion of what it might be, and he was too sleepy and hungover and randy to put more thought into it. He rolled on his side, ran his hand along the girl's leg and up her belly and caressed her breasts. She began to wake, smiled, squirmed a bit, and Jack felt his ardor growing.

He could not recall her name.

"Come on then, Betty, let's have a bit of that," he murmured in her ear, running his calloused hand softly over her cool, perfect skin, just barely touching her, like she was the most fragile of objects.

"Mmmm," she sighed, opened her eyes, shuffled away from him. "Don't you 'Betty' me, you bastard . . ."

Jack smiled, pushed closer. Something in the stuffing of the straw mattress pricked him and he shifted. His body ached in various places, his joints stiff, sore from sleeping on a thin mattress tossed over a rope-strung cot. He was thirty-six years old, not a young man anymore, and his body was starting to feel the effects of its hard use.

The same could not be said of his libido, however. That had not dulled or weakened, not even after twenty years of giving it free rein.

The girl put her hands against his chest as if fending him off. "Sir, you take liberties . . ."

Jack smiled. This little bunter, who was at that moment naked and in bed with him, was coming it the coy maiden. She was even convincing in her act and it excited him.

God, but he did love women! There was nothing, nothing that John Rackam loved more than women; teasing them, flirting with them, holding them, undressing them, humping them.

There was no aspect of piracy that he loved so much as he loved women. Not fighting, not drinking, not plundering a rich, fat merchantman. None of it could compare to the feeling of having some lusty young thing thrashing away under him.

And there was no one whom the women loved more than him.

Calico Jack Rackam: handsome, square jawed, with an audacious mustache that turned up playfully at the ends. Hair long and curly, falling over his shoulders and his back. Any wigmaker would have been rich if he could have created a head of hair as perfect as that which God had given to Calico Jack. His body was still lean and hard, not gone to fat, or scarred and battered, or with teeth and hair fallen out from the scurvy like so many of the brethren.

When he wasn't naked he was generally tricked out in coats and waistcoats and even breeches in bright printed calico, dandified clothes of which he was well proud. Quick-witted, dashing, generous, Calico Jack Rackam the pirate.

Jack pushed the girl gently on her back, lost in the feel of her, the smell of her, the soft, smooth skin of her shoulders and neck.

On the street below the window the commotion was growing louder, building like his own desire. And just as he was ready to enter her he heard the name "Rogers" float in through the window, shouted from the street below.

With that one word he understood what the uproar was about and all his desire was stamped out like an ember under a bootheel.

He leapt out of bed, tossing the sheets aside, ignoring the girl's surprised and angry shout.

"What in hell has got into you?" she demanded.

Jack was bouncing on one foot, pulling his breeches on. "Bloody Rogers . . ." Jack said, getting the second leg in and grabbing up his shirt. "Bloody Woodes Rogers must be in the offing."

Woodes Rogers. He was as much a pirate as any of them, or had been, at least, during the last war. Plundered the Spanish in the Pacific, came back to England a rich man, with money and reputation enough to win him respect.

Now he had been appointed Captain General and Governor in Chief of the Bahamas and he was rumored to be on his way with a force of ships of the Royal Navy. He was reportedly coming to sweep Nassau clean of pirates, make it safe for honest settlers.

The girl sat up in bed, watched his frenetic dressing. "Woodes Rogers, the new Governor? Are you afraid of him?"

"Not afraid, darling, not afraid." Rackam buckled his belt around his slim waist, adjusted the angle at which his sword hung. "But I don't reckon Vane'll be waiting for his pardon, and I don't care to be left on the beach, is all."

He pulled on his coat. Calico, a floral print, hundreds of tiny roses on a white background. Not many would have the flair and style to wear something like that, and none who tried could have pulled it off like Jack Rackam.

He dug in his purse, relieved to find one coin left there, a doubloon.

He tossed it to the girl and she squealed in delight. He blew her a kiss, lifted the wooden latch on the door, and stepped into the dim hallway. That doubloon was the last of his money, but he reckoned they would be under way by nightfall, and the generous payment would guarantee her affections when next he was in town.

If, indeed, there would be such a time. Perhaps he would not return. No one knew what Rogers was capable of doing, or what he even intended to try. Most thought that once the navy was gone, Rogers would be like the others; corrupt, bribable, eager to make his fortune in partnership with the pirates.

But Rackam was not so certain. Rogers had a reputation, and the rumors that had swirled around Nassau had all indicated that the man meant business.

Deep, deep down, in a part of his mind that would never find voice, Calico Jack Rackam understood that he was, in fact, afraid. Afraid of this grand, heedless way of life coming to an end. Desperately afraid of the noose.

He staggered down the narrow hall. Through thin walls he heard others dressing, talking, copulating. He stuffed his silk stockings in his pocket as he hurried down the rickety stairs and out the door that opened onto Bay Street.

Jack took the morning sun full in the face and he held up his hand and with his sleeve brushed the tears away. His head had felt surprisingly good, despite the wild night he had enjoyed, but now it throbbed in the brilliant glare. He pushed his cocked hat down on his head and stepped into the street, paused as a dray rumbled past, then crossed the dusty road to the waterfront beyond.

Nassau, lying along the northern edge of New Providence Island, was mostly waterfront. The sun beat down on the town and the shallow water, unrelenting, raising a pungent odor of brine and discarded conch shells and fish viscera and the rough cooking of the people who lived by the water.

Pirates did not congregate where it was cold. Cold was not conducive to their lifestyle.

All along Bay Street, wooden docks thrust out into Nassau Harbor, a strip of water sandwiched between Hog Island to the north and New Providence Island to the south. Beyond the docks, riding at their anchors, pirate sloops and pirate brigs and pirate ships and the rotting wooden corpses of prizes and old pirate vessels abandoned to the ravages of the tropics. Decay was everywhere, in the streets, in the air, on the water.

A crowd of people were jammed onto the longest of the docks and staring east toward that entrance to Nassau Harbor. Jack pushed his way through, snarling, "Give way there, you whoreson" and "Bloody step aside!" In Nassau, Calico Jack held certain privileges, he felt, including the right to be at the head of any mob he chose. He was, after all, quartermaster to the famous Captain Charles Vane, and in his own right a well-known, well-loved figure.

At the edge of the dock he spotted Ben Hornigold, grand old man of the Nassau pirates.

Jack had seen Ben kill a man in an argument over a spilled drink, had once personally hauled the corpulent villain out of a ditch, after finding him there, delirious with drink and covered in mud and his own vomit.

But now Ben was dressed like a country squire, with a

velvet coat and silk waistcoat, powdered wig on his head. The silver buckles on his shoes glinted, and his thick fingers and meaty, calloused hand rested on top of a gold-headed walking stick. The sweet trade had been good to Ben Hornigold.

"Halloa, there, Ben. What's acting?" Jack sidled up beside him, looked in the direction he was looking.

"John Rackam!" Ben Hornigold looked Jack up and down and his eyes took in the bare feet stuffed in his shoes, the shirt and waistcoat as yet not buttoned. "Dress in a hurry, boy? Was her husband coming in the door?"

"Nothing of the sort, Ben. I told her, says I, 'I must go now, Mrs. Hornigold, lest your husband need my help.' "

"Need more than you, young Calico Jack. See yonder is H. M. S. *Rose,* and if Woodes Rogers ain't aboard her, then he's aboard one of the other three men-of-war in the offing."

Off to the east Rackam could see her, a frigate with forecourse and topsails set, sailing across the mouth of the harbor. Just as she began to pass from sight beyond the far end of Hog Island she tacked smartly and settled on her new course, back and forth across the mouth of the harbor. The blockade had begun, the first offensive thrust in Woodes Rogers's war against the pirates.

"Well, damn my eyes, Ben, this whoreson Rogers must want to see you hang something awful, to send such a force."

"Perhaps." Hornigold stared off at the *Rose,* thoughtful and somber. "Rumor has it Rogers brings with him a pardon to any will give up the sweet trade. Some of the lads are thinking on taking it, get us a bit of breathing room, see what this Rogers is made of. See if he wants to play with the devil once his little men-of-war are gone, and it's but him and us, eh?"

A pardon? Sure, you fat old son of a bitch, easy for you to say, Jack thought, running an eye over Hornigold's rich clothing. Old Ben had been at the business for years, probably figured his luck had run its course anyway. Ben had not just given over his last bit of coin to some doxy whose name he could not recall.

"You're a respectable man now, Ben Hornigold, a right gentleman, and I wish you pleasure on your retirement. But as for me, I should rather greet old Rogers with a cannon full of shot rather than tugging my forelock with my hand outreached, so I'll be off to my ship."

Hornigold took his eyes from the distant frigate, met Rackam's. "Captain Vane's ship," he corrected.

"It's all of one."

"If you'd have command of a privateer, Jack, you had best make your move, and soon. This life—" he made a sweeping gesture with his hand, taking in the crowd on the dock, the town of Nassau, the pirate ships riding at their moorings "—will not be around so very much longer."

Jack smiled, chuckled a bit. "If in all the world, Ben Hornigold, there is but a canoe with a fistful of groats aboard, there will still be fellows such as us to take them. I don't reckon that will change soon."

"Perhaps not," Hornigold said, but there was no conviction in his words. "Godspeed to you, Calico Jack."

Jack shook hands with the old man and pushed his way back through the crowd and down to the strip of sand where the boats were pulled up. He found a crew, just shoving off, who would take him out to his ship.

Captain Vane's ship. The pirate brig *Ranger*.

Jack came up the side, stepped through the gangway into the waist. There was Vane up on the quarterdeck rail, one hand on the main shrouds to steady himself, looking east through a glass.

The rest of the men, about thirty in all, were in various states of sobriety. Some were sleeping, some eating or drinking, some working at repairs to the running gear, each after his own whim.

Empty bottles that had been tossed into the scuppers rolled slowly back and forth and clinked against each other as the brig rocked in the swell. A roasted goat, partially eaten, hung from a spit over the portable cookstove. Great heaps of cordage were piled up on deck. The old fore-topsail, torn beyond repair, lay partially folded in the bows, the task of striking it below abandoned before it was half-completed.

The pirates were sailors to a man, but they did not pay much attention to the niceties of seafaring tradition. They had had their fill of that in their former lives, as merchant seamen and men-of-war's men. There was no one now to tell them their duty. The pirates did nothing that they did not care to do.

Richard Corner came lumbering up. He moved slow, seemed too huge and too stupid to move fast, but his lethargic appearance was deceptive. Rackam had seen him in many a fight, wielding a cutlass like it was a twig, a powerful and dangerous man. Corner was always the first to plunge into any brawl, seemed to crave a fight the way Jack craved women, as if he had no understanding of danger.

He held out a bottle of rum and Rackam took it and swallowed, let it settle and swallowed some more. "If I'd known you was coming aboard, I'd have taken a boat over," Corner said, "waited for you."

"Never you mind, Dicky," Jack assured him. "Didn't know myself till an hour ago I was coming back so soon."

Jack took another swallow, handed the bottle back, nodded his head toward the quarterdeck. "I best go see himself," he said, and Corner nodded, watched him as he stepped aft. Good to have the love of a fellow like Corner, Jack thought. It was like having a big, vicious dog as your loyal pet.

Up on the quarterdeck, and Captain Charles Vane took the glass from his eye, looked down as Rackam approached. "Ah, Quartermaster, I was afraid we might leave you on the beach."

"Are we to get under way directly?"

"Oh, we shall see. I have sent message out to this rogue, Woodes Rogers. Offered to accept the buggering King's buggering pardon if we can keep all of our booty. Told him we'd bloody well fight if he didn't agree." Vane laughed out loud at that, at his own audacity. "We'll see what the bastard says to that, eh?"

Captain Charles Vane was not some small-time picaroon or petty sea robber. He was a pirate, a genuine pirate. He was what civilized people pictured when they thought of a pirate: a sword on his belt, pistols thrust into crossbelts on his chest, the long locks of a once fine wig tumbling down his back. A red silk coat and a red silk sash around his waist.

He was bold but not reckless, smart, daring, utterly ruthless. Rackam had seen him burn an uncooperative captive's eyes out with a lighted match. He was one of that small cadre of pirates who were considered not merely troublesome, but a genuine menace because they were so vicious and so successful at what they did.

Jack Rackam was his quartermaster, which in the hierarchy of the pirate ships meant he was second-in-command, sort of a go-between for the captain and the men.

The Rangers looked up to Rackam, like they looked up to Vane. Both smart men, both ruthless, with a certain flair that was beyond the nature of most of the simple, rough seafarers who drifted into the pirate life.

But Calico Jack alone understood that in him they had the trappings of a ruthless and charismatic leader, and in Vane they had the genuine article. Quartermaster Rackam liked Captain Vane. And he wanted to take his place. And he feared him.

"You expect a reply soon?"

"Aye. Yonder comes our longboat, standing in with the lugsail set."

The longboat swooped up the harbor and when at last it drew up to the *Ranger*'s side, Jack could see that the crew were well into a good drunk, flinging bottles at their comrades aboard the *Ranger*, shouting and cursing Woodes Rogers's name.

George Fetherston climbed up the side of the ship and staggered aft to the quarterdeck. "Captain Vane," he called, "the bloody bastard would not even see me, can you believe it?"

"Did he give you word as to his intentions?"

"Aye, the sodomite. He sat in his cabin like the fucking

lord and master, sent one of his little arse-lickers out to tell
me he would not be sending a reply to your demand. And
me being the soul of reason, saying we but want to keep
that what we earned through our own hard work."

Jack watched Vane, waited for his reaction. He could not
always tell which way Vane would go—he was not the
most stable of men. But this time Vane laughed and made
an obscene gesture in the direction of the blockading frigate. "Well, bugger him then, the sheepbiter. I'll burn his
goddamned ships for him. But first we must be away."

"Now?" Rackam asked. Did Vane intend to try fighting
his way past the *Rose?* An unsettling thought, and even if
they managed it, there were the other ships coming up behind.

Vane was generally more sensible than that. He would
take risks, sure, but he would not plunge in when the odds
were that much against him.

"No, no, not now, Quartermaster, you fire-eating son of
a bitch!" Vane said, and slapped an arm over Rackam's
shoulders. "Wherever are your manners? We have to welcome the grand fucking Governor proper, and then we shall
take our leave."

Midnight, and Calico Jack Rackam stood on the sloop's
deck, idly swinging his sword back and forth.

The first time he had set foot on that deck, two months
before, he had been the cocksure, swaggering Jack Rackam,
pirate quartermaster, and the sloop had been another in a
string of victims of Captain Charles Vane and company.

The sloop had run from them, for a bit, but the *Ranger*
was fast and had quickly overhauled them. The sloop had
struck her British merchant ensign to Vane's black flag with
its leering death's head.

Vane beat the captain senseless, in part for having had
the audacity to run, in part because he wanted to.

Calico Jack strutted it in front of the terrified crew of the
little sloop. It amused him to play at the vicious killer; he

took pleasure in the terror he could evoke without drawing a drop of blood. He had been bold then, when there was nothing aboard the little captive sloop that he need fear, the heavy-armed pirates outnumbering the unarmed crew ten to one.

They spent hours tearing the sloop apart, drinking the wine they found aboard, terrorizing the crew. Finally they put the frightened men in a boat, took the sloop with them. It was the kind of plundering Calico Jack most enjoyed.

He was not so calm now, though there was no one aboard the sloop but his own shipmates. There were no lights burning, no activity, beyond the murmured conversation of the others, hunkered down on the deck aft and drinking steadily.

Below his feet, in the low hold of the sloop, cask upon cask of gunpowder. And between the casks, stacks of straw, canvas covered with oil, old barrel staves, anything that would burn. They were standing on top of the most volatile cargo imaginable, and when the time came, Jack would have to set it on fire and get away before it blew him straight to hell.

This was Charles Vane's idea of welcoming the new Governor. He had left it to Jack Rackam to execute, presented him the task like it was some kind of a goddamned reward, and Jack did not dare act otherwise.

He paced fore and aft, slashed at the air with his sword.

How long had they been waiting there? A long damned time. Vane had guessed that Rogers would send the big ship in to try and take them before they sailed. But perhaps Vane had guessed wrong.

He heard a muttering aft, and then the soft padding of bare feet and George Fetherston was there, still as drunk as he had been that afternoon. "I think I sees them now, Quartermaster. Son of a bitch coming right up under topsails, the whore's son."

Rackam walked aft with Fetherston, stared out into the dark. Yes, there it was, a big ship, coming up out of the night, and not so far away. In the darkness and with the quantity of alcohol they had consumed, the Rangers had allowed the frigate to get within two hundred yards before spotting her.

Jack swallowed, tapped the deck with his sword, watched the frigate approach.

"You have a match lit, Fetherston?"

"No."

"Well then, light a buggering match. Corner, get your ax and stand ready to cut the cable. The rest of you, get the boat alongside."

Dark shapes shuffled off. Richard Corner came looming out of the dark and stepped forward, grinning wide. The *Rose* fell off a point, a ghost ship in the starlight. Well handled, closing fast.

Damn, damn, damn, damn, Rackam thought. Had to time this perfect. If he lit the sloop too early, it would be mutterings of cowardice, and next he would find himself marooned on a spit of land, with only a pistol and a single bullet to put through his head when the thirst became unbearable.

Light it too late and he would be blown into fragments, tiny pieces of his beautiful body dropping like rain into Nassau Harbor where they would be eaten by the fish. The last of Calico Jack Rackam, crapped out a fish's arse.

Jack watched the *Rose* looming up through the night. A voice shouted out, the cadence of an order, and then a deep rumbling as the frigate ran her great guns out.

"Fetherston! Light her up! Corner, cut the goddamned cable!"

A glow amidships as Fetherston touched the match to a torch of oil-soaked rags and then the torch burst into bright flame that illuminated the entire deck. From forward, the *whump, whump, whump* of Corner's ax, hacking at the cable.

Eager hands pulled the main hatch open and Fetherston tossed the burning torch down into the volatile hold. Jack tensed, gritted his teeth, waited for the sloop to explode under him. The fire in the hold flared, crackled, shot up through the hatch, but the vessel did not blow.

Jack felt the sloop moving under his feet, sweeping sideways, and he knew the cable had been cut through.

"You men, in the boat, get in the damned boat!" Jack shouted, but the men, fearless drunk, just watched with amusement as the fire in the hold built higher and higher.

"Get in the damned boat, you stupid bastards!" Jack roared, and finally the men tore themselves from the great pyre and began to climb down the low-sided sloop and into the boat, floating alongside.

The fire was rising up from the hold like a great yellow and orange spirit. It grabbed hold of the main boom and the mainsail stowed down on top of it, and in a flash the dry canvas was burning, the fire running along the length of the spar and lapping over the various lifts, sheets, and halyards made fast to the fife rail at the base of the mast.

Big Richard Corner came loping aft. The fire played over his face and his thick beard and would have made him look utterly demonic were it not for his wide, stupid grin.

Jack wanted to slap him, to shove him down into the boat. Instead he opened his mouth to urge the idiot to hurry, but before he could speak there was a loud snap, a rending of wood aloft, a flash of flame from the hold.

Rackam and Corner looked aloft at the same instant, looked up just in time to see the long, thin gaff plunging down from the masthead, the halyards burned through, the line whipping through the blocks. And then the heavy triple block of the throat halyard, fifteen pounds of wood and rope and iron, plunged down from the dark and slammed into Richard Corner's head and sent him sprawling back.

The gaff landed with a crash on top of the burning main boom, scattering the fire in a hundred directions, igniting the sloop fore and aft. The deck was all but covered in flame, and the fire in the hold was roaring, leaping up, ready at any moment to blow the powder casks.

From over the side the men in the boat were calling out. Forward, Jack could see Corner's body sprawled out on deck, could see it plain as day in the bright fire that ringed him.

Leave him, leave him, he's dead, he's dead, son of a

bitch, he's dead anyway, Rackam assured himself. He took a step toward the side and stopped.

"Aarrrr!" Jack shouted. "Goddamn it!" He plunged forward, through the fire, not thinking, because if he thought about it, he would not do the thing he knew he must.

Forward, and he grabbed Corner's motionless body by the arm, pulling him up just as the main boom fell and sent a shudder through the sloop and Jack thought that the gunpowder had gone off. He pulled Corner up, got his arms under Corner's arms, dragged him to the side of the sloop.

Now what, now what? he thought, but there was George Fetherston, climbing up over the side, and together they tossed Corner down into the boat and then leapt after him, heedless of how or on whom they landed.

"Pull, you bastards, pull!" Jack shouted. No need to appear calm now, everyone in the boat was near panic. They leaned into the oars and the boat drew away from the sloop, and the sloop, now carried by the wind and tide, whirled away from them, spun into the path of the man-of-war.

And in the light of the burning vessel they could see the *Rose,* the mighty *Rose,* putting her helm up and running for all she was worth back toward the harbor entrance.

Forecourse, main course, the big sails tumbled from the yards and were sheeted home. The fire from the sloop illuminated the great spread of canvas, reaching high enough for them to see the topgallants being set as well. The light lapped over the yellow stripe along the frigate's side, the black muzzles of the great guns, still run out, the towering stern windows as the man-of-war fled from the awful sight of the inferno bearing down on them.

The longboat was a hundred yards or more away from the sloop when it finally blew. The concussion from the blast rolled over the men, hit them like a solid object, tumbled them into the bottom of the boat.

They pulled themselves to their knees, looked back across the harbor.

Blast after blast shattered the night with each barrel that went off, great columns of flame shooting up from the sloop's wrecked hull, and the cannon along her side, loaded and shotted, firing off into the dark, as if the vessel herself were lashing out in her death throes, making one last attempt to strike her tormentors before she died.

And between the deafening explosions of the powder casks, Jack could hear cheers, howling, curses from around the harbor as the pirate community celebrated this act of defiance, this spitting in the face of the man who had vowed to rout them out.

Jack threw his head back and howled as well, howled, shouted, let all the pent-up fear and anxiety out with each wild animal cry. He screamed in triumph, in exhilaration. He screamed in pure, sweet relief.

Chapter 4

IT WAS TEN MILES TO THE FRENCH POSITION OUTSIDE Brecht, and the detached regiment of light horse, over two hundred riders strong, covered most of the distance in the dark.

Mary Read kept well behind them, following undetected. The sound of her horse could not be heard over the thunder of an entire regiment. The scouts from the raiding party were sent out ahead of the main body, she knew, but they would not scout behind. There was no danger behind.

She kept her distance as long as she could. She knew the ribbing she would take from her fellows, the lewd suggestions, the half-serious questions raised by men incredulous that she should voluntarily ride into harm's way when she had every right to be, at that moment, safe in camp.

It was not the first time she had turned out for duty to which Frederick had been assigned and she had not. She was ready to fend off the jokes, the queries, but she would put them off as long as she could.

An hour of riding and the sky to the east began to grow

light, the sun illuminating the thick cover of cloud. It would be another overcast, dreary day in Flanders.

When at last Mary could make out the dim shapes of the riders farther up the road she put spurs to her horse and closed quickly with them, as if she was just catching up, as if she had not been following them the whole time.

The rear guard swiveled in their saddles as she approached, a trace of alarm in their tired and anxious faces, and then they saw her and smiled.

"Well, now, Corporal Read, and what the fuck are you doing here?" one of them called as she pulled up with them, slowing her horse to match the pace of the regiment.

"Damned if I'll let you girls have all the glory," she said with a smile. Mary Read was as proficient as any man at the kind of rough verbal dueling of comrades. Better than many, in fact.

"Here, Heesch, your tentmate's arrived!" Halfway up the line Frederick Heesch turned and looked back, confused at first, and then his eyes met Mary's and he smiled, a look of resignation. Shook his head in disbelief.

"I think he fancies you, Heesch!" one of the troopers called out, and another, "Best sleep with your arse to the tent wall tonight, lad!"

Ribald laughter and Mary spurred her horse forward, drew up alongside the man who had made that joke, whacked him a solid thump on the back of the head. "You can kiss *my* arse, Chandler. Forage party means food, and I'll be goddamned if I let you get it all. Haven't had a bloody decent bite in a month and I'll be happy to kill all the Frenchmen I have to to get one."

"Silence in the ranks!" a sergeant called down the line, and that was the end of the banter. Mary rode with the others near the back of the regiment, far from Frederick. There would be opportunity later to get close to him, but for now she was better off keeping her distance, lending some credence to her claim that she was there for her own good alone.

The morning light spread farther and farther along the horizon, though the sun was not to be seen through the

impenetrable clouds. Mary breathed deep in the clean
morning air, took in the smell of the wet grass and the
horses and a touch of woodsmoke from some distant fire.
The gathering dawn revealed patches of dark and light
green fields and little bursts of trees spread over the rolling
country through which they rode. Here and there a house,
a farm, a tiny village tucked amid the downs.

It seemed an unlikely location for a bloody raid. But out
there, somewhere, Mary knew, was a French foraging party,
scouring the countryside for whatever food and firewood
they could gather, a systematic search for those things that
would sustain an army in the field. And covering those
foragers would be infantry and perhaps even cavalry, to
keep their own people from deserting and to protect them
from exactly the kind of attack that was about to take place.

But from where she sat, high on top of her horse, looking
out over the countryside as it was revealed by the morning
light, it was as peaceful a scene as she could hope to see.

Perhaps they are wrong about the grand forage, she
thought. *Or perhaps the French have fallen back to their
lines.* Mary wished that bloody war did not have to intrude
on that fine morning.

And then over the sound of their trotting mounts, the
sharper sound of horses at the gallop. A buzz ran through
the light horsemen, orders shouted down the line, and the
combined regiment reined to a stop. The scouts were back
with information about the enemy's position. Mary did not
have to hear or see them to know that. She had been in
that place enough times to recognize what was happening.

Colonel Richmond, commanding the combined regiment,
wheeled his horse away from the front of the line, rode
down the flanks, captains, lieutenants, sergeants trailing behind like a comet's tail. "There's infantry cover for the
foragers, spread out on the open ground beyond the next
rise," he called out, his sword in his hand for emphasis. He
made a stirring, martial sight, sitting atop his chestnut stal-
lion, his long red coat vivid, even in the dull light, as he
passed orders along the line.

"We'll take them on their flanks, attack around either

side of yonder rise. Richmond's regiment, form up under your captain to the left! Walpole's regiment to the right!"

No more orders than that were needed. The troops, well trained, experienced in more of these sorts of attacks than any could count, moved swiftly from the file formation in which they rode to a long line abreast in which they would sweep down on the enemy.

Mary thrilled at the maneuver, despite her unwillingness to see the peace of the morning destroyed. There was something awesome and terrible about a cavalry attack. Unstoppable. Infantry in the field had no defense against the horsemen who came charging down on them, blades flashing. No defense other than to form a square and hold the horses off with lances and bayonets, but it was the rare infantry company that possessed the discipline and courage to do that. Usually they broke and ran, and when they did that, they died.

Only artillery could stop a cavalry charge dead, but a grand forage would not have artillery. That was for a real battle.

Mary wheeled her horse to the right, joined in with the other troopers from Walpole's regiment. In the brief, confused shuffling as the riders formed into their line she managed to sidle up beside Frederick, held her horse at a stand beside his.

"Good morning, Frederick." She smiled at him.

"Michael, whatever are you doing here? Half the troopers here would have missed this day if they could have, and here you are when you do not need to be."

"One gets a taste for such things, you know. Like drink. Or rogering country girls in exchange for chickens."

Frederick sighed. "You will never answer me straight, will you?"

"I don't know how much more straight I can be."

There was no need for a straight answer. Frederick knew full well why she was there, and he appreciated the concern, genuinely appreciated it even if he could not fathom why Michael Read felt as he did.

Mary looked away. *This cannot go on,* she thought. She

could not endure this playacting any longer. She had to make her confession to Frederick. But the thought of that was more frightening even than the battle into which she was about to ride.

On the open ground before them the captain took his place in the front of the troops, and arrayed behind him the lieutenants, and behind the lieutenants, the sergeants. And behind the sergeants, a great unbroken wall of horses, and mounted on them the men of the light cavalry, their long red coats hanging down over their thighs, their tall black boots gleaming dull in the overcast.

The horses shifted, pawed the ground nervously, whinnied and snorted. Like the men, the animals had been there before, and they understood the great thundering action into which they were about to plunge.

And in front of all, Colonel Richmond, his sword drawn and held aloft, his gauntlet-clad hand gripping the hilt, the heavy handguard inlaid with gold. Mary felt her heart race, her hands sweating inside her own gauntlets. She looked at Frederick, met his eyes, and smiled with the thrill of it all, and Frederick, with considerably less enthusiasm, smiled back.

And then the colonel swept his sword down and his horse moved out, and behind him, the captains, the lieutenants, the sergeants, and then the great scarlet line rolled forward, gathering momentum as the riders let their speed build from walk to trot to canter.

They were an avalanche of horses and riders, rolling down on the enemy, unstoppable. Holding their straight line, controlled, disciplined, ready to charge or break right or left at their officers' orders, relayed by the trumpeters who rode on their flanks. A disciplined tidal wave, lightning striking on command.

Down across the field, down the rise, the high ground still between the riders and the screen of French infantry. The canter built to a gallop as the light cavalry surged forward. Mary felt the wind rushing through her queue-bound hair, felt the tears streaming down her cheeks from the cold morning air rushing over her eyes, felt the madness of the charge overtake her and she wanted to shout with the intensity of the moment.

But she was a disciplined soldier and she kept quiet. The line of cavalry reached the bottom of the hill and started up the next in their great thundering attack. Mary reached across her belly, grabbed her big cavalry saber and pulled it free, gripping the reins in her left hand, holding her sword cocked over her shoulder with her right.

She glanced over at Frederick. He was leaning forward in his saddle, driving his mount, so caught up in the drama of the thing that he had forgotten to draw his blade. She reached over with her sword, gave him a tap on his back. He looked over, his eyes moving from her face to her sword, and he nodded and drew his own saber and held it like Mary held hers.

Up, up to the top of the low hill, over the crest, and then below them an open wheat field. Mary's well-trained eye swept the ground below, took stock of the strategic position even as the two companies broke right and left, pounding down the grassy slope to strike the enemy on their flanks.

Spread over the field were the blue coats, the bright white breeches of French infantry. They were in a wide formation, like a skirmish line, perfectly situated for cavalry to cut them down.

At the far end of the field, tucked into a corner, a farmhouse, stone walls, thatched roof, and behind it a barn, built of boards and battens. The house was strong, could be used as a small fortification. A potential problem. The barn could be hiding more troops, even French cavalry.

At the far end of the field, a line of thick trees. Good cover for the fleeing infantry. The light horse could not penetrate there. Had to strike the Frenchmen down before they reached that tree line.

All this she thought as she scanned the field below through streaming eyes, her sword held high, a battle cry building in her guts, waiting only the moment when she could let it out, when she could ride down on some fleeing Frenchman who at the last minute would hear her horse, turn, raise his bayonet in one last futile attempt to live and be struck down by her sword. She could see it all before her. She had seen it many times already.

The scarlet line reached the edge of the plowed field and surged across it. In front of them, the gray puffs of musket fire as the French infantrymen took their one shot and then turned and fled for the tree line. There was no time to reload in the face of a cavalry charge.

Mary saw a trooper shot from his horse, saw another drop his sword and grab his shoulder, but Frederick was unharmed and the fight was already out of the French infantry. They were running now, as fast as they could, flinging muskets and haversacks aside in their wild flight for the trees.

Right in front of her and fifty feet away Mary could see a man running, running, stumbling as he made for the tree line. She raised her sword, jammed the spurs in her horse's flanks, closing fast with him. Frederick was still there and they charged on, side by side, carrying death to the French.

And then the tree line erupted in a cloud of smoke, spurting out over the field, and the air was filled with the roar of field artillery, the unearthly scream of flying grapeshot, and men and horses were knocked down like toys.

Colonel Richmond, sword raised high, was whipped from his saddle by a blast of grape and his crumpled body vanished in the tall stalks of wheat. The light horse stopped as if it had run into a brick wall, horses wheeling, officers bellowing orders that no one could hear.

"What the hell!?" Mary shouted, pulled hard on her reins, tried to get her horse under control. She looked back. Frederick was still mounted, still unhurt.

Again the tree line belched smoke and grapeshot ripped through the cavalry, tearing bloody holes in the perfect scarlet line. A single note from the trumpeter and then he was blown away, a blast of grape tearing him apart and flinging him from his wild horse.

A trap! A bloody damned trap! The infantry had been sent out ahead of artillery, hidden in the trees. Infantry, spread out across an open field, irresistible to attacking cavalry.

Mary wheeled her horse, looking for the lieutenant, the captain, any of the officers, but all she could see in front of the line were horses screaming and thrashing their lives away in the waist-high wheat, glimpses of scarlet where the officers lay dead on the ground.

Another volley, the flat report of field cannon, the scream of grapeshot, the scream of dying horses, dying men, frightened men. They were being cut down where they stood, with no one in command.

And then Mary saw Frederick's horse surge forward, rear up, eyes mad with terror. Foam streaked from its mouth, blood pouring from a gash under the animal's neck where the grape shot had torn up its flesh.

Frederick shouted, yanked on the reins, but there was nothing he could do. There was no rider on earth who could have controlled that panicked beast.

From the tree line the artillery blasted away.

Chapter 5

MARY RACED FORWARD, KICKING HER HORSE, FORCING it to approach Frederick's wild mount. She tossed her sword aside, reached out, grabbed Frederick by the collar.

The artillery was relentless, the murderous grape tearing through the ranks, stabs of muzzle flash from the trees and now from the stone house as well. They were in a cross fire and they were being killed like deer driven into a pen.

"Get off your horses! Get off your damned horses!" Mary shouted, again and again. She dragged Frederick from his frantic mount, pulled him over to her, and then her horse was shot out from under her, its neck and chest torn apart by grape. The animal collapsed with never a sound, like it had never been alive, and together Mary and Frederick fell with it, tumbling in a heap to the plowed earth.

"Son of a bitch!" Mary shouted, pulled her leg from under the dead animal. She looked frantically around, but Frederick was there, just a few feet away, pale, terrified, but alive.

"Frederick, are you hurt?"

"No, no. A little cut, it is nothing. You?"

"No." She pulled her carbine from her saddle and then looked up, quick, her head just over the top of the wheat. All around her were terrified horses, charging in every direction and dying in the hail of grape coming from the trees and the stone farmhouse.

But they were riderless. The troopers must have heeded her words, or figured for themselves the folly of remaining on their tall horses where they were perfect targets for the men laying the guns.

So now they were dismounted, hidden in the waist-high wheat, and it was only a matter of time before the infantry sortied out again, in force, and killed them all.

Damn it! They had ridden right into it, like bloody fools. And now there was no one left alive to give orders.

Well, Mary thought, *someone has to, or we'll all die right here, so it might as well be me.*

"Walpole's regiment! To me! To me!" she shouted from her kneeling position. She found her sword and snatched it up, leapt to her feet. The tree line and the farmhouse were blanketed with smoke, and the guns continued to add volumes more to the roiling cloud. Blasts of grapeshot whistled past and the air was filled with the cries of men and the ghastly shriek of dying horses.

"Walpole's regiment! To me!" Mary shouted, waved her sword, and from the wheat men stood, raced toward her, bent almost double, and dropped to the ground around her.

Another burst of artillery and a horse just ten feet away took the full blast of grape and was blown from its feet by the impact. Time to get down. Mary threw herself to the ground. The grape screamed overhead.

From her crouched position she looked around. There were two dozen men hunkered down in the wheat field around her, bright scarlet coats against the green plants. No officers that she could see. And she, a corporal, realized she might well be the ranking trooper there.

"Here, Michael," Frederick said. He was smiling. "Do you wish yourself back in bed now?"

"Shut your gob and listen up. All of you!" she said, loud, and all eyes turned toward her. "They'll fucking murder us if we try to get back the way we came, and they'll murder us if we stay here, but I reckon we can roll up the flank of that artillery in the tree line. You men follow me. Hands and knees. They see us coming we're dead. Frederick, stay right next to me."

Mary turned and on hands and knees she crawled away, pushing the wheat down in front of her, making for the right side of the tree line. And behind her the others followed. Mary knew that they were grateful to have someone giving orders, someone in charge. If they did not have something to do, some active part in their own salvation, then they would go mad with fear.

She crawled on, fifty yards, one hundred yards, her knees aching, her hands brown with the rich soil and cut with a dozen tiny lacerations from the stiff wheat stalks, as was her face, but she did not even think about that. Her whole mind was on the tree line, getting to the tree line.

She was breathing hard. It seemed as if they would never reach it. Was she leading them in a circle? She could see nothing beyond the wheat. The sun was too low and too indistinct to be of any help in navigating.

And then they were there. The wheat ended and there was twenty feet of cleared land and then the trees. The artillery was still firing, a near continuous barrage, and she wondered who they were firing at, what part of the light horse was foolish enough to still be standing up under that murderous hail.

That was not her concern.

Mary peered out from the cover of the tall crop, looked right and left. She could see no French troops and she hoped that meant that no French troops could see her. She retreated a few feet back into the field, turned to Frederick and the others behind her. "I'll go. If I don't draw fire, then follow me, two at a time."

Heads nodded and Mary turned and crawled back to the edge of the wheat. She pulled herself into a crouch, drew a deep breath, and then launched herself into the open field, in full view of anyone who might be looking in that direction.

She ran as fast as she could, her thigh boots flapping, the tails of her regimental coat slapping her legs. It seemed an impossible distance to the shelter of the woods.

And suddenly she was aware of someone running beside her. She looked over. Frederick was there, running all out at her side.

You idiot, you damned idiot! she thought, but then they were at the edge of the woods. They plunged through the bracken, into the shade of the big oaks, collapsed to the ground, gasping for breath.

When Mary had recovered enough to speak she said, "I will tear your fucking heart out for that . . ."

"Save my life . . ." Frederick gasped, "just to tear my fucking heart out?"

Before Mary could respond, a pair of troopers crashed through the undergrowth, and a second later another pair, as two at a time they crossed the open ground and found shelter in the trees, the same trees from which the French artillery was firing, quite ignorant of their presence.

Five minutes of that and all the men who had followed Mary were drawn up into the woods. In that time the artillery had fallen silent, an odd sensation to ears that had become accustomed to the continuous roar of the guns.

"I think they've sent the infantry out again," Mary said in a loud whisper. "We'll roll right up their flank and turn their artillery on them. Come along."

She turned and headed through the woods, stumbling through the undergrowth, and then from the jumble of trees and brush a trail emerged, making its twisted way through the tree line. Mary stepped onto it cautiously, unslung her carbine, and jammed the plug bayonet into the end of the barrel. Behind her the men followed. More than half of them had also thought to snatch their carbines from their saddles, and they fixed bayonets as well.

She picked up her pace. The artillery had to be arrayed along that path.

Up the trail they moved, through variegated patches of dull sunlight and shadow, their footfalls silent on the soft earth. Around a twist in the path and there was a French infantryman, a picket, protecting the approach to the artillery park.

A picket, but not looking down the trail. Rather, he was looking out over the field at where his comrades were spreading out, searching for the English cavalrymen hiding in the wheat. Hoping to see some fun, no doubt.

Mary leveled her bayonet and charged and the soldier caught the movement out of the corner of his eye. He wheeled around, his musket came up, his mouth opened and a shout of surprise formed in his throat, and then Mary drove her bayonet through his chest and he fell choking in his own blood.

The first time Mary had killed, close up, she had stood over the man, watched him die, then vomited, over and over. She cried all night, silently, in the dark, unseen. It was not an unusual reaction. She had since seen plenty of men do the same after their first blood.

She had puked the first time, suffered terrible remorse, but that was a long time ago.

Mary jerked the bayonet free of the picket's body, and her pace did not slacken. She raced up the trail and she could hear the heavy footfalls of her fellows behind her. She slung her carbine back over her shoulder, pulled her pistols from her belt. Her hands were too small to cock the pistols with her thumbs, the way the men did, so she cocked the locks of each with the palm of the opposite hand.

Around a twist in the path and right in front of her, not ten feet away, was the first of the field cannon. The artillery crew were lounging around their charge, leaning on rammers or with their backs against the tall wheels of the gun carriage or sitting on the trails. Their work was done, or so they thought.

An officer straightened, shouted *"Qu'est-ce que c'est?"* His hand went for his sword and Mary Read shot him in the chest.

She threw the pistol aside and with the one in her left hand shot a quick-thinking gunner who was swinging his rammer in a great arc at her head. The man was knocked back against the gun, slumped to the ground, and then the rest of the dismounted cavalry surged over the gun and crew, shooting them down, striking them down with carbines and cold steel.

In fifteen seconds it was over, but now the crews of the other guns up the trail were alerted and would not be so easily taken by surprise. Mary scanned the distant wheat field. She could see the blue backs of French infantry, moving cautiously over the ground, like pheasant hunters trying to flush out the hidden English troops.

"Three of you, stay with this gun, start firing on those bastards out there!" She pointed over the barrel of the big gun, toward the field. "The rest of you, reload and follow me! Take their firelocks—" she indicated the clutch of dead and wounded Frenchmen at their feet "—if you've none of your own."

She unslung her carbine, pulled the bayonet from the muzzle, and held it in both hands as she charged up the trail again. The next gun was no more than forty yards away, though they could not see it through the thick wood until they were almost on top of it. The crew there was not milling around as the first had been; they were alert, small arms ready, unsure of the source of the gunfire down the trail.

But they were only nine men, and ready as they were, they were not prepared for the surge of running, screaming, crazed troopers who suddenly burst from the wood and rolled right over them. Guns popped off, Mary saw one of her men fall, but it was not Frederick, and then she shot one of the French gunners with her carbine, plunged her bayonet like a knife into another. She was screaming, she realized, shouting at the top of her lungs, and so were the others behind her. Ten seconds and that gun crew lay dead, strewn around the fieldpiece they served, and the light cavalry charged on up the trail.

There were eight guns that had been dragged into the cover of the woods, arrayed along the trail, waiting for the vulnerable infantry to lure the British cavalry into their arc of fire, and Mary Read led her troops right up that line, killing the gun crews or sending them running into the wheat field.

The gunners were skilled specialists, trained at serving their field artillery fast and accurate. But they were not battle-line soldiers, not trained in the kind of hand-to-hand combat that was the standard work of light cavalry, and their resistance was minimal and weak.

The end of the trail, and Mary stopped, breathing hard. Through a gap in the woods she could see the stone house. There were no more guns between herself and that post. They had taken all the artillery in the tree line.

Hands on her hips, gasping for breath, she turned and looked out over the wheat field. The French infantry were not much farther along than they had been the last time she looked. They were moving cautiously, prepared for a surprise from in front.

Mary glanced impatiently down the trail, wondering why that first gun had not yet fired. But just as the gunners were not skilled in hand-to-hand combat, so the cavalry troopers were ignorant of the ways of artillery, and she could not expect them to load and fire with any great efficiency. What was more, she had left only three men at each gun when normally they were served by three times that number.

And just as she was thinking that, the gun went off, loud in the relative quiet, the gray smoke spurting out across the field, the wicked grape blasting into the French skirmishers.

She saw two men drop, but the soldiers were spread out across the field, not an ideal target for grapeshot, not like an unbroken line of cavalry. Still, the effect of the blast far exceeded the casualties the gun doled out. Mary saw men wheel in surprise, back away from the tree line, then wheel again, recalling the possible threat from the English troops hidden in the wheat.

Then the next gun spoke, another blast of grape, and the Frenchmen in the field did not know which way to run, did not know where their lines were, where the enemy was hiding. Mary knew very well how exposed they would feel, there on that open ground, the guns in the trees hurling their deadly loads. Not an hour before it had been her there, her and her beloved Frederick.

Another gun fired, another blast of grape added to the confusion and mounting panic, and the French infantry knew at last, knew for certain, that the guns were not in the hands of their fellow soldiers. They broke and ran, making for the stone house, and another gun blasted into their flank, firing with great effect, blue-coated bodies hurled in the air, scarlet bursts of blood over the green crops.

Those men who had come with Mary the full length of the trail wheeled their captured cannon around and pointed the muzzle at a place in front of the running French.

Frederick stood at the muzzle, ramming the grapeshot home. He was grinning like a little boy, his sweet face at odds with the bloody work they were doing. He pulled the rammer free and another of the troopers stepped up to the touchhole and applied the match and the cannon roared out, a deafening, earth-shaking noise. It leapt clean off the ground, rolled back ten feet, and Mary and her men were engulfed with gray, choking smoke.

"How much goddamned powder did you put in there?" Mary shouted, barely able to hear herself through dull, ringing ears.

The ad hoc gun crew grinned and slapped one another on the back. Someone actually giggled.

Bloody stupid men! Mary thought. They must have put more than twice the proper load in there, just to see what would happen. *God, but they are nothing but a goddamned bunch of little boys!*

When the smoke was finally carried away she could see that the last of the French infantry had reached the protection of the stone house. The gunners there would turn their cannon on the tree line, and once they had blasted away for a while the French infantry would once again come after them. Time to go.

"You boys, load this gun again," Mary ordered. "Round shot this time, and no more than two ladles of powder! If that goddamned barrel explodes, it will kill us all. Train it around to bear on the stone house. One shot and then join us down the trail and we'll go. I'll pass the word. Frederick, come with me."

She turned, headed down the trail, Frederick following dutifully behind. If those lunatics wanted to make the gun blow up in their faces, at least she and Frederick would not be in the way of the shrapnel.

They came to the next gun and Mary gave the same order and then she and Frederick walked down the trail to the next artillery position. They arrived there in time to see the first gun fire at the stone house. The ball struck a low wall, sending up a shower of rock splinters, as deadly as grape.

They continued on down the trail, rounding up the men as they went. "Michael," Frederick said as they walked. "What you did today . . . you saved us all."

"Not yet I haven't," Mary said, and said no more. She was not in the mood for praise.

Each of the eight former French guns blasted its round shot into the stone house, and then the English gun crews abandoned the pieces and assembled on the trail, just beyond the first gun they had captured.

Mary looked over the men. Nearly all of those who had come with her through the wheat field were still there, and she was happy for that, but Frederick was there as well, and that was all that really mattered.

She led them down the trail, past the place where they had entered the woods. Behind them, the guns from the stone house opened up, the men there having finally dragged their guns around to fire on their own gun emplacements. Round after round tore into the trees, firing at the abandoned guns, but the only men they could hit there were French, and they were dead already.

They came at last to the far end of the tree line. Mary led them across a patch of open ground where the French artillery would have massacred them, if their gun crews had still been alive. They made their way around the hill over which they had charged, and then they were hidden from the stone house and the wheat field, and the sound of the French guns was muted and distant.

They tramped wearily across the open fields, and found the road down which they had ridden to the attack that morning. It seemed impossible to Mary that it had only been that morning. It seemed they had been a week at least in that wheat field, that tree line.

A mile down the road, trudging back toward their camp, and they met up with another regiment of English cavalry. These fresh troops had been dispatched to help with the disaster, word of which had reached headquarters by way of a few lucky troopers who had escaped the slaughter.

Corporal Read stood at parade rest and reported to the colonel in terse words what had happened that morning, how she happened to be there at the head of two dozen tired and defeated troops.

The colonel listened, nodded. "Well done, Corporal, good show," he said at last. The survivors of that morning were mounted up behind the fresh troops and the regiment returned to camp. The colonel deemed further action against the French inadvisable.

They returned to camp just before nightfall, exhausted, wounded, defeated. They had no horses to attend to, few weapons left to clean, and those that they did have went ignored. They wanted nothing but rest, to lie down on their blankets, to close their eyes, to let sleep wash over them, to let that day pass from painful reality into unpleasant memory.

Mary Read pulled her tall boots off, let her regimental coat fall in a heap, her sword and belt on top of that, and lay down full length on her blanket, inside her little tent.

Beside her, she heard Frederick do the same, heard him give a little moan as the weight came off his feet. She opened her eyes, watched him for a moment in the light of a single candle, guttering in a lantern, that filled the small tent with a warm, soft glow.

She closed her eyes again, but her mind was whirling, and it was not about that bloody day that she was thinking. Rather she was thinking about their situation, the two of them, together in that tent.

Every night for almost a year they had lain down together, side by side, slept as close as man and wife. Mary had known plenty of married couples who did not share the warmth, intimacy, and love that she and Frederick had. But Frederick, of course, did not see that. Only she could think of it that way, because only she knew the truth.

She could stand it no longer. So what if Frederick was scandalized, so what if he rejected her, reported her to the colonel, had her thrown out of the regiment? After that morning she had had her fill of cavalry attacks in any event. The bloody death that had stalked them all that day, their wild attack on the artillery park, improbably successful, the horror of slaughtering men, the near miracle of their escape, all combined to fill her with a reckless, careless abandon.

She let out a little groan, flexed her arms. "Are you hurt, Frederick?" she asked, her voice low, soothing.

"I am hurt all over," he said, "but nothing mortal, I think. You?"

"I am the same. But I took a bad hit on the ribs. I fear one might be broken." She reached a tentative hand to her neck, unfastened the top button on her loose-fitting shirt. It took some great resolve to make her fingers work the buttons, one after the other, with the necessity of keeping her sex hidden so ingrained in her.

Her shirt fell open and the cool air touched her skin. Her breasts were not large—had they been, she would never have been able to get away with her guise for as long as she had—but they were full and round and unmistakably feminine.

She closed her eyes, overcome with a sense of finality, more afraid than she had been all that day, more afraid than she had been in the wheat field or running up the line of artillery emplacements. This was the sensation of taking wedding vows or stepping up to the gallows: final, irreversible. She felt her recklessness melt away. What if Frederick did reject her?

She ran a hand over her ribs, as if probing for a broken bone. Tensed, waited for Frederick to notice. She felt her panic mounting, wished she had not done this, wondered if it was too late to stop.

"Do you . . ." Frederick began, and then he gasped, a sound of pure shock, and Mary startled, her terror no longer an act. She sat up fast, pulled her shirt closed over her breasts.

She looked over at Frederick, her eyes wide in genuine fear. He was staring at her, his mouth hanging open, half up on his elbow, and she thought, *The die is cast.*

For a long time they were silent. Mary turned her face away. She felt the tears welling up, felt one roll down her cheek. She had so long envisioned this moment, had long calculated how she would feign embarrassment and fear and uncertainty. She had not counted on those feelings being real, but now that the moment was upon her they were very real indeed.

"Say something, goddamn it," she said at last, her voice low and husky, choking back the tears.

"Dear God . . ." Frederick managed, "you are . . . Are you . . . Dear God, are you a woman?"

Mary looked up at him. The tears were flowing now, down her cheeks. *Tears, dear God, after all I have seen!* she thought. There were times when she had wondered if she would ever cry again, if all of her femininity had been stamped out of her, living so long in the guise of a man, following her brutal calling. But here she was, and she felt not like a woman at all but like a frightened little girl.

"Yes, Frederick, yes. I am a woman. My . . . I'm . . . My name is Mary."

Frederick shook his head, looked away, and Mary wondered what possible revelation could be more shocking to him than that. Was there anything at all that could more completely shake his understanding of the world than to find out that his tentmate, his comrade-in-arms, was a woman?

"But you . . ." Frederick stammered, "you have served with the regiment of foot . . . and you told me you served aboard a man-of-war as well . . ."

"I did. I did not lie to you."

If he had replied that her whole life had been a lie to him, she was ready to point out that she had never explicitly told him she was a man, but he did not say that. Rather, he asked, "How have you managed . . . this?"

Mary sighed, pulled her shirt tighter around herself. "I have been playing the man most of my life. My mother, she was a good woman . . . Her husband was a sailor, you see, and once, soon after they were wed, he went off voyaging and he never returned. Lost at sea, I reckon. But he left her with a child, a boy. Some time after, my mother was tempted by another man. It happens, you know, even to good women, particularly when they are grieving as my mother must have been. This man got her with child . . . me . . . and abandoned her."

Mary paused, threw her head back, closed her eyes. She had never told this story to anyone but herself. These were memories long put away, and it was with great agony that she now wrenched them from their hiding place. "The boy, my brother, died soon after my birth. My mother was desperate, but she could not apply to her husband's family for help, not with a bastard child. So once I had grown a bit she dressed me as her lost son, passed me off to her husband's family as their grandson, and they supported us.

"I spent most of my life thus. A boy. My grandmother died when I was thirteen and I went to work as a footboy to a noble Frenchwoman but had no stomach for that, so I entered aboard the man-of-war. I have been from the one place to the other ever since." She gave a weak smile. "Like so many other young fellows."

For some moments Frederick was silent, thinking about this, trying to get his mind around this extraordinary turn of events. Finally he said, "This was no accident just now, you revealing yourself to me, was it?"

Mary bit her lip, shook her head.

"Why? I was in no way of discovering you."

She closed her eyes again, and the tears ran down her cheeks. She felt sick, in the pit of her stomach, a fear like she had never known. She opened her eyes again, wiped the tears away. Charge right into the guns, it was the only way. "Because I love you, Frederick. I love you and I could not stand to live another moment without you knowing the truth. God, we were nearly killed this day! Perhaps we will be killed tomorrow. I did not want to die with you never knowing."

At that Frederick chuckled, shook his head, and Mary felt a flash of anger. "You think this funny?"

"No, no, I do not. There are so many thoughts, all crowding together . . ." Frederick paused to let those thoughts settle. "Yes, I suppose it is funny. We were nearly killed today, in battle, two troopers in a regiment of light horse. But you saved us, saved us all. A woman."

He shook his head again. "So much makes sense now . . . How could I have not seen this?"

"People do not see things where it does not occur to them to look. That is how I have passed for a man for so long."

They were silent again, and then Mary said, "Do you hate me? For this?"

Frederick looked at her, and his face was kind, thoughtful, concerned. He seemed surprised by the suggestion. "Michael . . . Mary . . . no, no. I could never hate you. You have saved my life many times, showed me so much kindness. Just because I find you are a woman, that is not changed."

Mary smiled with relief. How many men would have felt that way? Every man Mary knew would have been furious at the thought of a woman helping him, protecting him, giving him advice on soldiering. But not Frederick, and it only served as further proof of how justified was her love for him. "You are a beautiful man," she said.

He shuffled closer to her, put his arm around her back. "My God, Mary, you cannot know what this means to me. I . . ." He shook his head, looked up again. "I . . . you see . . . I . . .'Tis a relief, for I have come to love you, too. Do

you see? Dear God," he chuckled, shook his head again at
the wonder of it all.

"I thought there was something wrong with me, can you
imagine, thought I was turning into some kind of bloody
buggerer! My God, my God . . ." He smiled, a full smile
of profound relief. "Do you see what a salvation this is?"

And Mary smiled as well and the tears rolled down her
cheeks in a steady stream and she thought she might burst
with happiness, joy like she had never know. Never, never
in her wildest fantasies had she envisioned Frederick at that
moment professing his love to her.

And then he sat up, beside her, and put his arms around
her. Their faces were inches apart. Mary looked into his
brown eyes, those eyes she loved so well, those eyes she
had stared at so often, but never this close.

And then they pressed their lips together and Mary was
swept away in the tenderness and passion and love and joy
of it all. She put her arms around him, ran her rough fingers
through his thick hair, kissed him with the pent-up passion
of a year and more.

He pushed her gently down on the blanket and lay beside
her and they kissed in desperate longing. She felt his hand
on her bare stomach, his long, gentle fingers running over
her skin, and it thrilled her and she felt a shiver run through
her. She pulled his head closer to her, wanted to consume
him with her kisses.

His hand moved slowly over her warm flesh, over her
firm breast. He cupped her in his big hand and gently
squeezed and it was heaven to her, but it was not right.

She put her hand on his, gently moved it away. He leaned
back, looked down at her.

"I love you, Frederick. I'll do anything for you. But I
won't be your whore."

At the close of the campaigning season they were married.

It was with no small fear that they revealed the truth of
Mary's gender to the captain of their company of Walpole's

Regiment of Light Cavalry, and announced their plans. There were many possible outcomes to their deception. Hanging was not out of the question.

But they were not hanged, not even close. The revelation of Mary's sex stunned the captain, indeed it stunned the entire army, just as it had stunned Frederick Heesch. But so well liked was Corporal Read, and so respected, that the news was greeted with amazement, then good humor and delight. The story of two troopers marrying became the great joke of the age.

And when at last they did marry in the small church in Rijsbergen—Frederick in his regimentals, Mary in a silk dress happily donated by Colonel Walpole's Flemish mistress—the church was packed to standing room only with all of the officers of all the regiments of horse and foot and artillery, along with a few select troopers, and the courtyard was jammed with those who could not get in the church.

The captain stood as Frederick's best man, Colonel Walpole himself gave Mary away.

For a wedding present the two were given their honorable discharges from Walpole's regiment.

A collection was taken up for the young couple to set up housekeeping, and so enthusiastic were their former fellow soldiers that Frederick and Mary Heesch found themselves in possession of a significant sum of money.

They went with the army to winter quarters in Breda, and there, not far from the great castle that dominated that city, they bought an inn, under the sign of the Three Trade Horses. With the city crowded with soldiers the inn would have been a success in any event, but the great fame that now attended the couple assured them a steady flow of officers, eating and drinking and taking their ease at their establishment.

Nor were any of the guests disappointed by the fare or the accommodations. With Frederick's affability and his skill in the kitchen, the Three Trade Horses was soon known as the finest, most congenial ordinary in Breda.

Frederick set the mood, but Mary ran the place, with her quiet efficiency and command presence. She supervised the servants, kept the books, dealt with the farmers and dairy-men and brewers and distillers who supplied the inn. There was never a military outfit that was more well organized or efficiently run.

She wore silk dresses and let her hair flow free under cotton mobcaps. Frederick put his arms around her, told her how much he loved her. At night, in front of the big fire-place in their bedchamber, they made love, tenderly, pas-sionately, with the abandon of two people completely devoted to one another and completely at ease in each other's presence. Sometimes Mary felt as if she could no longer tell where she ended and Frederick began, and she was delighted by that.

For a year and a half Mary's life was rapture. She felt as if she had finally arrived at that place she had been seek-ing all her life, and now that she was there, on that height, she would remain, content, for the rest of her days.

A year and a half. Then one morning Frederick woke with a cough. A week later he was dead.

Mary struggled on. She kept the Three Trade Horses go-ing. She kept it going for Frederick, though she herself was no more than an empty vessel, just the shell of Mary Heesch, with all the stuff inside torn out.

The Peace of Utrecht was signed and the war ended. The army went away and there was no business anymore for the Three Trade Horses. So, when all of her money was gone, when all of her servants had been let go, when every-thing that could be sold had been, Mary Heesch once again donned men's clothes.

There was no living to be had for a penniless widow in a foreign land. Mary Heesch could no longer survive, so once again she remade herself into Michael Read. She did not use the name Heesch, because every time she said it, it was like a knife through her chest.

She served for a while in a regiment of foot in a frontier town in Holland, but it was a living death. She could no longer stand to be in the Netherlands, could not endure the army life. As long as she was there she was constantly faced with the memory of what she had had, what she had lost.

She drifted to Amsterdam. Recalled her time in the navy. The life of a sailor had not been so bad. Thought that perhaps she would try that again.

Shipboard. It seemed as good a place as any to work and to live and to wait for her life to be over.

Chapter 6

NASSAU WAS A DREAM MADE SUBSTANCE TO ANNE Bonny, and something less than that to her husband.

They had been married a fortnight when they arrived at that island. The first two days of their union had been mostly taken up with making love, awkwardly and clumsily—sex, to James Bonny, had always been the end result of a financial transaction, and he was not accustomed to bedding a woman who wanted more than money for her effort—and arguing about what next to do with themselves.

In the end Anne had won out, concerning their future, as she knew she would, though with more effort expended than she had counted on.

Nassau it was.

James secured a berth as seaman aboard a ship bound for Nassau. The difficulty had been in finding such a ship; there was not so much trade with New Providence, and most honest shipmasters were loath to sail into that pirates' lair.

But Nassau, like any town, needed supplies: food, cloth, rum, manufactures. And unlike most colonial towns, there was ready money to be had there, in the form of the disparate coin that the pirates took from honest ships of every nation. For a shipmaster who did not mind the risk of sailing into the lion's den, and was not overly particular about where the coin in which he was paid had come from, there was real money to be made in trading with New Providence.

Once such a ship had been found, hiring on was not a problem. There was a dearth of seamen in the colonies, and fewer still who wished to sail in harm's way.

The next day Anne used half of the money she had stolen from her father to buy passage aboard that same ship. She sailed under her maiden name. No one knew that she and the new seaman were man and wife. In this way, though Anne had to pay for her passage, James was paid for his, so it was as if they were making a voyage for free. Except that James had to work.

The ship was a week sailing to New Providence. It was the first time that Anne had been at sea since she was eight, since sailing from Ireland to the colonies. She remembered little of that voyage, having only vague impressions of fear and loneliness, the ache of leaving the only home she had known, the terror of the big sea and of a future in an unknown and wild land.

And here she was again, she realized, leaving home, off to some dangerous and unknown place; but there was no fear in her heart now, no loneliness or despair. She was in rapture with all that she saw, the beautiful ship that towered over her, the blue, blue water through which they plowed, cleaving their long wake, startling white against the blue sea. The dolphins, the flying fish, the hundreds of little sounds that made up the orchestra of a ship at sea, she loved it all.

After four days under way she prevailed upon the master, who was quite taken with her, to let her go into the rigging aloft.

He had been shocked at first, flustered at the suggestion. But Anne was persuasive, and the master relented. She donned her coarsest working clothes, and with the master as her guide, clambered into the mizzen shrouds and ratlines that formed something akin to a rope ladder up the mizzenmast, and started to climb.

The master was attention itself, showing her how to hold

the shrouds and not the ratlines, how to maneuver around the running gear that threaded its way between the black standing rigging. He put his arm around her waist in a most protective manner, even augmented her safety with a helpful hand on her ass now and again, but Anne ignored those liberties, because her spirit was soaring.

Up and up she went, with the ship growing narrower below her. Up into the great arcs of canvas, gray and black tar-stained against the blue sky.

She paused under the platform halfway up the mast.

"That there is what we call the 'top,' " the master explained. The shrouds were narrow there, where they came together near the masthead, forcing the master to press hard against her. "In this here case, the 'mizzen top,' on account of its being on the mizzenmast, do you see?"

There was a hole through the top, an easy way up onto that platform, but she had never seen any of the sailors use it. Rather, they had clambered out onto a smaller set of ropes that ran from the lower shrouds up and out to the edge of the top at a near forty-five-degree angle. Climbing over those meant hanging backwards from them as one made his way over the rim of the top.

"What now, Captain?" Anne asked.

"Well, ma'am, if you would go into the top, it would be best if you was to climb through that hole there, which we call the lubber's hole."

"Lubber's hole? A disdainful name. I have never seen any of the sailors use it."

"No, ma'am. That's why we call it the lubber's hole. A proper sailor goes over the futtocks, which is them short shrouds there. But, ma'am, you ain't a proper sailor."

"Indeed I am not. But like a proper sailor, I say, 'Sod the bloody lubber's hole.' "

Anne smiled at the master's visible shock. *Such a coarse bitch I am,* she thought. *Is it any wonder he thinks he'll have me betwixt the sheets by voyage's end?*

Then with three quick steps she was up the futtocks and over the edge of the top, no easy task in skirts, which were a terrible nuisance.

And if the master objected to her brashness, Anne guessed that the view of her legs afforded him as she hung backwards on the futtock shrouds more than compensated. In any event he followed her with never a word about it.

It was magnificent up there, with the horizon making a great unbroken arc as far around as she could see before the view was blocked by the lovely curve of the sails. Below her, the run of the deck from the bow aft, the long line of wake running down her side. How very narrow the ship looked from up there, far too narrow to remain upright, as if she should just tip over under the weight of her masts.

The motion, too, was unlike any she had experienced; a plunging back and forth, much more pronounced than it was on deck, along with a circular kind of swaying as the ship rolled, pitched, yawed, and the height of the mizzen top above deck exaggerated every move.

"Oh, sir, I see why you men love sailing so! Is there anything more magnificent than this?" Anne cried, and though she was addressing the master, it was herself to whom she was speaking.

"Indeed, ma'am. When the weather if fine, it is a wondrous thing."

She spent the rest of the voyage soaking in as much as she could of the shipboard life. She watched her husband working high aloft and sweating at the sheets and halyards with his fellows, smiled at him as he shot black looks aft at her, unhappy with the attention she was receiving from the master but unable to do anything about it. Her world was the quarterdeck and his the forecastle head at the bow, and as long as she was a passenger and he a sailor before the mast, there was nothing that could change that.

Six days out and they raised New Providence, low and green on the horizon. Anne remained on deck throughout the day, watching with eager anticipation as more and more detail of the island revealed itself, gratefully accepting the master's offer of the use of his telescope to scan this place she had so long dreamed of seeing.

Nassau, the pirates' haven. Wicked, depraved Nassau.

The breeze failed with the setting sun and it was not until

late morning of the next day that they stood in between Hog Island and New Providence, threading their way through the tangle of shipping there.

"Sir," Anne said to the master. She was standing on the quarterdeck, as usual, dressed now in fine, demure silk and taffeta, a parasol protecting her fair skin from the tropical sun that beat down on them. "Sir, pray, you had said there was not much shipping bound for New Providence, but I perceive a great number of ships here. More than ever I saw in Charles Town Harbor."

"Bah," said the master. "It's those rogue pirates, do you see? They'll have a ship, and when they are done with her, why, they'll just let her rot.

"To be sure they careen their vessels, by which I mean they take them up on a beach and roll them on their side and thus get at the weeds grown there. They have to, have to keep them fast, or else they'd never be able to run their poor victims down, or escape from the men-of-war. But beyond that the lazy dogs will do nothing. So these ships here, castoffs, old prizes, rotten pirate ships. Wreckage, no more."

Anne nodded her head. Fascinating. Her first lesson in piracy.

"There's not half the number now as there was," the master continued. "This new Governor, this Woodes Rogers, he's making a clean sweep, fore and aft. He come here with a pardon from the King. Full amnesty to them will foreswear the pirate life. Half the villains here have accepted his pardon, and half have lit out before he hangs them. But they are still a vicious lot of rogues, to be sure."

"I have no doubt," said Anne.

They stood on, into the harbor, taking in sail as they worked toward a clear place to anchor. Anne could see James Bonny up aloft, his skinny posterior pointing skyward as he bent far over the foreyard, handing the sail.

The master put on a great show of bellowing commands to bring the vessel to anchor, being manly for Anne's benefit, and once the anchor was down she was not surprised to find him seeking her out.

"As a gentleman I am honor-bound to warn you, Miss Cormac, that it ain't safe for a woman alone in this place."

"As I have said, sir, I shall be visiting my brother, who keeps a small farm in the interior of the island. I am in no doubt but he is ashore now, watching our arrival, and will be at the dock to greet me."

"But if he is not, ma'am, I would entreat you to consider staying aboard, under my care."

Under your care indeed, you randy old dog, Anne thought. There was a certain wantonness about a young woman traveling unescorted, and Anne imagined that the master took encouragement from that, as well as from her other brazen displays. But before she could politely decline, the mate stepped aft. "Anchor's holding, sir. I've veered half a cable. And the new fellow, that Bonny, says he's ruptured himself."

The master, the mate, and Anne looked forward. On the forecastle head James Bonny was doubled over in what Anne thought to be an excessively histrionic display of agony.

The master sighed. "Bloody convenient, eh? All right, let us pay the rogue off and see him ashore. He has a mind to go a-pirating, I'll wager."

"Oh, sir," said Anne, "if you are sending that poor fellow ashore now, perhaps the boat could bear me as well?"

And so they went ashore, James and Anne Bonny, to set foot in Nassau for the first time.

They wandered away from the dock and along wide Bay Street, which fronted the water. The taverns, the rickety inns and smattering of shops, the men and women in their outlandish, brightly colored clothing, the smells of cooking and rotting fish and the briny odor of the sea, the hot sun, the laughter, and singing, it was mesmerizing to Anne Bonny, like a place from a storybook, a wicked fairy tale for grown-ups, a place beyond laws, common or statute.

In her excitement she hardly noticed James Bonny, whining at her elbow, and took little notice of his complaints about the improperness of it all, the villainy of that town, his concerns over how he would protect her virtue in such a place. His voice was like the screaming of the cicadas back home: loud, grating, high-pitched, and incessant, but easy to ignore after a few moments of listening to it.

"Anne . . . we needs secure some kind of lodging . . . before you are off on your grand tour . . . I can't carry our things all bloody day . . ."

That complaint had some validity and so Anne stopped where she was, an intersection where a sandy dirt road branched off from Bay Street and ran between a smattering of ill-conceived wood-frame buildings, the bright paint peeling off their shudders.

James Bonny dropped his seabag and Anne's small chest filled with all the things she had smuggled from her father's house. He took off his battered, wide-brimmed hat and wiped his brow with his sleeve. "Just like I reckoned, not a place fit for a lady to stay, not a one on this whole damned—"

"I am terribly thirsty, James. Let us go to that place there and have something to drink." She pointed across the street to a two-story building on the opposite corner. A few small windows looked out over the road. A sign above the single door read The Ship Tavern.

"What, there?" As they considered that establishment the door swung open and a great bearded hulk of a man staggered out, his hat askew, his coat half-off. He managed a few steps down the street before he fell in a heap on the dusty road and lay there, unmoving.

"Yes, there," said Anne. "It looks as reputable a place as any in this town, and they may have rooms to let as well."

"If you are thirsty, Anne, I can fetch . . ." James Bonny began, but Anne was already halfway across the street before he finished the thought, leaving him with nothing to do but pick up their worldly possessions and hurry after her.

She stepped boldly across Bay Street, marched up to the door of the Ship Tavern, and pushed it open. After the brilliant afternoon sun she was nearly blind in the gloomy interior. She could make out a smattering of tables, a bar against the far wall. The smoke of a dozen pipes hung in layers beneath the low ceiling and swirled in the current of air created by the swinging door.

The place was crowded; bearded men, their long hair tied in queues and clubbed, wearing the blue jackets and wide-legged trousers of sailors, or battered silk coats, once-fine breeches, and silk stockings. Bare feet or square-toed shoes, even a few silver buckles, every stratum of the pirate community was gathered there in the Ship Tavern.

The smell of the place wrapped around her, reminiscent of the ship she had just left; pipe smoke and unwashed men, cooked meat, tar. But also the tangy smell of strong drink, and perfume as well, for as her eyes adjusted to the gloom Anne could see that she was not the only woman there.

It was a filthy, mean, dangerous, and unwholesome place. It was everything she imagined Nassau to be.

Anne stepped boldly through the door, swept across the floor to the bar. She could see heads turn, could feel the eyes on her. She might not have been the only woman in the tavern, but she was the only one who did not look like a prostitute, and, in fact, the only one who was not.

She stopped at the bar, turned with a flourish, and looked back across the room. James Bonny was struggling through the door under his load. He deposited it on the floor and hurried over to his wife, as if she might be violated in the three seconds it took him to thread his way between the tables.

"Anne . . ." he said in a low tone.

"Rum," said Anne, loud. "That is what you sailors drink, is it not?"

"Well, yes, sailors—"

"Let us have some rum then! A whole bottle of it!" She turned away from the room, away from the many eyes that were watching her. "Publican, pray, a bottle of rum here, and two glasses."

The publican considered her over folded arms. He had the look of a man who had seen plenty in his time and was not impressed by much of it, but he pulled a bottle from under the counter, set it down with two glasses.

Anne tipped the brown liquor into her glass and into James's as well, then without asking or being asked, topped off the glass of the man who stood on her other side.

She lifted her drink, and, with a nod, bid her husband do the same, which he did, reluctantly. "To a new life in New Providence!" she said, and someone in the dark tavern called out, "Hear her, hear her!"

She put the glass to her lips, tipped it back the way she had seen men do it. The liquor burned, the fumes swirled in her nose and down her throat. She felt as if she might gag, but she fought it. Tears welled up in her eyes. It was a sensation like none she had had before, burning, noxious, and at the same time sweet, thrilling, warming her from the inside as it went down.

Rum. It ran like a river through the West Indies. It was a trade good, a medicine, a refuge, an easy pleasure for rich and poor alike. It was a staple of the pirates, as much as food and water. It was the taste of heedless abandon.

She poured herself another glass. And that was how her new life commenced.

Woodes Rogers looked out the window of his office in the Governor's House at the work being done to the walls of the fort.

It was with an inner smirk that he used the term "Governor's House." He doubted that that title had ever been applied to a more pathetic structure than the one he now occupied. It was not even a house, really, but a small stone building inside the small fort that overlooked the western entrance to Nassau Harbor. It had been built as an officers' barracks, but for lack of anything better, Rogers had taken it over as the Governor's official residence.

The captain and lieutenant of the small company of soldiers that he had brought with him from England lived in the other building within the fort. The troops were housed in their tents, no great hardship in such a climate.

The Governor's House was a shambles and the fort was

a shambles. Soon after taking possession they had cleaned it out, removed most of the debris, and evicted the few hopeless drunks and madmen who had taken residence there. The soldiers and settlers were housed within the limited safety of the fort's walls. But the entire structure was crumbling. As a shelter it was barely adequate. As a fortification it was useless.

Under the hot Caribbean sun, under Woodes Rogers's critical eye, soldiers and hired men labored at rebuilding the walls against the possibility of Spanish attack. The hired laborers were pirates to a man, men who had accepted the King's pardon and were playing at honest work.

Not that they were working overhard. Half of them at any one time were sitting down, and half of those sitting were asleep. They were all drunk. It was pathetic. But that was the laboring population from which Rogers had to draw.

Behind him, Ben Hornigold poured another drink, smacked his lips loud, and sipped.

"No, I couldn't raise old Vane for the life of me," Hornigold continued his report. "He's still out there. So is this Stede Bonnet and Teach as well. But they know now you means business. That word is spread. They know you ain't going to run like a puppy if they come sailing in."

"Good."

Rogers was pleased with old Ben Hornigold. Hornigold had not just accepted the King's pardon, he had agreed to join with Rogers in routing the pirate threat from Nassau.

Easy for him, he was a wealthy man who had already made his fortune on the account. Rogers knew better than to ask he return that stolen booty. Let him keep it, he was more valuable to England as a privateer than his stolen fortune would be sitting in the treasury. He was the kind who would be loyal to the side he thought would win. For now that meant Governor Rogers.

"Do you think Vane will return?" Rogers asked.

A merchant ship, the *John and Elizabeth,* had come limping into Nassau some months earlier, and her master had a message for Woodes Rogers, given him personally by

Charles Vane. The message was an unequivocal threat.

From most, such a threat would have been mere bluster, but not from Charles Vane. Vane was a madman. Vane was a man who had beaten uncooperative merchant captains to death with his bare hands, a man who had stuffed oakum into his victims' mouths and lit it on fire, had put a thin cord around men's heads and twisted, twisted until their eyeballs burst from their sockets.

A threat from Vane was worth considering, even for Woodes Rogers, a man who would not be intimidated.

Rogers had dispatched Hornigold to hunt Vane down. Hornigold had been gone so long that Rogers reckoned he had gone back to the pirating life. But the day before, Hornigold had returned, his pledge to the Governor intact.

"Vane return? That I can't say. Are you afraid, Governor?"

"No," said Rogers, and it was true.

"Well, revenge, it's a costly thing, you know. Don't know if Vane will care to do it in the end. And he ain't sailing a man-of-war. His men have to agree as well. Faith, his men have to agree to damn near anything he wants to do, unless they are in a fight, or chasing or running. It's the way with the pirates, as you know. I don't think young Calico Jack Rackam is of a kidney to sail right in here and burn your ship just for the pleasure of Charles Vane."

"Hmmm." *Calico Jack Rackam.* Rogers had not heard that name before. He tucked it away in his mental catalog.

One of the men working on the wall had produced a bottle of rum and was passing it around. Rogers wondered if he should go out and put a stop to such egregious behavior. He was walking a razor's edge between maintaining discipline and not pushing so hard that these men would just piss on their pardons and go pirating again.

A self-conscious cough and a soft, "Beg pardon, Governor?" and Woodes Rogers turned toward the door. There was a young sailor standing there, a skinny fellow with a weak chin and a few uneven patches of whiskers on his face.

"Yes?" He would have to appoint a secretary to intercept this kind of intrusion.

"Sir, beg your pardon . . ." The young sailor took a step into the room. He held his hat in front of him, like a tenant farmer addressing the lord of the manor.

If only all of these bastards were as cowed as this one, Rogers thought. "What might I do for you?"

The sailor's eyes darted toward Hornigold and back again.

"Whatever you have to say you may say in front of Captain Hornigold. He has my complete confidence." The former pirate nodded, poured himself another glass.

"Well, Governor, I had heard . . ." the young man stammered, "that is to say, it was my understanding . . . I thought you was willing to pay, sir, for information, about them that was going back to their pirating ways . . ."

Rogers nodded. He had made it known that he would pay for such information. He deemed it necessary, as loath as he was to do it, as disgusting as he thought such a man must be who would take him up on the offer. "That is correct. What have you to say?"

"Well, sir . . ." Eyes darted at Hornigold again, but the old man was firmly planted in his chair and showed no signs of leaving, so the sailor went on. "Sir, I heard . . . overheard, that is to say, one Nathaniel Nelson saying as he was fixing to go on the account, and the King be damned . . . Beg your pardon, that was what he said. Said he would be sailing within the week. And another by the name of Billy Oglethorpe, he cursed your name, sir, something wicked, and says he's for pirating too, once he's careened his sloop, sir."

Rogers nodded. Nelson and Oglethorpe were vicious rogues, and he had never been much impressed with their sincerity in accepting the King's pardon. Very well, he would have them watched. Let them make one move and it was the gallows for both of them.

The sailor was still shifting from foot to foot, abusing the brim of his hat with nervous fingers.

"Is that all?"

"Yes, sir, but, sir, I'll keep my ears open, you know, keep a weather eye out, and if I hears more, then you'll know it, sir . . ."

"Good. Thank you, I am grateful." *God, what a pathetic weasel,* Rogers thought. He hated such men, hated the necessity that drove him to countenance them. He dug in his purse, produced a shilling. "There you go, son, for your trouble."

The sailor took the coin eagerly. "Bless you, sir. Thank you."

"What is your name, lad?"

"Bonny, sir. By your leave, James Bonny."

"Well, thank you, James Bonny."

"You're welcome, Your Honor, to be sure . . ." James Bonny said, then with a bit more bobbing and scraping, he was gone.

Rogers watched him hurry away through the dust and rubble of the fort. "What think you of this fellow, Hornigold?"

"Bloody pathetic, the little worm." Hornigold stared at the floor, frowned, and then said, "Yes, yes, now I recall. Saw him last night, down to the Ship Tavern." He chuckled.

"What of him?"

"Him? Nothing. Just more of the trash that drifts through this place. But the damndest thing. He has a wife, name of Anne. Lovely girl, damned lovely, and making quite a show of it. Drinking and carousing with all those dogs at the Ship, acts like she's been pirating her whole life, though I was told they've only been here but three weeks or so. Quite a woman, I can't recall the like."

"A whore?"

"No, she ain't, as I hear it. Just a girl who likes her fun."

"And she is married to this Bonny?"

"For now. I'd warrant him for a dead man within the month. But this Anne Bonny, she will be trouble for you, my dear Rogers." Hornigold poured another shot of rum, tossed it back, laughed. "She will be trouble."

Chapter 7

AMSTERDAM WAS COLD, WINDSWEPT. NUMB-FINGERED, wind-like-needle-pricks-in-the-face cold, under leaden skies. A few flakes of gray snow whipped around, clung to frozen iron and wood and brick, but the air was too frigid and brittle for real snow.

There were some fine places in Amsterdam, lovely places despite the bitter winter weather. Grand old buildings that stood like monuments to age after age of Dutch fiscal responsibility and plodding work. Canals that cut through the city, as lovely as might be found anywhere in Europe. Beautiful parklands, manicured and tended, theatrical houses of Roman proportions, hushed office buildings, all leather and paneling and epic scenes in oil on canvas.

There were some fine places in Amsterdam, but the waterfront was certainly not one of them.

It was not lovely along the waterfront, but then it did not have to be. The people who lived and made their livings there were not the people for whom beauty was created. They were the meanest of humanity: the dockworkers, sailmakers and chandlers, the stevedores, the sailors. They were not the recipients of wealth, they were the conduits of it. Their work was to carry things of value from the Netherlands out into the world and back again, and they kept for themselves just the tiniest part of it, the merest scrapings.

The ships were crowded against the docks, shoulders braced to the wind that whipped off the IJmeer and whistled through their bare, spindly masts and yards, like so many dead trees in a long dead forest. Small waves piled up against the mole, pushing the line of detritus and flotsam against the seawalls again and again. Everything was colored shades of brown and gray.

Captain Dirk Bes, master of the 240-ton merchantman *Hoorn*, ran a handkerchief under his nose and then with the cuff of his coat wiped a tear from his cheek. The wind bit into his face and made his eyes water when he looked up. His cocked hat was tied to his head with a wool scarf that was knotted under his chin. He was miserably cold.

He glanced down into the waist to assure himself that the sailors and stevedores were stowing the cargo down well enough that he could turn his attention elsewhere, for a second at least. *"Voorzichtig met die vaten, jullie uilskuikens!"* he shouted, then turned to the young man who was waiting patiently for his attention.

"Zo jij bent een zeeman?" Bes said. "So you are a sailor, then, not some miserable creature from the slums?"

"Aye, sir. I was three years in a man-of-war."

The master nodded, looked the young man up and down. Faded red wool coat, wool shirt, wide-legged trousers, wool stockings, battered square-toed shoes. Quite unremarkable. But there was a tenseness, a rigidity about him, like he was close to standing at attention. Not the posture of a merchant seaman, the liberal dogs. Navy usage, perhaps, but the master did not think so.

The boy's Dutch was as flawless as that of any native speaker, but the accent was not native-born.

"Dutch navy?"

"No, sir. Royal Navy. Royal British Navy."

Ah, the master thought. "You are just off this navy ship, then?"

"No, sir. It has been a few years."

Bes nodded again. He noticed the darker patches on the coat over which insignia had once been sewn. Now he understood. "You were a soldier then, in the late war?"

"Aye. Cadet in a regiment of foot, and then I rode with a light infantry unit, sir."

Of course. The Low Countries were full of them, young English soldiers who had been sent across the Channel to fight in Flanders and France and Spain. They fought to stop the threat of a reunion between the Austrian and Spanish Hapsburg line or the Bourbons of France and Spain. It was a wildly convoluted political circus, and the master had often wondered how many of those poor bastards slogging through the mire and filth understood or cared.

The war was four years gone now, but still legions of them remained. They were wanted men in England, or married to women in Holland or Flanders, or just too shattered from their experiences of war to return to their homes.

The master looked back to the waist, shouted an unnecessary admonition to take care with the stay tackle, then turned back to the boy. He was young—early twenties, perhaps, his chin quite devoid of whiskers. A handsome lad with short, black hair and striking blue eyes. Faraway eyes, a combat veteran's eyes, eyes that were much older than the rest of him.

Captain Bes was no newcomer to the ways of the wicked world, but he could only imagine what this youth had seen in his brief years that gave his eyes the look they had.

"Very well. But see here, the docks are crawling with sailors, able-bodied men, with years more time at sea than you. I can't pay you but a boy's wages."

The young man nodded. He did not seem to care.

The master coughed. He had expected some protest. In fact, he was prepared to pay the boy an ordinary seaman's rate if he had argued. There was something about the youth that he liked, some sadness that elicited sympathy for his plight, whatever that might be, whatever it was that drove him back to sea after all these years.

Sympathy was not an emotion Bes felt on any regular basis, particularly not when it came to sailors.

But the young man did not protest being rated ship's boy, he just accepted this offer with stoicism, and it put the master momentarily off balance. And it told him something more. The boy was not going to sea to seek his fortune. He was running away.

"We're taking this lot to Stockholm," Captain Bes went on, nodding toward the stack of casks on the dock and those being swayed down into the hold. "Then I reckon we'll be for the Med, or the West Indies. Been to the West Indies?"

"No, sir."

"They got the yellow jack there, and pirates swarming like flies to horseshit. But at least you don't freeze your damned balls off."

"No, sir."

"All right, then. Stow your dunnage forward, then lend a hand in the waist."

"Aye, sir." The boy lifted his seabag and tossed it over his shoulder in one smooth, practiced motion.

Dirk Bes watched the boy as he headed forward, watched him drop his seabag down the forecastle companionway and start to clamber down after it.

The young man had gone directly to the forecastle, had not had to ask what was meant by "stow your dunnage forward." That, and the fact that he could so deftly handle the act of getting down a narrow companionway with a big seabag, an act that confounded the landlubber, proved he had not been lying about his experience aboard ships.

"Oh, yes," the master called after him. "What's your name? For the books?"

The boy paused, halfway down the ladder, his chest level with the deck. "Read, sir. Michael Read."

Mary watched the seabag plunge down the dark hole of the forecastle scuttle, watched it hit the deck with a soft thud, then swung her leg over the combing and scrambled down the ladder. It had been years, but the lessons of shipboard life had been drilled into her at a young age, and with the uncompromising exactitude of the Royal Navy. She had not forgotten.

She stepped off the ladder into the gloom of the forecastle. There was a lantern lit over the long table that ran down the centerline of the ship and took up a good deal of the space, but its light was weak and most of the forecastle was lost in deep shadow. She could see the berths that lined either side, three high from deck to overhead. Most had curtains drawn across them; scant privacy, but better than she had in the navy.

Larboard side and all the way forward she saw a berth with the curtain pulled back and no sign of occupation, so she hefted her seabag again, maneuvered around the table, and tossed the dunnage into the bunk. The straw in the thin mattress made a crackling sound under the weight of the bag. She sat on the edge and looked around her new home.

Lord, how it all came rushing back! The soft sway of the ship as she was pushed around by the waves, the slap of water against the hull. The dim-lit space. The smell of unwashed men and their wet clothes. The smell of tar, linseed oil, paint, wood, marlin, bilge. The remnants of a thousand meals eaten at that table. Man-of-war or merchantman, first-rate ship of the line or coasting brig, the smell was the same.

Mary shook her head. So long, so long. And here she was once again in men's clothing. Michael Read, off to sea once more.

Frederick, oh, God, Frederick, how have I come to this again? Why were you taken from me?

She thought about her new shipmates, whom she had yet to meet. Had they, for all their masculinity, seen the things that she had seen? Had they killed as many men as she had in bloody combat? Had they known love and loss? Were they strutting cocks of the forecastle, or wounded and half-dead like her, no longer seeking happiness, just trying to run away from despair?

Whatever else they were, they were her shipmates. The closest thing she would have to a family for the duration of the voyage.

She put her face in her hands and began to cry.

Chapter 8

EIGHT WEEKS ON NEW PROVIDENCE ISLAND AND ANNE Bonny was already bored.

She never thought it would happen, not there. Not in Nassau, with all its wicked delights, a bountiful source of excitement. She did not think she would tire of the thrill of associating with such dangerous men, such sinful and un-inhibited women as those who inhabited the island's taverns and ordinaries, its streets and beaches.

She had thought she could spend her whole life exploring the town and the interior of the island, making herself wel-come on the pirate ships that rode at anchor in the harbor or strolling along the stretch of beach that served as home to most of the sea robbers there.

Anne, with James in protesting tow, would amble down wide Bay Street, accepting the nods and lustful stares of the men she passed, down along the hot sand, stop and chat with those pirates with whom she was acquainted.

As dusk fell they would make their appearance at the Ship. Then the revelries would begin in earnest, the long bouts of swilling rum and rumfustian, punch, gin. There were frequently musicians there, rough dancing, bawdy songs, the close-by sounds of fornicating, wild and unbridled. It was exactly the unfettered existence that Anne had craved during all those long years she had chafed away in her father's fine house.

Anne was the center of attention, the loudest, the most raucous, the most bawdy, the toast of the taverns. She was the object of all of their desires, and she enjoyed the atten-tion, the unrequited lust, while James sulked and whined and tagged after her on their nightly bacchanal.

Not so long before sunrise they would return to their

room above the Ship Tavern and if Anne was not too disgusted, and if James was not too angry or drunk or both, and if they were still speaking to one another, they would make love.

Mechanical, uninspiring, and not overly satisfying, James would sweat away. He reminded Anne of a little dog humping its owner's leg.

When it was over they would sleep until noon, rise, and do it all again.

As insane as it all was, still, it was turning into the one thing she detested. It was becoming routine.

Now she sat in the Ship Tavern at her usual table, the now familiar taste of rum in her throat, a film of sweat on her face and neck from the exertion of dancing with some great brute of a fellow who had been with Blackbeard himself aboard the *Queen Anne's Revenge* before Teach had shed himself of that ship.

James was sulking, angry with Anne for dancing with the man, but too afraid of both the pirate and his wife to make much of a protest.

The night outside was cool and lovely, but in the dark tavern room of the Ship it was sweltering with the close-packed clientele and the heat from the lanterns hanging from the rough-cut beams, the candles guttering and swirling and searching for air enough to stay lit in the thick layer of smoke.

The musicians were playing, loud and fast, music for dancing, music for terrorizing a prize into surrender. Rogues crowded around the round tables, heavily armed, laughing loud, with whores in gaudy dresses on their knees, pewter mugs in hand.

It was a mad, crazed bacchanal, the desperate exuberance of the damned, and already Anne felt more at home there then she had at all the cotillions in Charles Town.

She picked up the bowl of punch, took a long drink.

But I am bored, she thought. She realized that she was just putting into conscious thought something she had understood for a week or more.

Not that Anne hadn't tried to stir things up a bit. One

night James had caught her in the hammock of one of those villains, copulating wildly to the creaking of the manila cordage that held the hammock up. There had been considerable fireworks following that event, screaming and threatening, but in the end James Bonny had not the heart or the guts to do anything about it, and that made Anne despise him all the more.

It was time for something new.

"James, dear, what think you of moving on?" she asked.

James looked around, confused, said, "What? Off to our room?"

"No, what think you of leaving Nassau? Go to Jamaica or Barbados, perhaps? See some more of these islands?"

James Bonny scowled. "We've just but arrived here, and now it's off again?"

"We've not just arrived. We've been here two months, at least. We've seen what Nassau has to offer. I should like to take another voyage by sea, I think."

"Humph," James Bonny said. He had not been much pleased with the goings-on during the last voyage. "And where will I get the money then, eh? What should I do for work on them islands?"

"What do you for work now, my dear?" Anne asked, and as she did, it occurred to her that she did not actually know how they were managing to live. James always seemed to have some money. Not much, but some, and she did not know from where it came. His wages for that one voyage from Charles Town could not have lasted that long, not the way she was wont to spend.

She had hoped for some weeks that poverty would force James to ship out again, leave her there alone, where she could enjoy herself without feeling as if she had an anchor tied around her neck, but he showed no inclination to go.

"How *do* you get your money?" she asked again, curious now.

James smiled a cunning, knowing smile, an expression that did not suit him. "I have a special arrangement, do you see, with some very important men. Damned important men."

Anne squinted at him. She was on her way to being drunk, but not yet so far in her cups that she failed to see something was afoot. "Very important men" did not generally mix with the likes of James Bonny, nor did he have much to offer such people.

"What, exactly, is your 'special arrangement'?" she asked slowly.

"It ain't for your ears, and you a woman."

"What is it?"

"I said, it ain't for your ears. Now, you are my goddamned wife, will you bloody well act it for once, and not concern yourself with how I earns a living?"

Anne glared at her husband. There were two ways she could pry this information from him: the sweet way or the bitchy way—and she was in no mood for the sweet way. "You are a liar. There are no important men would give you the time of day."

"Humph. You think not, eh?"

"I know it. Speak no more on it."

"You think I got nothing to offer no one of quality? Just simple Jack Tar, am I?"

"I said no more of your lies."

"Oh, lies is it?" James's voice dropped to a conspiratorial whisper. "Well, Governor Woodes Rogers himself, he don't see it as lies."

Woodes Rogers? The new Governor was anathema to Anne, who took her opinions on such matters from the Brethren of the Coast, but she chuckled and said only, "Woodes Rogers indeed!"

"Hush up, you daft woman!" James hissed, glanced around quick. "Aye, Woodes Rogers. And old Ben Hornigold, what is now in His Majesty's service, they are both most interested in what I have to say."

"And what might that be?" Anne spoke soft.

James leaned forward, spoke softer yet. "I tells them things, see? Keep them informed of what is going on, the things I hear. Who is going on the account, who has the King's pardon but don't intend to honor it, that sort of thing. And aren't they grateful, and willing to pay good coin for their gratitude?"

Anne leaned back, putting distance between herself and James Bonny. "You loathsome little worm!" she said, loud. She could see her husband begin to panic, as well he might, though her voice could not penetrate the din unless she actually yelled, nor were any paying attention. "You little bastard, you filthy son of a bitch!"

James looked furtively around and held up his hands in hopes of shutting Anne up.

Anne glared at him, letting the contempt show in her face, but she did not enunciate his crimes. As vile, as verminlike as he seemed to her at that moment, she could not do that. She knew what the men in the Ship Tavern would have done to her husband if they knew he had been telling tales to Woodes Rogers, and she would not have that on her conscience.

Still, she regarded him with the purest hatred. The boy who had tried to rape her, for him she had felt fury, outrage. For her father, bitterness at his trying to constrain her. For James Bonny, she had always felt a touch of love, a bit of affection, and pity for his weakness.

But now that was gone. She hated him, reviled him, loathed him. He became suddenly something hideous to look upon. For the moment she was unable to move. She wanted to spit in his face, to kick him into the dirt. Perhaps she *would* make a general announcement of his perfidy.

And then the front door of the tavern swung open—not the crack of someone slipping in or out, but flung open, a great, bold gesture. The cool evening air swirled the clouds of pipe smoke in patterns like the smoke of a battlefield and the blessed fresh draft wafted over Anne's sweating brow.

All heads turned toward the door. Anne looked as well. The noise dropped off to near silence.

A man was standing there, framed by the entrance, a tall man, well built. In the dim light of the tavern Anne could make out little of him, but he stepped in through the door, his arms spread, as if he was welcoming the crowd like they were guests at his home. She could see fine clothes, long, dark hair tumbling in curls down a nearly white coat.

But not white, there was a pattern to it, and the cloth of his breeches was striped in a bold pattern. Calico? It looked to be.

She recalled hearing of one of the well-known figures in Nassau, gone off pirating with Charles Vane, who was given to such dress. Could this be he?

Then the tavern erupted. Men leapt to their feet, crowded around the newcomer, slapped his back, and shook his hand. They pulled him into the room, and under the glow of one of the lanterns Anne could see the square jaw, the sculpted face, the thick, groomed hair, the white teeth under the audacious mustache. He would have been considered a handsome man among the gentry of Charles Town. Among the pirates, he was extraordinary.

The swarm of men pulled this newcomer toward the bar, still pounding, still shaking his hand. Anne sat up straighter, watching the procession as it passed, intrigued and a bit piqued. She was the newcomer, the center of attention. She had not seen such a fuss made over anyone since her own arrival.

From all corners of the tavern men and women called their hearty greetings and Anne heard "John" and "Jack" and "Calico Jack Rackam" shouted out with drunken bonhomie.

The men pulled Jack Rackam to the bar. The publican already had a bottle of rum freshly opened, and he placed it in Jack's outstretched hand. Jack put it to his lips and quaffed it to the cheers of the others. He was some sort of prodigal son, this Calico Jack Rackam, and Anne watched, interest growing, trying to see through the press of men.

Then, like the quirky way that fog will swirl away and open up a vista, previously hidden, so the men around Jack parted and there was nothing but smoky air between herself and Calico Jack.

Jack thumped the bottle down on the bar, was turning his head, looking at nothing in particular, laughing, saying something, when like iron to lodestone his gaze caught

Anne's and he stopped and whatever he was saying died on his lips.

He straightened, then leaned back against the bar, his eyes never leaving hers.

Anne did not know what to do, so she held his gaze, gave it back as brazen as ever she was. She heard James Bonny make some whiny noise of disapproval, but she ignored him, hardly registering his protest or even his existence. She had forgotten his treachery, and in that instant she had forgotten him.

There, across that dark, filthy room, Anne Bonny held Calico Jack Rackam's eyes. Neither moved. And in that instant Anne knew that her whole world was about to turn over again.

Just three hours before, Jack had ordered the *Ranger's* anchor let go and the pirate brig found herself once more fast to the bottom of Nassau Harbor. It had been a long cruise and Jack was glad it was over.

In July they had given Rogers his fiery welcome and slipped away. At first light they had run out of Nassau Harbor through a narrow, reef-bound channel and had run away to the northeast with such a lead that the British men-of-war could not hope to run them down. They did not even try.

As the pirates had sailed past the *Rose* and the *Milford* and the *Delicia* and Woodes Rogers's other armed consorts, they had lined the *Ranger's* rails, howling, jeering, firing pistols, exposing themselves, flinging bottles, urinating in the direction of the men-of-war. It was a grand moment. The perfect way to begin a cruise for plunder.

Jack had sailed away as quartermaster of the *Ranger*, and now he returned as her captain. He had deposed Charles Vane three months before, and seen himself installed in command. It was a masterful bit of trickery.

The *Ranger* had crossed paths with a French man-of-war, and Vane—vicious, but not stupid—had opted to run. It was the only sensible thing to do, as Jack well knew, but some of the others began to mutter cowardice, and Jack saw this as a glimmer of opportunity.

He encouraged their grumbling, treated them to absurd tales of what he would do were he captain. He knew he was safe from any chance of having to act on those plans. As long as the *Ranger* was being chased, Vane had absolute authority. It was in the pirates' articles.

Once the *Ranger* had left the frigate astern, the men voted Vane out and put Jack in his place.

November 24, 1718. Vane was put in a small sloop they had taken, along with those still loyal to him, and Jack took command of the *Ranger*. It was the position, and the responsibility, that he had always craved, and once he had it, he found that it frightened him near to death.

More than two months had passed since Jack had deposed Charles Vane. Two months, for Captain Rackam, of the most dreadful kind of anxiety, trying to figure where the best hunting was to be found, watching his back, listening for mutterings of discontent among his pack of wolves with their tenuous loyalty.

The men who remained with Jack had elected Richard Corner as quartermaster, and that went far toward securing Jack's position, since Corner would never do to him what he had done to Vane.

For all his worry, they had not been without success. They had cruised around Jamaica, taken a big Madeiraman stuffed full with a valuable cargo. They held her for three days, tore her apart, consumed her best cabin stores. They terrorized the crew, but they did not harm them.

Jack discovered—and it surprised him—that he had no stomach for Vane's brand of random cruelty. He enjoyed the power he had over his victims, enjoyed strutting around, using his big sword like a walking stick, making certain that the captive crew understood that he, Captain John Rackam, held absolute power over their lives—that, God-like, he could smite them down.

And they understood: they believed it, deeply, with a near-religious zeal, and that was enough for Jack. He did not have to torture them or kill them. And with him setting that tone, the others felt likewise.

They stood off the shore of Jamaica and came to a small island, rarely visited, and there they careened the *Ranger* and cleaned her bottom and spent their Christmas ashore, celebrating that holy Christian holiday in a wild, drunken debauch. They put to sea again soon after and scooped up a few more prizes, decent captures, but nothing of great value.

By then the *Ranger* was a tired vessel. Careening her had helped some, but still she was leaking fast through a hundred defects in her bottom. She was faster for being clean, but the growth on her bottom had also been slowing the inflow of water. With the weeds gone, the sea came in at such a rate that the pumps had to be manned watch and watch, and there were no slaves or captives aboard to man them, so the pirates had to do it themselves, and they were not happy to do so.

Her hold and 'tween decks stunk. They were damp and filthy and infested with vermin—so many fleas and lice and rats and whatever else inhabited those dark and moldering places that all the brimstone and vinegar in the world would not free the men from their torment.

Her rigging was slack and stretched so far there was not much more to take up. Rot spread like gangrene in her spars; Jack found he could pull great hunks of the main lower mast out with his bare hands.

Jack was tired as well. Like the ship, he felt spent, weak, rotten from within with worry. Every success they had only made him aware that the men would expect more, every prize they took made him think about the time they would see a vessel he did not wish to fight, and then it was off with him, just as he had see old Vane off.

He had heard a story once about a boy who stole a fox, Greek boy or Roman or some such, and hid it under his shirt. The boy was stopped and questioned and with a stony face he denied the crime, over and over, and all the while the fox was chewing away at his belly.

That was how Jack felt. His fear was the fox, chewing,

gnawing, tearing at him, and all the while, the stony countenance, the bold pirate swagger. No one had ever seen
through it. He was certain of that, because if they had, he
would have been called on it. If he had ever shown cowardice in battle, he would have been hanged. It was the way
of the pirates.

But what if he did flinch? What if his fear showed, just
once, just briefly, against his will, despite all his efforts to
keep it hidden? It would be marooning for him: a strip of
sand surrounded by ocean, a bottle of water, a pistol and a
single bullet.

It was time to give it up. Jack waited for the right moment to make the suggestion, and when it came, he knew
it.

That moment was during a spell of bad weather, driving
rain, howling gales that forced the men aloft to reef topsails
and send topgallant masts and yards down to the deck. The
storm's relentless wind found all of the *Ranger*'s chafed
lines, old canvas, rotten spars, and tore and snapped and
smashed all that it touched, springing masts, splitting sails,
shredding rigging like it was spun yarn.

Two days of that, with all hands on deck nearly all the
time, the winter rain cold, the big seas boarding the brig
again and again, washing men and gear away, and the only
relief from that, the leaking, wet, filthy, vermin-infested
lower deck. Two days, and Jack called all hands below into
the relative shelter of the great cabin and said, "Lads, I've
been thinking. We've had a good cruise, damned good, and
we've had the main fortune our way, I reckon."

Heads nodded at that. They had squandered quite a bit,
but each man there was still far richer than he had been
when first they sailed.

"That whore's son Rogers, new Governor in Nassau, he
has been issuing pardons, as you know." Jack was talking
loud, nearly yelling over the terrible sound of wind in the
rigging and the seas pounding the hull. "I'm thinking, time
we sail for Nassau, take the King up on his offer. Don't
mean we leave the sweet trade, but it is a reprieve, like.
Give us a good run ashore, and never the fear of being

taken and hanged. Dry taverns, all night in with some little bunter to warm your backs. What say you?"

They said yes. They said it with enthusiasm, and Jack could see each of those exhausted, bedraggled, hungry, wet, vermin-ridden men thinking of how fine it would be, at that very second, to be sitting in the Ship Tavern, punch bowl in one hand, pipe in the other, whore in his lap.

Once the weather had moderated enough that they could do something beyond running before the wind and seas, Jack set a course for Nassau. They stood into the crowded harbor in the late afternoon, dropped the hook as the sun was setting.

The booty they had divided long before. There was nothing to be done around the ship. She was done for. To keep the sea any longer, the *Ranger* would need far more work than could be done in Nassau, more work than the pirates were willing to do anywhere.

Jack knew, as the anchor plunged into the lovely, light blue water, that there the brig would stay. The *Ranger,* pirate vessel that had terrified so many, that had been the scourge of the Atlantic from Maine to Florida and throughout the Caribbean, would end her life rotting at the end of her anchor rode and then sink into Nassau Harbor until she was just so much mud.

We should all have so easy an end, Jack thought. He climbed down the brig's side, took his place in the longboat, and they pulled for Nassau's waterfront.

Nassau! God, how he loved the place, mean and vile though it might be! All those familiar smells enveloped him, delicate and unique and refreshing to one whose nose had grown accustomed to the smell of filthy bilge and filthier men packed together aboard the brig.

He walked slowly down the length of the dock and on to Bay Street. Nothing was changed in the half a year he had been gone; the same taverns and ordinaries, a few shops, a few houses, it was all as it had been and Jack was grateful for that.

He ambled down Bay Street, taking it in, listening to the sounds of the night: laughter, music, gunfire, yelling, singing, it all mixed together like the disparate ingredients in a pirate burgoo, all melding to form a unified whole. He was home, and he was happy.

He was worried as well. He, Calico Jack Rackam, was a popular figure in Nassau, but so had been Charles Vane. There might be some who would consider Jack to have betrayed Vane, even though Vane had been voted out all legal and in accordance to the articles.

For that matter, Vane himself might be there, though Rackam did not think his former captain would risk the wrath of Woodes Rogers, not unless he could show up with a significant force of men at his back.

All this Jack considered as he ambled along, taking in the atmosphere of the town that by default he thought of as his home, as much as any who followed the sweet trade could have a home.

He had no destination in mind, he was just walking, but still he was not surprised to find himself in front of the Ship Tavern. It was where he found himself almost every night he was in Nassau. His feet moved to the Ship as thoughtlessly as his hand might move to scratch an itch.

He paused outside. Behind the heavy wood door he could hear the raucous sounds, as if the door were a dam, holding it back, a dam that threatened to burst under the pressure of the sound, to blow out from the sheer weight of the noise behind.

Jack reached for the latch and paused, felt the fox gnawing at him. How would his return be met? Had his old friends gone over to Woodes Rogers, would they arrest him, see him hanged?

He grabbed the latch lifted it, threw the door open. *One broadside, then board 'em in the smoke,* he thought. He had to go in, find out. He had no place else to go.

The door swung open and Jack was hit with the cloud of tobacco smoke and the noise from the crowded tavern. He could see little of that dark interior, just crowds of people under the few lanterns, and shadowy forms off in the corners.

He stood there, hands outstretched, thought, *I am here. Kill me or embrace me, as you will.*

Then the sound died, the laughter, the arguments faded from the people's lips as they turned to this brazen new-comer, and Jack felt a wave of panic building, building until he heard the familiar voice of Hosea Batchelor shouting out, "Damn me to hell, it is Calico Jack Rackam!"

A form materialized out of the dark—it was Batchelor—and he grabbed Jack's hand and pumped it and slapped him on the back, and then more and more familiar faces crowded around and they all were slapping him, taking his hand, leading him into the tavern.

It was a triumphant return, it was Caesar riding into Rome, it was more than Calico Jack would have ever hoped for. There was the publican with a bottle of rum, out-stretched, and Jack took it and gulped the hot liquor down. He could hear shouts, people calling out, his own name echoing around the tight space. Pipe smoke, perfume, un-washed pirates, all the smells of the Ship Tavern swirled around him, all the familiar faces appeared in front of him, all those well-recognized voices welcomed him home.

He put the bottle down on the bar with a thump, turned to inquire after—what the hell was her name?—the little whore whose company he had so enjoyed.

The question was half off his lips when suddenly the crowd around him parted and he saw a woman, the vision of a woman, sitting under one of the lanterns and just for-ward of it, the light filtering through her hair and making her seem to glow.

He stopped, the sentence unfinished. This was a new face, not like any he had seen in the Ship Tavern or in Nassau or in all his ramblings, a sharply defined face, full red lips, eyes that flashed defiance. Thick blond hair tum-bled down the front of her dress, her low-cut dress, the skin above her large breasts glistening with sweat in the hot tavern.

She met his gaze and held it, brazen as any whore, but somehow Jack knew that this was no whore. This was a woman, beautiful, alluring, dangerous.

He leaned back against the bar and his eyes did not move from hers as he tried to make sense of what he was seeing. What was such a fine woman doing in that mean place?

She looked like God's new-made creation, and she looked like someone he had known for all eternity, all at once.

Chapter 9

JAMES BONNY SAID SOMETHING, BUT ANNE DID NOT hear it. The tavern was louder now, even louder than it had been before this Calico Jack Rackam's entrance, but Anne could make out no individual sounds, only a great swell of noise, like the surf, or a gale of wind in the trees.

She straightened, cocked her head a bit, her eyes never leaving Jack, Jack's never leaving hers. He was teasing her. She knew he would come over, make his introduction. There was no way he could not. But he was holding back, letting the tension build and it was irritating and intriguing all at once.

And then Jack reached around and took up his rum bottle and called to the publican for three glasses, which he took in one hand, all the while his eyes never leaving Anne's.

With a nod and a soft apology to the company who stood with him at the bar, Jack pushed his way through the men, stepped slowly up to their table. He paused, looking down at them; a tall man, Anne thought, not awkwardly so, but just tall enough to be above average.

"Good evening," he said. His voice was deep and his tone light. "I had thought there was no one in this place I did not know, but I find you two are strangers to me." He was ostensibly speaking to them both, even managed a glance at James, but there was little question as to whom he was addressing.

"We ain't been but two months here," James Bonny said, sullen, the words coming grudgingly.

"Ah! And I have been abroad for near six."

"And now we're off for Barbados," James added.

"Perhaps," Anne said, "or perhaps not." She did not look at her husband as she corrected him.

"Well, in any event, I pray you will allow me to make my introduction. I am Captain John Rackam. It pleases the people here to call me Calico Jack, for my preference in dress."

With that Jack Rackam bowed, an elegant move, arm across the waist, leg extended.

Anne had seen many pirates bow, indeed it was a favorite means of greeting, but they did it to mock convention, not adhere to it. When the pirates bowed it was with a great flourish, a sweeping of their hats high in the air, bent nearly double at the waist. They bowed in jest, in the same way that they delighted in referring to one another as "your lordship" or "your ladyship."

But not Jack Rackam, not then. His bow was elegant, serious, as fine in form as anything one might see in court, and when he straightened his expression was not in the least mocking.

"Good evening, Captain," James muttered, making some attempt to match Jack's elegance of tone. "I'm James Bonny, and may I present *my wife* . . . which is Anne Bonny?"

"The pleasure is mine. It is always a delight to see a new face."

Jack's eyes were once again locked on Anne's. He had no visible reaction to James's characterizing her as his wife, seemed to take no notice of the special emphasis he put on the words. It was as if he understood their relationship and knew that it had no bearing on him and Anne, as if there were no one else in the room, in the town, in the whole world, but them: Calico Jack and Anne Bonny. "Might I offer you a drink?"

"Well, we—"

"Yes, Captain," Anne interrupted her husband's excuses,

"we should be delighted, would you sit and drink with us."

Jack nodded, smiled, and with his foot dragged a chair over to the table and sat, facing Anne, with James on his right hand. He set the glasses down, filled them with the dark, pungent-smelling rum, and the three of them picked them up.

"To new acquaintances!" Jack said, and they drank to that.

"Calico Jack Rackam?" Anne said, and her voice came out more husky than she had expected. "You are a well-known figure around this town. I have heard much."

"I pray you will not believe idle gossip, madam."

"Been gone these six months?" James Bonny interrupted. "Have you been to sea, then?"

Jack made to speak, but Anne interrupted him, looking at her husband for the first time since Jack's entrance, staring her hatred at him, an expression she did not think Jack would miss. "Pray, sir, do not be too free with your speech around my . . . *husband* . . . He is sometimes too free with his own."

James looked at her and returned her scowl, then he stood, so fast he toppled his chair behind him. "And I'll thank you to keep your tongue still. The hour is late. Let us go now."

"No, sir. Go if you will, but I should like to tarry a bit."

"I said, let us go. I'll brook no argument from you, woman!"

At that Anne laughed, quite involuntarily and despite the fury that was raging inside her. James Bonny, playing the overbearing husband! It was a role that did not suit him, one he could not pull off with any conviction, but he was not done trying.

"Damn it!" He slammed the flat of his hand down on the table. "You come with me, wife, I'll not suffer your lip!"

Jack made to stand. "I fear I am in the middle of something that is not my affair."

"No, sir, pray, sit," Anne said, pointing to the chair, and Jack sat.

She turned to James, turned her full-blown fury on him,

like the height of a building storm. "If you would have me come, I suggest you make the attempt to remove me by main force." Her hand crept down her long, smooth leg; her fingertips played over the handle of the dagger she had secreted there. "If you do not dare try, little man, then pray be gone."

James Bonny stood glaring at her, lacking the courage to do what he wished to do.

At last he pointed a threatening finger at Anne. "I'll not embarrass myself by dragging you out of here, woman, but we ain't done with this." Then, with the precious little dignity he had remaining, he turned and stormed out of the tavern.

She watched him go, watched him push and stumble through the crowd and out the door. *Filthy little worm.*

And then Jack's voice, steady, consoling, apologetic. "I would not have wished to start a fight between a man and his wife."

"There was no man involved, I assure you." She turned to him, her fury not yet abated. "And you, sir, what manner of rogue are you?"

"The very worst kind, ma'am." His voice was smooth, his look assured, a man who did not hope to get what he wanted, but expected to. "I am the kind of rogue who breaks poor women's hearts."

"Are you indeed?" Anne felt the fury melt away like butter in a hot pan, and with it went all thought of James Bonny. "But I think you are not so honest a rogue, for you introduced yourself as Captain John Rackam, when I have heard tell that you are but Quartermaster John Rackam, second to that wicked pirate Charles Vane."

"I was that, when I sailed this summer, ma'am. When I exploded the fire ship under the nose of Woodes Rogers I was indeed quartermaster to Charles Vane. But I return as captain, and where Vane is now I do not know."

"You deposed him, sir? And how, pray, did you manage that?"

Jack picked up his glass and sipped. "By being a greater rogue than he."

Anne sipped as well, holding Jack's eyes over the rim of her glass. "But sure you are yourself a wicked pirate," she teased, "to depose so great a villain as Charles Vane. Are you not afraid that Governor Rogers will hang you?"

"Hang me? No, never in life, and me an honest merchant captain. But for any sins I might have committed, I believe the Governor has extended a pardon, for them will take it. Besides, there is to be war with the Spaniards, it is thought abroad. The worthy Governor needs all the fighting men he can muster. I reckon on a privateering commission soon. Then any piracy becomes all legal, like."

They were silent, but it was not the awkward silence of two who have exhausted their conversation. Rather it was a charged silence, crackling, as if their communication had move to a place beyond words.

"Then you shall be a great hero," Anne said at last, soft. "Another Drake, I'll warrant."

They were speaking words, but the words had nothing to do with what they were conveying to one another. It was all sex play, it was something entirely new to Anne. Jack was arousing her with his eyes, the cadence of his meaningless banter. She felt herself flushing, felt hot, feverish, as if a big fire had suddenly been stoked up in the middle of the room.

She put her glass down, leaned over the table, leaned close to Jack Rackam, and Jack leaned close to her. "I think you will not break my heart, Calico Jack Rackam."

They stumbled up the narrow, rickety stairs, giggling, running hands over one another, bouncing off the thin walls. Anne was full up with rum, full of desire. She wanted only to peel her clothes off, to rip his off, to feel him all over her.

Up onto the second floor and down the hall, filled with the sound of couples copulating behind thin walls. Anne felt her own need swell.

She stopped in front of her door, let Jack run his hands

behind her neck, kiss her deep as she fumbled for the latch. James Bonny might be in there, she realized, his scrawny form might be huddled under the sheets of their bed, but Anne did not care.

She could not think straight, could not reckon on what she would do if her husband was indeed there, did not think about it at all. Her head was whirling with the rum and the consuming need to be sated and she could not think.

She pushed the door open, stumbled back into the dark room. Jack's breath smelled of rum and tobacco as he explored her mouth with his tongue. Moonlight streamed in through the unshaded window, casting the room in a blue light.

James Bonny was not there.

Jack's hands ran along her waist, over her breasts, compacted as they were by her bodice. His fingers moved expertly over the laces, loosened them and peeled her clothes away as she shucked his coat off his broad shoulders and worked the buttons on his yellow waistcoat.

She was breathing hard already, desire sweeping her away, like tumbling in the warm surf. She reached behind her head, pulled off her mobcap and pulled the pin from her hair, letting all of her long yellow locks tumble free.

Jack moved with authority, with assurance, as he gently pushed her bodice and her shift off her shoulders, let them fall, caressed her breasts with calloused hands, gently pinched taut nipples between strong fingers.

Anne pulled at the buttons of his shirt, fumbled, her hand shaking. She could not get them loose, so she grabbed either collar and pulled, ripping the buttons from the fabric, pushing the torn cloth aside. She ran her hands through the dark, curly hair on his chest and over his lean stomach.

How long have I pictured this moment? she thought. In her most erotic fantasies it was just this: a shoddy room, a buccaneer, tall, well formed, handsome, a man who would be rough and gentle all at once, a man who knew how to please a woman. A dangerous lover.

In her more rational state she assured herself that such

men did not exist, that the pirates were all a depraved and brutish lot.

And yet here he was, her fantasy, made flesh. Calico Jack Rackam. There could not be another like him.

Jack hooked her skirts with his thumbs and pushed down and suddenly she was naked, petticoats and shift and bodice piled around her feet. It was a wild and new sensation, something she had never experienced, standing naked before a man as he explored her body and she his. Her head swam with it.

The cool air came in through the window and played over her flesh and she felt herself shudder. Jack wrapped his arms around her, attacked her neck with his lips, ran his hands down her back, over her buttocks, pulled her close.

She could feel his cock through the fabric of his breeches and she fumbled with his sword belt, but he pushed her hands aside and in a few swift moves dropped belt and breeches and stockings. He swept her up, carried her over to the bed, laid her down and lay down beside her.

Anne was on her back, arching, expecting Jack to mount her, wanting desperately to have him inside, but he did not. He ran his hands over the length of her body, covered her with little kisses, caressed her breasts, explored her with fingers and tongue. She squirmed under him, moaned loud, felt the pressure building, building, thought she could not endure it a moment more.

It was all new, like losing her maidenhead again, but much, much better. Anne had not even suspected that such a degree of pleasure was possible, had never imagined that a man could understand so well how to please a woman.

She wrapped her hand around the shaft of his cock, stroked him, listened with satisfaction as he breathed louder, moaning himself, his kisses growing in passion and strength, his hands groping her just rough enough to be exciting.

"Oh, Jack, Jack, pray, make love to me," she moaned, certain she could bear no more. She rolled on her back again, pulled him to her, but he guided her up from the bed, lay back himself, gently moved her over him.

She understood at once what he wanted, though she had never conceived of making love in such a fashion.

She straddled his hips with her strong thighs and guided him into her and slowly, slowly, began to move, up and down, and he began to move against her.

Her head lolled around in a circle and she moaned, feeling her long hair ticking her skin. "Oh, yes, oh, yes . . . so damned good!" she managed to gasp.

It was all so wicked: the tavern, the adultery, these new ways of fornicating, and with a pirate, the genuine article, fresh from the sea! The sensations and the rum and the sinfulness and the novelty of it filled her up, like a barrel packed tight, bursting at the seams, threatening to explode.

Her legs were beginning to tire, but she could not stop. Rather, she moved faster, relishing the burn of her muscles. She leaned forward, put her hands down flat on his broad chest, and he reached up and caressed her breasts as she and Jack moved together, faster and faster.

Anne felt her thick hair tumbling around her head. She swept it out of her face and her moaning became rhythmic, in time with their motion. She felt her whole body compressing in, tighter and tighter, as if she would collapse in on herself.

And then, out in the hallway, footsteps, and Anne listened as her whole body jarred up and down, listened as the steps stopped outside the door, listened as the latch lifted and the door swung open, slow, careful.

She stifled a scream of pleasure. The thought of James Bonny standing there, watching her, watching them, made her wild, drove her to a new plateau of excitement.

She bounced hard on Jack's hips and then threw her head back again and screamed, screamed with absolute abandon. She felt as if her body, compressed in on itself, was bursting out now with release, as if all the parts of her were flying out in a thousand different directions.

Under her she heard Jack groaning loud, felt him explode inside her, and she collapsed on his chest, heaving for breath, sweating, her sweat mingling with his, their slick bodies pressed together.

She heard the door close, heard the footsteps retreat down the hall.

For a long time they just lay there, Anne on top of Jack, warm with pleasure, letting their heaving breath subside. They were both coated in sweat, lathered up like race-horses. Anne felt as if her skin were melding into Jack's.

Finally Jack moved, ran his fingers through Anne's tangle of hair and down her back and gently over her bottom.

"Anne, darling," he whispered, soft, careful to preserve the mood, "was that your husband?"

"Not anymore," she sighed.

Chapter 10

THE *HOORN* MERCHANTMAN WAS STRUGGLING IN heavy weather, and Mary Read was trying to sleep.

It was her time below, a well-earned rest after an exhausting day's work, followed by another four hours on watch as she and her fellows were lashed by the building storm.

She lay in her bunk, all the way forward, wedged between her seabag on the one side and the hull of the ship on the other, jammed in as tight as she could get to keep from being tossed from the bunk.

The *Hoorn* heaved, pitched, and rolled in the mounting seas. The single lantern illuminating the forecastle swung in great irregular arcs, making fast-moving shadows and patches of dull light across the table and bunks.

The small space was filled with sound—the smash of the seas against the hull, the creak and groan of the ship's timbers, the scream of the wind in the masts as it was carried by the rigging to the vessel's fabric, the slosh of the water running inches deep on the forecastle deck.

Mary felt the ship rise on a wave, pause, and then go down, down, rolling as she went, rolling over on her beam ends, farther and farther. She gripped the edge of the bunk, thought, *Dear Lord, come up, come up* . . . And then just when it seemed the ship would roll clean over, she paused, lurched, and righted herself again, coming up with a shudder as she shed the tons of water that had crashed over her decks.

It is a peculiar thing . . . she mused. Her spirit was weary of life, ready to be shed of it. And yet her flesh could only react as all living things did, with a desperate need to keep on living.

The *Hoorn* was not a happy ship. The misery started at the quarterdeck and spread forward. It was not Captain Bes; he was a good man, a good master, but he had little to do with the daily running of things. That was not the master's job.

Claude Waalwijk was the mate, a bully and a coward, a brutal little man who was wont to use fists and belaying pins and rope ends to see his orders carried out, orders that would have been obeyed in any event. He liked to hit people. Mary, enduring his cruelty, wondered how he would act around men who could hit back. But she had seen his type before, craven petty tyrants, and she knew the answer.

Captain Bes did nothing to stop him, either from ignorance of his brutality or indifference or tacit approval. It did not matter. He let Waalwijk turn an otherwise difficult voyage into another tier of hell altogether.

The *Hoorn* was not a happy ship, but neither was she very unusual.

Mary was in her bunk, still wearing her oilskins and hat. There was no reason to take them off. Her clothes were wet clean through, despite the oilskins, despite the lines lashed around wrists and the belt around her waist to keep the water out. Her bedding was wet clean through. Four inches of water ran back and forth over the deck in the forecastle, crashing like surf on one side or the other as the ship rolled, and more was streaming in through leaking deck seams above.

She had no means of drying her clothes other than wearing them. Even then they would never dry completely without a stretch of fair weather, and that was not likely to happen anytime soon. And then would come the saltwater sores, the patches of skin rubbed raw from the continual chafing of dried salt crystals in wool clothing, the lacerations that would not heal on hands made soft by continual soaking in seawater.

The North Sea in winter. Mary was no stranger to it, but she had forgotten what an unmitigated misery it could be.

She could hear the sound of the wind rising in pitch, could feel the increased laboring of the vessel. When she had come below, an hour before, they had been struggling on with just the barest amount of sail showing—fore and main topsails, deep reefed—but soon even that little bit of canvas would be too much. She did not think her rest, such as it was, would last long.

She lay there, eyes wide, staring into the dark. Her stomach twisted in hunger. For the past four days the weather had been too severe for the cook to light the galley fire, and they had had nothing to eat but ship's biscuits, snatched whenever they could. Her ankle throbbed from having twisted it while struggling with the main topsail halyard, hauling with her fellow sailors, knee-deep in the water that surged over the bulwark.

Her fellow sailors. They were a decent crowd, she had found, the usual smattering of forecastle rats and boys after adventure and old sailors who like herself had nowhere else to go. She liked them well enough and they liked her.

They had no notion that she was anything other than a young man seeking his fortune at sea.

Oh, Frederick, dear Frederick . . . she thought, then thankfully the ship gave a wicked roll and she braced herself and the sudden real possibility of drowning forced those memories aside.

The ship came up again, slower this time, and Mary eased her tensed muscles. If she had never had her life with

Frederick, if she had never known real happiness, then her present misery would not be so acute. But she could not change what had been, could not blot out her remembrance of that joyful time. Nor would she, even if she could. Her memories were the only pleasure left to her.

Oh, Frederick . . .

The hatch opened overhead and Mary heard the roar of the wind, felt the blast of cold, clean air as it whirled through the close, fetid atmosphere of the forecastle. She tensed again, knew what was coming.

"All hands! All hands!" the mate's hateful voice boomed. The words were loud even over the howling storm, but Waalwijk's bullying cocksure tone was absent, frightened out of him by the storm.

Bloody coward. . . . Mary rolled out of her bunk, sat for a second with her legs hanging over the edge. Waited while the ship rolled away and then stood as the ship rolled back and nearly tossed her across the forecastle with the momentum, as if to say, *Up, up, and attend to me!*

She staggered along with her hands on the table for balance. She paused as Hans Franeker, the youngest on her watch, struggled from his bunk, wide-eyed, confused, and she wondered if he had actually been sleeping.

Ah, youth!

She grabbed Hans by the collar, helped pull him to his feet. She liked him, found she had something akin to a maternal affection for this boy who was probably sixteen years old, ten years or so her junior. It was his first voyage and he needed watching.

"Hans!" she said, yelling to be heard over the din of the storm, even belowdecks. "It'll be a goddamned misery up there! You stick close to me, keep clear of Waalwijk, you hear?"

Hans nodded and Mary nodded and she pushed past him. Fore and aft the rest of the men from her watch groped their way from their bunks, staggered aft, each as wet, as miserable, and as frightened as she.

They moved as fast as they could along the heaving deck, struggled up the ladder.

Mary stepped through the hatch into a foot of water that ran over the deck, cascading off combings and rails and shooting into the air like breaking surf. The night was black, the air filled with water from the spray that broke over the bow and the great surges of green water coming aboard and the rain that drove down in sheets. The scream of the wind in the rigging was inhuman. The whole world rolled, bucked, heaved under them, and all they could do was stagger from one handhold to another.

Mary moved out of the way, making room for her fellows to gain the deck. She grabbed hold of the foremast fife rail and a big sea surged over the bow and ran down the deck, nearly up to her waist. The water pulled at her legs, filled her boots, crashed against her chest. She sucked in breath as her clothes, which had warmed up somewhat during her time below, were soaked with the icy water once more.

She held tight as the flood tried to pry her from the rail, tried to whirl her away along the deck and toss her over the bulwark and into the sea. They had lost a man already that way, two days before.

She turned her face from the surging water, could see it crashing into the combing of the forecastle hatch, could see it flooding down the open scuttle and into the forecastle, the cramped, festering place where they lived. Now instead of being inches deep on the forecastle deck, it would be feet deep, and all their gear swept away, floating, surging back and forth with the roll of the ship, their bedding carried away by the water. Now their lot would be even more miserable, as impossible as that seemed.

Waalwijk loomed up, moving hand over hand along the lifelines run fore and aft. In his right hand he clutched a knotted rope end, but he held it more like a talisman than a weapon. There was no violence in his face now, only fear.

When the last of the watch was up from below he shouted, "The storm gets worse! We must lie to, reefed mainsail, backed foresail hung in the brails! *Van een goed wind, een kwaaden maken,* make a bad wind out of a good one! You men, take in the main topsail!" His voice was hoarse from shouting, from swallowing salt water when he did.

Mary nodded. Lie to, that was what she expected. If they had been in the open ocean, they could have run before the wind, just let the storm have its way until it blew itself out. But they were not in the open ocean, they were in the North Sea, with its ship-killing coasts on every hand. They did not have the luxury of a thousand miles of open water in which to run, they had at best a couple hundred miles under their lee before they piled up on some shore or other.

They had to lie to, to stop as best as they could, let the ship bob in place like a seabird, drifting as little downwind as possible. That meant hauling up the foresail with the lines on deck, which was relatively easy. It also meant climbing aloft, fifty feet up in the violent night to stow the topsails, which was not easy at all.

Slowly, fighting for each step, Mary worked her way toward the pinrail, joined the clutch of men there struggling with the lines, hauling away to pull the sail up. She reached through the crowd of men who were tugging and swaying on the clewline, got her hands on the rope, added her weight to the effort.

Another big sea came over the bow, rushed waist-deep along the deck, knocking the lot of them sideways, but they clung to the clew-line like grapes on a vine, pulling, struggling on despite the frigid water that tried to sweep them away.

The topsail was attached to the topsail yard, a great tapered wooden pole that crossed the mast at a right angle, forming a sort of a cross, fifty feet up. Mary and her fellows hauled on clewlines and buntlines and pulled the topsail up to the yard, the once taut sail now a great flogging bag of canvas, threatening to beat itself to death against the mast.

Mary stepped back, looked aloft, blinking away the spray and the rain. There was the easy part done. Now it needed only for them to climb up and stow the sail, lash it to the yard.

To a landsman, just being on deck in such weather would

seem madness. But to the mariners the deck was safety, and the real work lay in climbing aloft, with the wind howling and driving the freezing rain before it, and the ship rolling and bucking like a wild thing.

And then once aloft, they would shuffle out along the yard, leaning over the yard itself, their feet on a rope slung beneath. There they would wrestle with the topsail for an hour or more as it flailed out, with the motion of the ship greatly exaggerated by the height of the mast.

To a landsman it would all seem quite beyond the pale.

But to Mary and her fellows it was just what they had to do, what they would do, and when they were done their actions would be considered no more heroic than scrubbing the deck.

Hans Franeker stood beside her. She slapped him on the shoulder, pointed aloft at the topsail, made a "follow me" gesture.

Franeker nodded, and Mary took a firm grip on the main shrouds, stepped up onto the pinrail, and then swung out and around to climb up the ratlines toward the topsail yard.

In fair weather, even moderate weather, the seamen would race aloft, taking the ratlines at a running pace and swarming up over the top. But not that night. Now they went step by step, fighting for every foot.

Mary took care with each fresh grip on the shrouds, tested her weight on every ratline as she worked her way up. The ship heeled to leeward and the wind pressed her to the shrouds, and she was able to scramble up a few feet. Then the ship rolled back with a quick snap that tried to throw her from the rigging into the boiling sea below, and she could do no more than cling tight, arms wrapped around the shrouds, and hang on and wait.

Below her, Hans Franeker did the same, and on either side of her, the others from their watch, as slowly, one torturous step at a time, they fought their way aloft, fifty feet up, where the sail pounded away, demanding to be stowed. The deck below became indistinct in the night and the driving rain and spray, the ocean a wild black pit, invisible save for the great foaming breakers along the tops of the giant waves.

Just under the main top the shrouds narrowed as they came together and the sailors had to go one at a time up, over the futtocks and then up the main topmast shrouds to where they could step out onto the yard.

Mary waited her turn, arms wrapped around the thick standing rigging, one minute pressed into it, the next tugged away as the ship rolled. She glanced down. Hans was just below her, his face a foot below her feet, looking up, blinking away the water. She smiled at him, hoped to bolster his courage, but he did not see.

And then it was her turn and she stepped up, one ratline, then another. Her long oilskin jacket beat hard against her legs; water streamed down her face and worked its way under her clothes—sharp, cold rivulets against her skin like the blade of a knife where her body had managed to make her clothes just a little warm, if not at all dry. She gasped, sputtered, climbed on.

Up, up and over the futtock shrouds and once the wet sole of her boot slipped off the ratline and she thought she might plunge from her precarious perch and in that flash of terror wondered how long it would take her to die in the water. But she did not fall, and she found her footing again, and made her way up into the topmast shrouds and up again.

Slowly, slowly, one after another, like weary men at day's end in a slow-moving paymaster's line. Then Mary's waist was level with the main topsail yard and it was her turn to step onto it.

The sail twisted and banged and whipped around, gleaming wet canvas, and Mary could hear nothing beyond the crack of the sailcloth as it filled, collapsed, and filled again. Her whole world, her whole madly tossing, banging, soaked world, was reduced to that section of shroud, the yard, the footrope, the sail.

She reached over and found a handhold, took a firm grip, and reached out with her foot and set it on the footrope. She paused, half on the yard, half on the shrouds, waited for the ship to roll the right way, then stepped across and onto the footropes.

A step out along the yard, then she stopped, turned back. Hans was there, clinging to the shrouds, eyes wide, and Mary was afraid that he had spent all of his courage just getting to that place.

She reached out a hand for Hans and he reached out and took it, and then when the ship pitched forward he used the momentum to step on after her.

Side by side they shuffled out along the yard, bellies pressed against that long wooden pole, feet on the footrope slung below it, and fifty feet below them, the ship, rolling and pitching, green water surging over the bows and burying the deck under a foaming blanket.

The sail reared up in front of them—wet, half-frozen canvas, as stiff as a board. It smacked their hands and faces, slammed them in the chest as they clawed their way out, finding what handholds they could as they moved.

At last Mary came shoulder to shoulder with the man just outboard of her and she was as far as she could go. She reached out and began to gather the sail up under her arms, pressing it against the yard in an effort to subdue it. Her wet fingers pulled at the thick canvas, trying to catch enough of a fold that she could grip the cloth and pull it in.

Inch by inch they fisted the sail, working together as best they could, ignoring bleeding hands and torn fingernails and the bitter, bitter cold. They did not think on how perilous their situation was, because if they did, they would not have been able to go on.

And just as they felt they were gaining on the sail, just as they could feel a respectable pile of canvas under their arms, the wind would catch it from behind and billow it out again, and all their clawing and grabbing could not hold it back. And then they would start over again.

For half an hour they fought canvas, but they were no further along than they had been when first they worked their way out on the yard, and Mary could feel the strength going from her arms. On either side of her she could see the movements of the others becoming more awkward, slower, as they, too, grew tired and the numbing cold began to work on their fingers and hands.

The sail blew out, and then collapsed in a fluke of wind, and Mary's hand shot out and she got a fistful, pulled it toward her, and on her right Hans did the same. She reached out, grabbed another, thought, *There now, we shall get this in . . .*

And then a gust, more northerly, a burst of wind and the sail billowed out, and from the corner of her eye Mary saw Hans's arms knocked aside by the wild canvas. She twisted, saw the young man falling back, arms flailing for something, anything, to grab, fingers clawing in air as he toppled back.

Mary seized a line with her left hand; her right hand shot out. Her fingers scraped down Hans's oilskin as he fell and then she hooked his belt as his feet came off the footropes and for a horrible instant Mary thought he was going down and she was going with him.

Then everything seemed to stop, the terrible moment frozen. Hans hung by the belt in Mary's fingers and Mary hung from the line in her left hand, her feet still on the footrope, her body half-twisted around. She felt the rough fibers of the line across her palm as the wet rope began to slip from her grasp. She wondered how long she could hold on, if Hans's belt would break, if the line would break, if she and Hans would plunge into the sea or hit the deck.

And then the men on either side turned as well, reached down and hauled Hans up to the yard, grabbed Mary before the line slipped from her hand, before they fell down, down into the sea below.

It had been mere seconds that she had held Hans suspended in air, and that realization surprised her, because it had seemed so much longer. It seemed she had lived her whole life on that yard, like she could not remember a time when she was not out on that cursed yard.

The others set Hans back on the footrope and with never a word they fell back to stowing the topsail, beating the canvas with numbed hands, grabbing up folds when they could, holding it under their arms against the yard.

They were at it for another forty minutes before they finally had the cloth subdued, before the foot of the sail came to hand and they had it all against the yard. They passed their gaskets around and around the sail, hauling tight, binding it carefully to the topsail yard so that the wind's prying fingers would not find a tiny loose bit and pluck away at it, pulling it from its lashings, until it had the sail free once again and had torn it to ribbons and negated all their work and suffering.

At last they headed back to the deck and the going down was far worse than the going up, for now they were exhausted, their arms like rubber, their hands bleeding and numb with cold. They could barely feel the shrouds in their grips and had no faith in their ability to hang on, but one by one they made it down to the lowest ratline and swung inboard and dropped to the flooded deck.

Mary had been one of the first up, so perforce she was one of the last down, and when she hit the deck she found Hans there, waiting for her, just as she had feared.

"Michael . . ." Hans began, yelling over the wind and the working of the vessel. "I . . ."

Mary held up her hand to stop him, shook her head. She could not bear to hear gratitude. It was not their way, not the way of sailors. She did what she did, she would have done it for any of them, even the most despised denizen of the forecastle. She did not expect thanks, did not want it, would not give it to another who had done the same for her. It was their way.

Hans looked uncertain, made to speak again, then shut his mouth. Then instead of speaking he nodded, just nodded, a simple recognition of what Mary had done, and she nodded back. *Smart boy,* she thought.

And then Claude Waalwijk loomed up among them and shouted, "About bloody goddamned time you were done! Were you buggering each other up there, or what were you?"

The wind had increased in strength, pulling at Mary's oilskins and the hat that she had lashed firm to her head, but the *Hoorn*'s motion was easier now, with the ship lying to, riding out the storm like a gull sitting on top of the water.

Mary was wet to her skin, numb, exhausted, battered and bleeding. The fingernail on her right middle finger had been torn clean away, but she could not recall when that had happened. She had wrenched her shoulder in holding Hans by his belt and knew from experience that it would hurt like hell in a few hours. She was alone in the world and once more playing at being a man. She had no home. Her misery was absolute and compete.

The ship rolled again and she staggered against the bulwark and clung to a backstay, staring down at the ocean roiling black just a few feet away. She wondered why she put so much effort into staying alive. As she stared into the water, the foaming depths began to look inviting, comforting. *Better perhaps to just slip away into that blackness.*

They were bound away for the West Indies. They had taken their cargo to Stockholm, had carried another to Riga, and now had a hold full of sundry goods they were carrying to Port Royal, Jamaica.

The West Indies. She had never been, but she had heard enough about it.

She had heard about the yellow jack and the bloody flux and the pirates who would be found there, but those things did not concern her. She thought instead of the blue skies, the gentle trade winds, the clear, aquamarine water. Palm trees, long white-sand beaches. Warmth. All year long, warmth. Just the thought of it lifted her spirits a bit.

So, for a while at least, she would be in the West Indies and she would be warm.

And then back to Europe, the Baltic, the North Sea. She felt herself sag, physically and emotionally.

The thought of reaching paradise and then leaving it again made her spirits sink to a place even lower than they had been.

Mary Read stared down at the black water, rolling and crashing below, the foaming crests reaching up to her, beckoning her, and she wished that she had the courage to throw herself into that void.

Chapter 11

ODDLY ENOUGH, AND TO JACK RACKAM'S GREAT amazement, James Bonny was not so quick to recognize the dissolution of his marriage.

Jack would have thought that the extraordinary humiliation that Anne had served him out, there on their first night of wild copulation, would have been enough to dissuade him from further pursuing her. Most men, he imagined, who were not of a kidney to seek revenge, would have dismissed her as a whore and would have been done with her. Most men would not have exposed themselves to the further and thorough humiliation that she doled out at their every meeting.

And those meetings were more frequent than Jack would have preferred. James Bonny clung to them like a shadow. When they strolled arm in arm down Bay Street, James Bonny was invariably a block behind. When they made their nightly appearance at the Ship Tavern, James Bonny was lurking in a dark corner. When they went up to what they now thought of as their room, Jack did not doubt that James Bonny was listening on the other side of the door.

He could not imagine that James Bonny liked what he heard. Anne was no virgin, of course, but she was no whore either. Her knowledge of the art of lovemaking was limited, and from what she told Jack of her husband, she had received no decent instruction.

But she was an avid student, a quick and eager learner, and every night, for half the night, they exhausted themselves on the bed, on the floor, on the windowsill, trying everything in Jack's extensive repertoire and then improvising beyond that. Jack had been with a lot of women, far more than he could recall, but he had never had one like Anne.

Their conversations never flagged, their eyes never wandered from one anther, their desire was not sated even by their nightly and energetic coupling.

Six months on the account, and Jack had amassed a hoard of booty. That wealth he poured over Anne: jewelry, clothing, the finest of everything that Nassau had to offer, which admittedly was not much, but Anne seemed entirely pleased.

When that dross ran short, Jack considered taking a berth on board a privateer. But he was torn between his desire for more wealth to pour over Anne and his not wanting to leave his beloved alone to endure James Bonny's badgering.

Anne assured him that she could handle her husband and he knew that she could, so he went. He shipped aboard a vessel captained by a former pirate named Burgess who had accepted the King's pardon and now hunted only Spaniards. After a short and successful cruise they returned to Nassau with several prizes, one laden with coconuts, the other with sugar, both of which sold quickly to the factors who came to that place specifically to buy prize cargoes at a bargain.

Wealthy again, and reunited with Anne, he took up with her as if he had never sailed. James Bonny, Anne assured him, had been no more than a minor annoyance, like a mosquito in one's bedroom at night.

Jack was as happy as he had ever been—happier, in fact. He had the Governor's pardon, so he had no fear of hanging. He was ashore and so he was safe, free from the possibility of death from an enemy's sword or drowning as some rotten ship sank from under him or being marooned by his men. He was still a local hero, beloved in Nassau, which left him free from fear of being murdered by some compatriot of Charles Vane's, or by Vane himself.

And he was in love. It was a novel sensation, as novel to him as Anne's newfound heights of sexual ecstasy were novel to her.

Calico Jack had never felt this way before. He had

known few women with whom he wished to spend even ten minutes after he had satisfied himself. He had never known a woman with whom he wanted to spend every waking hour, whom he thought about every minute, whom he dreamed about, who could keep his eye from wandering to any other female flesh.

That was how he knew it was love.

He considered that as he sat at their usual table in the Ship Tavern, the usual riot going on around him, waiting for Anne to return from the privy. He stared off across the room, toward the corner and the dim form of James Bonny, who was sitting there. Jack could not see his face, but he knew Bonny was staring back.

That little puke is something of a splinter in my side, Jack thought. James Bonny was no threat, but he was an annoyance, the one flaw in Jack's otherwise perfect contentment. *Perhaps I shall do something about this.*

Jack pushed himself to his feet, not overly steady—he had been drinking for some time—and made his way through the crowd.

He could hear the whispered conversations. There was no one in Nassau who was not aware of their particular triangle. Calico Jack Rackam and Anne Bonny were already famous in the pirate community, each in his or her own right. Their union was the talk of the island, and everyone in the Ship could see that Jack was setting a course to confront the third party in the issue.

He stopped in front of Bonny's table and Bonny looked up at him, sullen, angry, but still defiant. Jack stood there for a moment, considering the little man, as Bonny considered him.

Jack Rackam knew he was damned lucky that Anne's husband amounted to no more than this pathetic creature. If James Bonny had been an Edward Teach or a Charles Vane, then he would still be firmly entrenched as Anne's husband, with never a threat to his marital rights.

But James Bonny was not Charles Vane or Edward Teach. He was nothing of the sort. He was a pathetic coward, more afraid than Jack on his worst day, and he would not try to win Anne back through force of arms. Apparently he was trying to wear her down.

"See here, Bonny, you can't be insensible to the fact that Anne don't want you for her husband," Jack said at last.

Bonny glared at him. "Don't matter, does it? I am her husband, it's the main truth, and she gots to come back to me. There are laws against adultery, in case you don't know."

"There are also laws which allow one to buy the divorce of another man's wife. I'm willing to be most generous."

"You reckon me for the kind of man will be bought off?"

"I reckon the only issue is the price."

James Bonny spit on the floor. "Sod off!"

"Sod off?" With a great flourish of the tails of his calico coat Jack kicked the table over, reached across his stomach, pulled his sword.

James Bonny, his eyes wide, leapt to his feet, stumbled backward.

"Sod off!?" Jack roared.

Bonny pressed his back against the wall and slid sideways, his eyes flicking from Jack's face to the wicked tip of his sword, which tracked his movements, slowly, like a snake. "You kill me, it's murder! And me unarmed, and the husband of the woman you fancy. Rogers'll hang you, you son of a bitch!" James hissed.

"Yes? And who here you reckon will say it weren't self-defense, and you drawing on me?"

James continued to move away and Jack took a step closer, kept the tip of the blade within striking distance. He alone knew that he would not strike. Bonny was not wrong—Woodes Rogers had been hanging men with abandon—and Jack was not willing to risk his precious pardon, or his neck, for killing the likes of that little weasel.

"Get out of here. I'll spare your life this time, but I don't want to see you following us, I don't want to see you in here, I don't want to see your filthy face again, hear?"

James paused for a moment, held Jack's eyes. "Sod off," he said again, then bolted for the door, hit it running, flinging it open, and then disappeared down the dark street.

Jack watched him go. He did not try to follow, hoped that would be an end to it.

And then he felt small hands on his shoulders; his nose caught the familiar perfume of Anne Bonny. "Jack, darling, what are you about?"

"Trying to drive away vermin with a little vinegar and brimstone."

"Quite a bit of vinegar, it would seem."

"Too much perhaps."

They were quiet for a moment. Jack slipped his sword back in the scabbard and put his arm around Anne.

"I fear, my beloved Jack," Anne said at last, "that you will just have to kill him."

The abruptness of that remark, the casual tone, took Jack somewhat aback. They were the first words that Anne had ever spoken to him that did not move over his ears like sweet music. "You would have me kill him? You would think nothing of it?"

Anne shrugged. "You are the only man for me, Jack. No other life is of any importance to me, save yours."

Jack smiled and kissed her. Such a perfect love she had for him, he could not think why he found it somewhat disquieting.

After that encounter, James Bonny was more circumspect, but he was not gone. He did not come to the Ship Tavern any longer, did not lurk in the hall outside their room, but he still followed behind them, though now a few blocks back at least. He maintained a safe distance, but he was there.

Two weeks of that, and Jack Rackam was growing weary of it. He sat with legs splayed out in front of him at a table set just outside the front door of one of the ordinaries on Bay Street. Before him, a nearly uninterrupted view of the harbor, with its crowd of ships—some legitimate merchantmen, most not—and beyond that the low green hump of Hog Island. The sun was hot, but the table was in the shade of the building and so it was quite comfortable.

Bloody damned near heaven, he thought.

He glanced up and down the road, trying to catch a

glimpse of the little vermin, but he could not and thought perhaps that they were shut of him for the moment.

Across the table from him, lovely as ever, her skin turning golden brown in the sun, her hair bleached out to a shimmering yellow, sat Anne. Between them, the remains of their dinner on wooden plates, glasses with a rough red wine, half-drained.

"The sweet trade, Jack. Piracy. It must be damned exciting," Anne said, lazily. Their days had a dreamy, languid quality.

"The sweet trade? Oh, it has its moments. Not much in life can match the feel of leaping down on the deck of a prize, you know. Pistols and cutlasses, the smoke from a broadside. Makes a man feel alive, to be sure. Don't reckon there's anything got my heart pounding as well, until I met you, my dearest."

"Hmm," Anne said, her contented coo that Jack loved so well. "It sounds such a thrill."

"But don't get any wrongheaded notions of it. We call it the 'sweet trade' in jest. It's a hard life. Filthy ships, food so rotten it would throw you down. Out at sea for months at a time, keeping a weather eye out for the navy, with always the possibility of drowning or the noose. There's few is in the sweet trade more than a year or two before they meet their end by one means or another. You've seen enough of them poor broken sods that lives on the beach yonder to know what it can be like."

"Hmm," Anne said again, as if she had not heard any of Jack's caveat. "Do you think of going back to it again, at all?"

The answer was no, emphatically no, not with the life he had now. But he could see Anne was developing some romantic ideas, and he did not want to disabuse her of them, for fear she would think less of him, so he said, "Oh, to be sure, I think on it. But I think I shall wait for a privateering commission from the Governor, which is the main chance, you know. That way there is no bother about being hanged, and that is one less concern, at least."

"The Spaniards would hang you, was you taken."

"No, love, they would burn me at the stake."

"There's a comfort. But the people are saying that Rogers will not grant any more commissions. They say he reckons he has pirates enough in his employ."

"Ah, but he does not have Calico Jack!"

Nor, it seemed, was Rogers interested in having Calico Jack. Jack had heard the same rumors that Anne had, and an additional word from Ben Hornigold, whom he had encountered one morning while Anne was still abed. There would be no commission for the likes of Calico Jack Rackam, former quartermaster to Charles Vane.

But that was just as well. Jack didn't really wish to go privateering any more than he cared to go pirating. As it was, he could continue to impress Anne with his bravado and still not have to risk his neck.

"Calico Jack Rackam!" Anne said, as if trying the name out for the first time. "You are such a dashing figure, Jack, so bold and colorful. You are just what civilized ladies with a notion for romance think of when they think of a pirate. But I fear you are unhappy with your idleness, that you will resent me for keeping you from your wicked ways."

"Never, my dear, never in life. You are just the thing that my life was wanting for."

"If you were to go back on the account, Jack, however would you do it? Would you take the *Ranger* to sea?"

"The *Ranger* is done for, I fear." Jack leaned forward, tried to see that ship at the far end of the harbor, but she was hidden from his view. "You cannot see her from here, but did you see her yesterday, when we was walking along the shore? She is down three strakes already and I do believe she carries a bit of a larboard list. I give her no more than a fortnight before she rolls right over and sinks to the bottom."

"Then how would you get a ship?"

Jack gave a dismissive wave of his hand. "It is easily done, you know. Any ship at anchor here could be had, nearly. Why, see that sloop there, the one that is stern to us? She is called the *Nathaniel James* and is all but ready for sea. I could make good use of her as a pirate. I wouldn't reckon her to have more than a handful of men aboard. Go out at night with muffled oars, steal aboard her, and she is mine, with never a worry."

"Oh, you are a wicked rogue," Anne said in that tone she used when she was delighting in the proximity of villainy. "But I could help you, you know."

"And how could you help?"

"I could go out for a visit in the daytime. Have myself rowed out in my finest silk dress with its scandalous decolletage and a wanton display of breasts. They would invite me aboard, the randy dogs, tell me anything I asked them. How many aboard, how well armed, what kind of a watch they keep at night. There would be not one surprise left when I was done with them."

"You think you could? You reckon you could pry from them every secret they had?"

"Jack, darling . . . could you, of all men, doubt my ability to get whatever I might desire from a man? Be it information or whatever?"

"No, my dear Anne. I do not doubt it. But how could I ever go on the account and leave you on the beach?"

"I could go along as well. Disguise my sex, dress as one of your buccaneers. I can fire a pistol as well as any man, I was bred to it in my father's house."

"Disguise your sex! As if you could do any such thing!"

"I could, you know. I have done so already. My father dressed me as a boy until I was five years of age or so."

"Why in the world would he do such a thing?"

"He was pleased to pass me off as the son of a relative of his, said he was raising me to serve as his clerk. He was trying to fool his wife into thinking he had no contact with his mistress and bastard daughter, which was my mother and me, so that she would not stop his yearly allowance."

"The dog! But sure, it is one thing for a mere girl to pass herself as a boy. How should such a fine woman as you ever pass for a brutish, hairy man?"

"I should pass for a brutish, unbearded young man."

"Then you would be as wicked a villain as I am."

"I have turned adulteress for you, why not pirate?"

"If you could be half as good a pirate as you are adulteress, then you should sweep the oceans clean." Sex seemed to ooze from their every conversation. "But could you kill a man, my delicate flower? Could you shoot a man, or run a sword through him?"

"Do not doubt it, my dear Jack."

And Jack did not doubt it, not for a minute. But it was just in fun, all this repartee, and Jack was relieved to think that he did not have to consider acting on any of these fantasies.

And then as if by magic James Bonny appeared in front of him. Jack sat bolt upright as his hand moved toward his sword and he yelled, "You are a sneaking little puppy! Did you come through the kitchen, then, you damnable little coward?"

"Nay, hold!" James Bonny yelled. He had obviously plucked up his faltering courage for this encounter and with great difficulty he held his ground. "I told you, there's laws against adultery, and I got the law on my side. Here."

He thrust a paper at Anne and in her surprise she took it, unfolded it and read. Jack watched her eyes move back and forth. Her eyebrows came together and the terrible clouds of rage gathered in her expression.

"Been sniveling to the Governor again, have you, you little bastard?" Anne hissed, and half crumpled the paper in her hand.

James Bonny folded his arms, mustered a look of defiance. "The Governor is the law here, and all I'm asking is the law be enforced, and that means you're my wife and you'll commit no more adultery! And if the Governor has to whip you till you see that, then be it on your head!"

"Bastard!" Anne shouted. She grabbed up her wineglass and hurled it at James Bonny, who twisted so it bounced off his shoulder, and then twisted further to deflect the plate and knife and fork she hurled next.

"Little goddamned worm, you fucking vermin!" Anne screeched. She cleared her throat, summoned up a mouthful of mucus, and spit it into the summons that James had handed to her, crumpled it up and threw that at him as well. "Son of a bitch!"

By now Jack was on his feet, his sword drawn, though how he could be more intimidating than Anne, he did not know. James Bonny was backing away, was ten feet from them, when he straightened again, and shouted, "It's the law, Anne! And damn me if I won't see it carried out!"

"Get out of here, you son of a whore, you little puke!" Anne screamed, and over her curses James Bonny shouted back, "I'll give you till tonight to think on it and if you don't come back to me, I'll have the law on you, damned if I won't!"

Jack took a step toward him and James turned and fled down Bay Street and it was quiet again, and in the quiet Anne's breathing sounded loud. "Oh, Jack, Jack, whatever shall I do?" she said at last.

"What was that he showed you?" Jack asked. He was relieved that she had rendered it unreadable so he did not have to admit that he could not read.

"It—" she scowled, nodded toward the crumpled paper in the street "—is an order from the Governor that I return to my husband. If I don't, he says he'll have me whipped as an adulteress. Jack, I could not bear that."

"No, no, nor would I ever permit it," Jack said. He sheathed his sword, sat, reached for Anne's hand over the now cleared table. "We'll not let this happen. We'll think of something."

"But we have, Jack. We have thought of it. It needs only for us to act now."

"What . . . ?"

"Our plan. For taking the sloop, yonder. Our idea of going on the account?"

'Our plan'? Dear God, she can't be serious! Jack thought. *Does she think such talk anything more than play-acting?*

"The sloop? But, my beloved, we have no crew, no—"

"Your fellows will join us in this. George Fetherston, Dick Corner, John Howell, Harwood, Earl, the lot of them would follow you, and they are but down at the Ship, or on the beach. Small sloop like that, we would need a dozen men no more, and they are to be had at a snap of your fingers!"

The more Anne talked, the more excited she became and the more inextricably Jack felt himself being pulled in. He had not been lying about the relative ease with which they might take the sloop, and she had not been wrong in thinking she could easily scout out the vessel first and make her capture even easier.

What objections could he raise? That he did not want to go pirating? God, she loved him exactly because she thought him some dangerous rogue! That he was afraid? She would spit in his face the way she spit on the Governor's summons, and then off to the bed of some bastard who was a real fearless villain, and not just a sham of a one dressed up in bright calico clothing!

Jack managed a half smile, an unimpressive effort that he hoped she would take as concern for her own safety. "Let us do it then, and the Governor and his pardon be damned."

Chapter 12

ANNE LOOKED GOOD, DAMNED GOOD, AND SHE KNEW it. It amused her to think that she was now embarking on a new life, one more wild, more villainous than any she had known or even dreamed of, and she was using her oldest skills of seduction to do it.

She still had the beauty and the allure to work her will on men. Life among the pirates had not ameliorated that in the least. If there was any doubt in her mind, then she had only to look at the men at the oars, Richard Corner and George Fetherston, who were facing her as they rowed her out to the sloop *Nathaniel James*.

Fetherston, to starboard, was stealing glances whenever he could, his eyes flicking to her face, her breasts, her ankle which she left exposed for the men's pleasure.

To larboard, big Richard Corner was staring, unabashed, his eyes locked on her breasts like he was seeing some holy vision. His mouth was even hanging open, the unsubtle dog.

But as blatant as they might be in looking, they were both of them loyal followers of Captain John Rackam. They knew that she was his lady, and so they would never do more than look.

Anne didn't mind the looking, didn't mind letting the men think what they would. She enjoyed it, encouraged it, with a glimpse of ankle and an occasional lean forward, back arched, to give them a better view. If Jack were going to kill men for looking, for lustful stares, then he would have killed half of Nassau by then.

The small boat moved fast over the placid water of the harbor, the oars double-banked, pulled by the strong arms of Fetherston and Corner.

There was an urgency about their mission, not a moment to spare. James Bonny had gone whining to Woodes Rogers, reported Anne's abuse of the Governor's orders. Rogers had summoned Anne to appear in person, and when she did he reiterated his promise to have her publicly whipped. To that threat he added a new twist—he would order John Rackam to do it.

That was too much. Despite Calico Jack's reluctance to take her pirating, which he assured her was owing only to his concern for her safety, they both knew it was time to act. Nassau was a safe harbor no longer.

The boat weaved between the vessels that floated in the clear, blue-green water of the harbor—the pirate ships and their prizes and their abandoned hulks, the fishing boats and island traders and vessels from England and the colonies that had ventured into that unsafe harbor. Anne held her parasol demurely aloft to keep the brilliant sun off her skin, looked at each passing ship with a delighted expression, as if she were seeing the harbor for the first time.

Finally they came alongside the *Nathaniel James,* which seemed to loom over the small boat, though it was itself of no great size. Corner and Fetherston tossed oars, the boat bumped alongside, and Corner grabbed on to the chains with his meaty hand.

A head appeared over the bulwark, looking warily down. Anne could see the barrel of a musket that the man held at the ready.

"Pray, sir, do not shoot me!" Anne cried out, and watched the man's expression change from wary concern to surprise and delight as he looked down into the boat's stern sheets.

"No, ma'am, never fear of that!" he said. "Might I help you?"

"I wish to speak to the captain."

"Captain is ashore, ma'am. I am the mate. Might I be of help?"

"Well, Mr. Mate, must we shout at one another, or might I come aboard so we can talk in civilized tones?"

"Oh, forgive me, ma'am, of course, of course! Allow me to see a bosun's chair rigged!"

"You are very kind, sir, but there is no need. I am no stranger to the ways of ships." She stood and stepped toward the cleats fastened to the sloop's side for use in climbing aboard. "I shall be but a moment," she said to the men at the oars, as if they were watermen for hire, "and I require you wait for me."

"Yes, ma'am," said George Fetherston.

Anne handed her parasol up to the mate above, grabbed on to the cleats, and climbed, her eyes down so she could see where her feet were stepping, giving the mate a good look at her cleavage. Three steps and she was up to the deck and took the mate's proffered hand.

"I had thought this an honest merchant vessel, sir, but I see you are armed like some buccaneer." She nodded to the musket. "You will not take me captive, I pray."

"No, no, ma'am, never fear." The mate smiled at her concern. "We are honest merchants, to be sure. Please, allow me to introduce myself. I am Paul McKeown, mate of the sloop *Nathaniel James*."

"Good day to you, sir. I am Miss Patricia Clark."

"My pleasure, ma'am. As to the musket, in truth there are a wicked lot of pirates in Nassau, and it behooves us to be prepared. We keep the one musket on deck and charged, but that is it."

"Such precautions are sensible, and speak well of your vessel," Anne said. There was one other man besides McKeown on board, and he smiled shyly and nodded his greeting. Arrayed along the sides were eight four-pounder cannon, their tackling neatly coiled down, belying the mate's assertion that they were but honest merchants.

"Might I be of assistance to you, Miss Clark? You had mentioned wishing to speak to the master?"

"Yes, just so. I am looking to take passage, and I have heard abroad that your vessel might be bound away for Barbados? Is that right?"

"Right indeed, ma'am. We'll be taking passage to Barbados once our cargo is put down."

"I am pleased to hear it. I am in a great hurry. But would you have room for a passenger on so small a ship?"

"We have one cabin, ma'am, and it is not generally taken. It is small, to be sure, but clean, and comfortable. If you would like, I could have it fresh scrubbed, even painted this afternoon, so it would be to your liking."

"Scrubbed would be fine, sir. There is room on the floor for my servant girl?"

"Yes, ma'am," the mate assured her, though he did not sound so sure himself.

"Good. Might I see?"

"Certainly, ma'am. This way, if you please." McKeown led the way aft and down a tiny scuttle that led to the cramped deck below. Anne followed, bending low to avoid hitting her head, counting the stairs, fixing in her mind the location of handholds, doors, obstacles that might trip her up in the dark.

"This here is the cabin, ma'am," McKeown said proudly, holding open the door to a room that was half as tall and a quarter as big as the closet she had enjoyed in her father's home in Charles Town.

Anne looked it over, nodded her approval. "But what of that door, back there?" she asked, pointing to a door in the bulkhead all the way aft.

"That is the door to the master's cabin, ma'am. And this here—" he pointed forward toward the forcastle "—is crew berths."

"It must be terribly crowded, all of you men aboard this little sloop."

"It can be, ma'am. But for now the captain is sleeping ashore, and it is only me and the other fellow aboard."

"I see . . ." said Anne.

They made their way back on deck and Anne said, "Your vessel seems quite adequate, sir. When might I apply to the captain for some notion of when he might sail?"

"I fear Captain Denney will not be aboard before noon on the morrow. If you could tell me where you are staying, I could send word to you."

"That is kind, sir, but it is not necessary. I do so like to get out on the water. Perhaps I shall call again tomorrow?"

"That would be my greatest delight, ma'am," the mate said, and his words were entirely genuine.

"Tomorrow, noon, then." She met his eyes, giving him her most seductive smile. "Or perhaps I shall return even before then. One never knows."

Two A.M.

That would be . . . Anne tried to recall, *four bells . . . no, three bells. Three bells in the middle watch.* She wondered if the pirates worried about such niceties.

The raucous sounds of the Ship Tavern, one floor below, had abated enough that Anne could hear, faintly, the cries of "All's well!" from Woodes Rogers's soldiers as they paced their watch along the crumbling walls of the decrepit fort.

"All's well!" another cried, and Anne thought, *Such they know*.

A swell of noise from belowstairs drowned out anything more from the window. Anne stood, took a few tentative steps in the unfamiliar square-toed shoes. Once they were under way she would start going barefoot, get her feet toughened up, but for now it had to be shoes.

Not so bad. The fit was good. She could feel the places where they would hurt until they were broken in, but for now they were tolerable. She picked up her shoulder belt, slung it over her shoulder. At the end hung a cutlass, the weight heavy on her shoulder, pressing against her breasts, but she liked the way it felt. She rested her hand on the weapon's hilt, took a turn around the room. *Yes, yes*.

She wished she had a mirror, but that was not an amenity with which the squalid rooms above the Ship were provided. She looked down at herself in the light of the two candles on the washstand. Square-toed shoes, wool stockings, and loose, wide-legged sailor's slop trousers. A wide leather belt around her waist, a sheath knife in the small of her back.

Tucked into the trousers was a big cotton shirt, purposely oversized to hide her breasts, which it did, to some degree. The shoulder belt hid them a bit more. Over that she pulled on a man's coat, blue wool with wide lapels and big silver buttons. Jack had already plaited her hair and bound it up with a strip of leather. She could feel it thump against her back as she moved, like a soft cudgel. She tied a red cloth around her head and pushed a cocked hat down over that.

She put her hand on the hilt of the cutlass once again and struck a manly pose. She smiled, then laughed out loud, carried away by the dash and boldness of the thing. She had thought it daring to marry the penniless James Bonny, to browbeat him into running away to Nassau, but that was a trifle compared to this, embarking on a career as a pirate. A genuine, full-fledged pirate!

She laughed again and shook her head. She picked up the brace of fine pistols that Jack had bought for her, tied together with half a fathom of bright ribbon, draped them over her shoulders and tucked them under her coat. She looked around the small, ugly room that had been her home since arriving in Nassau. So many memories it held.

But memories were for old women, and she was not that, nor did she think she would ever be. A short life and a merry one, that was what the pirates said, and that was for her.

Time to go. She blew out the candles and stepped through the door, relishing the novel weight of the weapons slung over her shoulders, the way they thumped against her as she walked.

Gone were the heavy skirts and petticoats that twisted around her legs and impeded her movements, the tight bodices with their damned whalebone stays, the ungainly false rumps and panniers.

Now she was dressed like a man, like one of the dangerous fellows gone on the account. Simple, functional clothes, they did not slow her down. They were clothes designed for action, not so much slipcovering to turn a woman into a living ornament, a human decoration that could do no more than oversee a household.

Her spiritual freedom felt complete with this newfound freedom of movement. Along with her bodice and her petticoats she had shed the last vestiges of her father and his stifling social concerns and what he considered proper female decorum, and she liked the feel of it.

Down the narrow stairs to the low, smoky tavern where those who had not yet staggered off or passed out were still carousing. Half the men in the room—nine, including Jack Rackam—were there for the same reason as herself: preparing for the night's work. For Anne that meant donning the mantle of a pirate. For those who were pirates already it meant fortifying themselves with rum.

She stepped down the stairs and one after another of those rough men noticed her, stopped, grinned at her approach. This was her grand entrance, like she had made at her coming-of-age party, three years before. But oh, how different were her circumstances now!

"Here, now, this is a proper buccaneer!" Jack shouted

out, a lusty cry that was taken up by the huzzahs of the others, who crowded around her and slapped her on the back hard as if they had no notion that she was indeed a woman.

"Well done, Annie, well done. I near pissed my pants in fright, just at the sight of you!" Jack said, putting his arm around her and kissing her, to renewed shouts from the crowd.

And then the door opened, and one by one the men fell silent as James Bonny came pushing his way through. His hands trembled. Anne reckoned he had used every last bit of his courage to come to that place, to confront her this one last time.

He stopped in the middle of the room and swept the men with his eyes, pausing for a beat on Calico Jack, then looked right past Anne. He was half-turned around when he stopped, whirled back, seeing Anne at last. His mouth hung wide.

The silence in the room broke like a thunderclap, men roaring in laughter, shouting, "He looked right past her, damn my eyes!" and such. It was a marvelous joke to them.

James took two steps toward Anne, stopped a foot away from her. "What the devil are you about?" he hissed.

"Be gone. This is no place for you," Anne replied.

Bonny's hand lashed out. He grabbed her arm and he began to pull her toward the stairs, away from the crowd, but before he had completed two steps Jack Rackam's pistol was raised, cocked, pressed to his temple.

"Stay, Jack," Anne said. She wrenched her arm from her husband's grip. "I will have a word with him. In private."

Jack's eyes moved from James to Anne and back again, and then at last he lowered the pistol, and now it was Anne who led James to the end of the room, to the base of the stairs, out of whispered earshot from the rest.

"Anne, this is too much!" James said in a harsh whisper. "Adultery's crime enough, but now you dress against your sex, which to be sure is agin the law, and I won't have it!"

Anne closed her eyes, took a deep breath. When she felt she could speak, she opened her eyes again and looked at

James. "It's not a matter of what you will have, James. Do you not see that?"

"You are still my wife. By law."

"Yes, but there are things bigger than laws. I am not your wife anymore, and all the threats and proclamations from that bastard Woodes Rogers will not change that. Now, James, I pray you just leave and forget me, forget we ever met. It will go easier on both of us."

James cocked his head, squinted at her. "What are you reckoning to do? Are you figuring on running off with these bastards? You ain't . . . you ain't turning pirate with these whore's sons?" The truth began to dawn on him. "Good God, that is what you're figuring to do, ain't it!"

"James, I beg you, ask no questions. Just be gone."

"I won't stand for this!" James Bonny raised his voice. "No, damn you, I will not tolerate this!" Heads turned toward them.

"James, shut your gob, damn it! Are you mad?" Anne hissed. "This could go hard on you!"

James lowered his voice, but his tone did not change. "If you do not come with me this minute, then I am off to the Governor's, and won't we see what he thinks of your dear Calico Jack breaking his pardon?"

"James, please . . ."

"I mean it, Anne," he said in a harsh whisper, "I'll not stand for this! I'll see the Governor turns the troops out this night, puts a stop to whatever you have a notion to do."

Anne closed her eyes again. As much as she despised James Bonny, she did not want to see him dead, there in that ugly place, not after he had come all that way for her. For the sake of what little pleasure they had once had in each other's company, she did not want that to happen.

But Jack and the others were her fellows now, and they were off on a job of work, and their success was more important than anything, more important certainly than the life of one miserable toady of Woodes Rogers's.

If she did not stop him, then he would go to the Governor, and no doubt Jack would hang.

She did not want to choose between them, because she knew what the choice would be.

"James, do not make me do this. For your sake, I beg you, just go . . ."

"We leave together, or so help me, it is the gallows for your beloved Jack!"

"James, it is your life I fear for. I beg you, go."

"No. And that is an end to it."

Anne shook her head, slowly, sadly. It was such a waste, so unnecessary, but he had driven her to it.

"Let it be on your head, then," she said soft, and then pushed him hard in the chest, sent him reeling back and shouted, "Oh, you'll go to the Governor, will you? You'll tell the Governor tales of what we are about, just like all them others you betrayed? How many men have you sold out, eh, for your bloody pieces of silver? How many have hung because of you, you rat?"

James Bonny had regained his balance, was shaking his head, moving toward the door, but there was a wall of men between him and safety, a wall of armed and angry men who were hearing every word of Anne's accusations.

"Jack, we must be off, before my . . . *husband* . . . runs to the Governor with tales of our enterprise. He has done it to others, he told me as much, and he promises he will do it to us." She turned to some of the others there, men who were not a part of their scheme, said, "Pray, will you detain this whore's son for an hour more, so that we might get safe away?"

Big hands grabbed on to James Bonny, pulling him farther into the tavern. His eyes were wide, his face white and waxy in the lantern light. He was shaking his head and looked as if he wished to speak, but nothing would come.

The nine men and Anne Bonny hefted their weapons and their meager seabags, and filed out the door, into the early morning quiet of Nassau. Anne was the last to leave. She stopped, looked at James, and held his stare. "I begged you, James. Now, good-bye."

She turned and followed behind her fellow pirates.

James Bonny watched her leave, her feminine walk all but masked by her men's clothing, the cutlass on her hip. The room was spinning around. Huge, hairy faces loomed up in front of him, big hands gripped hard on his arms and shoulders.

They would not hold him, he understood that. They would kill him for what he had done. He would not see another sunrise.

He was not afraid. He had moved to a place beyond fear, the place where men are when they climb silently up the gallows steps, or shout out some heroic thing or other as they stand before the firing squad.

Oh, Anne, I love you so, do you not see that?

Then a big knife flashed before his face and he could not tell who of all those men was wielding it. He tried to flinch, but the others were holding him tight. A shot of fear came through the numbness, like lighting on a black night, and then he felt the burn and dull pain of the knife as it was driven into his gut, pulled out, and driven in again and again.

He doubled over and the blood came like vomit and the dull pain of the stab wounds welled up into an unbearable agony, a burning, like red-hot irons had been thrust under his skin.

The hands released him and he fell, saw the floor coming up and was unable to do anything about it. He hit with a jar that sent shudders through his body, and the pain that a second before he thought was more than he could bear double, tripled, engulfed him in a torment that was well beyond what seemed possible this side of hell.

He realized that he was going to die. Not sometime in the next hour or day, but now, there on that filthy tavern floor, his blood mixing with the rum and spittle that covered the bare pine boards, and he realized that death would be a welcome thing if it made the pain stop.

His eyes were bulging. He opened his mouth and blood

trickled out and when it had stopped he said, so soft he could barely hear himself, "Anne, oh, Anne . . . you done for me now . . ."

They were the last words that James Bonny ever said in life. He closed his eyes and suddenly the pain was not so bad.

Chapter 13

ANNE FOLLOWED THE SMALL BAND ACROSS BAY STREET, their shoes making scuffling sounds on the hard-packed sand. Nassau was cool and quiet at that hour. A light rain had begun to fall, which seemed to muffle all other sound. The night was black, well suited to their enterprise.

The damp air was heavy with the scents of the harbor and the ocean and hints of the island vegetation. It was a Nassau that Anne had rarely seen: peaceful, sleepy, quiet. The silence only served to heighten her tension, her sense of intrigue and danger.

Across Bay Street and down a block or so and then out along a battered old dock. The smell of conch shells and rotting fish was heavier now. Below them, the sound of small waves washing against the beach, and from out over the dark water, the slap of rigging and spars as the vessels at anchor rolled in the tiny swell, the occasional burst of laughter, bits of song.

It seemed to Anne that it took an extra effort to engage in piracy on so tranquil a night, a struggle to fight the languid effects of wine and a big meal.

At the far end of the dock, and floating five feet below, was a boat, and seated on the thwarts were Corner and Fetherston. It was a bigger one than they had used that afternoon to transport Anne out to the *Nathaniel James* for her spy work and she wondered where all the boats were coming from. Figured that was part of it, this life on the account, taking what you need.

Silent, the men began to clamber down the short ladder and step into the boat, settling on the thwarts, stowing their dunnage in the bottom. They were all experienced seamen, seasoned pirates, and they went about this business calmly, silently, despite the great quantities of rum they had consumed.

Anne watched them, the way they moved, the look on their faces. She tried her best to imitate it, stood waiting her turn with one hand on her waist, the other on the hilt of her cutlass, scowling, glancing around, ignoring the rain that fell on her cocked hat and soaked through her jacket.

Sweat stood out on her brow, despite the cool evening; her palm was slick on the steel of her cutlass. She felt as if tiny bolts of lightning were running along just under her skin. She wanted to shout, to run, to do something.

It was not fear, but the thrill of the thing, the danger, the wickedness. She thought she might explode, like she felt that first time in bed with Jack. But she was a pirate now, and she stood unmoving, stoic, waiting her turn to go down into the boat.

Finally it was just she and Jack, and Jack put one hand on her waist and with the other gestured for her to go down. She nodded, turned to face the ladder, stepped down like she had seen the others do, placing her feet with care on the slippery rungs. Three steps and then her foot found the bottom of the boat and she stepped in and worked her way aft, hands on the men's shoulders for balance. She stumbled, nearly fell, said, "Goddamn it!" through clenched teeth. She made her way all the way aft, took a seat on the stern sheets.

A second later Jack was there, seated across from her. He took the tiller, nodded to the men, and with never a word spoken, Corner shoved off and the men began their slow, rhythmic stroke with the long oars, the shafts muffled in the tholes with rags and oddly quiet, the careful dip of the blades all but inaudible. .

Anne settled herself in her seat and kept her eyes mostly

right ahead, despite her desire to look around, to take it all in. It seemed much tougher and piratical to look disinterested, the way the others did, so she held her face grim, as much as she felt like smiling, like laughing out loud.

The raiders threaded their way through the anchored vessels, Jack steering the boat with little motions of the tiller. They pulled through the light rain, the hulks of ships rising dark around them.

Finally Jack leaned toward her and whispered, "There she is. Stand ready." How he had found the *Nathaniel James* among all those shadowy vessels on the black water, Anne did not know. She hoped he had indeed found the right one.

And then a sloop was looming up over them just off the boat's starboard side, and it looked like the *Nathaniel James*, though Anne would not have bet on it.

Jack nodded, a single nod, and the men at the oars took one last pull and then the oars came inboard and were laid along the thwarts and the boat's momentum carried it along the sloop's side.

Corner in the bow grabbed the chains with the boathook and stopped the forward motion as half a dozen hands kept the boat from thumping against the sloop. They paused, silent, waiting for some challenge from the deck above, but there was no indication that anyone aboard was awake.

Anne felt as if her every nerve were firing at once, as if her whole body might start twitching, as if she could not contain herself. Corner went aboard, quick and silent, amazing for a brute such as himself, and Fetherston went next and then Anne. She gained the deck, stepped aside as more men came after her.

Now she recognized the sloop, the deck she had stood upon that afternoon, the passageways of which she had taken careful note.

Last of all, Jack Rackam stepped up on deck. "Where will the crew be at, Annie, dear?" he whispered.

"Below and forward. I shall see to them." She stepped off across the deck and Richard Corner followed behind. The short scuttle doors were shut. Anne set her fingers on the latch, gently, and gently lifted it and swung the doors wide. She turned and nodded to Corner, then for the second time that day ducked low through the entrance and stepped below.

One, two, three, four . . . She counted out the steps as she descended and when she reached four she knew she was on the lower deck, though she could see little in the dark cavern of the ship. She reached out and felt the lockers that lined the side of the vessel, ran her hand along as she stepped softly forward. Behind her, Corner made the slightest of sounds as he followed.

Ten feet, twenty feet, and in the dim light that filtered below Anne could see the door that McKeown had told her was the door to the forecastle in which they slept.

Her hands were shaking, as if all the surfeit of emotions were looking for an outlet. She balled her fingers into a fist, then opened them and wiped her palm on her jacket, and then silently pulled her sword from its sheath and held it in her right hand. With her left she took up one of her pistols. She felt tense, electric, as if she wanted to bite down hard of something, or scream out loud.

She palmed the lock of the pistol back. The click was loud in the dead still air. She heard a rustle in the forecastle and took three bold steps forward, her heavy shoes loud on the deck.

"Who's there?" McKeown's voice, edged with panic. Anne was in the cabin and she could see McKeown's vague form, sitting up in his bunk. She brought the pistol up level, straight arm, the end of the muzzle not three inches from the mate's forehead. "One move, one word, sir, and I shall blow your brains out, damn me if I will not!" she shouted. The words sounded to her ear as natural as any she had ever spoken.

"Up, up, sir, and be quick!" Anne ordered, and McKeown threw off the sheets. Three minutes later she and Corner were back on deck, pushing the sleepy, confused, frightened crew members before them.

Jack stood by the gangway, ran his eyes over the men as they were hustled along. He had a presence, a calm efficiency about him that Anne found impressive and alluring. He glanced around once and began to issue orders.

"You men." He pointed to five of the pirates. "Bind the hands of these stupid bastards and set them in the bow. Corner, see to getting the cable in. Fetherston, take a gang and get the gaskets off them sails and see the halyards laid along. Annie, get you aft on the quarterdeck and see there's no boats bound our way. Quiet, the lot of you."

The men nodded and fell to their appointed tasks. As Anne turned to go she noticed the mate, McKeown, staring at her, wide-eyed, like he was trying to understand but could not. She met his eyes, gave him a sweet, demure smile. She waved the barrel of her pistol at him, like a wagging finger at an overeager suitor, then stepped aft.

She went back by the taffrail, peered out into the night, but there was no movement there, no indication that anyone knew what they were about. She could feel her heart pounding in her chest, could feel the excitement tinged with fear and a dreadful feeling of being exposed, of being watched, of armed men closing in on her and Jack.

Footsteps behind, and George Fetherston and his gang swarmed over the big boom, casting off the lines that held the sail in place. From forward came a steady clack clack clack as others heaved the handspikes in the windlass and pulled the anchor cable aboard.

Anne turned and looked astern again, but still there was no movement on the water, no sign of excitement on the still night. No alarm, no boatloads of soldiers coming after them, no sound of the guard ship getting under way.

They must have held James, as I asked them, she thought, and did not allow herself to think beyond that, to think about what she knew they had really done to him.

Jack stepped up onto the quarterdeck, grinning, and gave Anne an elaborate bow. Anne grinned as well and bowed back, a man's bow.

From forward came a muted cry, "First anchor's aboard!"

"Very well, Corner, let the other go!" Jack called back,

as soft as he could and still be heard across forty feet of deck.

By way of reply came the low rumble and slight tremor underfoot as the cable to the sloop's second anchor ran across the deck and snaked out of the hawsehole. And then it stopped and the *Nathaniel James*'s bow began to turn, the dim shapes of anchored ships sweeping past as the light breeze and the current got hold of the sloop.

George Fetherston took up the big tiller, kicking off the beckets that held it in place and swinging it slightly to starboard, but the tiller seemed to have no effect. With no sail set, the sloop drifted sideways down the harbor, slowly, inexorably, entirely in the grip of wind and tide.

Jack came aft, climbed up on the quarterdeck rail, one hand on the main shrouds, and stared forward into the dark. The tails of his white calico coat flapped in the breeze and draped in folds over the cutlass that hung from his belt. His long, curly hair was wet and nearly straight as it fell back over his shoulders. His face was set as he looked out ahead. He looked dashing, dramatic, the more so because for once he was not trying to look that way.

The few lights still burning ashore seemed to drift by, hazy and unfocused in the rain. Anne tried to guess to which buildings they belonged, or to which camps on the beach, but she could not.

"There's the guard ship," Jack said, nodding toward a distant light, and Fetherston grunted his concurrence, but how they knew that, Anne had no idea.

A certain tension settled over the deck, grim faces, little talk, and what talk there was in hushed tones. Men leaning over the rails, looking forward, astern, larboard and starboard. Dark, anchored vessels seemed to sweep by, some barely discernible, some startlingly close.

Then from the night came a voice, so close sounding and so unexpected that Anne jumped and almost shouted in surprise.

"What ship is that?" The speaker was using a speaking trumpet.

"*Nathaniel James!*" Jack shouted back. He sounded

composed, perfectly natural. Anne guessed that the challenge had not taken him by surprise, that he had expected it.

"Why are you under way? Where are you going?" It was unsettling, this voice from the night. It had to be someone aboard the guard ship, the small man-of-war stationed in Nassau to protect that place from smugglers and pirates.

"Our cable has parted. We've nothing but a grapple aboard, which will not hold!" Jack called back in exactly the tone of voice one might expect from a seaman in that circumstance.

It seemed to satisfy the guard ship, for no more word was heard from that quarter.

The *Nathaniel James* was moving well, drifting toward the western entrance of Nassau Harbor. Right under the guns of Woodes Rogers's fort, but when the fort hailed them, as the guard ship had, and Jack gave them the same story, they, too, seemed to accept it.

Five minutes, ten minutes—an hour perhaps—they drifted silently down harbor. Anne could not tell how long it had been; in that tense atmosphere the minutes seemed to crawl by, it seemed they would never fetch the end of the confined water. She had no urge to laugh now. She was swept up in the universal tension aboard the sloop. It felt like they were all holding their breath.

Then suddenly she felt the deck drop away, as if it were falling out from under her. She stumbled and the bow rose up and up, hung there for a second, and then came down and the quarterdeck seemed to rise and the tension on board broke like a fragile skim of ice.

"Yeah! Kiss my arse, Rogers you bloody sodomite!" someone shouted from the waist, and a chorus of jeers and shouts and obscenities followed, hurled back at the town of Nassau passing astern.

Orders flew along the deck, spoken in loud voices, commands that Anne did not understand but the others apparently did because gangs of men fell to the halyards and the sheets and began to haul away. The big mainsail rose up, unfolding itself off the boom and spreading out, gray against the dark night's sky. Forward the jib began to jerk up the forestay.

Anne leapt aside as another gang of men hauled away on the mainsheets, nearly trampling her as they pulled the boom amidships.

The sloop seemed to pause in midswing, as if uncertain of where to go. And then, making up her mind, she began to gather headway, the big mainsail full and curved in an elegant sweep of canvas, the water making a musical gurgling sound down her side.

"Jack!" Anne staggered forward and grabbed on to the rail for support. In an instant the calm, stately motion of the sloop had changed to a wild, corkscrew ride. "Whatever is happening? Why is the boat moving thus?"

Jack was grinning wide. "Why, my beloved, that is the feel of the deep-water rollers. We are free of the harbor, don't you see? We are in open water now, with never an alarm raised, and Rogers and all his toy soldiers can kiss our sweet arses!" He laughed, an infectious laugh, and Anne joined in, let it all out, all the tension, all the thrill and fear and regret and anticipation she had felt raging within her for the past twelve hours.

Jack pointed toward the bow. "Bring those fellows aft!" he called, and the sloop *Nathaniel James*'s two unhappy crew members were brought back to the quarterdeck and stood in front of Calico Jack.

"What cheer, fellows? See here, I am a charitable man, so I will offer you both the main chance. I will give you leave to join with us gentlemen on the account. What say you?"

"We've no taste for piracy and we'll not go willing with you." McKeown spat the words and the other man nodded.

"Very well, you sniveling puppies, I shall send you crawling back to your master. Put these rascals in the boat!"

Richard Corner and four others grabbed the men roughly and pulled them back to the gangway. "Pray, give our service to Woodes Rogers!" Jack called after them. "And let him know we shall return the sloop once we have had a little use of it!"

The men's hands were freed and they were hustled down the boarding cleats and into the boat, and a moment later the boat was lost in the gloom astern. Jack stepped back to the quarterdeck, leaned against the windward rail, and Anne took her place beside him, as close as she thought proper, which was not very close. After all, they were shipmates now, brothers in arms, not lovers. Not at that moment.

This is it, she thought. They were in open water, Nassau was astern, and under their bows, the Caribbean, the Spanish Main, the American coast, wherever they wished to go.

They had stolen the sloop *Nathaniel James* right out of Nassau Harbor, and her part had been the most active of all of them, hers and Jack's, and that made them the first candidates for the gallows.

She was an outlaw now; there was no going back. She was a pirate.

Chapter 14

THE CARIBBEAN WAS BLUE-GREEN, A WARM AND UN-failing breeze, humps of high, jungle-covered mountains in the far distance. It was as good as Mary had hoped it would be.

Fifteen knots of wind blowing over the starboard quarter, blowing so steady that they had not had to go aloft to set or take in sail for four days, had not even needed to tend a sheet or a brace. The air was warm but not hot, a temperature that matched hers so perfectly that it seemed neutral, as if there were no temperature at all.

Overhead, the sky was a robin's-egg blue, with big white anvil-head clouds building on the horizon, but safely to leeward. They might mean a squall for some unlucky mariners, but not for those aboard the *Hoorn*.

She lay stretched out on the foredeck, her head propped

up on the forecastle hatch combing. Bare feet, loose, wide-legged trousers. She wore a big soft canvas duck shirt as well and over that a faded red waistcoat of the same material—an unusual piece of clothing for a sailor, but then sailors were given to adding their own idiosyncratic touches to their kit, and no one thought anything of it. They certainly did not think that the waistcoat was there primarily to compact and disguise her breasts.

Her shoulder-length black hair had been plaited and clubbed by a shipmate, sailor fashion. Her reemergence as a seaman was complete.

It was the middle of the forenoon watch, ten o'clock in the morning. Normally she would have been on watch, taking her trick at the helm, or standing forward lookout, or at day work, up aloft overhauling running rigging or slushing masts with rancid tallow or any of the myriad jobs required on shipboard.

But it was Sunday, a day off. Dirk Bes, master of the *Hoorn,* was a good man—Mary could see right through his facade of hard-bitten ship driver—and he was not the type to deny his crew the simple pleasure of four hours free time once a week, as much as Waalwijk would have loved to work them.

"This is your first time in the Caribbean?"

Mary opened her eyes. Hans Franeker was sitting beside her, fiddling with a piece or rope, attempting to tuck an eye splice.

"Turn that over . . ." Mary waited while he obeyed. "Now take that third strand and tuck it right to left . . . right to left . . . there. That is the hard part done. Now over and under with all three strands."

Hans smiled at his eye splice, correct now after a dozen attempts. "This is your first time in the Caribbean?" he asked again.

"Yes."

"Hmm."

"You seem surprised."

Hans grinned, a sheepish look, shrugged his shoulders. "It's just . . . well . . . it seems you've done so much, had so many adventures, it is hard for me to think of something you have not done."

Mary smiled. God, but he was young! He had taken to following her like a little brother, or a puppy or some such. She could see the worship in his eyes. All because of her one instinctive grab as he fell, and the sheer luck of catching her fingers in his belt. But she did not mind, because she liked him and she could keep an eye on him if he was close by.

Lord, if you knew the truth of me, wouldn't you be surprised! she thought. It was not a thought that she had very often. She had been too long among men to think about it much anymore.

She moved her eyes up to the rigging overhead. The sails of the mainmast rose up and up above her—mainsail, main topsail, main topgallant sail. They bowed out in great, round, elegant curves, like the belly of a pregnant woman with the fabric of her dress stretched taut over it.

Oh, Frederick, why did we not have children? Then there would be a piece of you still alive for me to love.

They were not childless for want of trying, but never was she able to conceive. Mary had come at last to believe she was barren, that perhaps playing the man for so long had somehow affected her womanhood in that way.

Where would she be if she had had children by Frederick? Not here, that was for certain. She would never have abandoned them, would never have forced them, or even allowed them, to live the life that she had been made to live.

"You have been on the Continent, then, these years?"

Mary looked over. Hans was still trying to pry information from her about a life that he reckoned was rife with fine adventure. She gave him a thin smile. "I have been on the Continent since . . . 1710, I believe. Cadet with an infantry unit at the outbreak of the late war, and then I rode with Walpole's Regiment of Light Cavalry."

"It must be a fine thing, to be a trooper of horse."

"It can be." Mary recalled the exhilaration of the attack, the martial sound of drum and bugle, the pounding of the horse under her as she charged, saber held straight out like a lance.

And she recalled the hidden artillery opening up on them, the screams of dying men and dying animals, the desperate fear for Frederick's life, for her own.

"It can also be an absolute hell. War is not a fine thing, Hans, it truly is not."

"I believe you," Franeker said, though it was clear he did not.

Mary closed her eyes again, let the warmth wash over her. This was just the thing she had envisioned, back during the torment of the North Sea. Why did anyone live in Europe when such a place as this existed on earth? she wondered. The ship moved under her in a steady rhythm: down, up, a slight corkscrew motion and then over again, like a giant cradle rocking her to sleep.

Once they had found good weather south of thirty degrees north latitude, Captain Bes had given them leave to rinse their clothes in fresh water—just two buckets for the entire crew, but it was enough to wash away most of the salt.

The sun was warm on her face. Her stomach was full. Her clothes were fairly clean and entirely dry and she was dry and warm. At that point in her life she did not feel there was much more she could hope for. That was enough.

And then the forward lookout's cry of "Sail, ho!" and she sat bolt upright, every muscle taut.

"Where away?" the master called from the quarterdeck. Everyone seemed to be frozen in place, everyone staring at the lookout.

"Three points off the weather bow! Topgallant up."

Weather bow. Topgallant up. Most of the vessel was still below the horizon, at least from the deck, so there was no telling what she was. Still, the same thought flashed through the mind of every sailor in those waters at the sight of a distant sail: pirate.

"You there, Ratten, up to the main crosstrees with a glass!" Bes called. Able-bodied seaman Ratten grabbed up a telescope, flung himself into the weather main shrouds, and scrambled aloft. He clambered up into the crosstrees, extended the glass, and put it to his eye. There was a moment of silence as he stared out at the horizon and everyone else aboard the *Hoorn* stared at him. At last he called, "Sloop, with all plain sail set and coming down fast!"

Sloop. It was a popular and common rig in those waters. Popular with honest traders and with pirates as well.

A moment more of silence and then Bes called, "Is she altering course at all?"

"No! Wait . . . she . . . she's set stuns'ls, sir, topmast stuns'ls!"

Stuns'ls. Light sails set on the outer edges of the square sails to give the vessel every inch of canvas she could carry. This stranger was not turning away at the sight of the *Hoorn*. Rather, she was closing with them as fast as she could.

Mary met Hans Franeker's eyes and she could see that he was afraid. Even he understood that the pirates were the only ones in those waters likely to close a strange vessel.

In the momentary silence Mary said, "Now, Hans, you will see what grand adventure is really like."

Before Franeker could reply, Captain Bes exploded in a series of rapid-fire orders, turning the ship as directly away from the pursuit as he could, sending hands to trim the sails to their maximum efficiency, setting the *Hoorn*'s stuns'ls as well.

Waalwijk paced fore and aft, applying his rope end to the shoulders of those who did not work fast enough. The speed with which the crew set sail now had a direct bearing on his own personal safety, and that brought a powerful motivation to his beatings.

Twenty minutes of furious activity and the fat Dutch merchant ship was fleeing the distant sloop as fast and as directly as she was able.

They ran for an hour and then Ratten called from the main crosstrees, "Just hull up now, on the rise!" For all of their effort, the sloop was still gaining on them.

"All hands, lay aft!" Bes bellowed, and all the crew of the ship crowded around the base of the mainmast, looking up at the quarterdeck and the master and mate. The murmuring was loud, the buzz of speculation in fast, guttural Dutch, but there was little doubt in Mary's mind what Bes would say.

"See here, lads," the master began, and the murmuring died away. "I don't know what yonder sloop is, but we got to reckon on the worst, that she's a pirate and she's chasing us. We're running best as we can, but it looks like that ain't going to be fast enough. So if she overhauls us, and they're pirates indeed, we have to decide, do we fight or do we surrender?"

That is the question, Mary thought. It was well known among mariners that often the pirates would not harm those who surrendered, and show no mercy to those who fought back. But not always. It was a gamble.

"I reckon you men know what can happen, do we fight and lose," Bes continued. "This ain't a decision I can make for you. I'll give you a minute to talk on it, then we'll vote."

Mary listened to the talk, back and forth, heated opinions expressed with force. She did not participate. She had seen men in this state before, fear mixed with bravado and ignorance, and she knew that debate was pointless. No one would be swayed. *Let us vote and be done with it,* she thought.

Five minutes of shouting and then they voted, and the vote was to fight.

Mary voted that way as well, realizing that her years in the army and naval service had made the thought of passive surrender anathema to her.

We shall fight then, and see what comes of it. She sighed. Was there no place on earth where she could go to be free of this violence?

And then Claude Waalwijk shouted, "And let me say this, if any of you bloody cowards tries to run below, by God, I'll shoot you myself!"

"Michael . . ." There was Hans Franeker, wide-eyed. "That was the right decision, weren't it? Fighting, I mean?"

Mary looked at the boy and thought of all the answers

she might give. But the young man did not need any of her weary philosophy at that juncture, so she just said, "Yes, it was the right decision. Don't you worry, we'll do for these bastards."

The relief in Franeker's face was at once gratifying and disturbing. *Lord, don't look to me to save you,* Mary thought, *I've made quite a hash of my own life.*

For four hours they ran, south by west, with the breeze all but right astern and the sloop growing larger and larger in their wake. The strange vessel had run up a Dutch flag, which was meaningless. The only fact they knew for certain about the vessel following was that it *was* following, and trying to overhaul them, and that was all they needed to know.

Up through the scuttle came two men bearing between them an arms chest, and then more men carrying pikes, cutlasses, boarding axes—all the meager assortment of weapons the merchantman carried. They dumped them all unceremoniously on the deck.

"Very well, you men, take up the arms you want!" Bes shouted from the quarterdeck, and the crew swarmed around the pile of weapons like children to free candy.

Mary managed to push her way through. She picked up a cutlass, felt the heft in her hand. It was lighter than a cavalry saber, but not as well balanced. She tried a tentative feint and recover. It would do.

Beside her Hans had one pistol in his belt, another in his hand, and a pike in the other. He was grinning.

"Not the pike, Hans," she said. A pike was useless in all but the most skilled hands, and Hans's were most assuredly not that. "One loaded pistol in your left hand, another in the belt, and a cutlass in your right hand." She found a cutlass for him. "Here."

Hans looked disappointed, but he laid the pike down, took the cutlass from Mary. Then over the sound of the men's speculation and the clash of weapons and the working of the ship came a flat banging sound that sent Mary reeling back through the years, stirred up memories of morning guns in camp and the opening rounds of artillery duels as she waited for her turn to charge into the fray.

It was a cannon shot, a ranging bow chaser from the sloop astern. A spout of water shot up one hundred yards off their starboard quarter and all of the cocky high spirits of the men were blown away by that single round.

Weapons in hand, they raced to the rail and up the shrouds to stare at their pursuer. The Dutch flag was gone, and in its place a black flag, with some pattern they could not make out from that distance. Not that it mattered.

"That's it, it's pirates then, and they means to take us . . ." Hans said, as if trying to convince himself that any hope of it being otherwise was gone, as if hoping someone would tell him his conclusion was wrong. But it was not.

"Yes, Hans," said Mary. "We'll be grappling with them in an hour, I should think. Perhaps less." She pointed with her cutlass to a spot on the deck, to her left and two feet behind. "You stand there. No matter what happens, you stay this close to me, on this side. When the fighting starts I don't want to have to wonder where you are."

Hans nodded, and though they were still an hour from the fight, he took up the position Mary had indicated.

Good lad. She hoped something would happen so that they did not have to fight. If they did fight, she hoped they would win, she hoped that none of her shipmates would be killed, she hoped that she would survive.

But all that was too much to hope for. So instead she would try to keep Hans Franeker alive, and if she could achieve just that one tiny thing, then that would be something, at least.

Chapter 15

ANNE BONNY SAT ON THE SLOOP'S QUARTERDECK, AFT by the tiller, and sewed, looking for all the world like a young Jack Tar stitching his clothing on make-and-mend day.

She was dressed in her loose sailor's trousers and a big cambric shirt she had stolen from Jack. Her long-tailed blue coat had been exchanged for a short blue jacket like the sailors wore. Her head was bound in a bright red cloth, and the cocked hat that she generally wore over that was on the deck beside her. Her thick reddish blond hair was tied back with a length of yellow ribbon.

Like all of the brigands aboard the sloop, she was barefoot.

She had put away her square-toed shoes two days after sailing. Shoes were no more than a hindrance in that fine weather, and Anne relished the feel of the hard, warm deck planking against the soles of her feet. There was a brazen freedom about going barefoot, walking around in the company of rough men with her legs entirely bare from midcalf down. She loved that. Her father would have had an apoplexy if he could have seen her.

Overhead the sky was clear and blue, with big Caribbean anvil-head clouds building to the southward. The ship rose and dipped and rolled in a steady, hypnotic manner.

They had been prowling the sea for a month, but still had little to show for the effort. A few fishing boats around Eleuthera, a small island trader bound away for Great Abaco, their victims were poorer and more ill equipped than the pirates, so they had plundered their vessels for what little was worth the effort to lift and let them go on their way.

Their prizes, such as they were, did not run and did not fight. A shot across the bows and their sails came down fast and the buccaneers swaggered aboard in the face of their wide-eyed and trembling victims.

It was not exactly how Anne Bonny had imagined it, none of the smoke and thunder of great sea battles, none of the massive fleets of a Henry Morgan from an earlier age. Just fishing boats, small traders. Not an ounce of fight in them.

Still, the crew of the *Pretty Anne*—she was the *Pretty Anne* now, the name painted on the fresh plank that replaced the one on which *Nathaniel James* had been carved—seemed content enough with things as they were. They offered their victims the chance to join the sloop's company, and as often as not they agreed, so their numbers were somewhat increased now.

They had stopped once in Tortuga and taken on supplies—rum, food, prostitutes—and then sailed to a small island in the Windward Islands where they careened the sloop and caroused on the beach for a week before setting off again.

If the others did not seem restless for some real action, then Anne reckoned she probably should not either.

Far from restless, the pirates lolled around the deck, drinking furiously, constantly, eating when it struck their fancy, keeping a desultory sort of watch. They lived much the same life they had lived ashore in Nassau, save for the close quarters and increased discomfort and somewhat worse smells aboard the small sloop.

Anne had always thought the sea a treacherous place, a place where only constant vigilance could stave off a watery death. But after a month of cruising the Bahamas, she began to understand that the Caribbean was an altogether more benign place than those seaways she had heard about.

There was no one aboard, not Jack or Richard Corner or George Fetherston or Noah Harwood or any of the experienced seamen, who seemed overworried about a threat from wind or weather, and so Anne did not worry either.

Rather, she lived as the pirates did. She ate, slept, drank

wine and rum. She humped furiously with Jack in the small cabin aft. She did what work she could aboard the ship, and though she was learning to be a sailor, she was still unfamiliar with most maintenance tasks, and she was of little help. It frustrated her. She chafed at her forced idleness and her lack of knowledge.

But she had been raised as a lady, and one thing a lady could do was sew, so she sewed.

She sat with her back to the bulwark on the weather side of the quarterdeck, in a place and manner that would never be allowed aboard a legitimate ship, doing work that would never be done in that place.

Spread out on her lap and tumbling along the scuppers, a great spread of black cloth, a sturdy number five canvas. In her hand, a sailmaker's palm, the rugged seagoing equivalent of the thimble she had learned to use when her mother had schooled her in the fine art of sewing and embroidery. Awkward at first, but once she was used to working needle and palm together, she saw her speed increase in a satisfying manner.

She was making a flag. It was a labor of love for her man, Calico Jack Rackam.

When he had brought the limping *Ranger* into Nassau, when he had returned to accept the King's pardon, unsure of whether it would be extended or not, he had had the foresight to dump all evidence of his pirating over the side.

Down into the depths went anything that bore the name of any ship they had taken, over the side went any instrument or journal or ship's log that might be claimed by its owner and held up as evidence. And into the sea went the black flag.

Now it was time for another.

The design was Jack's, one he had conjured up during long hours as Vane's quartermaster, thinking on how things would be when he was captain. A black field, and on it, a death's head, and below that, crossed cutlasses. Simple, elegant, terrifying. Anne quite approved, and her needle flashed in the sun as she built a new one for Calico Jack and the *Pretty Anne*.

She took the last stitch on the crossed cutlasses, checking both sides to see that they were aligned, that the sail twine had gone through both, and then, satisfied, she finished it off with a few crossed plunges through the cloth.

A shadow fell across her work and she looked up and Jack smiled down at her. "Annie, you are the master of all that you touch. Sailor, seamstress, is there nothing you cannot do?"

"No, my dear Jack, there is not."

It was true that she was picking up the sailor's arts quickly, and she had many an enthusiastic tutor among the *Pretty Anne*'s company. None of them had ever met a woman such as Anne, a woman who was not just a means to sate their sexual appetites but rather a fellow pirate, a woman who could dress like a man and drink and curse and work and plunder side by side with them.

She was the captain's woman—bedding her was not an option—but the fun and novelty of having such a woman aboard outweighed the frustration of keeping hands off.

They showed her how to sweat a line, to heave and belay and coil, how to lay aloft and cast off gaskets, how to sheet home a sail and how to stow it again. They taught her the trick of keeping the ship on course with small adjustments of the helm, how to box the compass, how to tie a bowline and a sheet bend and a reef knot. Anne was smart and eager to learn and she learned quickly. And the more she learned the more she wanted to know, and the more eager the men were to teach.

"You'd best get that finished up, my dear," Jack continued. "We're nigh on halfway betwixt Bermuda and Grand Bahama, and there'll be some fine hunting here. I should think anyone who sees that flag will piss their trousers and then fall to the deck in surrender."

"Might we get ourselves in the way of something more valuable then barrel hoops and salted fish, Jack?" she asked, and saw the anger flash across his face, the unintentional wound delivered. She did not mean to impugn his leadership; she thought she was commenting only on their poor luck.

She opened her mouth to try and correct her blunder, but by then the anger had passed from Jack's face like a cloud before the sun. He smiled down at her. "Yes, my dear, it should be fine hunting here."

He looked out to weather, as he always did, every few minutes, and Anne ran her eyes over his profile, lit up with the sun above and a little behind him.

John Rackam was a magnificent man. He was wearing his striped calico breeches and a cotton shirt with big sleeves that fluttered in the breeze, a waistcoat of calico that perfectly enveloped his torso. His clothes hung on him with an ease and fit that the finest gentleman would envy. His long light brown curling locks fell over his shoulders and stirred in the quartering breeze. He was slim but not dandified, courteous and smooth but nothing of a fop.

For all the attention she received from the others, he showed not the least signs of jealousy and she gave him not the least reason to be jealous. There was no one aboard that sloop, or in all of Nassau, for whom it would be worth leaving Calico Jack Rackam.

"This flag will do you justice, dear Jack. A flag to proclaim to the world, 'Beware! Calico Jack Rackam in at sea once more!' "

Before Jack could respond to that, there came a cry from the masthead lookout, the only station other than the helm that was manned with diligence and consistency. "Sail, ho!"

Jack made a little involuntary gasp and his head jerked back as he looked up at the lookout and Anne did the same.

Sail, ho! It was the call for which they waited during every moment of daylight, their operative phrase, their clarion call to action.

Fore and aft the others looked aloft, a reflex action, since looking aloft would garner them no new information. Anne wondered if aboard that distant ship they had seen the *Pretty Anne*'s sails, if on that other deck men were staring aloft to hear their own lookout's report.

"Right on the loo'rd beam. Ship rig, reaching to west southwest, I reckon," the lookout called down.

Nodding heads, smiles, wolfish grins passed among the

fifteen or so pirates aboard the sloop. Ship rig meant a big vessel, and since the pirates had no national loyalties at all, there was no vessel that was not a potential prize, save for a man-of-war, and it was unlikely that she was that.

Jack looked down at her, grinning as well, and his face showed avarice and pleasure and not a little relief. It occurred to Anne that Jack bore the responsibility of finding prizes, and a heavy responsibility it was, with the dubious loyalty of his crew depending on his success.

"Sew like the devil, Annie, dear, we'll need that flag directly, I'll warrant."

"It is a done thing, my dearest," she said. She hopped to her feet and presented the bundle of black cloth to him and he took it, let it spill out onto the deck so he could see the emblem, the grinning death head, the crossed blades. He smiled. His delight was genuine and it filled Anne with pleasure.

"See here, lads!" Jack turned and addressed the rest of the deck. He gave the flag a shake so it opened up full, eight feet long, six feet on the fly, and the Pretty Annes cheered and Anne grinned, happy through and through.

"Come, you lazy bastards!" Dicky Corner shouted. "Let us tend to them braces and run yonder poor sod down and put Annie's fine work to some use!"

The men raced to the lines, hurried on by this new motivation to leeward. Anne crossed to the weather main brace and cast it off, kept a turn around the belaying pin as she had been taught, and as the *Pretty Anne* swung off the wind, pointing her bow toward her intended victim, so Anne eased away the line until the yard was braced around right. She stopped it there and let the men on the leeward side take up the slack. With a flick of her wrist she cast a loop around the pin again and thought, *Damn my eyes, if I ain't becoming a proper sailorman!*

"Stuns'ls now, boys!" Quartermaster Corner called out, and the men raced into the shrouds and up, and Anne along with them. There were none who moved any swifter or more sure at their task than she, of that she was certain.

She loved working the ship, and she was proud of her ability.

It took no more than ten minutes to set the four stuns'ls and the outer jib. Ten minutes, and then the *Pretty Anne* was flying through the water with everything she could carry set to the breeze, plunging into the rollers and sending the spray back over the deck in brilliant showers. Anne felt the flying water hit her face and her neck, felt the sloop bucking under her, and she wanted to yell with exhilaration.

It was like sex, this wild ride, and the climax would come when they plunged down on their victim's deck, swords flashing, guns blasting away.

"Ha!" the lookout called from aloft. "They've smoked us now, the sorry bastards, haven't they, and running for all they're worth! It'll do you no good, you miserable bugger!" His report was tumbling out like he was narrating events for his own benefit.

"Fenwick!" Jack called out, his voice a bit peevish. "What see you of her?"

"She's turned now, Jack, my beauty, and running right away from us, isn't she? Ah, there they go, getting the fore and main topmast stuns'ls set, and a fucking clumsy job they're making of it!"

This seemed like troubling news to Anne. She had somehow thought they might steal up on their victim, remain unnoticed until it was too late. But this other ship had set stuns'ls as well, and being bigger, she would in theory be faster than the *Pretty Anne*.

"Jack, what does this signify? Are we to lose them?"

"Eh? Oh, no, I don't reckon so. Great fat lumbering merchantman, they should be no match for us, with our new-cleaned bottom. We'll fly over the waves, my dear, be up with them before they've had a chance to give themselves a good thorough scratching."

Anne thought to ask Jack if this might be a richer prize than those they had taken, but she recalled his defensiveness on that subject so instead asked, "Do you think they will fight at all?"

"Might do. Ship rig, they'll have a bigger crew, no doubt

as many as we are, perhaps more. They might well decide to fight when they see they can't outrun us."

"Oh . . ."

"Are you afeared, my Annie? I don't think the men will hold you to fighting, like they do with one another."

"Afeared? No. No, not at all." Her thoughts had been moving on quite another tack. She was thinking about the fight, the madness of plunging in with pistol and cutlass. Not just an opportunity for wild abandon, but an absolute need for it, a moment when hesitation and reticence could mean her death.

Killing a man who was trying to kill her. A basic, savage reflex. Life distilled to its purest essence.

When she thought about it, she felt the little bolts of lightning shooting down her arms and out her fingertips. Her limbs felt as if they wanted to jerk and spasm with all the energy she was holding in check.

No, she was not afraid.

Chapter 16

CALICO JACK COULD STAND IT NO MORE. HE WRAPPED his hand around the hilt of his big straight sword and pulled it from the scabbard, slashed at the air with it as he paced and waited for the next gun.

Damn them, damn them, sons of bitches . . . he thought.

The merchantman—Dutch, by the flag—was fighting back. The *Pretty Anne* had chased them for four hours, overhauling them cable length by cable length. They had approached to within half a mile and they had broken out Anne's flag, a magnificent piece of needlework, terrifying in its stark bold pattern, unequivocal in its meaning. They had fired bow chasers.

But the merchantman continued to run, and when the

Pretty Anne came within the arc of her small cannon she began to fire back. Jack could not shake the images of all the men he had seen who had been horribly disfigured in fights of one kind or another. Visions of their wounds swam in front of him. Noses, ears, limbs gone, whole sections of face slashed away, he could not get them from his mind, could not decide if he would rather be dead than thus maimed.

A jet of gray smoke from the Dutchman's side and a quarter second later the bang of the gun. The round shot skipped by and dashed water up into Jack's face and made him start and wince in surprise.

"We'll make them pay for that, Jack, dear, eh?" cried Anne.

You don't need to yell, you stupid bunter, I'm ten feet away, he thought.

"Yes, damn them, that we will, Annie."

She seems to be enjoying this, the little tart, doesn't know enough about a sea fight even to be scared.

Jack growled, paced, flailed around with his sword. It seemed that his fear must be obvious, the fox tearing at his innards, but no one had ever noticed before and they did not seem to notice now and so he guessed he was safe from detection.

How many of you have foxes hidden away? he wondered. *How many of you are really afraid right now?*

From what they could see of the Dutch merchant ship, she had a full crew, as many men as there were aboard the *Pretty Anne.* They were just merchant sailors, of course, but hell, every man aboard the pirate sloop had once been just a merchant sailor, and now they were a bloody pack of cutthroats indeed. Could be they were just as fierce a crew aboard the Dutchman.

He turned, paced the other way, and Anne caught his eye and smiled and he made himself smile back.

She must be afraid as well, he concluded. It was not possible that a woman could face this circumstance—going into a fight against an armed and equal opponent—and not be at least as frightened as he was.

And if she was not, it had to be ignorance. Calico Jack did not like to think on the alternative, that she was in fact bolder than he.

"You look as fierce a buccaneer as ever strode a deck, Annie!" he called.

Anne had donned her long-tailed blue coat, which better disguised her sex. Over that was a shoulder belt from which was slung her cutlass and a boarding ax. Two pistols were draped over her shoulders by a length of ribbon tied to their butts and a third was shoved in the wide belt around her waist. Her head was bound in a red cloth and her cocked hat was pushed down over that. Jack did not think that anyone would guess her a woman.

Another shot from the Dutchman, and that one slammed into the *Pretty Anne,* up near the bow, and set the men howling and jeering, like a flock of birds startled by the blast. Jack leaned over the rail, looked forward, but he could not see any damage done.

They were no more than a cable length away, perhaps less, perhaps closer to 150 yards. They would be up with them soon. *Waiting, always so much damned waiting . . .*

Jack lifted his glass, scanned the deck of their victim. He could see cutlasses and pikes and pistols too. *Oh, Lord, oh, Lord, this will not be an easy thing,* he thought.

He felt his fingers slick on the leather wrapping around the telescope. "Quartermaster, see them grapples ready, and hand grenadoes as well!" he cried, glad to have thought of an order to give. Made him look in control of the situation.

"They're laid along now, Captain!" Corner called.

Jack looked forward. Dick Corner had already prepared the things they would need to grapple and board.

Two of the *Pretty Anne*'s four-pounder guns went off, one after the other, slamming inboard to renewed shouts from the men.

Oh, we are having a merry time . . .

But Corner had called him "captain," and such he was. Here they were, going into battle, and that gave him unquestionable authority. He was Captain John Rackam. After all those years, here he was. Captain Rackam.

He felt his faltering courage get a little boost from that. He turned and began to bang his sword against the side of the ship, began to chant, "Death, death, death . . ."

Anne watched Jack surreptitiously as he paced, slashing at the air, and she was worried about him. It was clear to her that he was afraid, and she was certain she knew the reason.

It was the Dutchman.

A rich prize if they could get up with her, but she was not as slow a sailor as Jack had thought she would be. Jack was afraid the prize would get away, that the big ship would sail from their grasp and he would not be able to lead his men into a fight on her decks or to secure for them the riches she held in her hold.

She wanted to put her arms around him, to tell him that it would be all right, that there would be other fights if they missed out on that one. That his men loved him and she loved him and they would follow him anywhere, even if they did lose the Dutchman.

But she did not. It did not seem right that she should do that. Stoicism was the sailors' way and so she made it her way. And in truth, she had never been very good at that sort of thing. She was not the comforting type.

Rather, she tried to show Jack through her actions that she supported him, and that she was not afraid.

She knew he would worry, would be concerned that she was terrified by the impending fight, and she wanted to ease his mind, show him she was not afraid, which indeed she was not. In truth she was wild to get into it, thought she might explode if they did not board the Dutchman that instant.

Ten feet to her left the Pretty Annes touched off two of their four-pounder guns in rapid succession.

The concussion of the gunfire hit her like a solid thing, made her stagger, knocked the voice from her throat. She put her hand down on the cap rail to steady herself. Then, like a second concussion, the thrill of the cannons' power overwhelmed her and she screamed, the high, keening shout of her Celtic ancestors plunging into battle.

A bit aft of her Jack started in on the vaporing, banging his sword against the side of the sloop and shouting, "Death, death, death . . ." and around her more and more of the Pretty Annes took up the chant.

The Dutchman was less than one hundred yard away and the *Pretty Anne* was flying down on her. Anne could see the activity in her waist as they loaded and fired their pathetic guns as fast as they could, trying to knock something away before the pirates overwhelmed them.

Too late, too late, too late for you . . . The thought ran through Anne's mind, over and over. She glanced up at the big black flag snapping at the masthead, took joy in her handiwork. *Too late for you, it says.*

She reached across her taut belly, grabbed the hilt of her cutlass and pulled it out, held it over her head and waved it, shouting her Irish war cry in time with the chanting of the others. The noise circled her, embraced her, carried her up and up as she yelled and chanted and banged her sword.

The vaporing terrified their victim and whipped the pirates up into a frenzy. It was unrestrained madness, like the Norse berserkers. She jerked the pistol from her belt, fired it at the Dutchman, realized that it was a waste of a loaded weapon.

Forty yards and the Dutchman's guns went off again and iron shrieked overhead, a banshee cry, and ten feet to her left David Wolcot was torn near in two by the gunfire.

Anne watched his body as it hurled across the deck, the viscera spilling out on the planking, the eyes wide, dead before he came to rest. She watched with a detached fascination—not frightened, not sorry, not revolted—just interested. Here was a part of the whole thing. Train the cannon an inch to the left and that would be her, but that thought did not bother her either.

She pulled her eyes from the horror on the deck. The vaporing had broken down to random screaming and clashing weapons. The pirates were firing off their pistols at that impossible range.

Twenty yards away and now she was looking up at the high-sided merchantman and she realized that they would be attacking up, climbing up and over the bulwark rather than leaping down onto the deck. She felt a touch of fear, a taste of apprehension. But all around her her fellow pirates were screaming and clambering up on the sloop's rail, wild to be at them, and Anne took comfort from that and forced the fear down.

"Let 'em go! Grapples away!" Jack shouted, and a bold sight he made, standing on the quarterdeck rail, one hand on the main shrouds, waving his long straight sword at the Dutch merchantman, his long hair flowing and his bright calico jacket swirling around as he moved.

Those men who had grappling hooks stood at the rail and on the channel, swinging the hooks in small arcs. At Jack's command they drew their arms back and let them fly. The hooks soared through the air in great elegant arcs and fell from sight on the Dutchman's deck. The Pretty Annes grabbed on to the lines and heaved and heaved, drawing the two ships together.

To Anne's right, four men leaned into the line, heaving away, then collapsed to the deck in a heap as someone aboard the Dutchman thought to sever the rope tied to the hook. But there were other grapples and the gap between the vessels fell off to ten yards, then five yards.

Dicky Corner elbowed her aside, pushed a glowing match into the short fuse of a hand grenado, and flung it over the side, and with it went half a dozen more from the *Pretty Anne*'s deck. A few seconds pause, and then a series of deafening explosions and the high-pitched scream of a dying man.

Something flew back toward the sloop, landed on the deck, bounced, and Anne saw it was one of their grenadoes. Someone aboard the Dutchman had thrown it back. The fuse sputtered, threw off sparks, was too short even to see.

Anne whirled around, collided with Corner standing beside her. She grabbed him around the waist, pushed him over one of the four-pounder cannon and down to the deck, heard him yell, "Goddamn it!" loud in her ear, and then the grenado exploded.

She pressed herself down, could smell the sweat and grime and tar and spilled rum on Corner's clothing while around her the air was filled with the scream of the iron bits, the clang of metal hitting the gun barrel, punctuating the bass tone of the explosive.

The deck jarred beneath them, the screaming iron replaced by the sound of smashing wood and the screech of wrenched iron, and Anne thought, *Have I been hit? Has this grenado sunk us?*

She looked up and the Dutchman loomed over them and she realized that the two ships had struck, that the shudder was not the grenado, it was the collision, and with never a thought she was on her feet, cutlass in hand.

One foot on the cannon barrel, a step up, the next foot on the *Pretty Anne*'s rail and then she was on the Dutchman's main channel which thrust like a staging from her side, where the main shrouds terminated. Hand up on the shrouds, foot on a deadeye and she was up, up, her face level with the deck.

A pistol banged out, ten feet away. She felt the ball pass close and she kept climbing. She was screaming, cursing, a constant noise pouring from her mouth, had no idea of what she was saying, just let it come.

Up the main shrouds and then she stepped onto the rail. Fore and aft the rest of the Pretty Annes were pouring over the merchantman's side, heavily armed, bearded, wild pirates, splashes of color from their bright clothing, shouting, cursing, howling like wild animals, firing shot after shot, the air filled with the crack of pistols, the clash of steel as blade met blade.

There was Calico Jack, a little aft of her, engaging someone with sword and dagger. Anne let go of the shroud, dropped to the deck, hit the planks in a crouch, just as she had fantasized about doing so many times: tensed, alert, cutlass at the ready.

And then someone in front of her, screaming, charging, a great bearded seaman wielding a cutlass. He slashed at her, swinging the weapon in a wide arc, and she jumped back and the blade swished past, missing her waist by inches.

He cocked his arm to slash again, a backhand stroke from three feet away. Anne could see the rage in his eyes, the crooked teeth in his snarling mouth.

The cutlass came around and this time Anne reacted the way Jack had instructed, the way her own instinct told her to act. She brought her blade up, met the oncoming cutlass. The two weapons hit with an impact that sent a shudder up her arm, made her hand ache, and wrenched the cutlass from her grip.

It dropped to the deck and the man lunged. *Shit shit shit shit shit,* Anne thought as she twisted sideways and his cutlass pierced her coat, tangling in the cloth. He cursed, wrestled it free, stepped back to give himself room.

Anne was pressed against the bulwark, her cutlass at her feet as he stepped forward again, bringing his own cutlass back, his eyes locked on Anne's, his wicked blade winding up for a death stroke.

Her mind was in a fury, the edges of her vision dulled, all the noise around her blended into one great swirling sound, and through it all, as she stared at the blade that would kill her, she heard, *The gun, the gun, the gun.*

She did not know if she had said it, if she thought it, or if someone else had told her, but suddenly one of the pistols dangling around her neck was in her right hand and her left palm was pushing back the flintlock.

The man's sword was already coming down in a clumsy stroke when Anne fired the pistol into him. She had meant to put the ball right through his heart, but instead she hit his left shoulder. The impact of the lead sent him reeling back. The cutlass stopped in midswing as he instinctively clapped that hand over the wound.

He stumbled back five feet, six feet, but his wound was not mortal and the fight was not out of him. She saw him glare at her, heard him howl in pain and outrage as he stumbled forward again, cutlass raised, his right arm and shoulder unscathed.

Anne darted forward, snatching her cutlass off the deck as she moved, closing with him even as he came at her, bellowing like a bull, ready to deliver the coup de grâce blow that would cleave her head in two.

Right foot forward, arm extended, every ounce of power in her arm and shoulder and chest behind the blade and she lunged. She saw the deadly point touch the man's blue jacket, felt the resistance, then the give as it passed cloth and then flesh as she pressed the lunge home and the man's own momentum carried him onto the blade.

She heard the bellow turn to an agonizing cry and she took a step forward and pushed harder and felt the man's body yielding to the blade as she drove it home.

She looked him in the eye and he looked back at her, his eyes wide with disbelief. He made a coughing motion and blood spurted from his mouth. He began to waver and his eyes rolled back.

Around them the fight swirled, surging across the deck, men shouting, guns firing, blades clashing, but on that spot of deck Anne Bonny stood, silent, watching the man die at the end of her sword.

He fell to his knees and Anne pulled her sword free of his body and he fell sideways, dead before he hit the deck, his eyes still open, his arm twitching.

My God, my God, she thought, *so that is what it is to kill a man . . .* She felt the excitement boiling in her guts and she shouted out loud, screamed in triumph, let her elation vent from throat and mouth.

Then she stopped shouting and looked down at the man again, looked into his dead eyes, the pool of blood spreading from his wound. She found herself panting for breath. The elation passed like a warm puff of air and behind it came remorse, revulsion, emotions she would never have guessed she might feel.

Anne whirled around, bent double, vomited into the Dutchman's scuppers.

Mary was standing by the main fife rail when the pirate ship struck them, a solid collision that made the heavy *Hoorn* shudder and knocked her to the deck. Through numb ears she could hear the victory scream of the buccaneers and the wrenching of wood as the two vessel ground against one another.

She leapt to her feet, pulled Hans up by the collar, and shoved him back away from the rail. The pirates swarmed over the side from the fore shrouds all the way aft to the quarterdeck. Great bearded beasts of men, weapons hanging from belts and ribbons and shoulder belts, they screamed as they came over the bulwark and the Hoorns fell back, the merchant sailors, new to combat, overwhelmed by the ferocity of the attack.

Mary cocked the lock of the pistol in her hand, and glanced back to see that Hans had done the same. Her head was filled with the unreal, dreamy quality of the fight. It was such a familiar sensation, the horror and the numbness and need to move swiftly and to be aware of what was around you, all around you.

Some great brute of a man charged at her, cutlass raised, and with never a thought she lifted her gun and shot him and he fell and skidded to a stop at her feet.

Stupid bastard, she thought, tossed the gun away, pulled anther. There was Captain Bes locked into a fight with another of the rogues and she could see Bes was no swordsman.

She raised her gun, firing it at the pirate's head. She missed, and the bullet clipped off a part of his ear, but it took his attention from Bes and turned it toward her and that was good enough. Two more strokes and Bes would have been a dead man.

Hans Franeker was crowding her now and she reached behind, gave him a bit of a shove, wondered if there was time to snatch up her last pistol, all in the two seconds it took the man with the bleeding ear to disengage from Bes and come after her, slashing as he came.

No, no pistol, Mary thought as she caught his blade with hers, turned it aside, stepped forward and brought her heel down hard on his knee. He shouted in pain, stumbled away, and Mary thought she had him as she cut sideways with her cutlass. But the pirate's cutlass was there to meet hers, blade hitting blade in an oscillating clash of steel as the two combatants fell away from one another.

Mary glanced back. Hans was right behind her, safe, and there was no enemy at her back. She held her cutlass low and loose, beckoning to the limping pirate with her left hand. "Come on, come on, have at me, you bastard . . ." she said, "come on, you whore's son, you prancing French dance master . . ."

The pirate roared, and charged in a limping stride, entirely off balance, lunging at her. He had none of Mary's skill or training with a blade, but he nearly compensated for his failings with ferocity and brute strength.

Mary caught his blade with hers, was just able to turn it away, then lunged herself, missing as the big man stepped back.

He lunged again and this time Mary hit his blade hard, knocked it aside, thrust her cutlass at him, felt the tip bite and cut flesh, but again the pirate fell back before she could deliver more than a superficial wound.

Damn me, you'll take some killing . . . she thought, and before he could recover she was on him, cutlass moving fast, overwhelming him with speed of arm and foot. He cursed and worked his blade to keep hers away.

A step backward, and another. The bulwark was right behind him and Mary knew that when he hit it he would stumble and drop his guard and then he was hers.

"Bastard!" she shouted, attacked with a fury that drove him back another step. He hit the bulwark and stopped. He stumbled, dropping his guard, and his eyes went wide with surprise.

Mary knocked his sword aside, brought hers around, and then from aft the cry, in Dutch, "Quarter! Quarter!"—it was Waalwijk's voice—and the clash of weapons being thrown to the deck.

"No!" she shouted, turned toward her shipmates, and as

she did she felt the burn of a cutlass blade as it sliced through the flesh of her upper arm.

The pirate she was facing had lunged at her just as she had turned, and would have put his cutlass right through her heart if she had not wheeled around in surprise as her shipmates called for quarter.

She leapt back, *en garde,* ready for the attack, but suddenly the noise on the deck dropped off until it seemed silent in contrast to the raging fight of a second before.

Mary glanced side to side, fast, never taking her eyes from her adversary for more than a fraction of a second. She could feel the blood running down her arm, under the sleeve of her shirt.

No one else was fighting. Waalwijk was on his knees before two of the pirates, hands clasped in supplication, tears streaming down his face as he pleaded in Dutch. The rest of the Hoorns had dropped their weapons and had their hands in the air or were on the deck, bleeding.

Mary straightened. The man she was facing grinned at her, shrugged his shoulders. Pointed with his cutlass to the weapon in her hand.

In all of her years of combat, Mary had never surrendered to an enemy, and every part of her resisted doing so now. She looked around again. She was the only one of the merchantman's crew still bearing arms.

In disgust she threw her cutlass to the deck.

For all the Hoorns' high talk about beating the villains or dying in the attempt, they had called for quarter after all. They had surrendered themselves to the pirates.

And now it was up to the pirates to decide if they would live or if they would die, if they would scream out their lives in agony, paying the price for their resistance.

Chapter 17

IT WAS A LOW POINT IN MARY'S LIFE, SECOND ONLY, perhaps, to the evening when she held Frederick's hand and watched him slip away.

They had been overrun by the pirates. They had called for quarter. They had been herded like cattle up into the bows. They stood there in a cluster, those of the *Hoorn*'s company who could still walk, and waited for what horror the pirates would now visit on them.

But still the Caribbean seduced her. The sun shone down warm on her head and face, the trade winds blew steady over her. The gentle swells of the sea rocked the two ships, still bound together, in their hypnotic rhythm. Mary could not seem to conjure up the dread that she knew she should be experiencing.

Hans had come through the fight with a deep gash in his shoulder where a pistol ball had grazed him, but nothing worse than that. She hoped that he would not be harmed further. But other than that she could not seem to make herself care what happened next.

Am I so done in? she wondered. *Can I muster no interest in my fate?*

The pirates were tearing into the main hatch and carrying up from Captain Bes's cabin all of the alcohol and tobacco they could find, handing it around, swilling with abandon. For the moment they had no time for their captives.

The tarpaulins on the hatch were rolled back, the gratings removed, and the buccaneers leaped down into the dark 'tween decks to see what they had acquired. Then, from below, muffled shouts of enthusiasm, whoops of triumphant joy, as they surveyed the *Hoorn*'s valuable mixed cargo.

And all the while the Hoorns stood by and watched the

mounting bacchanal. The tension they had felt before, with the pirate sloop closing them, was nothing at all compared with waiting for the torture to begin.

They had all heard the stories—mouths stuffed with burning oakum, thin cords twisted around heads until the victim's eyeballs popped out, and sundry other horrors. Mary wondered when one of them would break under it and begin to sob or fling himself at the pirates or into the sea.

She did not love to think on it. So instead she studied the pirates as they went about their business.

Pirates. The stories of their doings were everywhere, and they ranged from romantic notions to terrified loathing. And here they were, in the flesh. Pirates tearing the *Hoorn* apart, in just the fashion that she had heard they did.

They were a frightening bunch. Big men, for the most part, but some of the small, wiry type—the most dangerous in a fight, in Mary's experience. They were dressed like common sailors, though their clothes were more filthy and tattered than most, and adorned with flashy embellishments such as bright cloth bound around their heads, or red silk sashes around their waists, or wild feathers in their hats, audacious points of color that proclaimed for the world what they were.

Except for the captain. He was dressed in breeches of striped calico, a waistcoat and coat of the same material, but white with little flower prints on it, a look that was almost foppish. His long curling hair tumbled down his shoulders, unbound, and under his proud nose a big, well-groomed mustache. He strutted around like a peacock, using his sword as a walking stick.

You're a dandy one, ain't you, Mary thought, and then her eyes moved to the brigand standing beside him, close, in a companionable way, but something more than that.

Her mouth fell open.

Dear God, that is a woman! Damn me if that ain't a woman!

She glanced around at her fellow sailors, wondering if any of them had made that startling discovery as well, but they all looked too stunned or frightened or despondent to notice anything.

Mary looked back at the captain and the pirate next to him. She was dressed as a man entirely, and her long blue coat did much to disguise her sex. Her hair was reddish blond and bound back in a queue, sailor fashion. But still there was no doubt in Mary's mind. The way she moved her body, her stance as she stood with arms folded across her chest, the way she smiled, her delicate hands. It was a woman.

What manner of pirate is this, where a woman ships aboard and fights with the men?

None of the other pirates paid her any more attention than they did anyone else. *Do they know their shipmate's sex?* Mary wondered. *Or are they ignorant, like the men of this ship are of me?* It did not seem possible to Mary that they could not know, when it was so obvious to her.

And then the pirates' initial exploration of the *Hoorn* was done and it was time to turn their attention to the crew. The pirate captain in his bright calico strode forward, still using his sword like a walking stick. Mary could feel the tension among the Hoorns rise as he approached in his insouciant manner, as if brutal murder were no more than an afternoon stroll to him.

"Good day," the captain said, bowing low. "I am Captain John Rackam, of the sloop *Pretty Anne*. They call me Calico Jack."

They call me Calico Jack . . . Mary had to force herself not to smile, despite the uncertainty, despite the terror that this Calico Jack's performance was striking in the others.

Lord, but we are carrying it high, aren't we . . .

"You people failed to strike, when we did run up our black flag, and that don't answer among the Brethren of the Coast. You're all dead men, by our practice, but—"

Mary took a step forward. "They don't speak English, Captain." In his eagerness to strut, "Calico Jack" seemed to have overlooked that possibility.

He stopped, whirling around in an impressive flurry of coat and hair. "Who speaks!? You? What say you?" He crossed the deck fast, stood three feet from Mary. "What say you?"

"I said they don't speak English, Captain. They're Dutch, the lot of them."

She could see the anger flash in his face. His cheeks turned a darker hue and then his sword was up under her chin, pushing her head up and back an inch, and she wondered if she had miscalculated, if he would slit her throat then and there. The needle point dug into her skin and she could smell the warm steel. She heard Hans gasp behind her.

"Does that amuse you?" Jack asked, his voice a snake's hiss.

Years of military service had taught Mary the art of deference, and when she said, "No, Captain," there was not the least hint of irony or amusement.

Jack eased, like the tension coming off a line, and lowered his sword. "You are not Dutch?"

"No, Captain. I'm English."

"But you speak this Dutch lingo?"

"Yes, sir."

The pirates were crowding around now. Mary guessed they had come to see a throat cutting, and she understood that they might still.

The big man with whom Mary had fought pushed his way through. "This is the one almost done for me, Jack. Mean little bastard, fierce as a snake. Look, he shot the tip of my ear clean away." There was no malice in his voice. He reported the fight matter-of-factly, perhaps even with a bit of admiration.

"You almost done for Corner, eh?" Rackam asked.

Mary shrugged. "It was a nice thing. Might well have gone either way."

And then the woman was there, the woman with bright blue eyes and her thick blond hair spilling out from under the red cloth around her head, and she said, "Oh, this is a pretty one, Jack. He's too handsome a lad for the likes of us."

Mary shifted her gaze to the woman. Their eyes met and

they fixed each other with their stares. Mary waited for some sign of recognition, some indication that this woman had smoked that the "handsome lad" was a woman as well.

But there was nothing. The look that met Mary's was one of interest, curiosity, amusement, but there was no hint that she had guessed at Mary's secret.

How can she not tell? Sure a woman should see through me. Is she but feigning ignorance? The questions raced through Mary's mind, and so absorbed was she that she was surprised when Jack spoke.

"You there." He turned back to Mary. "You tell them others they'll be put to work, swaying out whatever we please from the hold of this ship and stowing it aboard ours, and if they don't work like dogs, it'll go hard on them."

Mary stepped forward, translated Jack's words and then added her own suggestion that they should be very cooperative indeed, and perhaps they would not be tortured to death after all. She could see the relief sweep through the men, the all but unbearable tension easing away as they heard her words.

She turned back to Jack. "I have told them. I have told them to cooperate and they will. I am in no position to ask anything, but I would beg you to spare them."

Jack looked at her for a long moment. "You are right. You are in no position to ask anything. But if they do like I ordered, then we might spare their lives. We might, I say." He continued to stare at her, as if trying to see what was behind the blank "trooper at parade rest" expression on her face.

Mary had heard tales of pirates torturing and killing the officers of captured ships who had brutalized the men under them. It was their way of taking revenge for all the wickedness done to common sailors. She thought of telling Calico Jack about Waalwijk, and the kind of mate he had been, let them tear him apart. But she could not. That was not her way.

She thought of Waalwijk, on his knees weeping, calling for quarter. His authority was gone now, he had shown himself for the coward he was. No one would fear him again. That was punishment enough. It was the worst punishment for his kind.

"These Dutch frogs ain't of use to us," Rackam said at last. "However, seeing as how you are an Englishman, and all but bested my quartermaster, I'll give you leave to join us, if you cooperate too."

At that Mary did smile, taken aback. "Join . . . you? Turn pirate?"

"Yes. If you think yourself man enough."

Mary smiled anew. "No, to be sure, I do not think myself man enough."

"Very well. Get these men down into the hold and see that stay tackle cleared away."

He turned and walked aft and for a moment Mary could only stand there and watch him go. It was not three minutes before that she had been envisioning a horrid death. But instead she had been asked to join them, and her shipmates, it appeared, would suffer no worse torment than an afternoon's work.

She turned to the Hoorns, told them what Jack had said, suggested they get to work quickly and silently. And they did.

First they flung overboard the bodies of those few killed in the fight, pirates and Dutch sailors; together they went over the side with no more ceremony than that.

Then they sweated the afternoon and evening away, breaking out the cargo they had stowed down in Riga, heaving it up from the hold with the heavy stay tackle and then swinging it over to the pirate ship and down through their yawning main hatch. They worked fast and efficiently, as only frightened and motivated Dutchmen can, and an hour before the sun had set, the small pirate sloop was filled to where she could not contain a barrel more.

And all the while the pirates carried on their revelries, guzzling all the drink they could find on board, tearing into whatever food there was—the cabin stores first, the fine food Bes had brought for his own use and to serve to any guests he might entertain, and only when that was gone the salt horse served out to the foremast jacks.

They took little interest in what the Hoorns were doing, save for the odd glance to see things were stowed down right, or nothing of great value was being left behind. They jeered at the Hoorns and mocked them—taunts that had no effect since they were not understood—and on occasion threw beef bones at them, but the torment was no worse than that. The Dutchmen had been treated more inhumanely by their own first mate.

Mary stationed herself on deck, working the stay tackle, where she was able to translate those few orders that Jack or Quartermaster Corner had for the laboring seamen. There she had ample opportunity to observe the brigands, and she was intrigued by what she saw.

There was no hierarchy that she could identify, no deference to anyone, not even Captain Rackam, just a good-natured bonhomie, a mutual celebration of their successful plundering. To one who had spent her life in one military establishment or another, it was unprecedented. There was something even a bit frightening about that degree of freedom, that complete lack of structure or organization.

She had watched the woman particularly, trying to guess what secrets she held, what her status was among the pirates. A whore? A fellow brigand whom they all took for a young man? Mary could see no difference between the woman and the others. She boozed with the rest, ate her share of cabin stores, cursed, spit, laughed—as authentic a buccaneer as any of them. Extraordinary.

When at last the shifting of cargo was done, the Hoorns were rounded up and forced down below into the forecastle. One by one they went down the narrow scuttle and Mary stood near the tail end of the line, waiting her turn. The men's faces were grim once more. They did not relish being trapped below.

"Here, boy."

A voice behind her and she turned to find herself face-to-face with the woman. Her blue eyes were rimmed with red and she had something of a sagging quality, the effects of a day of fighting and drinking and carousing. Still, the setting sun illuminated her from behind, made her hair seem to blaze from within. The abuse she had endured at her own hand, the drinking and the sun and the violence, had not marred the perfection of her skin, the fine lines of her face, her trim physique, obvious to Mary even under the long coat and big shirt she wore.

Mary folded her arms. "Yes?"

The woman grinned, a sloppy grin. She was not sober. "You're a fine lad, ain't ya? And a regular shit-fire, eh?" There was a hint of Ireland in her voice. "Almost bested Corner, and that's no mean feat, great beast that he is."

"He is that."

"You have been watching me, I perceive. Do not think I didn't see you. For what reason have I caught your eye?"

Well, for starters, you're a woman, playing the man, just like me, Mary thought, but if this pretender was not going to admit to her sex, then Mary knew better that to let her know she had smoked the truth. "You are a singular pirate, I think," Mary said.

The woman gave a little laugh, as if to say, *You do not know the half of it.*

But I do, Mary thought.

"How do you happen to be here, then, on a Dutch ship?"

Mary gave a little shrug, her most noncommittal gesture. "I find work, now some and then some. This ship was a-wanting hands."

"You speak this froggy language, like a born Dutchman, but you're an Englishman. How does that happen?"

"I would not bore you with the story of my life. It is too dull a tale by half."

A spark of anger in those blue eyes, and the woman said, "You'll not speak, then? Are you too grand a fellow to talk to the likes of me? And what if I was to beat you insensible, would that loose your tongue? What say you?"

Mary studied her, this woman in pirate's clothes. She was capable of as much, Mary could see that. *There is a fire in this one.*

"It would not be worth the tiring of your arm for, rest assured."

The woman made to give reply, but then Calico Jack

Rackam was there, stepping quickly between them. He turned to the woman and said, "Prisoners down below."

"And what if I would have this one, for my own amusement?" the woman pirate said.

"Prisoners down below. Now."

The woman scowled but said nothing more.

Mary turned, walked toward the forecastle scuttle with never a word. That exchange, between Calico Jack and this woman buccaneer, told her more than she could have learned from an hour of questions.

I have been fighting all my life. For what? For what?

England? Less than half of my life I have spent there. How many men did I kill to stop Philip of France becoming King of Spain? Why should I give a damn who is the King of Spain?

Mary lay in her bunk, her thoughts whirling around Jack's one simple statement—*Seeing as how you are an Englishman, and all but bested my quartermaster, I'll give you leave to join us.* Over and over.

It was dark and quiet. She could hear the sounds of the pirates in their ongoing revelries, loud, but muffled by the deck. Their capacity was astounding, even by seamen's standards.

There was only that, and the sound of the water on the hull, and the occasional soft voice of the frightened men in the forecastle, quiet speculation on their fate—shot, drowned, tortured, the *Hoorn* set on fire.

"Read?" a voice called, soft. It was Captain Dirk Bes, who had been shut down with them. "Read, you speak their language. What say you? Will these villains murder us all?"

Mary was silent for a moment, thinking of her answer. *What manner of villains are these? Always heard that fighting and losing to pirates assured one an ugly death, but they have done none of that.*

This Calico Jack Rackam might think himself a cock of the roost, might strut like some upstart dandy on Pall Mall, but he is not a murderer. He has not killed anyone for vengeance or pleasure, and that is something.

Mary had seen so much killing. As silly as the foppish Calico Jack might appear to her, still she had respect for a man who could kill and chose not to.

"No, I do not think they will harm us. When they have had their fun, they will go."

He has not killed anyone for pleasure.

No, but he bears the blame for deaths enough, attacking us as he did, robbing us.

Robbing us? No. Robbing the fat rich merchant who put this cargo aboard in Riga. Who will collect the insurance money from the underwriter. That is what I nearly died defending.

Hers had been a life of campaigning, structured by the rigid hierarchy of the military, where people like her did not question the reason for which they fought.

And she never had.

But now she did, lying in her dark bunk, while over her head people just like her—foremast sailors, the most ill used of creatures—debauched themselves on the food and drink of the fat Riga merchants.

And they were doing more than debauching themselves. There was a symbolic quality to their madness. They were thumbing their noses at all rules and laws and any measure instituted among men for the purpose of holding such people as them in check.

Mary thought again of that great pyramid, with the nobility on top and herself and all her ilk making up that broad base. All but those pirates. They were not part of the base, they were not even in the pyramid.

The image of that woman haunted her. *What manner of people are these?*

She lay awake all that night, staring into the blackness, listening as the shouts of the pirates faded to loud talk, and then less and less of that and then quiet as they passed out, one after another.

These West Indies are so very beautiful. God, can I go back to the mud and the cold and the shit, after seeing this? The very thought of it made her feel sick. The warmth and the brilliant sun seemed to burn her misery away, and she could not bear the thought of leaving it. She did not think she would ever again have the strength to stand up under the heavy gray skies of Europe.

What allegiance do I owe to anyone? What allegiance have I ever shown for myself?

The *Hoorn* was a nightmare. She had been enduring Waalwijk's savagery for months. *Why must I suffer his punishment and that of the sea as well? By what law am I made to take such treatment?* The pirates did not stand for such. It was just this kind of injustice on which they spit.

But they are murderers, thieves. Wicked rogues.

And so I will meekly submit to more beatings from the Waalwijks of this world? To what end?

She was still awake the next morning when the forecastle hatch was flung open and the brilliant morning sun cut a square hole in the gloom and a hoarse voice called down, "Out of the roost, now, little chickens! Up, up!"

It was with renewed trepidation that the Hoorns once more clambered up on deck, blinking in the sun, tears running down cheeks from the onslaught of light.

They found the deck in shambles. Bottles, broken crates, stove barrels, and bits of food tossed everywhere. Halyards and braces were cut, lines falling limp off the pinrails or hanging down like bellpulls from aloft, swaying with the roll of the ship.

And they found the deck all but deserted. Most of the brigands were aboard the sloop, which was now held alongside by two lines only. The pirates were laying out their halyards, preparing to go.

There were three pirates aboard the *Hoorn* still, and one of them was Calico Jack. He gave an elegant bow, hat in hand, foot extended. "I thank you, people, for you hospitality. You have been the perfect hosts . . ." Mary could see the others grinning at this.

Is it all play with these people?

"But alas, we must be on our way. Good day to you all, and pray, clean up this mess."

That received an outright laugh from the pirates, and Jack with a flourish turned to go.

Mary stepped forward, made to grab his arm, thought better of it.

"Captain?"

Jack turned, still smiling. "Yes?"

"I've been thinking, Captain Rackam . . . about the offer you made . . ."

That one stammered-out phrase, and she was committed. Mary Read, man-of-war's sailor, infantry soldier, horse trooper, innkeeper, merchant seaman, now off on yet another odd byway in the bizarre route of her life.

Now she would be a pirate.

BOOK II

THE SWEET TRADE

Chapter 18

JACK'S SHOULDERS ACHED. HE FELT AS IF HIS ENTIRE body were being pushed down toward the Spanish tiles on the floor of the Court of Admiralty, as if the very hand of God were on his back, crushing him under His palm.

The drone of the secretary's voice as he read the Kings' Commission was intolerable. "It is among these things enacted, that all piracies, felonies, or robberies committed in or upon the sea, or in any haven, river, creek, or place . . ."

He could sense the restlessness of his fellow pirates. There was Big Dick Corner easing from one foot to another. Jack caught a whiff of perfume, and with it the unwashed bodies of his brethren, and from the open window, jasmine and a hint of the ocean.

". . . directed to all or any of the Admirals, Vice Admirals, Rear Admirals . . ."

"Sweet Jesus!" There was George Fetherston, calling out, "Hang us if you will, but don't bloody bore us to death!"

Jack felt his innards go liquid. *Dear God, you'll make it go harder on us, with your fool wit!*

Sir Nicholas's gavel came down, again, demanding order, but the court was silent. No one dared laugh at this effrontery, if, indeed, they found it funny at all.

The pirates thought it funny. A quick glance and Jack could see the grins on their ugly faces. *You lot aren't afraid to die, are you?* he thought. *Why should you bloody be, what do you have to live for?* His fellows would take this all as a great joke, just like they took all of life as a great joke.

A short life and a merry one . . . Those were words to live by, until you came around to the end of that short life, and then it was not so damned funny.

"Silence!" Lawes growled. "One more word from the prisoners and you all shall be gagged!"

The pirates were silent, their expressions just on the safe side of insubordinate. The secretary continued on.

Here I am . . . here I am . . .

Jack Rackam had always wondered how it would end. Had entertained thoughts of spending his latter years in some fine house he had built with the great riches garnered in the sweet trade. Living to a venerable age with Anne by his side. Rogering the house girls when Anne's looks deserted her. Dying peaceful in his bed. Or perhaps in one of their beds.

Who was I bloody trying to fool? Myself?

It didn't end that way for men like him.

Look at the others. Bold Charles Vane whom he had supplanted had now disappeared. Look at Edward Teach, that monster they called Blackbeard. Took five bullets, twenty sword thrusts to bring him down, but now he was dead. Fifteen of his men hanged, that idiot Stede Bonnet hanged, old Ben Hornigold thrown in with the British navy.

Black Sam Bellamy drowned three years back, his bones buried in the shifting sands under the waters off Cape Cod. Woodes Rogers sweeping the pirates from New Providence, using persuasion and the gallows in equal measure.

Men like us do not die of old age.

This was how it ended, in a Court of Admiralty, listening to the dull words that dull men wrote, "made for the more effective suppression of piracy." Listening to descriptions of your own crimes rendered in phrases so boring that it did not seem possible they were describing actions for which you would be hanged, and soon.

Sir Nicholas Lawes turned to the Chief Justice Nedham, said something that Jack did not follow—he was too distracted to understand much of what was happening—and then the women were taken away.

Jack watched them go, wished Anne would turn and meet his eye, give him that little cock of the eyebrow that he loved, the little half smile that told him she was not afraid, that together they could beat back all the civilized world.

But she did not look at him. She moved with a dignified grace, despite her manacled hands. Beside her, Mary did the same.

She blames me for this, but it is not my fault. What did she think, when she went out on the sweet trade?

It was because of them, he knew, that this trial was so well attended. Who would have come to see him and his men tried? Pathetic picaroons who robbed fishing boats, they were nothing, the kind of petty thieves who were hanged by the score all over the Caribbean.

It was the women who were of interest.

The secretary was no longer reading the interminable Act. Now Sir Nicholas was saying something and Jack looked up, sharp, in case it was something that had to do with him, but it was not.

It is my death they are debating here, and I do not even know what is acting.

At last the President turned and looked, not at the prisoners, but near them, and said, "Set the prisoners at the bar."

Rough, unsympathetic hands grabbed Jack's arm, propelled him forward until he was pressed against the low rail that divided the court.

"We shall proceed with the charges against Rackam and the others."

Jack glanced down at himself, at his torn and filthy clothes, now ill fitting as well. He had grown thinner, his appetite quashed by rotten food and gnawing anxiety. The once bright calico was dingy. He could feel the irritation of a week's growth of beard on his cheeks.

It's no wonder Anne won't look at me, he thought. *Come, play the man, don't look so bloody hangdog.* He pulled himself up straight, fighting the forces that seemed to be crushing him. He could not smooth his hair, his hands were constrained by the manacles, but he gave his head a toss to get the hair over his back. He squared his shoulders, faced the judge. *There.*

The crier stood, yet another sheet of paper in his hand, and read, "All manner of persons that can inform this honorable court, now sitting, of any piracies, felonies, or robberies, committed in or upon the high seas . . ."

It was the proclamation that called for witnesses against the pirates on trial. He read it three times, and as he did, several men from the galleries stood and moved toward the bar, and they were not men whom Rackam loved to see.

There was Thomas Spenlow, captain of a schooner they had plundered. Held him two days as their prisoner, he damn well knew their faces. And with him, two Frenchmen they had taken off Hispaniola, made them work the ship for weeks. They would give no help to the defense. And so it went.

The Register turned to the pirates, turned first to Jack Rackam. "What have you to say? Are you guilty of the piracies, robberies, and felonies, or any of them, in the aforesaid articles mentioned, which have been read to you? Or not guilty?"

"Not guilty." It was a reflex action, like shielding your face when a pistol is fired into it, and just as useless. Still, it had to be done. Any other plea and they were done for, then and there.

Down the line the Register went, and each of them, Corner, Fetherston, Davies, Howell, Bourn, Harwood, Dobbin, Carty, Earl, and Fenwick, each in his turn said, "Not guilty." The pleas did not raise one sound from the gallery, did not move the President's face a fraction of an inch. It was just another formality, like the reading of the King's Commission.

"This court calls one Thomas Spenlow, of Port Royal, in the island of Jamaica, mariner, master of the schooner in the third article."

Spenlow stood, stepping up to the witness stand with that same shuffling gait that Jack recalled from the two days he had held the man prisoner.

The court swore him in and he told his tale. He did not lie.

Oh, dear God, dear God . . . we are done for . . . Jack felt the panic welling up, the fox tearing at him with abandon. He thought of how the noose would feel around his neck, thought of his beautiful body coated in tar and hung from a gibbet as an example to all. His eyes pecked at by the birds. He thought he might be sick.

Oh, God, it is so damned unfair . . .

And then his more rational parts had to note that it was not, in fact, unfair. Spenlow was not lying. And when the Frenchmen, Peter Cornelian and John Besneck, stood and through an interpreter gave their testimony, they did not lie either, nor did James Spatchears, who had sailed in company with Barnet, who had tipped Barnet off to their location.

John Rackam, alias Calico Jack Rackam, was guilty of piracy. He knew the punishment for that crime even before he had signed aboard his first ship.

The testimony and deposition of the witnesses went on and on until Jack wanted to scream. It was torture of the most despicable kind. They were making the accused men stand there and endure the agony of waiting to discover what hideous fate would be theirs.

It was just what he had been pleased to do with his own prisoners, back in the day. Jack finally got the grand joke of it, and he did not laugh.

At last the witnesses were done and President Sir Nicholas Lawes swung his heavy face toward the pirates. "You have heard these charges and the witnesses against you. I will ask you each and severally if you have any defense to make or witnesses to swear on your behalf, or if you would have any of the witnesses who have been already sworn cross-examined. And if you do, I will tell you to propose to the court what questions you would have asked."

He stared down from his cliff of a bench, his meaty face framed by the white wig. "John Rackam, have you any defense to make?"

Jack swallowed hard. This was it, this was it, and he had not one damned thing to say. "No, my lord."

"Have you any witnesses?"

"No, my lord." Ah, it was the fight with Barnet all over

again, cowering away, too terrified to move, submitting to inexorable fate.

Sir Nicholas said nothing, turning his attention to Fetherston. "George Fetherston, have you any defense to make?"

"Yes, my lord, to say, we never committed an act of piracy, my lord, and we are not guilty of that what those witnesses said."

This was greeted with a murmur and a nodding of heads from the other pirates, and Jack wondered what bloody good they thought would come of that. This was their defense, to say again that they were not guilty?

Sir Nicholas did not look any more impressed than Jack. "Very well. Have you any witnesses to prove this . . . lamblike innocence?" That received a chuckle from the gallery, a nice touch of levity in an otherwise dreary procedure.

"No my Lord."

"Richard Corner, have you any defense to make?"

"Yes, my Lord." *What will he say now?* Jack wondered. *Why are they bothering?*

Because they are not cowards. They are fighting, not shrinking in a corner and taking it, like you did. Like you did with Barnet and like you did just now.

"My lord," Corner began, his voice earnest, "I wants to say just that our designs was against the Spaniards, sir, and never did we mean to hurt a fellow Englishman, and we didn't neither. It was just the damnable Spaniards we was for."

"Very well. Have you any witnesses, or do you wish to cross-examine those who have been already sworn?"

"No, my lord."

And so it went, with most of the pirates offering some excuse or other which only served to annoy and exasperate the Register, the Commissioners, and Sir Nicholas Lawes.

None had witnesses to their innocence. There could be no witnesses, because they were not innocent.

When it was over the prisoners were taken from the bar, taken through the packed courtroom and out the big door at the far end of the room. Off the waiting room was another door, and this was a holding cell, and into that they were thrust while the President and the Commissioners discussed the evidence and decided on a verdict.

In the cell were Jacob Wells and some of the others whom Jack had forced into their company. They were not being tried with the original Pretty Annes, and Jack did not know why. Perhaps the courts decided beforehand who was definitely guilty and who was possibly not guilty and tried them accordingly.

Whatever it was, he did not have the energy to care, so he ignored them and they ignored him. He sat down heavily on the stone bench there. The others were silent.

Jack thought of those turning points in his life, the decisions that had led him down one path, down another, down another, and ultimately here.

Running away from the blacksmith in Depford to whom he was apprenticed. Shipping out as cabin boy at twelve. Slitting the throat of that old sodomite who was trying to bugger him, then jumping ship in Nassau.

Deciding to throw in with Charles Vane rather than change his name and ship out aboard an honest merchantman. Choosing to manipulate the *Ranger*'s men, play their run-in with the French man-of-war to his advantage.

Falling for Annie, letting her talk him into going on the account one last time.

His life was a barrel rolling down a hill, bounding here and there off each imperfection on the ground.

And now, the bottom of the hill, perhaps. This moment would change everything, no matter what the verdict reached.

As if that verdict were ever in doubt.

Jack Rackam, sitting in his holding cell, waiting to hear from nine hostile strangers whether he would live or die. Sunk lower than he had ever been before.

He was a very different man from the Calico Jack Rackam who had left the *Hoorn* wallowing broken and plundered in his wake. Quite another fellow from the one who in his exuberance was wildly making love to Anne Bonny in the great cabin, a frenzied, victorious coupling, a kind of frantic release of tension and march triumphant, all in one.

He, propped up on his arms so he could see her beneath him, see her lovely thin shoulders, her arms flung back, hands gripping the edge of the table. See her neck, the sharp line made by her jaw when her head was thrown back. Her big, full breasts moving with his thrusts, her narrow waist, the flare of her hips right where they were joined. Her thick hair spread out, fanlike, along the cushion on the locker.

And her, below him, her strong legs wrapped around his waist, her heels dug into the small of his back. He could feel the calluses scratch his skin as she squeezed him into her. They moved together in a steady, building rhythm, back and forth.

Back from the *Hoorn* and by unspoken, mutual consent they had raced to the great cabin, tearing at one another's clothes, the bloodlust of the day before turned now to lust of the flesh. They had handled one another rough, squeezing and biting, pushing each other down, growling like animals, cursing.

And then they came together, wild, driving, moving together in perfect synchronization, him thrusting, her pushing back and forth with her legs, the sloop rolling under them in a quartering sea, it was all a perfect symmetry of motion.

They glistened with sweat. Anne's belly and chest had a sheen of perspiration; drops stood out on her forehead, and the sight of them made Jack hotter still. Jack could feel sweat dripping down his cheeks as he worked, their bodies making sucking sounds as they came together and apart, Annie's whole body jarring with each thrust.

He heard her breathing build until it was a gasping and then stifled moans and then shouts and then her body tensed, her back arched as she reached her climax and Jack exploded as well, teeth clenched, his whole body rigid, pushing, and then relaxed.

He collapsed on top of her, put the weight on his elbows so as not to crush her, felt his skin slick on hers where they pressed together. Her legs were still wrapped around him, he was still inside her. The *Pretty Anne* lifted and fell and rolled on the sea, swooping them along like a magic carpet, keeping them moving still, even as they lay quiet, letting their breathing return to normal.

Jack turned his head, looked out the salt-stained stern window. The dark blue sea reared up, obstructed his view, and then moved on under them, picking the sloop's stern end up. As they crested the wave he could see the Dutch merchantman's masts, just three tiny dark lines against the horizon.

She would be riding higher in the water now. Most of what she carried was stowed down in his own vessel's hold.

This is the pinnacle of life, he thought. This was the moment for which most common people worked and sweated and plodded and dreamed and never achieved, and it was his. He was on top, and under him—literally—a beautiful woman, a ship, his command, stuffed to the gunnels with loot.

Anne stirred, shifted, brought her legs down. Jack felt himself slide out of her and he moved as well. He would have been content to lie there for hours, but Anne always became restless and wanted to move, even after he had given her a good thrumming.

"Mmm, Jack," she said as she came up into a sitting position, her long legs tucked under her. Her breasts looked so fine, Jack though he might just be ready for another go in not so long a time.

He sat up as well, gave her a kiss.

"You should be well pleased with yourself, Calico Jack Rackam. A fine prize taken, and our hold quite full. And then you boarded me with as much vigor as ever you did the Dutchman."

"I might only wish the Dutchman had put up so little resistance as you, my dear."

"Do you think me a tart, sir?" she asked, playful.

"Aye, but my tart, and no other."

Her hair fell half over her face in a manner most alluring. She arched her back, stretched, brushed the hair away. "For those few we lost taking the Dutchman, you have made a fair exchange, I think."

"What do you mean?"

"The young lad who has come with us. Read. He is a good exchange for the others."

"Perhaps. We shall see."

"Well, he nearly bested Dicky Corner, and that is no mean feat."

"I said, we shall see." Why were they talking about this whoreson Read? There was only one pirate he wished to discuss at that moment and that was himself, Calico Jack Rackam.

"Well, you needn't get curt, Captain Jack, I was but saying he is a fair trade."

"And so you said, and it needs no more saying." His desire for another flourish was fading, and he could see from Anne's expression that the chances of his getting one were fading as well.

Anne's brow furrowed and a certain look came over her face—not quite the look she had had when she sentenced her husband to death by blurting out his treason, but approaching that. Under different circumstances, Jack realized, he might be frightened of her.

And then her expression softened as she made herself put the anger aside, and she leaned forward and put her arms around his neck. Her breasts pushed against his arm and he felt a spark of life in his groin. "Forgive me, my dear Jack. Do not think I could ever have eyes for another."

"No . . . I do not . . ." And in truth he didn't. It had never occurred to him that she might find any man more desirable than him. Until that moment.

Mary woke to the sound of the ringing bell.

"Damn it!" She sat up, fast. Eight bells, change of watch, and she was late. It was a great sin on shipboard to be even a moment late for watch. She should have been woken ten minutes before, to be on deck at the exact moment.

But she *was* on deck. She looked around, confused, let the memories settle into place.

She was not in her bunk, she was not aboard the *Hoorn*. She had collapsed on the pirates' deck, exhausted from the previous day's fight, and breaking bulk and stowing it down aboard the pirate sloop, and from lying awake all night in indecision. She had been wrapped in a blanket of sleep so thick that she was having difficulty putting all the events in order.

She had made her farewells to the Hoorns, shaking each man's hand, even those who only grudgingly gave theirs, disgusted at her turning pirate. But they had been family for that short time, in the way that a ship's crew will come together in their special bond for as long as they are at sea, and so they did not let her go with never a word.

She had told Waalwijk, softly, that he was a pathetic little man, but he was already too broken for her words to mean much. She had said farewell to a visibly distressed Hans Franeker. She had wanted to say more, but for all the good-byes in her life, she was still not good at it, so she clapped him on the shoulder, gave him a weak smile, said, "God-speed, Hans," and then collected her dunnage and stepped aboard the pirates' sloop. She had joined the Brethren of the Coast.

There was little ceremony involved. Five minutes after she had come aboard, the men were treating her as if she had been there for five years. She had proved her courage in battle, even if it was against them, and she had proved her spirit in joining with them, and that was enough.

She had jumped into the job of getting the sloop under-way, lent a hand on the sheets and halyards with the confidence of an experienced mariner, knowing where help was needed and what was needed to be done.

A few minutes of concerted effort and they were moving, with the *Hoorn* receding in their wake astern. To the pirates, they were leaving behind another victim in a successful cruise. To Mary, it was her very life she was leaving, and everything she had been up until that moment.

Calico Jack Rackam and the woman had disappeared. Mary could see the lightning crackling between them, recognized the signs of consuming lust, and she had no doubt as to what business they were off to attend to.

None of the others made comment, none of them seemed even to notice, so Mary concerned herself with her work and said nothing.

An hour or so later they were back on deck, Jack and the woman, and Jack had with him a document, a great rolled piece of vellum, which he carried with impressive solemnity.

"Here, Read, a word with you," he called. His tone was not overly friendly, and indeed he seemed the least welcoming of all the pirate band.

Mary put down the line she was long-splicing, stood, ambled aft, as did the others. "Yes, Captain?"

Jack gave a cough. "I have here what we call the ship's articles, and every man what will sail in our company must sign and agree to live by them. They are the rules of the ship. They must be obeyed, and if you think you cannot, then we'll put you ashore. What say you?"

Mary looked from Jack to the woman and back. "I say I'd be honored to read them, first."

That brought a snicker from the men, a flush to Jack's face. "Can you read, then?"

"Aye." Jack handed the articles to Mary and she unrolled the document, holding it out at arm's length.

There were ten articles, each enumerating an inviolable part of the pirates' code. Every man had a vote in affairs of the moment, and equal title to fresh provisions and liquor. Every man was entitled to an equal share of any prize, but if any defrauded the company of the value of a dollar, he was marooned. Lights and candles out by eight o'clock; after that, drinking and smoking on the open deck only. No striking another on board, every man's quarrels to be settled onshore with sword and pistol.

Incredible.

Populacy, democracy, here it was. An impossible system

of governance, the road to anarchy and confusion. Any born aristocrat would tell you that the common people could not govern themselves, and yet here were the most debased men on earth doing just that thing, and obeying their own laws like a bishop obeys the word of God.

It was unlike anything that Mary had ever experienced, Mary who was so accustomed to hierarchy, to officers layered upon officers for the better management of the lower sort. She could only shake her head in wonder at it, that such things could exist.

"Will you sign? Or no?" Jack asked.

"Yes. Yes, I will sign your fine articles, to be sure."

She took the quill he offered and set it on the deck. Two of her fellow pirates took the vellum and rolled it out flat for her and she knelt before it, felt like a religious taking her vows. At the bottom of the document, a few scrawled names along with a series of X's, and beside the X's, "John Davies, his mark" and "Noah Harwood, his mark" and such, written out in a distinctly feminine hand.

Mary took up the quill, tapped out the excess ink, and then with a flourish wrote "Michael Read" at the bottom of the page.

She looked up. The others were grinning at her. "Welcome aboard the *Pretty Anne*." Dicky Corner grinned and Mary grinned back at him. She felt like she was home.

It all came back now, as Mary sat up on deck, wrapped in the night, looking around. The bells had stopped tolling and dark shapes were rising around her, men who, like her, had been woken by the sound and were ready to go on watch.

"Here, Read, that you?" Noah Harwood's voice came out of the dark.

"Aye."

"Your watch."

That was it. Aboard every vessel she had ever sailed the change of watch was a formal affair, with the oncoming watch expected to be on deck and ready before the first bell rang. They would relieve the helm and relieve the lookouts with a proper exchange of information.

But not aboard the pirate, apparently. Here men staggered aft when it suited them, five, ten minutes after the bells, relieving a watch that was in any event none too watchful to begin with. The pirates hated formality, shunned structure and hierarchy, save for their precious articles.

She pulled herself to her feet, worked the kinks from her muscles, and stepped aft, winding her way through the sleeping forms of men who did not care to stand watch that night.

George Fetherston was first officer and in charge of Mary's watch. He stood on the quarterdeck, near the helm. He grinned when he saw Mary approach, but then he was grinning most of the time. Fetherston was so jubilant and content that Mary thought he must be mad.

"Ah, Read, you are alive! Wasn't sure, with you sleeping like a dead 'un. Worked you like a son of a whore yesterday, didn't we?"

"Aye, sir, that you did."

Fetherston threw back his head and laughed, a great bear's roar of a laugh. When he was done he wiped the tears from his eye and said, "Belay that 'sir' shit, Read, this ain't the fucking navy! We don't stand on that kind of thing, none of your 'hop to, yes sir, no sir, beat yer arse with a rope end if you ain't aloft fast enough' nonsense here."

"Aye . . ." It threw her off, to not say 'sir,' so she cleared her throat and said, "Aye," again.

"How was you rated, Read, aboard the froggy?"

"Able-bodied."

"You can hand, reef, and steer?"

"Aye, that I can."

"Good. Then what say you take the helm, and we'll have one trick at least with a sober hand at the tiller, eh?" He laughed again.

"Relieve the helm, aye," Mary said, struggling to be informal. It did not come easy, and she was surprised to find how very ingrained was her respect for authority and the chain of command.

She stepped back to the tiller, the five-foot tapered wooden bar that attached to the head of the rudder, a few feet behind them. Took the tiller from the tired-looking James Dobbin who held it. Dobbin, thus relieved, gave Mary a pleasant nod and headed forward.

"Ah . . ." Mary said, and Dobbin stopped, turned back.

"Yeah?"

"What course?"

"Oh . . ." Dobbin walked back, peered at the compass in the binnacle box, lit by a small candle. "Looks to be around south-southwest. I'd make it around there, then."

That was it. He nodded again, headed off forward.

Mary held the tiller with one hand and let it press against her thigh, felt the weight of the bar as the rudder held the sloop on course. A bit of pressure, but not too much.

"You got the feel of her, Read?" Fetherston sidled up, still grinning.

"Aye. A touch of weather helm . . . feels about right."

"Good, good. Here." He held out a bottle of rum, and with a second's hesitation, Mary took it from him. "Ain't ever had a sober helmsman, to tell the truth, and I reckon we don't want to start nothing new this night."

Mary grinned, nodded, put the bottle to her lips and tipped it back. Rum . . . She felt the liquor warm her mouth and throat and belly as it went down, let the pungent odor fill her nostrils.

Rum. The taste and smell were so integrally tied to so much of her life—her tot in the navy when she was just a girl, rations while campaigning. It was often their only warmth and pleasure during brutal winter encampments. Rum poured with abandon in taverns all over England and France and the Low Countries or wherever her peripatetic life had taken her.

Hot spiced rum in front of a big fire at the Three Trade Horses, resting in Frederick's arms, silent, watching the flames, drinking in the happiness.

The smell and taste of rum sent her reeling back through

the years. It seemed to be a part of so many moments in her life. But never, never, had she actually quaffed it while standing a trick at the helm. Just the day before she would have considered such liberties inconceivable.

She took another swallow, handed the bottle back to Fetherston, who took a swallow himself. "You're second-in-command then," she said, "so I reckon if you say it's all right, the helmsman having a nip, then it must be all right."

"Oh, to be sure. You've a power to learn about our ways, I reckon. Ain't never been on the account?"

"No. Merchant seaman. And a soldier before that."

"Ah, so that's where you've learned your skill with a blade. And that 'yes, sir' horseshit, too, I'll warrant. No, we don't do things the same here. Men on the account have had a bellyful of that nonsense. Fellow here obeys the articles, don't shirk in a fight, don't steal from his shipmates, well, he can do pretty near as he pleases.

"And as to me being second, that don't answer here. With the pirates it's the quartermaster is second. He talks for the men, like. Me, I just stand me watch, on account of I was rated master's mate once, in the navy. Dicky Corner's quartermaster. He's a good man, don't you worry, and he won't hold no grudge, and you nearly besting him. Fact, he thinks more of you for it. That Billy Bartlett's a mean bastard, and Dobbin is something of a chucklehead, but the rest is good men, too."

Mary nodded. Good men. They were pirates, sea robbers, men burnt in the hand, the scorned and despised of the civilized world. Their lives were debased, squalid, and short. And yet they, of all men, accepted each other on their merits, and gave not a damn what their parentage was, or how much they had per year.

It would take some thinking on, to get it all straightened out.

"I'll keep a clear hawse around Bartlett then. There was another, didn't get the name . . ."

She saw Fetherston glance over, then take a drink. He handed her the bottle. She held it as she gave the tiller a bump to put the sloop back on course, then drank as well and handed the bottle back. She could feel the rum now, working at her. Sober, she might not have pursued this line, but she was not sober now, not quite.

"The young fellow," Mary said, "the one keeps near by the captain? With the yellow hair?"

Fetherston was starting to grin, was fighting it back. "Yeah? What of him?"

"Well, for starters, he's a woman."

At that Fetherston threw back his head, gave his great bear laugh. When he was done he wiped his mouth with his frayed sleeve. "You smoked that, eh?"

"Yeah, I did." *Pretty bloody obvious.*

"Well, you're right, young Read, and a sharp eye you have. Didn't reckon anyone would see through that. Aye, she's a woman. Captain's woman, name of Anne Bonny. Met her in Nassau and she shipped aboard with us. A right hellcat, that one, fights like a man, like you seen. We don't treat her no different than any other man aboard. She's the prettiest thing you'll ever see, but don't you be getting no ideas. She's Calico Jack's, she dotes on him, and he's damned jealous of her."

"I know better than to get my nose into that, you can be certain."

"Don't care to mix it up with Calico Jack, eh?"

"No." She let that ambiguous answer hang in the air. In fact, the thought of fighting that strutting, dandy pirate captain would not have given her a second's pause.

"But see here," Fetherston added, his tone more serious than was his wont, "don't you let on I told you. If she wants you to know the truth of her, she'll tell you herself. Until then, she's just another one of us. Don't you give her no special attention."

"You have my word on it." *And wouldn't you be surprised, was you to know the real reason I've no interest in bedding this Anne Bonny,* she thought.

It was an odd situation, odd indeed. How many women could there be, dressed as men and sailing as foremast jacks, let alone pirates? And for two of them to come together on that spot on the great ocean? It would take some thinking, some real philosophizing to figure it all out.

But not now.

It was not time for deep thought. The night was warm and overhead the stars spread in a great dome down to every point on the horizon, the constellations like old friends, the cloudy band of the Milky Way marking its path in the sky. The *Pretty Anne* was well balanced and tracking straight on course with just the smallest adjustments of the helm. The rum was warming her, dulling her senses, slowing her racing mind, and it felt good. Fetherston was a great jolly bear and Mary found his company agreeable.

This was not so far from what she had imagined, back in the icy hell of the North Sea. She had been a pirate now for less than a day. There was still plenty of time to regret her decision, she knew, but right then she could not. And she did not think she would soon.

Chapter 19

THE *PRETTY ANNE* PLOWED HER LONG, STRAIGHT WAKE through the Caribbean, cleaving the rich blue water into two even lines of white during the daylight hours, and at night leaving behind a wide glowing swath as she agitated the phosphorescence in the sea. She was a restless hunter, prowling the sea lanes, never stopping, never pausing, even as her people slept, woke, ate, stood their watches, drank to insensibility, passed out, and then started the cycle again.

Anne sat on the rail just forward of the quarterdeck, leaning with her back against the shrouds. It was four days since they had taken the Dutchman. In that time they had run south by west under easy sail, enjoying steady winds and the flawless weather of the West Indies. They had seen no hint of another vessel, but the weather was so fine and their hold so full that no one aboard seemed to mind.

Indeed, Anne thought that another prize might be viewed as a distraction in that idyllic setting. And she, for one, had distractions enough.

Black smoke belched out of the galley stovepipe and rolled away from her, over the lee rail, but still she could catch a whiff of it; burning wood and boiling salted meat and dried peas. Their fresh food was gone and there had been none aboard the Dutchman for the taking.

She felt her stomach give a little growl. She was hungry.

But her thoughts were not on food. Her attention was directed forward and halfway out along the bowsprit. Where Michael Read was lashing new footropes in place.

They had to be near the same age, she and Michael. He had not a hint of a beard, and yet there was something about him that was not youthful either. He had none of the silly naïveté or the boasting, swaggering, childish self-confidence of most young men.

He was quiet, which was an anomaly among the pirates, and he seemed to enjoy working, which was utterly unique. But, of course, any man aboard the *Pretty Anne* was free to do as he wished, and if it was work he wanted to do, then no one would say anything about it. Certainly no one would object.

Anne reclined against the shrouds, her lean body relaxed, her eyes taking in Read's every action. There was a grace with which he moved that Anne found intriguing, a fluidity of motion, like a dancer.

Most of the men aboard the *Pretty Anne* were great brutes, blundering through whatever task they were about with tremendous strength and little subtlety, like bears at needlework. Jack was the most refined of the lot, by far, but even he could not match Read's finesse and easy carriage.

He wore his dark hair clubbed, like most of the seamen. He was dressed in worn slop trousers and a loose shirt, much like the one Anne wore, and over that a faded red waistcoat. It was an odd sort of a garment, but he was never without it. In the small of his back, a big rigging knife, and

his hand extracted it and sheathed it again with a thought-
less familiarity as he went about his work.

He had small hands. They looked almost childlike holding the big knife. But they were not child's hands. They
bore the scars and calluses of a lifetime's hard work.

Anne had spoken with Michael Read a few times. He
was always friendly, always reserved. She had not revealed
her own sex to him. She had not been able to pry from him
one real detail of his former life.

She found him at once frustrating and intriguing.

This is not good, she thought. She could see the path
down which she was heading. *Jack Rackam is my man, he
is unlike any other and I love him, truly. There will never
be another for me.* But assuring herself of that fact and
actually believing it were two different things.

"Annie, whatever has caught your eye?" She jumped at
the sound of Jack's voice, turned with a guilty flush.

"Ah, Jack, I thought I saw a sail, fine on the starboard
bow, and Carty aloft quite blind to it, but I was wrong."

Jack, of course, had to look in that direction, fine on the
starboard bow. It was an irresistible reflex. But when he
did, he saw that she might also have been looking at Michael Read, out on the bowsprit. Anne could see the cloud
pass over his face.

This is not good.

In Jack's hand were two plates piled with food. "Jack,
my beloved, have you brought me my dinner?"

"Huh? Oh, yes . . ."

She looked at him, innocence and seduction, playing the
coy mistress, an act that she knew Jack found quite alluring.
"Jack, you villain. Do you think for such a little kindness
I will yield to you the final favor?" She could all but see
the thought of Michael Read fly from his head.

"Will you be coy with me?" Jack teased. "Perhaps I must
ply you with drink as well."

Anne took the plate from him. "You *are* a villain, to rob
an innocent wench like me of my delight."

"Ah, but it is my delight to do so," said Jack, sitting
beside her on the rail.

Anne picked up her lukewarm salt pork, tore a piece off with her teeth, chewed it with no little effort.

Men are such dogs, she thought. It still amazed her, after six years of experience with the breed, how easily they could be manipulated. Just like a dog. Kick 'em again and again, and then offer them a bone—or the hope of a good thrumming—and they were back with tongues wagging and tails swishing.

She wondered if the same would be true for Michael Read, if he were to discover the truth about her. He seemed an altogether different creature from the men she had known. Would he be able to resist her charms, if she were to taunt him with her sex? How much encouragement would it take to set Read's tail a-wagging?

I cannot be thinking on Michael Read.

She tried to conjure up some topic she and Jack might discuss. She thought to ask him about his intentions for the cruise, or his thoughts on how their luck might run, but he always became defensive when those topics were raised.

Actually, she had nothing to say to him.

They ate in silence, and when Jack was done he dumped his scraps overboard and said, "I have business that calls me below, Annie, dear. Might I have the pleasure of your company? Eh?"

He gave her a cock of the eyebrows, a visual nudge in the ribs. Anne wondered if he had any business at all below, of if it was all about wanting a little after-dinner flourish. She suddenly found the whole thing irritating and distasteful.

"No, Jack, dear. I have promised Corner that I would put a patch in the number two jib, and I can put him off no longer."

Jack hesitated, as if stopped in midstride, thrown off balance by this. Anne could not recall any time she had refused him. His eyebrows came down a hair.

"I am sorry, Jack," she added. "I'll warrant you are not accustomed to pirates who have their time of the month."

"Yes, well . . ." That kind of thing always made him uncomfortable and was sure to cool his ardor, but she could

see he was not convinced of the truth of it. "Very well . . ."
She saw his eyes flicker up and forward, over the starboard
bow, and then he said, "Well, do what you must." He was
being civil, still, but it was with effort. He turned, stamped
aft.

This is not good.

A change of watch at eight bells and Mary Read found
herself sent aloft to perch on the crosstrees seventy feet
above the deck and keep a bright lookout at the horizon. It
was one of the few stations on shipboard on a pirate vessel
that was assiduously manned, and it was taken quite seriously. Spotting hapless victims, running them to ground,
capturing and plundering them, it was their raison d'être.

Mary was not on her high, swaying perch above ten
minutes before she saw the distant vessel. She sat there for
a while, staring at the two grayish patches on the horizon,
the unmistakable profile of a schooner making the best of
the easterly trades. She sat there and stared and pictured
the building terror on the schooner's deck as some poor
bastard aloft reported the presence of the *Pretty Anne,* if
indeed they had yet spotted her.

In her mind she saw the debate ranging across the distant
schooner's deck, to fight or flee or both or neither. She had
heard the same debate aboard the *Hoorn,* imagined it took
place aboard every vessel in those waters confronted with
this situation.

She did not want to put men in that situation. She did
not want to terrorize, did not want to kill. Not anymore.
Not for the sake of plunder.

Some bloody fucking pirate you are.

But she could not have it all ways. It was just hypocrisy,
to join with the pirates and then try to wriggle out of the
moral quandary that her own choice had put her in. Doing
so would be more cowardly than joining the attack on an
innocent merchantman.

Either you are a pirate or you are not a pirate, and I

signed those articles of my free will. Went out of my way to ask Jack if I might join.

"On deck!" she called down, decision made with no further thought. "Sail, ho!"

If they do not fight, she thought, *they will not be harmed. The choice is theirs.*

The odd circumstances of her life had taught Mary Read to see moral issues in stark black and white.

"Are you afraid?"

"Hmm?" Mary said. It was four hours into the chase.

"Are you afraid?" Anne asked again.

Mary looked up at her, held up her hand to shield her eyes. The late afternoon sun was almost directly behind Anne's head. The strands of her reddish blond hair that had worked themselves free from her queue looked like they were on fire.

Jack Rackam had kept Mary to it, ordering her to remain aloft and keep a bright eye on the schooner as the *Pretty Anne* raced after her. He did it, Mary had no doubt, to place her as far from him and Anne as he could get her, but Anne Bonny had joined her aloft.

Indeed, Anne had been going out of her way to keep Mary's company. This, despite Mary's being no more than polite to her, and giving Anne nothing that might be considered encouragement.

Anne's persistent attention had not gone unnoticed. Not by Mary, not by the crew, not by Calico Jack Rackam.

With one hand Anne kept a loose grasp on the topmast shroud. She stood easily on the crosstrees, as if she were still on deck, as if they were not both rolling around seventy feet up.

"Afraid of what?" Mary asked.

"I don't know. You look so very serious."

"Yes, I suppose I am."

"Indeed? And I took you for such a fearsome creature,

the way you near killed old Dicky Corner. Or fearless, I should say."

Mary lowered her gaze, shifted it outboard to the schooner, which was no closer than it had been four hours before. They had some stuns'ls set, and some sort of square sail set below the topsail yard, every inch of canvas they could scrape up and send aloft. It would be a close thing, with the schooner and the *Pretty Anne* nearly matched for speed.

"Fearless? No, not at all. But if you are wondering, am I afraid for my own skin, then no, I am not afraid for that."

"Then what?"

"I am afraid that we will have to kill some poor innocent in the plundering of yon schooner."

"Really? Whyever would you fear that?"

Mary sighed. "I just do not care to kill people. Certainly not poor merchant sailors trying to earn a living."

"I have killed a man. Several." There was a bit of confession in Anne's voice, a bit of the brag.

God, she is young, Mary thought, and wondered if there was ever a time when she herself would have found such a wicked delight in having killed.

"Have you . . . ?" Anne asked. "Have you ever killed a man?"

"Yes. More than several. And I have had a bellyful of killing, I can tell you."

"What an intriguing creature you are!" Anne was swinging side to side, pivoting on the shroud, and it was making the topmast sway. "Tell me all."

"No, forgive me. I think not."

"Why not? Is it something so awful?"

"No, not at all. Very ordinary sorts of things, soldiering, men-of-war's man. Just . . . nothing I care to discuss." Mary had come to the Caribbean to wash that away with clean aquamarine water, and the Caribbean was working its magic on her. She did not wish to go mucking about in all that now.

"You know," Anne said, "a woman would find such mystery intolerably alluring."

Oh, God . . . Mary thought. "Yes, well, alas, there are no women aboard."

"No, but in their absence, I shall be intrigued."

"And intrigued you shall stay."

It was nice up there, aloft, high above the deck. It was nice to talk woman to woman, even if Mary was the only one who knew that that was what they were doing. Despite her discouraging Anne's advances, which Mary feared were predicated on a desire for more than just conversation of the verbal sort, Mary found she liked the young woman's company.

Mary did not often find women with whom she had so much in common.

"Could I tell you something?" Anne asked. "A secret? Would you keep it to yourself?"

"Yes, I reckon," Mary said. She wondered if this was the moment that Anne would reveal herself for what she was. What should she say to her, how should she react?

"When I . . . the first time I killed a man . . . ran my cutlass right through him . . . I was delighted at first. Thrilled, right through. And then I was disgusted and ashamed. I puked. I turned and puked, right in the scuppers."

Mary smiled, amused and relieved. "That is not so uncommon, you know. I have seem plenty of young soldiers do that."

"Really?" There was a look of genuine relief on Anne's face. "Did you? Did you puke, when first you killed a man?"

"I did." Mary remembered the moment, like it had just happened. The chaos of battle rushing like wind around her, and she, bent over next to her first victim, her meager breakfast coming up again. The tears in her eyes, the burn in her throat. The tortured nights in her tent, seeing the young man's dead eyes looking at her. It seemed like yesterday and it seemed like a thousand years ago, all at once.

"You are so eager to pry my past from me. What of your past, then?" Mary said, as much to redirect the conversation as anything.

"My past? Well, I am not so secretive, you know. I was born in Ireland, nineteen years ago. We emigrated to Charles Town, in the colony of Carolina, when I was young. My father was a wicked rogue—"

" 'Was'? Is he dead? Or reformed?"

"I am sure he is not reformed. If he is dead or not, I do not know. He is a wealthy man, but he has disowned me, threw me right out of the house."

"You don't seem so very brokenhearted."

"Oh, my father was a right bully. Back in Cork when his wife took sick and had to move to a place where the air was better, he set right in to rogering the maid, who was my mother. Then his wife had my mother arrested on some charge of robbery, of which she was innocent. She spent near half a year in jail before she was acquitted and then I was born."

"My goodness, such an eventful life you had, and before you were even born!"

"Oh, indeed. And it gets worse. My father, you see, still held my mother in great affection, and me as well, but his wife was making him a yearly allowance and he would not jeopardize that. So for the first five years of my life he kept us a secret. Do you follow?"

"Perfectly."

"And then he bade me come live with him at last, but he passed me off as an apprentice to his law practice. Can you imagine?"

"The dog . . ." Mary said, but all she really heard was the fact of a father who loved his daughter so dearly that he would jeopardize his living to have her near. The thought made Mary ache inside. How she would have loved to have a father! How her life might have been different if her father had been there for her, to love her, protect her.

"So when his business fell to ruin, he packed us all up and took us to America, and there I was raised."

"It seems to me that your father loves you very much. He does not sound so terribly bad. If he could not keep his cock where it should be, well, that is the way we men are, is it not?" Mary looked up at Anne, smiled at her. "At least he is not a pirate."

"No, but he is a lawyer, which is as much as to say he is a pirate without the fear of being hanged."

Mary shifted her position and glanced down at the deck below. Jack was looking up at them from his place on the quarterdeck, and he shifted his gaze when Mary looked down.

"So you came late to the sea, and this pirating," Mary said. "The others do not hold your inexperience against you?"

"The pirates are a singular lot, you will have noticed. It is their custom to accept every man on his merits—black men, too—and they do not give a damn what he is about, as long as he is honest with his shipmates and bold in battle. It is quite unique. If you have any familiarity with finer society, then you will know how absolutely extraordinary such a view is."

Mary nodded. This was more insight then she might have expected from Anne Bonny, a wild nineteen-year-old, a pirate and a killer. She was impressed, pleased to see that Anne gave some thought to such things. "I have no familiarity with fine society, but I do understand how unique this pirating life is."

She looked out at the schooner again. It was no closer, perhaps had even gained a bit of distance. If they did not blow out a sail or carry away a spar, the *Pretty Anne* would not catch her.

Their intended victim, it appeared, was going to escape. Mary felt a great sense of relief, a distinctly unpiratical reaction.

She did not share her feelings with Anne.

Chapter 20

THE SUN SET INTO THE OCEAN WITH A REMARKABLE flash of green, and then the nighttime settled fast over the *Pretty Anne* and the schooner was lost from sight. They continued the chase on through the dark hours, though they had no notion if their intended victim had altered course. They could not even tell if they were still following her.

At first light Richard Corner went aloft, and after fifteen minutes of searching with a glass, announced that they had lost the chase. The men were disappointed, but not overly so, with the rich haul from the *Hoorn* still packed in the hold.

They took in the stuns'ls and the ringtail, and the pirates settled into their daily routine. Mary stood her watch, did some little bit of work, ate, drank, avoided Anne Bonny as best she could.

The sun set during the second dog watch. Another turn of the glass and then eight bells announced the commencement of the night watch, Mary's watch below, as the off-watch was called, but she had no thought of actually going below on so fine a night.

Rather, she lay up in the bows, her head resting on her rolled-up coat. Her belly was full, she could still taste the rum in her throat. She watched the stars overhead. They seemed to whirl about in small circles with the sloop rolling under her, rocking her like a giant crib.

Around her she could hear some of her shipmates talking softly, laughing, but subdued. The smell of tobacco smoke came faint to her nose. It was getting late, probably approaching eleven o'clock. The usual wild bacchanal of the evening was easing into something more mellow.

Lovely. Mary was still enjoying her sense of relief at the

schooner's escape. She hated the thought of disturbing this holiday with violence and crime. *Would we could just sail on like this forever.*

She heard footsteps approaching, soft on the deck planking. She knew who it was. She did not move, just kept her eyes focused up, and Anne Bonny stepped into her arc of vision.

"Evening, Read," she said.

Mary turned her head slightly, as if just seeing her now. "Evening."

"You are always in the bows. Never aft."

Mary cocked her eyebrow, like a shrug of the shoulders. "Some habits are hard to break. In the navy, or the merchant service, the bows are the place for the foremast jacks." And then, toying with her, added, "But you know that."

"Sure, sure . . ." Anne folded her arms, looked up at the headsails like she was scrutinizing their set. The sloop took a slight corkscrew roll and Anne staggered a bit, caught herself on the bulwark and then leaned against it, resting her elbow on the cap rail, deliberately casual.

Been drinking a bit, have we? Mary thought. *What will you do now, with some liquid courage in your belly?*

For a long while she did nothing, just stood there, leaning on the rail, and Mary lay on the deck at her feet and they enjoyed the companionable silence. Finally Anne said, "Read?" It came out soft, a throaty whisper.

"Yes?"

"Would you come with me? I would have a word with you. In private."

Mary was silent for a moment. *Good Lord, whatever does she intend? Is she making love to me?* Aboard the sloop it was not physically possible to get more than one hundred feet from Jack Rackam. This did not seem a healthy thing for her relationship with the captain.

Mary sat up and got wearily to her feet. *We had best get this over with,* she thought. "Very well, I will follow your leader."

Anne smiled, and Mary could see pleasure and victory

and desire in her look. She pushed herself off the bulwark and led Mary down into the hold, and taking a lantern from one of the overhead beams, led her forward to the cable tier, where the great coils of rope like sleeping serpents were stored on gratings to dry.

It was absolutely black beyond the feeble throw of the lantern's light, and the air was dusty with the dried mud from the anchor cables. It smelled more like a farmer's field than a ship at sea.

The two women skirted the great bulk of rope and made their way forward, and Mary saw that they were headed for the forepeak, a small room in the very bow of the ship in which paint and tar and sundry stores were housed. It was the most private place on the small sloop, save for the great cabin, which was the very last place Anne might lead her.

Anne paused just outside the low door to the forepeak, glanced back at Mary, gave her a significant look. Mary imagined that if she really were a man, she would be frothing at the mouth by that point. Instead she just nodded, and Anne opened the door and stepped into the small space.

Buckets and paintbrushes and tools and rags were piled up in a haphazard way, some lashed in place, some lying where they had fallen. It was enough to give a man-of-war's boatswain an apoplexy, but it was just how the pirates liked it. It was certainly preferable to the effort required to clean it up.

Anne hung the lantern on a hook overhead, put her hands on a low bench behind her and leaned on it, her back slightly arched. Her breasts pushed against the fabric of her shirt, and her thin waist and the curve of her hips were obvious in that position. Her full lips were parted, and she looked up at Mary with her head lowered, a wisp of hair hanging over her face, and even Mary could appreciate how enticing she was.

"Read, there is something I needs must tell you."

Mary folded her arms. "Yes?"

"I'm . . . I am, in fact, a woman . . ."

Mary could not help but chuckle and shake her head at this solemn confession. She saw the anger flash in Anne's face. "Do you not believe me, Read? Or do you think this funny?"

"No, I believe you. It's just that . . . I know."

Anne stood straighter and her eyebrows came down. "You know? Who has told you?"

"No one told me. It is perfectly clear to me that you are a woman. I could see it directly."

"You . . . could? No one else has, none that we have captured, no one who did not already know. I don't believe you."

"Don't believe me, if you do not wish to, but it's true. I have known all along. Do you think I could hide my surprise so well, if I did not know?"

Anne took a step forward, a new tack. She put her hands on Mary's shoulders, ran them up to her neck. "If you have known all along of my sex, then you cannot be insensible to my . . . feelings for you. You are not like the other men here."

"That is a true thing, I'll warrant. But what of your Calico Jack?"

"What of him? Are you afraid of him?"

"No. But I had thought you loved him alone."

"I love him. But he can be tiresome. And I have so much love." Anne was close now, almost pressing against her, caressing the back of Mary's neck. Mary could smell her, a womanly smell, not one she was accustomed to. She could hear Anne's breathing, soft and growing quicker.

Mary put her hands on Anne's wrists and gently encircled them with her fingers. Slowly, deliberately, she removed Anne's hands from her shoulders and held them in her own.

For a second they stood there, looking into one another's eyes, Mary holding Anne's hands in hers. They were soft—woman's hands—with just the beginnings of calluses, not hands that had seen two decades hard use, like her own.

Mary took Anne's hands and pressed them against her chest, held them there, pressing down hard. Her eyes did not leave Anne's. She watched the expressions play over the younger woman's face: desire, then uncertainty, confusion. Anne Bonny's eyebrows came together, her mouth turned down in a frown.

And then, realization. She gasped and jerked her hands back, like she was touching hot iron.

Anne half staggered and half leaned back on the low bench, stared at Mary with wide eyes. Her mouth hung open and her lips moved as if she was trying to say something, but no words would come.

Then an involuntary twitch, a smile flickered on her lips, then disappeared, then came again, and then a laugh—more of a grunt—forced its way up from her throat, and then another and another.

A second later and she could not hold it back. Anne Bonny was laughing, roaring with laughter, so hard she was gasping for air, bent nearly double in that small space.

The laughter was infectious, the absurdity of the situation overwhelming, and Mary could not help but laugh as well.

She sat back on the edge of a tar barrel, the laughter spilling out of her, releasing months, years of pent emotions, the all but unbearable anxiety of the past week. The tears streamed down her face as she laughed, and the sound of the two women, in their hilarity, filled the small room.

And then Calico Jack Rackam kicked in the door.

Chapter 21

HE HAD STARTED IN DRINKING IMMEDIATELY, HAD gone directly for the rum bottle that he had jammed between two of the cushions on the locker.

What he wanted was a bit of a flourish, had been thinking on it all morning, and it was not easy for a man like Calico Jack Rackam to change direction so abruptly.

God damn her eyes, he thought as he pulled the cork, felt the first warming draft of rum go down his throat.

She had never refused him before, had never even seemed in the least hesitant. There were even times when he worried about his ability to keep up with her. When he indulged himself in his dreams of a big house ashore, he sometimes wondered if Anne would slow down as she got older, give him enough of a rest that he might have some vigor left for the house girls.

But now she had rejected him.

"Pirates who have their time of the month . . ." She must have her bloody goddamned time of the month every fortnight. He took another drink, stared hard out the window at the blue sea astern, the long white wake. *"Thought I saw a sail . . ."* my fucking arse. Staring at Read, goddamned Read, I'll cut his fucking throat.

He took another drink. Read, Read. She had been staring at him from the moment they had taken the Dutchman. What the hell was it about Read?

Read. It seemed every time someone mentioned Read's name, it was followed with "He almost bested Dicky Corner."

"Yes, well, I could bloody well almost best Dicky Corner. Could bloody well best him, I could, the goddamned ape." Jack said it out loud, because that made it sound more believable to his ear, but he was not so far in his cups yet that he could in fact believe it. He could never beat an animal like Corner with a blade or a pistol. Might outwit him—a monkey might outwit him—but beat him? Never.

He sat down heavy on the locker, stared at the deck, and took another drink. He was sitting on the exact spot that they had last made the beast with two backs. He was aware of that and it made him more depressed still.

Come along, Jack, come along. You might not be the man for all this fighting and mayhem, but none is your equal with the ladies. Is there a man alive can take from you a woman? What woman would choose another man over you? Not Annie, never my Annie.

He took another drink.

No, never Annie. Not for some boy like that whoreson Read, barely off his mother's tit.

He took another drink. *Almost bested Dicky Corner.*

That was what Annie liked. Dangerous men, men who lived life like they had no concern for losing it. Why had she gone off with him? Because he was a dangerous buccaneer, or so she thought. And here was this bugger Read, fought the pirates like a madman and then joined them. Handsome, dangerous Read.

Oh, God, why did I not hang that whore's son when we took the Dutchman? Charles Vane would have, would have made him pay for fighting back, made him scream out his life for the men's amusement.

Jack was no Charles Vane. He knew that. It was a point of pride for him. He had never wanted to be like that madman. But now, oh, what he would do for just a bit of Vane's cruelty! And his courage.

And so it went, for the bulk of the afternoon and into the evening, as Jack watched the level of liquid in the rum bottle drop lower and lower and his thoughts became more and more disorganized, until they were not really thoughts at all, but just wild impressions, trails of logic that seemed so clear at first, but when he tried to follow them, just faded off into nothing.

Annie . . . just got to tell her . . . I love her . . . she'll see. . . .

He stood, with some difficulty, and staggered across the great cabin deck. The roll of the sloop coupled with his own instability made for a wild ride, and the simple act of crossing the eight-foot-wide cabin became a tricky exercise.

But he had a plan now, a good one, as far as his saturated brain could tell. He would find Annie, tell her he loved her, had to have her to himself. No woman could resist him.

He made it at last to the far bulkhead, a flimsy sort of wall that separated the tiny captain's cabin from the rest of the hold. Against the bulkhead, a ladder led straight up to the weather deck above. He paused there, one hand on the ladder to steady himself, and with the other smoothed out his long calico coat, nicely tapered at the waist and flaring slightly in the long tails.

He ran his palm over his waistcoat. He had spilled rum

on it, it felt wet, but there was nothing for that. He tossed his long hair over his shoulders, took a deep breath, then half climbed, half crawled up the ladder, emerging onto the open deck.

The night air was warm and fresh, the breeze steady, and he felt his head clear a bit as he breathed deep. It was quiet on deck. He could hear loud snoring from various quarters. He climbed carefully over the hatch combing and stumbled forward, searching through unfocused eyes for Anne Bonny.

"Here, Captain, steady now . . ."

Jack turned toward the voice, saw the ugly, pinched face of Billy Bartlett behind him, the close-set eyes, the wisps of what he styled his beard.

"Billy, what ho?"

"Ah, Captain, been at the old kill-devil, I see. And a good night for it."

Bartlett looked like a rat. Jack wondered why he had never noticed that before. Small like a rat. Mean.

"Yes, yes . . ." The words were not coming so easy. "Prithee, have you seen Annie at all? Looking for Annie . . ."

"Annie? Oh, Captain, I don't reckon I should tell you . . ."

"What?" Was Bartlett smiling?

"Well, it's just . . . I seen her, not ten minutes before. She was up in the bows, talking with that new fellow, that Read. And then the two of them went below."

Read. That name, and all Jack's thoughts of embracing Annie, professing his love, fled like smoke in a breeze. *Read!*

"Ah, the whoreson! I'll cut his fucking throat, I'll . . ." Jack staggered back toward the scuttle. The air and this shot of anger were clearing his head still more, giving stability to his legs.

"Now, Jack, don't do nothing stupid, eh?" he heard Bartlett say, but his voice was soft and with little conviction and did nothing to sway Jack from his action. He stepped onto the ladder that led back down to the great cabin, took a step down, and heard Bartlett add, "They might have gone to the forepeak, seems to me."

The forepeak . . . Jack staggered across his cabin, his legs gaining strength and momentum. In his mind he pictured Read fucking Annie in the forepeak at that very moment, perhaps on the little bench, the sundry pots and buckets swept aside.

On the cabin bulkhead, hanging from a length of ribbon tied to the butts, his two best pistols. He pulled them down, took up his powder flask, poured gunpowder down the barrels, then a lead ball in each, and then wadding over the balls and tamped it all down, all the while cursing under his breath.

He draped the pistols over his shoulders, and this time stepped through the narrow door in the bulkhead that communicated directly with the hold. "Bloody put a hole right through his fucking head, what I'll do," he said out loud as he stumbled forward, through the cramped berthing area where the men made their home, crammed with sea chests and seabags and ditty bags hanging from hooks, clothing and bottles and rotting food tossed in corners.

He stumbled along, past the stacks of casks piled on casks, containing food, water, rum, powder, all the things necessary to sustain the life on the account, along with the plunder that that life had thus far yielded.

Forward into the dusty cable tier, and as he left the feeble light from the berthing area behind he realized that he should have brought a lantern. He reached out a tentative hand and it came down on the big anchor hawse, ten inches around. With his hand on the rope, half for guidance and half for balance, he made his way forward.

Past the cables he could see the entrance to the forepeak, rimmed in yellow as the light from the lantern that someone had carried in there leaked out around the imperfectly fitting door.

Jack lurched toward it, stumbled, caught himself on an upright post before he fell. Cursed softly. He could hear no noise from the forepeak and he wondered what was going on in there. He steadied himself and stepped forward again.

Just outside the door he paused, because he had not forgotten that Read had almost bested Dicky Corner and such a man had to be killed before he could fight back. *Throw open the door, shoot the bastard, right in the heart. Show Annie who the dangerous man is.*

Then, from inside the forepeak, laughter. Soft at first, and then building, two voices, and one was Annie's, laughing like she was about to burst.

Is he fucking her right now? Are they laughing at how they've put horns on me?

One of those two possibilities had to be right, and both filled him with rage. All thought of impressing Annie was done. They were both dead, Read and Bonny. He would kill them both in midrut.

With a growl of rage building in his throat he snatched up both pistols, pulled back the flintlocks, cocked his leg, and lashed out at the door. It crashed in with the impact of his boot, splintering under his enraged kick, and he burst in.

Two startled faces looked at him, Read and Annie. They were not rutting, not even undressed, not even in one another's arms, but Jack was too drunk and wild with rage to care. He lifted a pistol and pointed it at Read's forehead, three feet away. Read sprung from the barrel on which he sat, went down in a crouch, and his sheath knife appeared in his hand.

Too late for you, bastard! Jack thought, and pulled the trigger and the lock made a loud snap, but no more, because Jack in his drunken rage had failed to prime the pan with powder.

"Son of a bitch!" he roared, and leveled the other gun as Read sprung at him in a great blur of motion. Read's left hand came down on the gun, jerked it aside as Jack pulled the trigger, heard another loud snap on another unprimed pan, and then that big knife was whirling through the air at his throat.

He had time enough to gasp and then Anne's hand shot out, grabbed Read's arm, pulled it aside before Read could plunge the blade into Jack's neck.

"Enough!" Anne roared, and Jack was stunned by the authority in her voice. Read let go of the pistol in Jack's hand and Jack staggered back a step, his eyes and Read's still locked.

"Jack," Anne said, but Jack was still too drunk and angry to listen, soothing as her tone was.

"God damn your eyes, Anne, I'll not have you rutting like some animal with this bastard, hear? Make a fool of me, I'll not stand for it. I'll take this bastard ashore, run him through!" Jack pointed at Read with his impotent pistol.

"Jack, damn it, shut your gob and listen!" And again Anne's voice was such that it would not admit protest. Jack stopped talking, lowered his weapon. His breath was coming hard.

"This is nothing as it appears," Anne continued, her voice now conciliatory again. "Read . . . Do you attend me, Jack? Read is not a man. She is a woman. Like me. A woman, dressing as a man."

Jack frowned, looked from Anne to Read and back. A *woman?* What sort of a story was this? Was this some monstrous lie . . . or did Anne mean that she and Read were engaged in some kind of unnatural act . . . or . . . Jack could not seem to get his thoughts around this news.

"A woman?"

Then Read spoke. "That's right, Captain. My name is Mary. Mary Read. I have played the man the better part of my life. No one was ever the wiser. But Anne, she smoked the truth directly, soon as ever I came aboard."

Now Anne was talking. "You can well imagine, my beloved, that Mary and I have had much to say to each other, what with the sameness of our circumstances, but we reckoned it best if the others did not know Mary's secret, and that is why we have been sneaking about. I am sorry, my dearest, but I should have told you. Forgive me?"

Jack looked at her, but his brain was still five sentences back. *Read is a woman? Read . . . almost bested Dicky Corner . . .*

No, it's not possible . . . no woman could stand up to that beast. And yet . . . there was always something odd about Read . . . the voice . . . the smooth chin . . . His manner had always seemed too old for a beardless youth . . .

It was more than Jack's rum-sodden mind could cope with. He looked Mary in the eyes, tried to focus. "You're a woman?"

"Aye."

"You swear to it?"

Mary sighed, seemed to come to some decision. "I'll prove it to you, if you wish." Her hand moved to her red waistcoat, began to unbutton the buttons, and Jack watched, stunned, mystified.

"No, no," he said at last. Somehow he could not endure it, seeing the proof in the flesh of Read's sex. It was too bizarre by half. "No, I believe you . . ." he stammered.

Then Anne was there, a comforting arm around his shoulder. "Come, Jack, my beloved, let us go to our cabin and have a lie-down. You have had a long day, I'll warrant, and are quite ready for sleep."

She said that, and suddenly the thought of sleep was delicious and Jack wondered if he would even make it back to the cabin before passing out.

Sleep was what he wanted. To close his eyes, have it all go away: the fear of Anne's infidelity, the shock of Read's being a woman. Let sleep whisk him away, let him forget all that had happened during the past hour, a single hour that had spun his world off on some new and hardly comprehensible course.

Mary took the lantern down from the nail, followed after Anne Bonny and Calico Jack as Anne led the drunk buccaneer aft, steering him around the various obstacles in the hold.

Her heartbeat was settling back to something like normal, the surge of energy was subsiding. She had come close to death before, plenty of times, but still there was no sensation quite like having a pistol stuck in your face and seeing the flint come down on the pan.

How the gun—both guns—had failed to fire, she could not imagine.

Her moves had been instinctual, an instinct honed over the years of fielding as a soldier. It was the primal reflex to run or to fight, and there had been no place to run. She had not thought to draw her knife, had no notion of how she had ended up thus, with her left hand on the pistol, her right hand stabbing at Jack.

Instinct. It had saved her life so many times. But it was Anne's quickness that had save Jack's life.

Mary watched young Anne Bonny maneuver Jack Rackam aft, watched her strong, feline body as she took most of his weight, and him near to passing out.

Anne had reacted well, Mary thought, to the startling discovery that she was making love to another woman. She had not become furious, or indignant or horrified. She had seen the absurdity in it, the wild coincidence. The humor. She had reacted well when Mary had nearly killer her lover.

And she had reacted well to Mary's lie, had picked up the thread of it and carried it along, the tale of how she, Anne, had known all along of Mary's being a woman.

Anne Bonny might be a bit of a slut, but she was quick of hand and mind. She could laugh at her own folly and support her fellow in a lie with never a pause. One moment she could order Jack around and the next soothe his inflated male pride.

Mary had been watching Anne from their first meeting, curious, trying to fathom who she was. Up until that point she had not been much impressed.

But the events of the past fifteen minutes had changed all that. Anne had laughed, upon discovering the truth, and that laughter did more to recommend her to Mary than all the words in the world might have done. Anne had kept her head when the weapons came out, had actually quenched the fire.

It gave Mary a whole new image of Anne Bonny. She thought that Anne might actually be a woman whom she could respect. Perhaps even a woman she could befriend.

Chapter 22

CALICO JACK RACKAM WANTED TO WIPE HIS PALM, BUT he was afraid.

He could feel the big sword slipping in his hand, he could not hold it securely with his sweating grip, but he was not sure what to do. *What if they should see me wipe my palm? What would they think about that, eh? Fearsome Calico Jack's palms are sweating, he is so damned afraid.*

He looked aloft, like he was checking the set of the sails, then let his eyes move over the deck. The men were all at the rail, all looking outboard, and so he rested the point of his sword on the deck and wiped his hand quick on his coat, then readjusted his grip on the weapon.

This is stupid, this is bloody fucking stupid . . . it is only a damned brig, six men at the most.

Back when he had been just another of the pirate band, even when he had been Vane's quartermaster, Jack's fear encompassed only the possibility of physical injury. But it was different now, now that he had the responsibility he had once so craved. Now, along with concern for his bodily safety came the fear of possible failure, the anxiety of humiliation, the terror that his crew might grow restless and turn on him.

For the moment they were content—they had been lucky in their hunting—but how long would that last? Would this brig put up a fight? Would it prove to be a worthless prize?

They had spotted her that morning, the second sail in three days. Jack had woken, fully dressed and splayed along the locker, to the sound of "Sail, ho!" and an all but unbearable pain in his head. His memory was blotted by the rum-induced fog from the night before.

Anne had been there, dear Anne, with water and a dram

of rum to ease his agony. When he was finally in a position to listen, Anne had gone over with him again the events of the evening, Mary's gender, the fact that she, Anne, had known all along that Mary was a woman.

It was hard to imagine how the other brigands aboard the *Pretty Anne* would react to Mary's secret, but it was possible, likely perhaps, that they would not react well. The women agreed it would be better if they did not know. Jack agreed to keep the secret.

"Yes, but see here, Annie," Jack said, then paused. The pain in his head was insufferable, and he was afraid to speak what was on his mind. But it had to be said. "See here, I understand how you two are friends, but you've made it look like a damned sight more than just that. No, hear me . . ."

He held up his hand to ward off Anne's protest. It was hard enough to say this; he did not want to be stopped once he was under way. "It does my authority no good for the men to think you've put horns on me. Don't think there have not been mutterings; there have, I know it. I'll thank you two to act the bully friends and no more. Remember, the rest will still think Read a man."

Anne said nothing, just nodded.

"Very well, then," said Jack, and there was an end to it.

So now I have this bloody secret to keep? he thought, pacing the quarterdeck under the relentless tropical sun. *What will these bastards do if they find I've held this secret close?*

What if we can't run this brig to ground, what if she sails us under, like the schooner?

And if not this one, what about the next?

Oh, Annie!

If ever he needed comforting, he needed it at that moment. He wanted to hold her close to him, to bury his face in her neck, to let the tears of his frustration and terror run down her hair, to have her help carry his burden.

He wanted her by his side, but now she was with Read, up aloft, where they could talk in private. *Mary* Read, he reminded himself, a woman, so he knew she was not rutting with her. But it was not rutting that he wanted at the moment. It was love and sympathy.

Who am I bloody well fooling? Anne was not the type to give sympathy, Read or no Read. What would happen if he were to confess his fears to her? Would she cradle him in her arms, stroke his hair, tell him everything would be fine?

No, not a bloody chance. She would be revolted by him, reject him, announce his cowardice to the world, just as she had sentenced that little worm Bonny to death by blurting out his perfidy in the Ship Tavern. He had fallen in love with a wild woman, and wild women were not maternal and they were not sympathetic, and all his wishing in the world could not change that.

Jack felt the overwhelming need to speak, thought he might explode if he did not release some words. "Harwood!" he called to the helmsman. "Start easing her over now, ease her over and we'll bring her alongside. See if these bastards'll dance to our tune. And let's have Annie's fine bunting aloft, eh?"

He glanced up to see if Annie had heard that, but she and Read were not paying attention to the goings-on on deck. They stood on either side of the topmast, looking out toward the brig, which was now less than half a mile away, proving to be no match for the *Pretty Anne*'s speed.

Jack stared at the two of them. They were laughing about something, he could see them laugh, though the sound of their laughter was lost over the noise of the sloop. He wondered what they were laughing at, felt a flush of anger and embarrassment.

What do these others think, seeing them bloody well together all the time?

There was something very unsettling about Mary Read. Jack guessed her to be in her late twenties—younger than he—yet there was a quality about her that made her seem much older. She seemed to *know* things, to understand.

He knew absolutely nothing about her background, save that she had spent most of her life dressed as a man, had been a man-of-war sailor for some time. He thought Anne had said something about her having been a soldier, but Anne apparently did not know much either.

Mary was secretive about her history, and that made her more unsettling still. She always seemed to be looking right through his skin when he looked at her. She had almost killed him, that night in the forepeak. He had not been so drunk that he did not recall the blade coming at his throat.

Mary was enjoying the company of her newfound friend. She liked standing on the crosstrees, high above the deck, talking aimlessly.

But it worried her as well. The others, save for Jack, still thought she was a man. Would they think she was making a cuckold of their captain? What would they do about that?

"The others, the men, I mean, they will not object to our keeping company?"

"No," said Anne. "It is not their affair. They might talk amongst themselves, but they'll do no more."

"Hmm," Mary said. Talk was not so benign a thing as Anne seemed to think, at least not in the close confines of a ship.

"If Jack cannot endure it, then it will be his responsibility to act. Challenge you to a fight or some such, but I do not think he will."

"I hope not." An ambiguous statement, and though Mary meant by it that she did not wish to kill Jack, which would certainly be the outcome of their fight, she did not clarify, nor did Anne ask for clarification.

Anne looked down at the deck, at the growing activity there. "We'll be into the fight with yon brig soon, I reckon. Best lay down to deck. If we are lolling about up here when there is fighting to be done, that they will not forgive."

Mary gave one last careful scan of the horizon to see that there were no other vessels, that there would be no surprises from another quarter while they were engaged with the brig. Then she grabbed hold of a backstay, twisted her foot around it, and slid down to deck in a controlled plummet.

Her feet hit the cap rail and she hopped down to the deck below. Preparations for battle were under way. The men had armed themselves, the four-pounder cannon along the side loaded with grape over round shot. A rum cask had been set on deck and the head stove in with an ax, and the pirates were dipping into it like it was a water butt.

And there was Dicky Corner, looming up over her, his big dog grin spread across his face, and Mary thought if he had a tail, it would be wagging furiously.

"Here, now, Read, are you ready for a fight, then? Ready to give out to these bastards like you done for us, eh?" He held his ear in his fingers, bent it toward her so she could see the ragged edge her pistol ball had left in its wake. It was mostly healed, but still it was not pretty to look at.

"Aye . . ." she said, and stopped herself just before the "sir" came out. She was becoming more accustomed to leaving off the "sir," but it was a habit that died hard. "And what of weapons, then?"

"Weapons? What happened to your fucking weapons?"

"Nothing. I've never had any."

"What? Ain't we been in a fight since we took your goddamned Dutchman?"

"No."

"No? Well, goddamn my eyes. Very well, come on then."

Corner stepped aft and Mary trailed along behind him. Set next to the binnacle box was a barrel that held a variety of edged weapons, like ax handles for sale in a dry goods store, and beside it a chest half-filled with sundry pistols and such.

"These here is weapons we took from some of the ships we've had, which none has claimed as his own. Take what you want, then," Corner said, nodding to the arms stores. Mary poked through the blades, found cutlasses and sabers and straight swords. A couple she recognized as having belonged to the *Hoorn*. At last she pulled out a curved saber, very like the cavalry sabers that had once been such an integral part of her life.

"Ah, there, there's a great beastly blade. Cleave some bastard from head to arse with that!" Corner was grinning his approval. "Recall, too, the articles says each man is to keep his weapons clean and fit for service, so you have a mind for that. Now, some pistols for you?"

Mary poked through the chest. Some of the pistols were very fine weapons indeed, plundered from ship captains or the cabins of wealthy passengers, no doubt. Mary picked one up, pulled back the lock and pulled the trigger, looked with satisfaction at the trail of sparks that drifted off the steel frizzen. "This one will serve admirably," she said.

"One? No, take a brace, take two braces."

"Two braces? How will I hold two braces?" She could not imagine jamming four of the big pistols in her belt.

"What we do is we use ribbon, you see? Tied to the butts, drape 'em around your neck. Makes them who we're attacking shit their drawers, just to see you come over the rail. Scares the fight right out of 'em, and that's how we prefers it, do ya see?"

"You rather they don't fight?"

"Damn my eyes, you're a shit-fire! Course we want them to not fight. You read the articles, great scholar that you are. If a man loses an eye or an ear, well, it's two shares for him, and eight hundred dollars from the public stock if he lose a limb. That's less money for all but the unlucky dog who's hurt, so of course we don't want them to fight."

Mary nodded. That made sense. She knew these men loved a good rough and tumble, but if fighting might mean some fiscal loss, then they would want as little of it as possible. "Did you get two shares, then, for what I done to your ear?"

"No, on account of you only taking off the one piece. Next bastard shoots at me, I hope he aims better."

"But not too much better."

Corner laughed, his deep-throated laugh. "No, not so much as to put a bullet through my head. No extra shares for a dead man, and I don't reckon I'd care much even if there was!"

He ambled off forward, still chuckling at the thought. Mary searched through the pistols, found the mate to the one she had chosen, and then two more. A bit more searching revealed a linen bag full of shot to fit the guns and a flask of powder as well.

She sat on the deck, cross-legged, and loaded the weapons, while around her the excitement built like thunderheads, men moving fast, talking loud, bursts of shouting, even the odd pistol fired in the air.

It is like sex, she thought, *the way this tension will build and then explode at last when we board this poor bastard brig.*

She had never thought of it before, but now that she did she realized how alike the two things really were, at least in the pattern they followed. She thought of how many things in life were like that.

She mused on that notion as she tamped the wadding down in the fourth pistol and then Anne's feet—shapely and feminine, yet big for a woman—appeared on the deck beside her.

"I have brought this for you. You will need them, now that you are a beastly pirate." She held in her hand two lengths of bright red and gold ribbon and a buff leather shoulder belt with a frog to hold the saber.

Anne Bonny looked very like a beastly pirate herself, as much as she was able with her young and pretty face. She was wearing her long blue coat. A cocked hat was pushed down over the red cloth around her head, a brace of pistols dangled from ribbons around her neck, and a rapier hung at the end of a shoulder belt.

Mary took the ribbon and the belt that Anne held out to her and said, "Thank you."

She tied the ends of the ribbon to the butts of the pistols, draped the shoulder belt over her neck and the pistols after that, and stood up. The weapons were heavy. They clattered against each other as she moved. But they did make her look fierce, piratical.

Perhaps we can frighten these poor whoresons into sur-render, she thought. *Perhaps we will not have to butcher them all.*

The brig was close now, just two cable lengths beyond the starboard bow, around four hundred yards away, rising and plunging through the sea as she ran for her life, like a deer running pathetically, uselessly, from wolves.

In any event, we shall know soon.

A cheer ran along the *Pretty Anne*'s deck, men yelling, weapons raised overhead, and Mary, who had been admiring the way the pistols looked draped around her neck, looked up.

The black flag was run aloft, the white death's head, the crossed cutlasses beneath. Mary stared at it, recalled how she had first seen it from the *Hoorn,* how fear had swept along the merchantman's deck at the sight of it. *These men know the game of the mind,* she thought. *They understand how terror works.*

"Do you like it?" Anne asked, looking up at the flag, smiling. "I made it, you know. It was Jack's idea, but I sewed it."

"It is a fine piece of work. You are the master of many trades."

"It is true. Seamstress, pirate, whore, I shall never be without a living."

George Fetherston passed a bottle of rum to Mary and she took it, took a deep drink, felt the rough liquor burn her throat and stomach, but the pain was in perfect step with her mood. She took another drink, handed the bottle to Anne, who drank as well and passed it on.

Two hundred yards to the brig. The Pretty Annes were lining the rail, standing in the shrouds. They wore long coats or waistcoats or were bare-chested. Some wore hats, some had bright cloth tied around their heads or waists, some let their long hair flog in the wind. They looked like impoverished gentlemen or fugitives from the madhouse, but they all looked dangerous, frightening, loaded down with weapons, screaming like the damned.

Mary followed Anne aft onto the quarterdeck and they

pushed up against the rail, joined in the shouting.

Just forward of where they stood, Calico Jack Rackam paced back and fourth, his big straight sword in his hand. He slashed at the air, shouted with the others, glanced aloft and over at the brig.

There was a jerky quality to his movements, a hesitancy that Mary had not seen in him before.

She looked closer, watching him when he was not looking in her direction. She saw him yawn, made a great show of looking bored.

He is afraid, she thought.

She had seen fear before, many, many times, and she knew its face. She had been afraid herself, more often than she could recall, but with damn more reason than Jack had now, racing down on some pathetic merchant brig.

Mary glanced around at the others. *Do they not see it?* Apparently not. But, of course, they did not see she was a woman, and the men of the *Hoorn* had not detected the same of Anne. Mary did not give much credit to the average man's capacity for observation.

Then a cannon went off, fired from the brig, and the noise jarred her from her thoughts.

The two vessels, the *Pretty Anne* and her intended victim, had been sailing near parallel courses, like they were racing for some distant point. Now, by Jack's order, the *Pretty Anne* was slowly inching over, closing the gap of water between them, until at last they would collide, side by side.

Mary caught Anne's eye and Anne grinned at her, a grin that said, *Isn't this grand, isn't this a thrill! This is the greatest wickedness! Risking life this way, it is life itself!*

Mary grinned back. She did not agree, but she knew how Annie felt.

The brig's shot punched through the outer jib, leaving a ragged hole in the sail, and the pirates redoubled their shouting and cursing and waving of weapons.

And there was Jack, calling out orders, and at last the men were quiet enough to hear.

"We'll give 'em a broadside! The bastards, fire on us? We'll cut them to fucking ribbons, blow them to hell!"

Mary could hear the edge of hysteria in his voice, but she knew the others were too caught up in the excitement of the thing to notice. It took years of experience under fire to remain as aware as she was of her surroundings when the energy was really starting to pulse.

The men came down off the rails, swarming around the starboard battery of guns. Anne raced amidships, snatched up a powder cartridge from the powder chest, and stood behind the line of guns ready to hand the powder forward if the men would reload. Mary stepped over to the powder chest, took another cartridge, took her place beside her friend.

The helmsman pulled the tiller to starboard, just a hair, and the *Pretty Anne* turned away from the brig, and when she had turned enough that all the guns would bear, Jack's voice cut through the din with one word.

"Fire!"

There were only five guns per side, and they only fired four-pound balls, but in that charged atmosphere it seemed like the battery of a ship-of-the-line. The gray smoke erupted from the muzzles, filled the air with its acrid and bellicose smell. The sharp sound of the gunfire was taken up with the shouts of the wild men who lined the *Pretty Anne*'s rail.

That was enough cannon fire for the pirates. They abandoned the guns and clambered back on the rails. Anne and Mary returned the cartridges to the powder chest. Mary thought to secure the lid, and then they joined the others at the ship's side.

Anne pulled her rapier, waved it, and joined in the shouting, her high voice in contrast to the bass shouts of the others.

Mary shouted as well, waved her saber, and let the tension and excitement vent, tried to mask her guilt with the rough language. She knew that she should be revolted by the whole thing, or at least not be so enthused, but the energy was infectious, like the cavalry charges, or plunging bayonet-first onto the field of battle when she was an infantry soldier.

"Death, death, death . . ." There was Fetherston chanting, standing on the rail, banging the side of the *Pretty Anne* with his big sword. The others took it up, "Death, death, death . . ."

And that was enough for the brig's crew. The vessel rounded up into the wind, her sails in a great disarray. Her flag came shooting down from the masthead in surrender.

One shot, and then they put their fates in the pirates' hands.

Chapter 23

THE *PRETTY ANNE* STOOD ON, CLOSING FAST WITH HER victim, which was now stopped in the water. "Death, death, death!"

The helmsmen swung the *Pretty Anne* away at the last second, lessening the impact, but still the two vessels came together with a mighty, shuddering crunch that made the pirates stagger and hold their grip for a fraction of a second before they leapt with their berserker screams from the *Pretty Anne* onto the brig's deck.

They came over the rail like a breaking wave, and Anne and Mary were at the crest, crashing down on the deck, blades and pistols in hand, looking for some resistance, some fight from the brig's crew. They raced fore and aft, chasing the terrified crew toward the bow or stern or up into the rigging. It was all so familiar to Mary, the surge of energy, the heightened awareness, the muscles tensed and ready to react, her body all potential power, like a drawn bow.

There was a sailor in front of her and he held a cutlass tentatively in his hand. Mary could read the uncertainty in his face. She lifted her pistol, aimed it right at his heart.

"Drop it, damn your eyes!" she shouted, and the weapon clattered to the deck.

There was more cheering all around, not the vaporing of attack but the wild release that comes with the end of the action. Mary kept the pistol leveled, looked around. She could see only a few of the brig's crew, huddled against the far rail, and a few more half up the main rigging, and she imagined that that was all there was. The brig was taken, not a drop of blood had been shed.

And now, the spoils.

Mary's education in pirating had been brief but intense, she having now seen pirates in action from the point of view of the victims and the pirates themselves. She knew from her experience aboard the *Hoorn* that the pirates were masters at the art of pillage, and they set in to practicing those skills again.

Corner and Noah Harwood were standing on the main hatch, slashing at the tarpaulins with their cutlasses, but that was not efficient enough for the rest. In a flash James Dobbin was there with an ax in his hand and with a few strokes he reduced the grating beneath the cloth to kindling. The pirates pulled the hatch away, let the sunlight spill down on what was now their property.

"Come along, Michael!" Anne shouted, slapping Mary on the back. "Let us get to the master's cabin before these beasts tear it apart!"

Mary lowered the pistol which she still held level with the sailor's breast, saw the relief on his face as his tensed body sagged. *Poor sod must have thought I was going to shoot him all that while.*

She followed Anne as she pushed her way through the wild pirate band and plunged eagerly down the after scuttle.

Mary followed more slowly, saber sheathed, two cocked pistols in her hands. Her eyes were everywhere. They were still aboard an enemy vessel, there was no knowing who might be hiding in the shadows, a thought that had clearly not occurred to Annie, who whooped and shouted as she threw open the doors to the small cabins that lined the narrow alleyway aft.

Mary could not shake the feeling of trespassing, of being where she had no right to be. Once, in Flanders, Mary's regiment had looted a great country house, and it had felt just this way. Pillage, she guessed, was an acquired taste.

At the far end of the alleyway was a door that Mary guessed must communicate with the great cabin. Anne stepped back, leg cocked to kick it in.

"Hold!" Mary shouted. Anne stopped, turned around. "You do not know what is behind the door, my dear. What if it is some frightened bastard with a pistol, ready to shoot the first soul through?"

"How right you are. You are certain you have never done such as this before?"

"I don't believe I ever said that. Here . . ." Mary pushed past Anne, shoved the pistol in her left hand back in her belt, and held the other pistol in front of her. She put her hand on the handle of the door, twisted, threw it open, and jumped back.

No shots, no screams, just the bang of the door as it swung against the bulkhead.

"Better off safe, to be sure," said Anne. She stepped past Mary, looked quickly into the cabin. "Empty."

Mary stepped in after her. The cabin was small, seven feet deep by twelve across, and modestly furnished, but still it had a neat, comfortable aspect. A chest was lashed to the deck, a sturdy table in the middle of the space, a small shelf of books secured for sea.

Under the after windows, a row of lockers like a couch, and on top of them, red velvet pillows made to fit like pieces of a puzzle. It was light and airy, all very different from the pirate sloop, which was growing increasingly foul, dank, and vermin ridden.

"You are bleeding," Anne said, pointing at Mary's hand.

Mary held her palm up. It was smeared with blood from a cut that ran from thumb to wrist. "I wonder how I did that," she said. She could not recall cutting herself.

Anne held up her hand. There was also blood on the palm. "I managed to cut myself as well."

"How?"

"I am ashamed to say it, but in all the tussle of jumping aboard, I seem to have cut myself on my own sword!" She smiled at the silliness of it, then paused, as if hesitating in some decision. She stepped forward boldly, grabbed up Mary's cut hand, and pressed her own to it. Mary could feel Anne's palm, slick against hers, the blood mingling.

"There," Anne said, with a sheepish half smile. "Blood sisters. Bloodied in combat together."

Mary smiled back at her. There was something so child-like, so innocent about that gesture, as if she and Anne were, for that moment, not genuine pirates at all, but little girls playing pirates in the garden.

"Blood sisters," Mary said.

And then Anne, embarrassed by the sincerity of the moment, pulled her eyes from Mary, spun around, arms extended, and shouted, "Ahh!" She crossed the cabin and sprawled back on the pillows atop the locker. "This is the life, eh?"

"It is very like home," Mary agreed. She crossed over to a small rack of bottles, pulled out one, and examined the label. It was French, she could read the words, but they meant nothing to her. Still, it looked like the kind of wine one saw in a gentleman's stock, so she picked up the corkscrew that lay beside the rack and liberated the cork from the neck.

She tipped the bottle up, let the wine run down her throat. It was smooth, almost buttery, with a hint of a fruit flavor. Delicious. She did not think the wine-maker had imagined it would be consumed in such a manner, nor had it been made with such as her in mind. She took another drink.

This is not so bad. They had not murdered anyone. She felt her earlier hesitancy melting away. *A short life and a merry one. Very well, I am for that.*

Anne was on her feet again, poking through the master's things. She flung open the chest that was secured to the deck, squealed with delight. "See here, Mary, dear!" she said, and pulled a silk gown from the chest, held it up in front of her.

"Lovely," Mary said, and she meant it. It was a beautifully crafted garment, rich colors, subtly contrasting textures in the fabrics. Was the master taking it home to his wife? His mistress? To market in Jamaica, where the wives and daughters of the British planters ached for the fashions of London?

"There are more," Anne said, poking through the chest again. "We must take them along. Who knows when we might have the opportunity to wear such as these?"

"Who knows? They are not much use when a-pirating."

"No, but I am with child to see you dressed in silk and lace, my dear."

And then heavy footfalls in the alleyway, the doors to the cabins banging open again, and Anne stuffed the dresses back in the chest, shut the lid, her face flushed with embarrassment.

The great cabin door burst open and there were Dicky Corner and Harwood and Billy Bartlett bursting in, practically filling the small cabin with their bulk.

"Ho! Leave it to you then, to be first to the finer things!" Corner roared with his usual bonhomie, but Bartlett's eyes were narrow, and he looked suspiciously at Anne, and then Mary.

"This here is the property of all," he growled at Mary.

"I am aware of that."

"It's death, you know, to steal the value of one dollar from yer shipmates."

Mary glared at him, held his eyes in her unwavering stare. "You calling me a thief, Bartlett?"

"I didn't say nothing, I'm just telling you—"

"If you're going to call me a thief, you best be ready to prove it . . ."

The atmosphere was tense, like the seconds before a thunderstorm, and then Corner laughed, an incongruous sound, a laugh that filled the cabin, and the tension collapsed.

"We're all bloody thieves here, Read!" Corner shouted. The others smiled at the observation and then turned to tearing the master's cabin apart.

Mary leaned against the table, took another drink of

wine. *I will have to watch that little bastard Bartlett,* she thought. *One of these days I will have to put a sword through him.*

There was no more than five minutes amusement to be had in the master's cabin, and when it was thoroughly looted the three men and two women stumbled back on deck again.

Most of the Pretty Annes were aft. The brig's crew had been rounded up, pushed back against the taffrail, and Calico Jack Rackam was addressing them.

Mary recognized the performance. It was the same as he had given aboard the *Hoorn.* Fearsome Calico Jack the pirate, using his big sword as a walking stick. He was a frightening sight, and she could see that the brig's crew were frightened indeed.

"What think you of my man, Calico Jack?" Anne asked, nodding toward the performance taking place astern. Her tone suggested that she herself did not think too highly of him.

"He knows how to put the fear of his wrath in men. He makes a wondrous pirate."

"He threatens them, but he never does anything, you know."

"So it would seem. But you sound as if you do not approve of that."

"Well, it sets me to wonder at times. I would not like to think he was afraid."

"It takes no courage to torture defenseless prisoners. I have known some damned cruel men, and they were all cowards at heart. I think your Jack does just the right thing, frightening them half to death and then showing them mercy. It is his most admirable trait, the fact that he does not hurt his victims."

"Well . . ." Anne said. She looked surprised. "I had thought, sometimes, that you did not respect my Jack."

"I respect him in that."

Anne nodded. "Then I shall as well. I think I have much to learn from you."

Mary chuckled. "Yes, you do. If you would learn how

to make an absolute hash of your life, then I am the one to teach it."

Anne smiled back. "In some things I need no instruction."

They had their way with the brig for two days, plundered everything that was worth the taking, which was not much, terrorized the crew, and then sent them on their way. Two days more and the *Pretty Anne* had settled back into her routine: desultory watches, eyes on the horizon for potential prizes or men-of-war, sleeping, eating, drinking, drinking, drinking.

Anne was in the great cabin. She was kneeling on the lockers aft, leaning out the small stern window, looking down at the lovely blue and white ocean, the furrow of their wake, the rudder as it worked side to side in the gudgeons, just little movements as the helmsman on the deck above worked the tiller to keep the sloop on course.

Ah, this is fine . . . she thought. Then the stern dipped in the quartering sea and rose up again with a fast, swooping motion and her stomach convulsed.

She leaned farther out the window and her meal of an hour before was back up again. She watched it plunge into the sea below. Her body tensed, the muscles in her abdomen clenched, and then she puked again and again.

She rested on her elbows, alternately gasping for breath and spitting into the sea. "Goddamn it . . ." she muttered.

The hatch above opened and she heard footsteps on the ladder. It could only be Jack. She wiped her mouth with her sleeve, rolled back into the cabin, and sat on the locker just as Jack reached the deck and turned toward her.

She could tell by his expression that she looked as bad as she felt. The smile died on his lips and he came over to her, sat down and put his arm around her, and said, soft, "Annie, my dearest, are you sick?" He put his hand on her forehead, but she knew that she did not have a fever.

"Just my stomach, Jack, dear, it is nothing."

"Nothing? Are you quite certain? We can get you to a doctor, if you wish."

"No, no, it is nothing." Jack's tenderness was touching, and Anne needed tenderness just then. She wanted him to cover her in tenderness like a thick blanket on a cold winter night.

"I love you, Calico Jack," she said, leaned her head against him. She could see the words were a warm breeze to him, a whiff of lilac, and his face shone with delight.

"I love you too, my Annie."

She nestled herself against him, relished his strong arms enveloping her. She hoped she would not have to puke again, she did not care to spoil the moment. They rogered like dogs in heat, she and Jack, but they so rarely enjoyed just the simple act of holding one another.

I am a cold bitch.

She knew that Jack loved her, unconditionally. And she loved him. But she never felt able to give him love in the final measure, not the way he did her. It had been the same with James Bonny, even in the beginning. The same with her father. *What is wrong with me?*

Sometimes she thought that Mary was the only person she could love, and the more time she spent with Mary, the more she felt that way. Their relationship was not complicated by physical desire or jealousy or a need to control or any of that. Theirs was a simple bond.

He is still the Jack Rackam I fell in love with, she reminded herself.

But he was different as well. He was not so much the carefree buccaneer she had known in Nassau. *He is captain of the ship, leader of this band of bloody murderers. Is it any wonder he is distracted?*

She pushed herself closer, put her arm around his waist. She knew that he needed her, needed her support and encouragement, weary as he was with the consideration of commanding the *Pretty Anne.* Men could be so fragile that way. She wished she knew what to say or do. She wished she were that kind of woman. She guessed that Mary would have just the right words, know just what to do, but she did not.

And what she had to say next would not help. But it had to be said.

"Jack, my love, I must tell you something, and I'll warrant it is something you have never heard from any of your fellow buccaneers before."

"Yes?"

She pushed herself away, just a bit. She met his eyes, his arms still around her. "Jack, dear, I am going to have your baby."

Chapter 24

THEY CARRIED ON WITH THE SWEET TRADE FOR ANother five months, cruising the great tracks between Bermuda and the northern islands of the Bahamas, but the hunting was poor. A pink from New England with pitch, tar, and stores, a small ship bound from Carolina to England laden with rice and meat in barrels. Anne wondered, as those barrels were swayed aboard the *Pretty Anne,* if perhaps her father had some financial stake in the vessel. It was entirely possible, and she enjoyed the irony of that.

They put into Marsh Harbor on Great Abaco and sold the accumulated plunder in their tight-packed hold for less than a tenth of what it was worth. That was the price one accepted from a merchant who was not curious about bills of lading and receipts and such inconveniences.

The pirates split the money into even shares, then each man and woman came up to receive his or her portion from Quartermaster Corner. For all of their discounting their haul, it still amounted to several hundred dollars per hand, and the Pretty Annes were well pleased.

They left Great Abaco, which was not in the main very

welcoming to their kind, and found a small island with which Jack was familiar. There they hove down the vessel and enjoyed a grand bacchanal onshore.

Anne was no longer puking by that point, but she was growing large in the belly. She slit her slop trousers up the seams and sewed additional pieces of cloth in to accommodate her increased waist size. Her smooth, feline movements were becoming awkward. She was not sleeping well.

Jack was increasingly uncomfortable around her. The life of a sailor and pirate did not make one generally acquainted with pregnant women, and Jack did not know how to act. He was afraid to touch her, never seemed to know what to say.

Anne found it frustrating, infuriating at times. She wanted her old body back, she wanted to be able to move the way she once had. She found herself sometimes angry, sometimes profoundly sad. Her emotions were like a leash, pulling her first one way, then another. She had no experience with that, and it made her angrier still.

Everyone aboard—every man aboard—treated her like she was diseased, or else like she was a fragile china doll. Only Mary seemed to understand that she was the same woman she had always been. It was getting so she could not stand anyone's company, save for Mary's.

"Annie, my dearest?" Jack approached her one afternoon. She was sitting on the main hatch, looking out over the empty sea.

"Yes?"

Jack had that tentative quality, like someone approaching a strange and potentially vicious dog, and it was irritating in the extreme. "My love, I think soon you will be in your confinement . . ."

"Yes?"

"This sloop is no place for that. I have some friends, a family, in Cuba. Fine people. Methinks we should go there, for . . . well, should I say . . ."

"For me to have my baby, Jack? Your baby? Can't you just bloody say it?"

Jack pulled back like she had threatened him with a

knife, and Anne was sorry for the outburst. Her expression softened and she saw the shock leave Jack's face.

"I am sorry, Jack, dear, I fear I do not know what I am about these days. Yes, Cuba . . . let us go to Cuba, then."

They made their course south by west, threading through the Mayaguana Passage and then turning due west to run along the north shore of the island of Cuba. They captured a brig bound from Havana to Madrid, emptied her of food and wine and some specie and other goods, and sent her on her way. There was no time to spend toying with her.

They kept a sharp lookout now, and it was not for prizes primarily. It was a lookout ahead, eyes on the clear blue water, alert for the killing reefs and sandbars that fringed the island. And it was eyes on the horizon, watching, looking sharp for the *Guarda del Costa,* the small Spanish men-of-war that jealously guarded the coasts of Spain's possessions in the New World.

The pirates were enemies of the world, wanted by every nation, and while they did not care to be captured at all, they wanted least to be captured by the Spanish. Being tried as a pirate was one thing. Being tried as a pirate by Spanish civil authorities and as a heretic by the Inquisition was another.

So they watched the glittering blue sea to starboard and the green jungle-covered mountains to larboard, the long stretches of white-sand beach and, when they were in close enough, the languid palms that waved like beckoning arms. They saw poor fishing boats and island traders and pettiaugers like big canoes, but never a vessel that was a threat to them, nor any that was worth their while in taking.

The mood aboard the *Pretty Anne* was easy, jovial, despite the threat of the Spanish patrols. Anne could see that Jack was more relaxed now, with their imminent arrival ashore. He was drinking more, and had been for the past month, which was annoying, and he would rarely touch her, never mind make love to her. But at least he seemed once more the carefree buccaneer she had loved in Nassau, and she was happy at least to have that Jack Rackam back.

Anne was glad to have Mary, and said so one afternoon,

as they sat alone in the bows watching the Archipelago de Camagüey slip past their starboard side.

"I am glad as well, for your friendship," Mary said. "I have never had a woman friend."

"Nor I . . ." said Anne. "Indeed, I'll warrant I've never had a friend at all. Lovers, to be sure. A husband even. But never a friend."

"Was your husband not a friend?"

"No. Once you put carnal desire into the thing, it changes everything. A husband is a fine creature, but he cannot be a friend."

"Oh, I don't know. My—"

She stopped short, so abruptly that Anne looked sharp at her. "Your . . . ?"

"It is nothing. Perhaps you are right."

"No, you were saying? Your . . . husband?"

"Yes, my husband."

"You are married?"

"Was. Annie, pray, I do not wish to discuss it."

"Very well."

They were quiet then, sitting there side by side and staring out at the archipelago's islands, like a blue-green necklace between the *Pretty Anne* and the mainland of Cuba.

"You have been wet through and through, have you not?" Mary asked. "Miserable, soaked by rain and a boarding sea?" Her voice was soft.

"Yes."

"And then the weather breaks and the sun comes out. The hot sun, like here in the Caribbean. You know that feeling, of having the sun dry your clothes? Of having been so miserable, and now you are warm and dry and you wish only to never be so miserable again? And you can hardly recall what the misery was like?"

"Yes."

"Well, that is me, my dear. Before . . . before I joined up with you lot, then I was wet and miserable. And now I am near getting dry again. Perhaps when I am fully dry, then I will be able to talk about it."

Anne glanced around to see that no one was looking their

way. There were some men lolling around aft, and some sleeping in the scuppers. Jack, she knew, was below, drinking. No one was paying them the least attention.

She reached over and took up Mary's hand and squeezed it. "I will never ask again," she said. "But if you ever wish to tell, I will listen. Blood sisters."

Mary smiled. "Blood sisters," she said, and squeezed Anne's hand in return.

They sailed on for the rest of the day, and the next morning felt their way in through a gap in the islands south of Cayo Fragoso. The shore of the main island, Cuba itself, which had been no more than a vague and distant line, began to resolve itself into individual trees and a line of small surf along a white beach.

Jack was on deck now, in command at the helm, directing the vessel through the channels with an ease that could only come with familiarity.

"There, now, Palmer," he said, loud, "do you see that house on the western side of the town? The big one? Make your head right for there. Yes, yes, good. Steady as she goes. Oh, Annie! What think you of this, girl? Is this not the finest place in the Caribbean, and those damnable Spaniards ahold of it?"

"It is fine, Jack, truly," she said, and she meant it. They were close in enough that they could smell the shore, even with the contrary sea breeze, and it smelled of warm sand and vegetation and the perfume of tropical flowers. There was smoke rising from several homes in the distant village, and they could smell that as well, burning wood and fish and meat cooking.

The richness of the aromas enveloped them and enticed them, they having been so long at sea with only the occasional tang of salt air and the stink of the sloop, which, in any event, they no longer noticed.

Anne was in a dress, one of the fine silk affairs they had liberated from the schooner and which she had modified to fit her expanded belly. If felt odd, encumbering. She had not had so much cloth draped over her in almost a year.

Beside her, Mary leaned easily on the bulwark, still one of the men.

"This is the village of Caibarién," Jack said. "Just a poor fishing village, in truth, but good people. I have had occasion to make friends here. They do not abide by that heretic nonsense and all the prejudice of old Spain, no, they will judge a man by who he is.

"There is a certain family here, name of De Jesús, who are particular friends of mine. Did me a good turn once, nursed me when I was sick. Palmer, let us come to anchor just astern of that fishing boat, there.

"Actually took a bullet out of me, then nursed me, but that is a different story," Jack continued. He was buoyant, Anne could tell, pleased to have arrived and no doubt pleased to know the pregnant woman would soon be off his ship, safe ashore and no longer his responsibility, ashore before she had the chance to give birth. But he was acting like the old Calico Jack, larger than life, and Anne was happy to see it. It was the Jack she loved.

"In any event, I have managed to make them a fair amount richer over the years, for their kindness, and we are like family still. They will be kind to us, dear, and Abuelita De Jesús—*Abuelita* means 'grandmother' to these Spaniards—she is physician to the town. Not really a physician, of course, no formal schooling, but oceans of experience with this sort of thing. I'd put her up against any of your quacks in old London."

"I am pleased to hear it." *God, he thinks this is some kind of new thing, like no woman has ever given birth before.* But for all her annoyance with Jack, Anne had to admit, to herself at least, that she was frightened as well. There were moments when she did feel as if she were the only woman to ever go though this.

They rounded up and let the anchor go and Anne Bonny stared over the taffrail at what would be her new home for . . . she did not know how long. A month or two at least. And she liked what she saw.

Caibarién was a small town, fifty homes perhaps, and unmistakably Spanish. The buildings were brick and stucco, whitewashed and brilliant in the sun. Red tile roofs. Most were one story, only a dozen or so larger than that. Biggest of all, a church with its tall bell tower, farther inland but still dominating the village.

A main street ran from the beach right up the center of the town, a sandy dirt road that was the same white color as the beach itself, giving no clear point where the beach ended and the town began. But that seemed only appropriate for a town that was completely oriented toward the sea, as the dozens of canoes and pettiaugers and sundry small craft pulled up on the beach or anchored just a few hundred feet off seemed to indicate.

Of all the vessels there, the *Pretty Anne* was the largest.

"It is quiet . . ." Mary observed.

"It is Sunday, Read, if I ain't mistaken," Jack said. "They are a God-fearing bunch here. And papist. That will never bother you, will it, Annie?"

"Papist, Anglican, Jew, cannibal, it makes no difference to me."

"Well said," Jack answered.

From where they were anchored, they could look right up the main street to the town square—a circle, actually— at the far end of which was the facade of the big, white church. The land on which the town sat seemed carved out of the jungle. Just several hundred yards beyond the farthest building the tree line began, like a besieging army, waiting patiently for the moment when it could sally forth and over-run the village.

Suddenly the still air was filled with the sound of ringing bells, lovely, bold, and melodic. Jack put his glass to his eye. "I do believe church is out!" he announced. "Sorry, lads, to get you here late for Sunday service. Let us clear the boat away, mayhaps the padre will count his beads for us anyway."

Jack ducked below, and Mary went forward to help the others cast off the gripes and rig the boat falls. Ten minutes later the longboat was riding in the water alongside the *Pretty Anne*. By then the church had emptied, and all the village, it seemed, had come down to the beach to see the new arrival. There looked to be several hundred people there, dressed in their dark Sunday clothing, the women's heads covered with their *velos,* men with their wide straw hats, children running in their heedless way.

Jack emerged from the great cabin scuttle. He had changed into his best coat, the calico with the small rose pattern, clean breeches, and silk stockings. His shoes were an unmarred black; the silver buckles stood out bold. At his hip hung a delicate rapier, tricked out with gold and jewels. He held his best, all-but-new hat under his arm, a great plume jutting out from the band.

"My dear Calico Jack Rackam, you are a fine sight!" Anne said. And he did look fine. Tall, square jawed, his chiseled face set off by the big mustache, dressed out in his best clean, tailored clothing, it excited her, looking on him.

"And you, my love," he said, taking her hand, holding it up, running his eyes over her. It was a gesture he had done a hundred times, but this time it was different, the look was different, the feel. It was not the smoldering regard he had always had before. It was something less than that, something more restrained.

Anne was ready to be done with her pregnancy. She wanted Jack to have that old look again.

"Might I help you down into the boat, my dear Annie?" he said, and there was warmth and love enough in his voice that it helped to mitigate some of Anne's misery.

She followed him to the boarding steps and glanced down. The boat was manned, six hands per side, and heavily armed, as the pirates always were whenever going ashore, even in the most amiable of ports. On the second thwart, starboard side, Mary sat with her oar held straight up, like the others. Their eyes met and Mary winked and Anne was very glad that her friend would be there with her. Her one, immutable friend.

Awkwardly she climbed down the three steps and into the boat, where helpful hands grabbed her arms and guided her to the stern sheets.

"Sod it, sod it . . ." she muttered as she sat heavily on

the small wooden seat aft. She was more agile than any of those apes, she prided herself on that fact, and she was not delighted to find herself so clumsy and in need of such help.

Jack bounded down the boarding steps, sat in the stern sheets beside Anne, and took up the tiller. "Shove off, give way," he called in a cheery tone. Anne could see that he was excited by this landfall, like some local hero coming back to the accolades of his public. *We shall see,* Anne thought.

But as it happened, Jack had guessed right. The longboat ground up in the sand and the men and women on the beach surged forward, surrounded it, olive-skinned faces smiling wide, and she heard, "Juan!" *"El capitán Juan!"* "Juan Rackam!"

The men splashed out into the surf, grabbed the longboat by the gunnels, and hauled it up the beach, so that the Pretty Annes could step dry from the boat onto the sand.

Jack stood. In the stern of the boat he was several feet above the heads of the crowd. He smiled and waved, and the people cheered. He looked like Caesar making his entrance into Rome, and Anne wondered just how much gold he had spread through that town to make himself so welcome.

He hopped out of the boat, down into the white sand, and the crowd parted as an older couple—in their fifties, perhaps, it was hard to tell—pushed through. The woman wore a dark dress and shawl over her plump, matronly body and a *velo* on her head. She unabashedly grabbed Jack and squeezed him and Jack called, "Abuelita!"

When she released him, Jack extended his hand to the man beside her, a thin man, the top of his head bald, with a meager mustache that drooped down on either side of his mouth. The man took his hand, shook it vigorously, said, "Juan!" and Jack replied "Abuelito! Abuelito De Jesús! *Como estás?*"

Abuelito replied in rapid Spanish and Jack nodded as he listened, then replied in rapid Spanish of his own. Anne was taken aback, impressed and surprised, all at once.

"Anne, dear, this is Senora De Jesús," Jack said, presenting her to the older woman. "You must call her *Abuelita,* everyone does. It is like . . . grandma, in the Spanish tongue. And Señor De Jesús. You must call him *Abuelito.*"

I never knew he had any Spanish, Anne thought, and here he was talking like a native, as best as she could tell. *What more surprises do you have for me, Jack Rackam?*

Then, as if in answer to her question, another person pushed through the crowd, a young woman, twenty, if that. She was tall, slender, and her conservative church clothes could not hide her perfect figure, her voluptuous breasts. Her head was draped in a black *velo,* like the other women, but rather than making her look penitent or devout, the lacy fabric made her look more alluring still, like she was trying to hide her beauty. Thick black hair tumbled out from under it, framing a delicate face, a light olive complexion, and big, dark brown eyes.

She stepped toward Jack with a feline grace. *Just like I could move, once,* Anne thought bitterly. The young Cuban woman put her arms around Jack's neck and hugged him with an exuberance that went well beyond camaraderie or sisterly affection.

Anne scowled, looked over at Mary, and Mary gave her a cocked eyebrow, a hint of a shrug. She looked back at the little scene below, saw Jack disengaging the girl, holding her at arm's length, his composure not what it was. "Marie!" he said with somewhat feigned enthusiasm. "Marie, *elle es mi esposa,* Anne."

He turned and Marie turned and looked up at Anne, and Anne nodded a greeting to the girl. She watched demurely as Marie's thoughts and passions played across her face— confusion, realization, and then anger, the profound anger of a woman betrayed—and Anne thought, *So that is how it is.*

Jack held up his hand to Anne, to help her out of the boat. Anne stood, awkwardly, and she heard Marie gasp, saw her turn and push her way through the crowd, and Jack, uncertain now, looked from Anne to the place where Marie had been, and then back.

"It would appear she has not seen a woman quick with

child before," Anne said, acidly, "or at least not quick with your child."

Jack said nothing, just scooped her up in his arms and lowered her until her feet hit the beach. "She is a girl . . ." he whispered, "a silly infatuation . . ."

"Indeed." *As if I do not recognize the look of a scorned lover.* Jack hadn't mentioned this little wrinkle. "Are there any other girls here with 'silly infatuations'?" she asked in a harsh whisper. "Will I find a horde of half-white children here, with brown curly hair?"

"You will not, I assure you. What Marie De Jesús is about, I cannot reckon."

"De Jesús?" Anne grabbed Jack, half turned him around until they were face-to-face. "She is never the daughter of the family with whom we are to stay?"

"Well . . . yes . . ."

"Oh, this is brilliant, Jack, just bloody brilliant!"

"What? I see no problem with it . . ."

"No, Jack, you don't. And that, my dear, is half the problem right there."

The Pretty Annes leapt out of the boat and onto the warm sand, and while they did not receive the same enthusiastic greeting that Jack did, still it was clear that they were welcome, that the people of Caibarién did not regard them with the same disgust and fear that most honest citizens did.

They feasted that night, on local fare—black beans and fish and spicy goat meat—and the food and wine the buccaneers had plundered from the Havana brig. Long tables were set up in the town square. Torches fringed the open area, illuminating the place, giving it an appropriately festive air. A quartet of musicians played their Spanish-sounding airs. It was a raucous but civilized affair, a restrained bacchanal, and at the head of the table, Calico Jack Rackam, and beside him, his ersatz *esposa*, Anne Bonny.

It was a fine feast, and Anne would have enjoyed it thoroughly had it not been for Marie De Jesús, who sat with her family just a few feet down the table from them and with folded arms glared her hatred at Anne. There was something about the dark skin, the dark eyes, that made Marie look particularly threatening, and while Anne was not intimidated—it was unlikely that any woman or man could intimidate her—still she could not thoroughly relax with the young Cuban glaring at her.

"Jack, dear." Anne leaned over and spoke in a soft voice. "However is it that the De Jesúses welcome you into their house after you have seen your way to rogering their daughter?"

"Marie? I have never laid a hand on her. The De Jesúses know that perfectly well. I am not so very stupid nor randy that I can show no control, Annie. Nor can I help it if the dear young thing gets some silly infatuation."

"Hmm." Anne did not know whether to believe it. Jack certainly sounded sincere, though Marie would be a hard one to resist. Harder still, perhaps, with a pregnant wife with whom he had not had a flourish in two months.

Perhaps I shall show this dear young thing how things sit, Anne thought, and she leaned over, nestled against Jack, gave him a hungry kiss which he returned with enthusiasm and not a little surprise.

For a few minutes Anne lost herself in Jack Rackam, let him put his arms around her, envelop her, as she pressed close. She let the silent bond build, even as Jack continued on his other conversations, bantering loud in Spanish to his friends from the town and in English to the pirates, sometimes translating for one or the other.

Finally Anne looked down the table, met Marie's furious eyes with her own, gave her a look that said, *There. Now you know who owns Jack's heart.*

Marie held Anne's stare for a moment, and then the tears erupted from her dark eyes. She stood fast, knocked her chair over, and fled into the darkness.

"That was not so kind a thing to do," Mary, seated beside her, whispered in Anne's ear.

"Did you follow that?"

"I did. I hope she will not be trouble for you."

"I think not. I do not delight in such cruelty, you know. But sometimes one must mark one's territory."

"Perhaps you should have just pissed on Jack's leg."

"I might yet."

The festivities carried on late into the night and one by one the good people of Caibarién drifted away until at last there were only a few of the rougher sort left, along with the buccaneers, well into their cups, and the very weary Abuelito De Jesús.

At last Anne announced with finality, "Jack, dear, it is time we were off to bed," and obediently Jack stood and they followed Abuelito back to the De Jesús home.

It was a single-story house, but its cramped size was deceptive. Abuelito led them through the brightly painted front door and Anne was surprised to find not a tiny, dark hovel but an open courtyard that stretched away fifty feet to the back of the house.

Lanterns hung at regular intervals illuminated the courtyard enough to see the rough layout, the tall, lush plants, the little tile paths that crisscrossed it in a spoke pattern. There were columns all around the perimeter of the open space that supported a roof, and under the roof, nearly lost in the shadows, doors that led to the numerous rooms of the house. It looked like a hacienda, a monastery, and a Roman villa, all at once.

"Very nice . . ." Anne said, soft.

"Pirate gold, my dear," said Jack. "Calico Jack Rackam is not one to forget a kindness."

Abuelito De Jesús took down one of the lanterns, led them along the corridor that bordered one side of the courtyard, and stopped at last at a door near the end, which he opened and beckoned them through with a sweep of the arm.

The room was twelve feet square with a shuttered window that Anne guessed must look out on the road that ran along the side of the house. There was a large bed and a cross on the white stucco wall over its head. A washbasin with pitcher and bowl and night jar, a big wardrobe made of heavy planks, the door supported by wrought-iron hinges. Spartan, clean, inviting.

Abuelito said something in Spanish and Jack replied, *"La recámara está bien, Abuelito, gracias!"*

Abuelito nodded. *"Buenas noches,* Juan, *y* Señora Rackam, *buenas noches."* He set the lantern down on the floor and left them alone. Anne crossed the tiled floor and sat wearily on the edge of the bed.

"Will this answer, my love?" Jack asked.

"Famously. I won't pretend to be unhappy about being off the sloop, for the time being."

"This is a great improvement, I'll warrant."

"But are you not afraid of young Marie stealing in here and cutting your balls off, dear? These Spanish girls are hot tempered."

"My dear, I have told you, she is only a silly girl. In any event, Abuelito tells me she has gone off to visit her cousins in Santa Clara, a thing she has longed to do."

"A somewhat sudden departure, but I'll not quarrel with her decision. Come, Jack." She patted the bed. "Come and sit by me."

Jack sat down beside her, kicking his shoes off. They landed with a thump in the middle of the floor. Anne put her arms around his shoulders. "You will not mind this, Jack, staying here?"

"Never in life. I am as relieved as you to be off the sloop."

"Thank you, my dearest. I do not think I could endure this without you."

"Of course, my love. Of course."

"But you will never miss the sweet trade? I do not know how long my confinement will be, but I think it likely we will be here for six weeks. Two months, perhaps."

"Oh . . . oh . . ."

Anne straightened a bit, so she could see Jack's face. "Is that longer than you had thought, my dear?"

"Oh, well, the thing of it is . . ."

Anne knew what was coming, even before he said it. She felt her stomach turn over, felt as if her entire body were slumping down.

"My dear Annie, I fear you mistake it. I could never remain here for such a time. But," Calico Jack added brightly, "at the very instant you can go to sea once more, I shall return for you."

Chapter 25

MARY AND HER FELLOWS HAD INTENDED TO GO BACK to the sloop that night, but they did not make it.

They staggered as far as the soft sand, which was cool underfoot with the sun long gone, but difficult to walk on, even when sober. They made it to the longboat and stopped, catching their breath, looking out over the water in silence.

"So, Read, I was a-wondering . . ." It was Billy Bartlett with his shrill, ratlike voice, his tone always on the edge of mocking.

"What?"

"Well, now, when Annie has this little brat, will it have Jack's ugly face? Or yours? What say you?"

Silence, and a palpable tension among the men, and then Mary pushed off from the boat, stepped over to Bartlett. He was not much taller than she was and she looked him right in the eye. "What mean you by that?"

Bartlett shrugged. "I don't know . . ."

"What mean you by that, I asked. If you will not answer, then perhaps cold steel will loosen your tongue." She was angry and not in the least afraid of the mean little bastard, Billy Bartlett. She knew that killing him would not be frowned upon by the others, not in that circumstance. She knew that such rumors had to be quashed.

"Cold steel, is it?" Bartlett asked. "Do you challenge me to a fight, you little whore's son?" Bartlett spat. "Very well, then, I am for you!" His hand wrapped around the grip of his sword and Mary grabbed hers and then George Fetherston was between them, looming over them both, and his big hands pushed them both away.

"That's enough of that! Drink's in and wit's out, I say. We'll have no killing on so fine a night, and these here people so kind to us!"

And that was an end to it, because Bartlett was, in his heart, a coward and because Mary was not in the mood for a fight and because Fetherston was big enough and carried enough authority that he could put an end to such a thing, if he so chose.

"Come now," Fetherston said next, "let's get this damnable boat in the water."

They made a halfhearted effort to push the boat off the beach, but the enthusiastic men of Caibarién had pulled it far up the sand, and the falling tide had left it farther still from the water's edge, so they soon abandoned the project.

They sat heavily, reclining in the cool sand, ostensibly to rest from the effort of pushing the boat, and soon they were all asleep.

It was bright daylight when Mary opened her eyes. For a moment she did not move because she did not know where she was and she reckoned it was best to continue looking asleep, or dead, or however she looked.

And then she recalled, and she sat up with a groan and looked around. A few of her fellow pirates were already stirring, but most were still asleep and snoring loud. Out on the water, which looked like a thick sheet of light blue tinted glass, the fishing fleet of Caibarién was already at work, the one- and two-man crews of the canoes and pettiaugers hauling nets, the larger vessels standing out toward open water. The *Pretty Anne* was riding comfortably at her anchor, like a child's toy in a pond.

She stood, shook the sand off her clothes and out of her trousers, scratched. Looked around. It was lovely there, the white sand stretching away east and west, the line of vegetation that marched down to the beach where human hands had not beaten it back. She could hear the sounds of birds in the jungle, smell food cooking. Beneath it all, the sea was the town's leitmotif, the surf rushing up the sand, retreating, rushing again.

I wonder how Anne is faring. It was the first conscious thought to come to her. The second was, *I wonder if that Marie has cut Jack's balls off.* If she had not, Mary imagined that Anne might just do it for her.

No, not yet. Annie needed Jack. He was the father of her baby, and she needed him by her side, if for no other reason than the surprising fact that he spoke Spanish, and there did not seem to be anyone in the village who spoke English.

Father of her baby... The thought of having a baby gave Mary a dull ache inside. She wished she had had a baby. She thought of such a loving and helpless bundle of flesh, mewing, crying, nursing, a tiny person she might have created with her own body and nourished with her own body, a part of Frederick that would have carried on long after he was gone. It made her feel wistful and sad.

She breathed deep, pushed that aside. Rubbed a sore spot on her hip where she had apparently slept on the hilt of her cutlass, then headed up the beach toward the main road of Caibarién.

She was not sure where she was going, what she intended to do. *May as well find Annie, see what's acting,* she thought. It occurred to her that she did not know what Jack's plans were, if he intended to send the *Pretty Anne* on her way, without her captain, and have the sloop return later, or if he intended that the pirates remain at anchor for the next month or so. She wondered how long it would be before they wore out their welcome. Not long, she did not imagine.

She walked slowly up the wide central street, aware of the curious eyes that followed her, the children who peeked out of doorways, the old women who stopped their sweeping to watch her stroll by. She looked a fearsome sight, she realized, with her sea-battered clothing and her cocked hat pushed over her red damask headcloth, loaded down with weapons, which was the buccaneer's way.

Probably don't get many English pirates in these parts, she thought.

The houses were neat and well tended, though a closer look in the glare of the morning sun revealed a poverty that was not immediately apparent. There were patches of stucco peeled away from brick which had then been white-washed over, sections of tile missing from roofs, crude, home-built tables and chairs sitting just outside doorways.

Mary stopped a young boy who was stepping boldly toward the beach, a fishing pole over his shoulder. *"Garçon,"* she said, and only after she said it did she remember that that word was French.

Regardless, it worked. The boy stopped, cocked his head. *"Sí?"*

"Ahh . . . De Jesús? Juan Rackam?"

The boy's face lit up. *"Sí! Sí! El capitán Juan Rackam!"* He beckoned her follow, then reversed direction and headed up the street, and Mary had to nearly jog to keep up with him. At last he stopped at the bright red door of a modest house a block from the town square. *"Es la casa de De Jesús! El capitán Juan se queda con ellos!"* the boy exclaimed.

Mary did not understand the words, would not have understood even if the boy did not speak so very fast, but she caught "De Jesús" and "El capitán Juan" and she could deduce from that that this was where Jack and Anne were staying. She fished in the leather purse that was tied to her belt, fingered the first of the odd assortment of coins she happened to touch and pulled it out. It was Spanish piece of eight: she handed it to the boy.

"Gracias, gracias!" he said, his eyes as big as the coin, and then, apparently afraid that Mary would realize she had made a mistake in giving him such an ungodly sum, he raced off toward the beach.

Mary watched him run, chuckling to herself. She liked children, though she could count on her fingers the number of times she had had any contact with them. Then she knocked on the door.

A minute later it opened and Abuelita De Jesús was standing there. Her head was covered with a bright cloth, tied behind, and she was dressed in a coarse linen dress, washed so often it looked soft and nearly white, with a bright pattern of embroidery around the neck and the hems, a big airy garment, perfect for that climate.

Mary paused for a second, taken with how very comfortable it looked, how heavy and stifling her own coat and waistcoat and trousers and linen shirt were.

Before she could recover to speak, Abuelita De Jesús said, "*El capitán* Juan?"

"*Sí.*" She thought that meant yes, judging from the way the boy had used it.

And apparently she was right, because Abuelita opened the door wider, welcomed her in. She stepped through and found the door opened into a cool inner courtyard, with a garden and paths and a roof that overhung the various doors along the three other walls.

"*Esta muy bueno,*" Mary said, another bit of Spanish she had picked up the night before. She turned to Abuelita, unsure that she had said the right thing. The old Cuban woman was staring at her, a mixture of surprise and curiosity. And then the expression was gone from her face, whisked away by her own will.

La, she sees right through me! Mary thought, and suddenly she was afraid. *Will she tell the others?*

But Abuelita smiled, said, "*Gracias,*" so Mary guessed that her words had meant what she thought they meant, and that her secret would stop there. Those people at the bottom of the pyramid, Mary knew, learned to hold their secrets close.

She followed Abuelita along the corridor that skirted the courtyard, to an open door near the corner of the back wall. Abuelita paused, knocked on the doorframe. Jack, unseen in the room, called, "*Sí?*" and Abuelita replied, something in Spanish that did not contain any of the half dozen words Mary now possessed.

Jack stuck his head out the door. He was dressed only in his shirt and breeches. He looked Mary up and down; did not look overjoyed to see her, but said, "Ah, Read, good of you to come. Come in, come in!"

Mary nodded to Abuelita, stepped into the cool, spare,

but comfortable room. Anne was sitting on the edge of her bed, wearing only a shift. The thin cloth was piled up on her belly, pulled tight and spilling off like a frozen waterfall. There was a tenseness about her, a tight-lipped quality, and the tension emanated from her, filled the room.

"Ah, Mary, how good of you to come," Anne said, biting the words off. "I was afraid I would not see you before you sailed."

"Oh? Are we to sail this morning?"

"Yes. Yes you are. Is that not right, Captain Rackam?"

Jack ignored the sarcasm, busied himself with the wash-basin, wetting his face. "Yes, yes, when the winds turn offshore we will win our anchor."

We? Mary did not understand.

"But you will be back in a few months time, is that not right? Dear?" Anne said.

"Yes, yes, a few months."

"I . . ." Mary said, "I was not aware . . ."

"You see, my dear," Anne said, in a mock matter-of-fact tone, "it would never do for the notorious Calico Jack to be found loitering about the Cuban coast. The *Guarda del Costa* and all that, and you know how beastly these Spaniards can be. Besides, such vicious pirates as Jack's crew would not suffer to wait around here for some doxy to have a baby, and they can't sail without the captain, so he must be away. But I am in good hands, never doubt it." There was not the least bit of sincerity in her words; the sarcasm was thinly veiled. It was clear to Mary that she was repeating the arguments that Jack had made to her.

"Jack," Mary asked, "you intend to leave her here? Alone?"

Jack was applying lather to his face, studying himself in the mirror, too intent to meet her eye. "Nothing for it, I fear. I am as distraught as you." There was a hint of accusation in his voice, as if to say, *If she does not care to be left, she should not have gotten herself pregnant.*

Anne made a disgusted sound. Mary did not know what to say.

For a long moment it was quiet, the only sound the

scrape of Jack's razor across his cheeks. Mary imagined that Anne was at that moment thinking of stepping across the room, snatching the razor from Jack's hand, and cutting his throat with it. She was thinking the same thing herself. He would leave her among strangers, in a foreign land, in her condition, with not a word of Spanish, and sail off?

"I shall stay," Mary said with finality.

"Pardon?" Anne asked.

"I shall stay. You cannot be here alone. I will stay with you."

Anne smiled. The look of relief on her face was gratifying.

Jack turned at last, met Mary's eyes, smiled. He looked relieved as well. Mary wanted to slap him.

"Thank you, Read," Jack said. "I—"

"I'm not bloody doing it for you!" Mary cut him off. He closed his mouth, frowned.

"Thank you, sister," Anne said, soft.

"You are welcome. Now let us see to some breakfast."

They stood on the beach, side by side, their bare feet in the warm sand, and watched the *Pretty Anne* fill away on a quartering breeze. Two figures appeared on the topsail yard, Quick and Howard, it looked to Mary. They loosened off the topsail and let it tumble off the yard and hang in a gray pile of canvas. A minute later that sail was set and drawing and the *Pretty Anne* picked up speed, leaving them farther behind.

"That sloop was an honest merchantman the last time she sailed without me aboard," Anne said.

"The last time I saw her under way from a distance, I was an honest merchantman," Mary said.

"Quite the pair we make." Anne pulled her eyes from the sloop and looked at Mary. "I cannot tell you what it means, you staying this—"

Mary waved her hand. "I think your Jack was as glad to have me off the ship as you are to have me here."

"It is a queer sort of lovers' triangle we have, when just two of the three are lovers. And those two just barely, as of late."

"It is more the shame that Jack should be jealous of our friendship, but he loves you very much and he doesn't care to share you. It is a compliment to you, really, in an odd way."

Anne made a grunting noise. "Would a man who loves me leave me here, alone? And I *would* be alone were it not for you."

"He is a man. And a sailor. He is hardly accustomed to women who are not whores, never mind birthing and babies and such. It frightens him, I'll warrant. Don't be too harsh."

"Well, this is a defense from a quarter I did not reckon on. But let's no more of it. We'll be here for six weeks at least, I'd imagine. Let us make the most of our holiday."

"A good place for it. It is like paradise here."

Together they trudged back up the beach and up the main street to the De Jesúses' home. Before he sailed, Jack had arranged that they might both stay with the De Jesúses, that they could treat the house as their own, coming and going as they pleased.

And already Abuelita De Jesús, with her open, maternal way, had made them feel as welcome as family.

They returned in time for a dinner of tortillas and fish and rice. After that, they retired to their rooms for siesta, a Spanish custom that Mary found entirely civilized and agreeable.

She woke in the cooler hours of the late afternoon, kicked the thin blanket off and sat up in bed. She was wearing only her loose linen shirt, which hung down to her knees. It felt good, in that hot climate, to be so lightly dressed. It was rare indeed that she had the opportunity and the privacy to disrobe to that degree.

She sat for a moment, surveying the room. It was much like the one Anne occupied, the one in which she had spent her first night with Jack. A guest room? Marie's bedroom? Mary did not know. It did not look lived in.

There was a wardrobe, a heavy thing made of big planks

that might have been taken off a shipwreck, much like the one in Anne's room. Mary stood and walked over to it, opened one of the doors. She had expected to find it empty, but in fact there were a number of dresses there, soft, worn linen dresses like the kind Abuelita De Jesús wore, and shawls as well.

Mary picked one up, ran her fingers over it. Wondered if Abuelita had put it there for her use. It was old, but in good shape. One of Abuelita's perhaps, one that had not worn out before her girth had increased beyond its limits? Suddenly Mary could not endure the thought of putting on her man's clothing again.

She reached for the dress and then paused. Abuelita had seen right through her, but the others had not. What would they think, to see Mary go in the room a man and come out a woman? Perhaps they would find it a relief, to know that she was not a dangerous pirate after all. Or at least not a dangerous male pirate. If there was any talk of making a cuckold out of the beloved *Capitán* Juan, that would put an end to it, at least.

But would the others be so sanguine about so odd a thing? Mary wondered if she might be surprised by the *Pretty Anne*'s return and found out. Might someone in Caibarién give her secret away?

And then she knew that she no longer cared. She was too sick of worrying to worry anymore. The Caribbean was luring her deeper into its arms. She could not endure her European clothes, not there. She would not play the man there in paradise.

Mary smiled, laid the dress on her bed, and stripped off her linen shirt. She stood there for a moment, naked, let the cool air that came in through the slats of the shutters caress her body. She ran her hands over her stomach, her breasts. It felt so nice, hands on skin, even her own hands. The breeze raised little goose bumps all over her and made her even more sensitive to her own caresses.

Lord, it had been so long! So long since she had been naked at all, let alone naked with a man. Always on her guard on shipboard, never able to strip down, even in the worst heat. Sneaking off to some dark corner to furtively change when it was time to wash whatever suit of clothes she had on. It had become ingrained in her, second nature, but that was very different from liking it.

Mary picked up the dress and slipped it over her head. It was light, like gauze, and felt wonderful against her skin. She stepped over to the mirror above the basin, looked at herself.

Judging from the garment's size, it had been Abuelita's, and it hung on Mary like a burlap sack. She grabbed her wide leather belt, slipped the sheath knife and the pistol off, and fastened it around her waist, drawing the dress snug against her. The loose fabric, taken up in that way, accentuated her feminine figure, the curve of her hips, her breasts. She nodded at herself in the mirror.

The white garment set off her skin, which was tanned to a bronze color. With her dark hair she looked very much like a Cuban peasant girl, and she liked the look.

She reached behind her, untied the ribbon that held her hair clubbed, and unwrapped the sharkskin that bound it up in a tight cylinder. She let it fall loose, worked her fingers through it, fought through the tangles, straightened it as best she could, and finally draped it forward over her shoulders, then examined the results in the mirror.

"Mary Read, you are an attractive woman," she said to herself, smiling, but she meant it. As objective as she could be—and she was not a particularly gentle critic, not with herself—she had to admit that she did look good.

She ran her hands down the dress, smoothed the cloth out, felt her hard body under the linen. There was almost nothing to the dress, just the thin cloth between herself and the cool air of the late afternoon. No linen shirt, no waistcoat, no long wool coat, no slop trousers, no shoulder belt with cutlass hanging from it, no sheath knife. She felt practically naked and it felt wonderful.

She adjusted her hair again. *I must show Annie,* she thought, and hurried from the room.

Outside Anne's door she paused, gave a soft rap.

"Come," Anne called from inside, and Mary swung the door open.

Anne was standing at the window, her back to Mary, looking out over the narrow street. She turned as Mary entered, mouth open to say something, but she paused and her eyebrows came together, confused, and for an instant Mary could see that she did not recognize her.

Despite herself, Mary giggled, and even as she did she thought, *Dear Lord, when was the last time I giggled?*

"Mary? Mary Read?" Anne stepped slowly across the room, then took Mary by the shoulders. "My God, will you look at this! You really are a woman! I was starting to doubt it," Anne teased, spun her around to see her from all sides, fingered her long, dark hair. "You look absolutely lovely, my dear. Does it feel wonderful?"

"Yes, it does. Annie, I cannot tell you."

"I have more of these silk dresses, the ones we took from the schooner, if you would fancy something more elegant?"

"Never, Annie, dear, and I would wish you would chuck those silly things and get a dress such as mine. The people here, they know a thing or two about living in this climate. It is folly to dress like it is London when you are in the Caribbean."

"You are right about that, Mary, dear. Abuelita left me a linen dress such as yours and I will put it on directly."

She crossed the room, closed the shutters, and peeled off her short jacket and petticoat skirts. "Be gone, London! Be gone, Charles Town!" she said as she tossed the garments on the bed. She peeled off her long wool stockings and discarded those, then lifted her shift over her head and tossed it aside as well. She was entirely naked.

Mary watched, a little uncomfortable, a little embarrassed, but determined not to show it. She did not know if she had ever been in the company of a naked woman before. But Annie seemed to have not the least embarrassment, which in the main was not surprising. Anne did not embarrass easily.

Mary watched her as she moved to the wardrobe, opened it, and found the linen dress. Anne Bonny was a beautiful woman. Her arms and face were dark tan, like Mary, and the rest of her a creamy white. Her skin was smooth, perfect, a sensuous run from her buttocks up the small of her back to her shoulders and neck, partially hidden by thick reddish blond hair.

Her belly swelled out full, like a sail in a good wind. Mary thought she would not look nearly as beautiful if she were not pregnant. There was a certain quality that being quick with child gave her. Mary knew that Anne thought herself clumsy, no longer sleek and feminine, but that was not the case at all. Now she looked like a woman, full of life, creating life.

Anne slipped the dress over her head, shuffled it into place. The fabric was just the slightest bit taut over her belly. "I guess this is one of Abuelita De Jesús's dresses," she said. "Fits well. She and I are of a size, it would appear."

"Yes, but you will be much reduced shortly. Now pray, do not whine about your big belly. It grows tiresome. Shall we promenade?"

"We shall. Though this ain't Pall Mall, I'll warrant."

"No, and we ain't fine ladies of the court, either, so taken as a whole, it is as it should be."

They left Anne's room, walked arm in arm along the little courtyard, and bid good day to Abuelita De Jesús as they passed. Mary was impressed with the old woman; she gave no more than an open smile, a nod of the head, a few friendly and unintelligible words in Spanish. No hint of a reaction to the drastic change in her houseguest.

"I suspect," said Anne, "that Abuelita is pleased to find you are not some brute of a pirate, even if she is a little surprised by your transformation."

"I am pleased myself to find I am not a brute of a pirate. But as to Abuelita, she saw the truth of me right off."

Mary opened the bright red door and they stepped out of the house. The shadows were long, the air warm and still in the early evening.

They walked slowly up the gently sloping road to the town square. The square was like the hub of a wheel, with

various roads like uneven spokes running in different directions in an unplanned, haphazard sort of way. There was
the main street of the town, which ran right down to the
water. Also the wide, uneven road that connected Caibarién
to the larger town of Santa Clara, fifty miles inland. That
road, and the sea, were the only avenues of communication
between Caibarién and the rest of the world.

In the middle of the square a low brick wall formed a
circle which contained within it a small flower garden, and
in the middle of the garden a statue of the Blessed Virgin,
who, despite her somewhat gaudy paint, looked serenely
out over the town of Caibarién.

Anne and Mary sat on the low wall, looked in the direction that the Virgin was staring. At their backs, the big
church, and beyond that, the jungle with its wild sounds.
The thick perfume of the vegetation engulfed them. Somewhere in the town someone was playing a guitar; the music
came soft on the air, like the smell of the flowers.

"If we are to be abandoned, I reckon this is the place for
it," Anne mused.

"Hmm," Mary agreed. It was peaceful, and peace was
something she had not known in a long, long time. And
she had a friend, and that was something rarer still.

It occurred to her that she could spend the rest of her
days there, that she would not be heartbroken if Calico Jack
and the others never returned at all.

Chapter 26

FOR A WEEK AFTER THE *PRETTY ANNE* SAILED, THE
women enjoyed a reprieve from work or consideration.
They explored the town, sampled the local fare, watched
with professional interest as the men put out in their boats

in the morning and returned in the afternoon, generally loaded with fish.

They strolled the town square in the evenings, taking the air the way most of the people did: bachelors out to be seen, pretty young women under their mothers' watchful eyes, large families whose children moved like schools of fish in the open plaza.

Anne and Mary were curiosities at first, the pirate's wife and the woman who had dressed like a man, and a pirate at that. But the people were polite, the men bowed, the women smiled friendly smiles, and Anne and Mary were careful never to do anything that might cause offense in that culture, strange to them.

It was a lovely, quiet time. Mary reveled in it. Anne chafed and grew more sullen.

She has not seen real hardship in her life, Mary thought as she watched Anne staring out to sea, silent and pouting. *She is a girl, she does not understand the luxury of quiet, the gift of such peace.*

As the first week folded into the second, Mary decided they should pitch in, help with the work of running the De Jesús household. Earn their bread. She was certain that a good dose of labor would shake Annie from her ennui.

Anne did not agree, and she did not care for Mary's suggestions to the contrary. By midweek Mary managed to prod her into a desultory stab at housework, but it was short-lived. Anne slept later each morning. Their conversation dwindled away to an uncomfortable silence.

Friday night Anne would not budge from her room.

"Come, Princess Anne, let us go for our promenade," Mary said, as brightly as she could.

"Not tonight. I am not well."

"You'll be a damned sight less well if you just lie about."

"Oh, you are so certain. Are you a bloody physician? Have you had a baby? You do not know how goddamned hard it is for me to waddle about."

Mary scowled, let the anger and pain she felt from those lashing words show on her face. Something had changed in Anne, something had broken. Perhaps she was collapsing under the weight of her concerns, the physical difficulty of bearing a child. Perhaps she was frightened; that would not be unreasonable. Whatever it was, it was time for Anne to bear up to it. Time for her to show some fortitude.

"No, I have not had a baby," Mary said at last. "But I have seen enough people waste away with despair that I know lying about is no help."

"Go bloody lecture someone else," Anne snapped, and turned away. Mary remained for a moment more, then spun on her heel with military precision and stamped out.

She did not see Anne at all the next day. To the best of her knowledge Anne did not emerge from her room.

Sunday morning and Mary woke to the sound of the church bells, tolling nearby. She sat up. Someone rapped on the door.

"*Sí?*" Mary was making an effort to pick up all the Spanish she could.

Abuelita De Jesús opened the door. "*Quieres ir a misa?*" she asked, but Mary did not understand. She shook her head, shrugged her shoulders.

"*A la iglesia?*" Abuelita asked again. She pointed in the general direction of the bells, made the sign of the cross, and said, "*En nombre de Padre, del Hijo y el Espíritu Santo . . .*"

"Ahh!" Mary said. *She is asking do I want to go to church!* Mary had never been one for church. She had gone regularly as a girl, and she and Frederick had attended while they live in Breda, but beyond that she had not really been much of a churchgoer. Soldiers and sailors tended not to be.

She certainly had never attended a Roman Catholic church.

But presented with the question, she found that there was something appealing in the notion. She nodded. "*Sí, sí.*"

"*Y la señora* Rackam?"

Anne. Mary was still irritated with her, her spoiled, girlish ways. Anne had to be dragged from the muck of self-pity in which she was wallowing, and again it fell on Mary to do it.

"Sí," Mary said. *We'll make Annie go as well,* she thought. *Do her soul some good.*

Mary dressed quickly, covering her head with a black *velo* provided by Abuelita De Jesús, and then went to Anne's room, knocked on the heavy door.

"What?" Anne's muffled voice came through the wood. Without invitation, Mary opened the door and stepped in.

Anne was lying on the bed, the blanket and sheets rumpled around her. The room was dark with just a hint of light leaking in around the shutters. Anne's arm was flung over her eyes. She did not look at Mary.

"Abuelita has asked if we wish to attend church. I am going. I think you should as well."

"Do you, now?"

"Yes. I do."

Anne lowered her arm, looked over at Mary. She heaved herself up on her arm, swung her legs off the edge of the bed, and Mary smiled, thinking that Anne was at last taking proper direction.

"You reckon I should go to a popish church? Are you asking me to accompany you, or ordering me to attend?"

Mary's smile faded. "I think it would do you good."

Anne nodded. "I'll bloody bet you do. And you my self-appointed guardian." Anne looked away, stared off into a dark corner of the room.

"What offense I have given you, I do not know," Mary said, the words like a growl in her throat, "but I'll not suffer your childish tantrums!"

Anne turned, looked back, held Mary's eyes. "Oh, no? Well, see here, Mistress Read, I've had a bellyful of you. I was pleased you wished to stay with me. You were my friend, or so I thought, and I needed a friend when Jack deserted me. But now you seem to style yourself my mother, or husband, or captain, or some damned thing that I neither need nor want. When you are done being those things, then perhaps I shall give a damn what you have to say."

"Well, then, damn you for an ungrateful wench! Do you

think I am pleased, rotting away here, holding your rutting hand, you simpering little brat?"

"Yes, I do. I think you are damned happy, and I think you are never so happy as when you are directing another's life. Why don't you try directing your own goddamned life, for once!"

Mary scowled. All of the replies that came to her mind crowded together, all trying to leave her mouth at once, and none could get out. She turned, slammed the door, stamped across the courtyard and out the big front door to the street.

Stupid, stupid girl. Stupid, spoiled, pigheaded little girl.

Mary stepped furiously up the street, smarting and silently cursing Anne and cursing herself for stupidly wasting time with such a foolish child. Without thinking, she joined the stream of people converging on the town square and filing into the big church.

In the two weeks they had been there, Mary had not been inside the church, and what she saw surprised her, so much that, for the moment, Anne Bonny flew from her thoughts.

The nave rose forty feet over her head. The roof was supported by a crisscross of plastered beams that made an elaborate geometric pattern. Mary studied it and the walls as well as she worked her way toward the chancel.

Along each wall, stained-glass windows twenty feet high depicting in their medieval style some saint or other. And between them, intricately carved bas-relief statues of the Stations of the Cross.

Over the altar the ceiling rose higher still, and every inch of space from the chancel to the back wall was covered with paintings of saints, paintings of scenes from heaven, Latin words picked out in gold. It was magnificent, entirely surprising in that little fishing village, a monument to their devotion.

Mary realized she was holding up the people behind her, stopping in the middle of the aisle and staring up. She stepped forward, saw that the others genuflected before entering a pew, so she did as well. She hoped her doing so would not give offense as she straightened and shuffled to her seat.

She knelt with her hands pressed together and her arms on the back of the pew in front of her because that was what everyone else did. She tried to think of God and Jesus and perhaps even conjure up a prayer, but her anger at Anne had flared again and she could get nothing else into her head.

Stupid, spoiled girl . . .

Mary had pegged her for a silly tart the first time she had seen her, and now she wondered that they had ever become friends, of a sort. What basis was there for friendship between them? Mary, with all she had suffered, and Anne, not but a silly girl, lacking the most basic understanding.

Mary stood with the others as the priest and his altar servers stepped solemnly down the aisle, cross and Bible held aloft. She let her eyes linger on his elegant robes and vestments, trailing down almost to the floor, richly embroidered. She was mesmerized by the slow swinging of the censer, the puffs of sweet-scented smoke coming out in little gray clouds.

She stood and sat and knelt with the rest as the priest, his back to the faithful, carried on the mass in a singsong Latin, couched in his thick Spanish accent. There was something old and comforting about the service, something solid and immutable, that gave her a profound feeling of serenity even though she did not understand a word of it.

Mary felt her thoughts calm and settle with the hypnotic rhythms of the ancient liturgy. She felt her anger change into something else. Pity. Sympathy, perhaps. Anne would never be anything but a silly, spoiled child if she remained so obstinate, if she could not understand the things that Mary tried to teach her. Like Frederick, Anne needed her. Like Hans and countless other soldiers and sailors she had helped.

Mary opened her eyes, stared off at nothing.

Why don't you try directing your own life, for once. She heard the words in her head.

Oh, dear God . . .

Might it be that Anne possessed more insight than Mary

had ever realized? Was it possible that silly, spoiled Anne Bonny understood something about her that she herself did not even see?

"Me lo das," Mary said, reaching for the basket of laundry in Abuelita De Jesús's hands, trying to get the woman to surrender it.

"No, no, está bien. Puedo hacerlo," Abuelita protested.

"No, yo puedo . . ." The closest that Mary could come to "I will do the laundry. I insist" in Spanish was "I do . . ." accompanied by the forceful removal of the basket from Abuelita's hands, but it made the point.

"Sí, sí, gracias . . ." Abuelita said, genuinely grateful, as she always was, for the help.

Mary held the basket at her side, resting it on her hip for support, and walked down the corridor along the courtyard to Anne's room. She paused at the closed door, took a deep breath, and knocked.

"What?"

Mary paused again. "Might I come in?"

A short silence, and then, "Yes."

Mary opened the door. The room looked the same as it had the day before, when she had asked Anne to join her at mass. Dark and unkempt. But now it was starting to smell of old sheets and Anne's unwashed body.

Anne was sitting on the bed. Her eyebrows were pressed together. She looked as if she was bracing for a fight. Mary maneuvered the laundry basket through the door, stepped into the room.

"What now?" Anne said. "Will you order me to the stream to beat shirts with a bloody rock? Would that be good for me?"

Mary did not respond. The past day had been one of great introspection, strolling on the hot-sand beach, examining her life. She felt that she understood more about herself than she had in a dozen years. She felt that some truth had been beaten out of her by Anne's lashing tongue.

"No, I will not try to order you. Nor will I give advice, ever again, unless it is asked of me. I am going down to the stream to do laundry. If you would come with me, I would admire your company." She paused and then added, "Without you I have no friend in the world."

Anne's expression softened, and her face took on an expression very like relief. For a moment the two women remained silent, regarding one another. Then Anne nodded her head. "I should be delighted to accompany you. I reckon some fresh air would set me up well."

She stood and pulled her sleeping gown off and walked awkwardly to the wardrobe.

Mary had a notion that most women would have broken down in tears, would have hugged one another and apologized over and over for their behavior. But she and Annie were not like most women, far from, and that was ultimately the bedrock foundation of their friendship. This reconciliation seemed just the right measure for who they were.

Anne was profoundly relieved to have her friend back. She loved Mary. She had loved her as a man, loved her more as a woman. But she was not such a chucklehead that she was blind to Mary's faults.

Mary was utterly self-assured, and Anne much admired that in her. But that same quality could make her patronizing, which Anne hated bitterly. She had spent a lifetime being patronized, had joined with the pirates to escape that very thing. She did not need more of it, especially from the one person from whom she would expect better.

On board the ship, before she was quick with child, Anne could smile and nod and say nothing. But her pregnancy had changed things. She was more sensitive, more easily offended, less able to endure the foibles of others.

At last she could take no more. The simple pleasure that Mary took in strolling around that insufferably dull town grated on her. Mary's insistence that she knew best what

was good for Anne was beyond endurance. When she finally lashed out at Mary, it was as vicious as she could
make it, using the words that would cut the deepest. She
hated herself for it, but she could not stop.

After Mary left that first night, Anne wept until she fell
asleep, remorseful and alone. She could not get out of bed
all the next day, but lay there on her filthy sheets and wal-
lowed in her loneliness and despair.

But when Mary returned with her cocky attitude about
attending church, Anne did it again. She could not hold it
in, any more than she could keep her child forever in her
womb. And again she cried herself to sleep.

Anne's emotions were like a stampede, out of control.
She wanted to apologize, to swallow her anger, but she
could not. When Mary stepped into her room carrying that
basket of laundry, the mere sight of it, the anticipation of
what Mary would say, made her wild.

But instead Mary held out the olive branch, and Anne
accepted it, gladly.

And Mary was true to her word. She did not lecture, she
did not patronize, and Anne loved her more dearly still.

She went with Mary to keep her company, and even
helped wash the laundry in the stream. They were friends
again. They promenaded in the evening. Three times a
week they did the wash. Sometimes they would go down
to the beach for walks by the water, sometimes to the river,
and if they were alone, they would go to the place they had
discovered where the thick jungle obscured the river and
they would strip down and plunge in themselves.

They talked and rarely ran out of things to say, and when
they did, the silence was never uncomfortable. Time slipped
by like a boat on calm water. Anne felt herself grow bigger
and more awkward and she hid her secret fears of childbirth
and felt the identity that she had so carefully crafted for
herself slipping further and further away.

*A month and a half, festering away in goddamned Caibar-
ién,* Anne thought, sitting on her bed, running a brush
through her hair. If Mary had not stayed, if they had not
come to a genuine understanding, then Anne was certain
she would have shot herself already.

She heard Mary's feet on the tiles outside her door and
then she appeared in the doorway, a basket under her arm.
"I am off to do laundry," Mary said. "Will you join me?"

"Laundry? You jest, I am sure. I doubt that I can fit
through the door any longer, let alone waddle down to the
stream and bang shirts with a bloody rock."

Anne was quite large, her belly button inverted, the skin
on her stomach tight as a drum. Abuelita said it would not
be long now, and Abuelita knew about such things.

Anne sat on her bed, brush in hand, seeing Mary and the
basket of wash, and thought, *She likes this. Dear God, she
likes this housekeeping horseshit.*

"I won't expect you to bang anything with a bloody rock,
dear," Mary said, "but I should like your company."

"Very well." Anne put her wide straw hat on her head,
tied the ribbon around her chin. "I shall follow your leader,
my Captain General." Anne, who chafed at routine and do-
mesticity, could not fathom Mary's enthusiasm for such
things.

*I suppose if I had lived Mary's life, I would desire a bit
of peace myself.*

Slowly, bit by bit, over the weeks, the broad outlines of
Mary's history had come out. Nothing very intimate—dates
and places mostly—but still Anne was getting a more complete picture of who her friend was.

Mary led the way down a side street that led to the thick
jungle that bordered the western end of the town. The last
of the dusty streets trailed off into a broken and rocky riv-
erbank, at the bottom of which ran a respectable stream,
twenty feet across and five feet deep, tumbling down from
the high mountains in the center of the island and emptying
into the ocean two hundred yards away.

The river was everything to the town: fresh water, washtub, moat to keep the western jungle at bay. It was the reason the town was built where it was.

Anne sat heavily on a big, smooth rock, wiped her brow with her hand. Even a short walk was becoming a real effort. She wondered if she was carrying twins.

Mary dropped the basket at the edge of the river. She pulled the back hem of her dress up between her legs, tucked it in her waist, "girding her loins" as women had done from biblical times, and earlier, no doubt. She picked up the basket, trudged a few feet into the river. She pulled out a shirt, submerged it, spread it out for pounding with a rock.

They were the only two there, which was unusual, but Anne was glad for it. She did not care to make fumbling conversation in her rudimentary Spanish.

"You like this," Anne said.

"What? Doing wash in a river? Not particularly."

"No, not just the wash. All this. This keeping house. Given all the adventure you have seen, I am surprised you can endure such monotony outside a week."

"Hmm," Mary said. "Well, it is a new thing for me. I can say that. Even as a young girl I did not do so very much of it because, of course, my mother was pretending I was a boy and she did not want to reveal the truth of me. I reckon if I had been bred to it, I would not be so enthusiastic."

They were quiet for a moment, the only sound the click of Mary's rock working on the shirt and the rushing sound of the water, the occasional screech of a bird. Anne wanted to ask more, tried to get a sense for Mary's mood. If her mood was not just right, the questions would be rebuffed.

"When . . . you were married, did you not set up house-keeping?"

Mary paused in her washing, looked up at Anne, squinting in the brilliant sun. For a few seconds she said nothing, just held Anne's eyes, as if trying to determine what to say, how much to reveal. Then she went back to her washing.

"No, I did not, not really . . ." Mary said at last. Anne sat silent, listening, not wanting to interrupt or break the train of Mary's thought. She knew her friend had been married once, had lived in Flanders, but she knew nothing beyond that.

"Believe it or not," Mary continued, "I had servants to do it." She gave a little chuckle at the memory. "Here I am pounding shirts with a rock, and then I had servants."

She looked up again. Anne was silent, did not move. "I met my husband while I was riding with Walpole's light horse. His name was Frederick. Frederick Heesch. And he was the kindest, gentlest man that ever lived. And he was brave, brave to a fault . . ." Her eyes looked far away; she did not seem to be looking at Anne anymore.

"I don't think I ever told him that, but it was so. Oh, he was not much of a soldier, wasn't cut out for that. But one can be brave, you know, without having all the skills one might wish. It is a dangerous combination, as you can imagine.

"After I fell in love with him, and that was not so long after I met him, I can assure you, I would not suffer him to go into a fight without me. Saved him many times, many times. No, bravery and a dearth of military skill, it don't answer.

"We were tentmates, Frederick and me, if you can believe it . . ."

Anne sat quietly and listened. Mary talked as she washed, spinning out an incredible tale of love in the most unlikely of circumstances, of shared dreams and a unique realization of joy. Anne was mesmerized, drawn by Mary's bluntness into the simple narrative.

She stumbled over the words, she backtracked, filled in bits she had missed. It had none of the quality of a story often repeated. Mary was pulling it from her inner self, unearthing it from a place in her soul where it had been long buried.

Anne understood the difficulty and the pain of that process. She understood the trust and the profound friendship that the telling of it represented, and she listened, respectful, silent.

"When I could no longer support myself I sold the inn,

let everyone go. I dressed as a man again, served a bit in an infantry unit near the wilderness . . ."

Dear God, dear God, Anne thought. *What this poor girl has suffered . . .* She listened to Mary's simple tale and felt as if she, too, knew Frederick Heesch and loved him as Mary did and grieved for his passing.

Lord, I willingly tossed away all the things that this poor girl has ever desired. What sort of a spoiled little doxy am I?

Anne flushed at the thought of her own petulant behavior, felt ashamed that she had ever thought that the things she had endured constituted suffering. As she listened to Mary she understood that she had not a clue as to what real suffering was.

Mary was tight-lipped as she spoke, holding back tears. "And then I went to Amsterdam and found a berth aboard the *Hoorn.* The rest I reckon you know."

Silence again, save for the rushing water. Anne stood awkwardly and waded out to Mary. Mary straightened, turning toward her, and Anne reached out with open arms. Mary fell into them, all but collapsing against Anne, and buried her face in Anne's shoulder. They stood like that for a moment, and then Anne could see Mary's shoulders convulsing in tears, could hear the sobs muffled by her own shoulder.

She said nothing. There was nothing to say. She just held Mary, let the tears pour out, soak through the thin fabric of her peasant dress. Mary's silence was a dam, and as long as it held, the tears would not come. But she had breached the wall now, she had told her friend the full tale, and the tears flowed unchecked.

It is better, it is better this way, Anne thought. Like draining a wound. It could not be healthy to keep all that inside.

At last Mary straightened, looking at Anne with red and puffy eyes. "Thank you . . ." she said.

Anne reached out, running her fingers along Mary's cheek, and brushed her hair away from her face. "I grieve that I did not have the chance to meet your Frederick," she said.

Mary nodded. "You would have approved of him, I'll warrant."

"I know I would have. It is a tragedy that his life was so short. Though if he had not met you, if you had not ridden out with him in battle, it would have been shorter still. And far less joyful. He would never have had his inn."

Mary nodded and the look on her face suggested that she had not thought of that before. "Thank you . . ."

"Of course, my dear. Frederick was no less than you deserve. And your telling me this, after all this time, it makes me think you are finding some happiness again in your life."

Mary nodded. "I am. Peace. I am finding some peace," she said, and then laughed, a short laugh. "I don't reckon most people turn to piracy to find peace."

"You are not most people. Far from it, my dear."

"I do not know why I remained on the Continent for so very long."

"Indeed. A short life and a merry one, that is our motto."

Mary smiled. "It's to be preferred to a long life of misery, I'll warrant."

"Come, let us go home now. In your enthusiasm you have beat those clothes near to rags. If I do not mistake it, Abuelita will have some of those fish things for our dinner, and I am famished enough that even those sound good."

Mary gathered up the wash, put it in the basket, and waded out of the stream. She let her dress down again and the two women walked back along the warm, dusty road to the De Jesús home.

"Quiet this afternoon," Mary said. The streets seemed deserted. "Is it siesta time, already?"

"It couldn't be. Perhaps it is one of the popish feast days. They seem to have one every other day or so."

"Perhaps . . ." Mary's instincts were telling her something was wrong; Anne could tell without asking. And that made Anne wary as well, because she trusted Mary's instincts more than her own.

They crossed the main street, also deserted, to the red front door of the De Jesús home. Anne opened it, holding it open for Mary to carry the basket through, and then stepped inside behind her.

Abuelita De Jesús was standing there, facing the door, her hands clasped together, clenching them nervously. She looked frightened.

"*Cómo estás?*" Mary asked, and then someone behind them slammed the heavy door shut.

Anne and Mary whirled around. Against the wall, half-hidden in shadow, stood soldiers, half a dozen of them. Their uniforms—blue coats with red facings, once white waistcoats and shirts—were stained and dusty. Some wore breeches, some the loose trousers worn by Cuban peasants. They held dilapidated muskets in their hands. Long stringy hair stuck out from under battered cocked hats. They each had the leer of criminals, depraved, avaricious. They looked like pirates, only worse.

One of the solders stepped forward, a greasy fellow with round belly and high boots. He had an epaulet on one shoulder, and Anne guessed him to be the commanding officer, if there was such a thing.

"*Ellas son los pirates inglesas?*" he asked.

Abuelita De Jesús shook her head. "*No, no, no hay piratas inglesas. . . .*"

Anne had little Spanish, but she did not need much to follow what was happening. The soldiers had been sent to find English pirates rumored to be in Caibarién. They must have come from Santa Clara, it was the closest town of any note. But how would they know about the pirates' visit?

And then it came to her: Marie.

Anne had to smile, despite the predicament they were in. Of course. A woman scorned thus would not pause before sending the soldiers to hang them all. She would have, were she Marie.

Now I wish I had just pissed on Jack's leg, she thought.

The discussion was taking place in rapid Spanish, and Anne and Mary could do no more than listen and try to guess what was being said. Whatever argument Abuelita

De Jesús was mounting seemed to have little effect. The Spanish officer was clearly having none of it, and the others were shuffling closer, grinning more lasciviously.

"Si no hay piratas para ahogar, quizás encontraremos placer con sus mujeres," the officer said. He stepped up to Mary, ran his fat fingers over her cheek. Mary shied away, with barely repressed revulsion.

What the hell are they doing here now? Anne wondered. It was well over a month since Marie had left town in her fury. But then, the Spaniards were never too quick to their duty.

Anne did not know what the officer said, but she understood his intentions clearly enough. The soldiers would have some satisfaction before they left. If they could not arrest pirates, then they would rape the pirates' women. First the officer, then the others, one at a time.

Maybe that is it . . . maybe they did not care to fight pirates . . . waited till the men were certain to be gone . . .

She looked around, searching for some way out. But the soldiers had managed to surround them, nearly. Six armed men against three unarmed women, one old, one nine months pregnant, and all the men of the village out fishing. She felt the first inkling of panic creeping over her. She could see no escape.

One of the greasy men in the tattered peasant trousers stepped up behind Mary, ran his bony fingers through her hair, and smiled, displaying his rotting and intermittent teeth.

Very well, Mary, what do we do now? Anne thought.

And then Mary did the one thing Anne did not expect, the one thing she would never have expected from her battle-hardened friend. Mary screamed. Loud, hysterical, feminine, a sound of pure runaway panic, of mindless terror.

She dropped the laundry basket and screamed again, her eyes wide, her hands balled up in fists. She pulled her hair free of the soldier's hand, whirled around, shoved two of the surprised men aside, and bolted for the door. She jerked it open as the soldiers lunged for her and missed and she ran shrieking out into the street.

Through the open door Anne could see Mary running, still screaming in terror, as she abandoned Anne and Abuelita De Jesús to their fate.

Chapter 27

MARY RAN AS HARD AS SHE COULD. IN FRONT OF HER, the dusty road, on either side, the whitewashed stucco homes, shoulder to shoulder, seemed to fly past. Her legs kicked at the long dress as she ran.

She was screaming, loud and hysterical, but the voice seemed disembodied, as if it were coming from somewhere else, and her throat, burning with the effort, was the only proof that it was really her making that unearthly sound.

Come on, come on, you sons of whores. Her mind was moving fast, like her feet. She looked over her shoulder, wide-eyed, and screamed louder, thought, *Three of them, at least . . . three are following me . . .*

Up the gently sloping street, where just the evening before she and Anne had gone for their stroll. Up ahead, bobbing in her vision, the big church, so familiar to her now, so comforting. She had thought at first to go there, but realized now that this business could not be done in that hallowed place.

Twenty yards more, another frantic look over her shoulder. The one who had run his hand through her hair was gaining, pulling away from his comrades.

Ten more yards, Mary's breath was coming fast. *Now, now, now!*

She stumbled on some imaginary obstacle, took a few faltering steps, and fell, face-first, hands outstretched to block her fall. She hit the road in a cloud of dust, rolled on her back, screaming, shielding herself with crooked arm.

The soldier, ten feet behind, came at her, his pace never slackening, his broken-tooth leer obscene. Mary screamed again. Three paces and he was over her and she braced herself with her elbows, cocked her leg, and drove her calloused heel right into his crotch, grunting with the effort.

The impact was solid and direct. Her leg jarred and the soldier was lifted inches off the ground and his eyes went wide and he doubled over, forward. But Mary was ready for that, because that was what they always did, and she snatched his musket even as he was dropping it and rolled clear as he collapsed in the place where she had been.

It was one fluid motion for her: roll to her left and push herself up to her feet, come up with musket held at the charge bayonet stance, butt at her hip, the end of the muzzle at eye level, sorry that there was no bayonet there.

Here was the next of the soldiers, still running hard to catch up, though she was no longer running. She could see the confusion on his face. He tried to stop, but his momentum carried him along and she drove the end of the barrel into his stomach.

The wind was knocked from him, blown out like the last breath of a dying man. He, too, doubled over forward, and as his face went down it met Mary's knee coming up and he was snapped back and fell spread-eagle in the dust.

He had not even come to rest before Mary was stepping over him, going after the third man, who had stopped short, who was not so callously plunging into the fray.

No gunshots, no gunshots, she reminded herself. She flipped the musket over, held it by the barrel, club fashion, and descended on the third man, who had come to a halt five feet from the crazy woman. He hesitated, took a tentative step back, as if trying to assess what had happened, how this amusing pursuit, this whimsical prelude to rape, had suddenly turned so completely around.

Mary brought the musket back, like she was chopping a tree with an ax, and then the soldier understood that the danger was real. He shouldered his weapon, thumbed back the flintlock, and tried to train it on Mary just as Mary's musket came around and slammed into the side of his head, knocking him from his feet. He hit the road on his right shoulder, sent the dust flying, and did not move again.

Mary stood for a second, catching her breath, searching the road and the perimeter of the square for further pursuit. She was not in the Caribbean anymore, not in the blissfully tranquil town of Caibarién. She was back in the mud and shit of Flanders, Spain, France. She was a soldier again, slipped into that frame of mind like an old coat, where survival was paramount, victory second, and moral considerations a far distant third.

The soldier who had caught the musket on the side of the head was not moving, and Mary did not think he would again, but the other two were thrashing, moaning, starting to recover. Bam, bam, the butt of her musket came down on their heads and they were still, and because they were no longer a part of her tactical considerations, Mary had no more thought for them.

She rolled the men over with her foot. They did not carry pistols, she was sorry to see, but pistols were an officer's weapon and she did not really expect to see them. She took up a musket, checked the priming in the pan, and slung it over her shoulder. She picked up a second one, checked the priming, pulled a bayonet from one of the motionless soldiers' belts, fixed it onto the musket barrel, and she was off.

Back down the road she ran, the familiar road, the familiar sight of a musket and bayonet in front of her, but the two did not go together. Twenty feet away, the red door of the De Jesús home, and her eyes were fixed on that.

The door swung open and out stepped the fat one with the officer's epaulet and an expression of mild irritation as he looked up the road for his absent men. His eyes met Mary's, his eyebrows came together in surprise, then his mouth came open in fear and then Mary drove the bayonet through his chest, drove it right up to the muzzle end with all the momentum she had gathered running downhill.

The officer made a strangled, gurgling sound and Mary

jerked the bayonet free, wheeled around, and charged through the door.

Anne and Abuelita De Jesús were on their knees, and flanking them, the two remaining soldiers. Mary thumbed the flintlock as she burst through the door, leveled the gun and fired into the soldier standing by Abuelita, and he was blown away before he even knew what had happened.

Mary let the gun fall, whipped the other one off her shoulder, thumbed the lock, brought it up to her shoulder, but she was a second too late.

The remaining soldier, rather than try to shoot her, leveled his musket at Anne's head, the barrel inches away.

"No! No!" he shouted, his rapid Spanish tinged with hysteria. Mary paused, just for an instant, and then they were at a stalemate, her gun pointed at his head, his gun at Anne's. No one moved.

Damn it, goddamn it, Mary thought, *why didn't I shoot this bastard?*

They were motionless, all of them. Anne on her knees, erect, teeth clenched, looking straight ahead, looking at nothing, the picture of stoicism. Abuelita had folded over as much as her girth would allow, and was weeping into her hands, but no one paid any attention to her. For long seconds her sobbing was the only sound in the room.

"Tira la arma! Tira la arma!" the soldier shouted, his voice rising in pitch, his eyes wild. It was clear enough what he wanted. Someone had to lower a weapon, and it was not going to be him.

Mary nodded. The soldier was young and he was profoundly frightened and that made him dangerous in the way of a cornered and panicked animal. He could easily blow Anne's brains out with an involuntary spasm of his finger, brought on by fear alone.

"Very well, very well," Mary said. Her tone was soothing, like a mother to a child. "Very well . . ."

Mary brought the musket down from her shoulder, lowering it slowly. The soldier nodded and Mary saw the tension drain from him as his eyes followed the butt of the gun coming down to Mary's hip. He did not notice that it was only the butt that Mary moved, that the muzzle never wavered from its aim, right at his chest.

The soldier was starting to smile and lower his own weapon when Mary pulled the trigger. The impact of the ball spun him around, threw him back. His musket discharged as he fell, blasting apart one of the red tiles on the floor. Mary could feel shards of the tile hit her legs.

The soldier fell back and Anne was shouting, "Shit! Shit! Shit!" She watched him fall, sprung to her feet, then doubled over in pain.

"Annie, Annie, are you all right?" Mary dropped her musket, rushed up to her.

"Yes, yes . . . Goddamn my eyes, woman, what the hell was that?"

"Oh, he would never have got his shot off before me," Mary assured her.

"You have done the like of this before?"

"No. But I reckoned it was so."

"Humph," Anne said, then, "Well, you scared me half to death, I'll warrant. Jesus, Mary, and Joseph, I've gone and pissed myself."

Mary looked down. Anne's dress was soaked through and there was a puddle of liquid on the floor where she was standing.

"Ay, Dios mío!" Here was Abuelita De Jesús, struggling to her feet, pointing at the puddle on the floor. *"Se rompió la fuente! Tú vas a dar a luz ahorita mismo!"* she said excitedly. The tears were glistening on her cheeks, her hands and lips trembled, but she was smiling.

Anne and Mary looked at her, shook their heads by way of saying that they did not understand. Abuelita patted Anne's tummy. "Baby . . . now . . ." she said.

"Now?" Mary asked, stupidly.

"Ohh," Anne gasped, grabbed her abdomen, doubled over in pain.

Two hours later the gasps had turned to teeth-clenching, deep-throated moans, the sound of a person in great pain who is set on a course of stoicism, and those sounds started coming at more frequent intervals.

Anne was stretched out on her bed, sweating with abandon, clutching Mary's hand until the muscles in her forearm knotted, and then relaxing as the pain passed.

Mary sat beside her, mopping her brow, holding her hand when the contractions came.

"Squeeze my hand, squeeze my hand!" Anne gasped, and Mary squeezed, not so hard as to cause Anne more pain, but Anne shouted, "Squeeze my hand, goddamn you!" and so Mary squeezed for all she was worth, squeezed with the considerable strength in her hand and her arm, and Anne gritted her teeth and then the pain passed and Anne said, "Yes, Mary, dear, like that. Pray, squeeze like that from now on."

"Yes, Annie, of course. Lemonade?"

It was all so beyond Mary's experience, and yet so familiar as well. How many times, she wondered, had she held the hand of some poor boy, racked with the agony of wounds inflicted by gunshot, grapeshot, saber, hand grenado? How often had she blocked her ears to the screams, the cries, as the boys called out for help that could not be rendered? This scene, here at the bedside, was so much a part of her history, even if the stucco walls, the brilliant sun, the cool room were not.

And yet . . . those boys with their bloody and gaping wounds had been screaming their lives away, and the only relief they found came when their souls finally abandoned their shattered bodies. But Anne was not wounded, and she would not die; at least Mary hoped she would not. Abuelita did not seem concerned, and Abuelita knew about such things.

"Oh, Mary . . ." Anne said, and she sounded tired. "Bless you, my dear, for staying with me . . ." She gritted her teeth against a spasm and Mary wiped her forehead with a damp rag. "How I wish my dear Jack was here . . ." she added, "so I could wring his fucking neck . . ." and then another contraction was on her and she grabbed Mary's hand and squeezed.

God, how well she endures the pain . . . Mary thought. After nearly a lifetime of playing the man, Mary had come to honor those things that men honored, and the stoic endurance of physical pain was one of them. She felt her admiration for Anne Bonny increase even as she wondered if she herself could be so hard in the face of such agony.

Abuelita said some soothing words and ran her hands over Anne's huge abdomen. Abuelita De Jesús was another admixture in this weird brew of the foreign and the familiar.

No one knew better than Mary the need for command presence, the absolute necessity of having a steady officer in charge during crisis. She had seen routine military evolutions crumble for want of steady leadership, and she had seen disasters turned to victory through the force of an officer's command.

Abuelita was in command now, and she was as competent, as self-assured, as totally in control as any field-grade officer Mary had ever seen. The sight of Anne's water pooling on the red tiles had driven from her mind the trauma of seconds before. With tears still streaking her fat, brown cheeks she began to shout orders, even as she led Anne to the bedchamber.

Servants scrambled in all directions. Abuelita nodded toward the bodies on the floor, shouted something else, and seemed to give no more thought to the two dead men in her house, the third lying just outside her door in a wide patch of blood-soaked dirt.

Abuelita guided Anne back to her room, had her lie on the bed, and her troops darted in and out with sheets, towels, water, lemonade, glasses, and bowls. Mary had never felt so eager to surrender herself to another's authority. She stood by, ready to carry out any orders she was given, but Abuelita seemed to need no help from her. Never had Mary been so grateful for another's competence.

"Here now, here now, squeeze my hand . . ." Anne gasped, half sitting up, the muscles in her neck standing out proud. Mary squeezed, but for all her strength she could not squeeze harder than Anne's crushing grip. Mary gritted her teeth as well and endured the pain that Anne was inflicting on her, and in a way was even glad for it, as if it helped her in her empathy, as if she could share Anne's pain and thus lessen it.

"Oh, dear God, oh, dear God." Anne collapsed back on the pillow, her eyes wide, staring up at the ceiling. Mary wiped her forehead with a damp cloth because she felt like she had to do something, and that was the only thing she knew to do. She wished it would end.

Abuelita De Jesús, all business now, placed her hands on Anne's big belly and gently pressed her fingers down, here and there, feeling the living thing underneath. She frowned, stared off at nothing as she felt the baby's position. She smiled, not a joyous grin but rather a small, intimate smile of satisfaction. She nodded, smiled wider at Anne, who ignored her, and issued another string of orders.

The afternoon dragged on, and the only real mark of time's passing was the moving shadows across the room and the ever-increased intensity of Anne's moans and the power with which she crushed Mary's hand in her own seemingly tireless grip.

Finally, with back arched, she said between clenched teeth, "I have to push, I have to goddamn push!" but Abuelita, who understood the intent, said, "No, no! No . . . poosh!" and then Abuelita made gasping sounds to show Anne what she must do.

Anne fell back again, muttered some words that made Mary glad for Abuelita's lack of English.

Some time later—it seemed like hours, but the sunlight coming in around the curtain put the lie to that—Abuelita again examined Anne, and with a genuine smile said, "Poosh, Hanne, poosh!"

Anne clenched her teeth, arched her back, and her face was a mask of pure determination as she pushed down. Mary, looking at her, could not begin to image what she was going through, what it felt like to be Anne Bonny at that moment.

"Poosh! *Bueno!*"

"Arrrrhh." Anne pushed, panted for breath, pushed.

Abuelita tapped Mary on the shoulder, nodded toward the place between Anne's legs, and since Anne seemed to have completely forgotten her presence, Mary stood and stepped back and looked.

There was blood and fluid everywhere. Mary was used to blood, but this was something different. Blood on the soaked white sheets, blood on Anne's smooth, gleaming, muscular thighs, blood on her stomach and matted in her soft reddish blond pubic hair.

Her vagina was stretched out beyond what seemed possible and it made Mary cringe and emerging from that bloody place, a pink hump of flesh, a tuft of light-colored hair. It all seemed to Mary as if it was going terribly wrong, but Abuelita looked not in the least concerned as she coached Anne in her soft Spanish and gently, gently eased the little head out.

Anne arched again, clenched and pushed, and suddenly the head was out and in a great welter of liquid and blood and gray flesh and umbilical cord the baby was free, blinking in shock at this turn of events. The room, it seemed, sighed in relief, Anne collapsing on the bed, the attendants in their delight, Abuelita deftly severing the umbilical cord and wrapping the boy—Mary saw it was a boy—in clean white swaddling clothes.

Mary stepped back to the head of the bed, took Anne's hand. She smiled down at her friend, who seemed to have finally succumbed to her exhaustion, lying still with eyes closed. "Annie, Annie darling, it is over," Mary whispered, and Anne nodded her head, just slightly, in acknowledgment.

Mary smiled wide. There was something so miraculous about a little life emerging from all that pain and blood, whereas in her past experience only death attended such things. She could hear the baby mewing now. A tiny life, a brand-new person.

"It is a little boy, Annie, a perfect little boy," Mary whispered. "Would you hold him now?"

Anne did not open her eyes. She turned her head away from Mary. "No," she said.

For an hour Mary sat in a straight-backed chair at the edge of the room and held the baby while Abuelita and her servants tended to Anne. Mary cradled the little bundle in her arms, looked down at the tiny face, the wide blue eyes which looked back at her.

She sang soft songs and the baby did not cry, did not fuss, did not make a sound. He just looked at Mary and Mary looked back. She imagined that the baby was trying to understand this profound change that had just happened and she hoped that he was thinking that it would be all right, that this new world might hold some joy for him. She was trying to show him that there was love to be found here, too, outside the warm embrace of the womb.

"Farewell and adieu to you fair Spanish maidens, farewell and adieu to you ladies of Spain . . ." Mary sung, soft. She did not know any songs that were really appropriate for children, but she sung soft and melodic and the baby was content.

Your first hour on earth. Whatever will the rest of them be like for you, little one? Mary thought. *Your aunt Mary could tell you much of what not to do . . .*

Mary did not know what was to become of the child. The idea of the birth had been so monstrous a thing to comprehend, she had given little thought to what might happen to the baby after he was born, nor did Anne appear very approachable on the subject.

She looked at his little face and suddenly the thought of parting with him seemed too painful to consider. She forced herself to admit, silently but consciously, that he was not her baby, and that realization made her ache as well.

Mary stood, keeping the infant tight to her chest, and stepped over to where Anne lay with eyes closed on the bed. Abuelita and her troops had cleaned her up, changed her dress and sheets, and now she was letting her exhaustion carry her away.

"Annie, dear . . ." Mary whispered, and Anne's head lolled over toward her and she opened her eyes.

"Ah, Mary. It's over now, thank God. Now perhaps we can get back to where we are meant to be."

"Back . . . ?"

"Back to sea, Mary, my beauty."

Mary nodded, but inside she felt hollow. Back to sea? It seemed so unhappy an idea, like rolling out of a warm, dry bunk to lay aloft and stow sail on a stormy night. Thoughts of remaining behind, of raising the little boy as her own, flashed though her mind. "Would you like to see your baby?" Mary asked.

Anne made a noncommittal sound, lowered her eyes to the bundle of cloth, and Mary pulled back the cloth so that Anne could see his tiny face. "Hmm," Anne said. "Odd-looking thing."

"What is to become of him?" Mary asked.

"Oh, Jack has it all arranged, dear. Abuelita will take him in, raise him as her own."

"But, Anne . . ." Mary did not know what to say. "Let another raise your child?" The thoughts and the emotions were coming fast and disorganized. "What of his welfare?"

At that Anne smiled a weak smile. "I am thinking of his welfare. Am I not doing the best for him, by not forcing him to suffer a mother so horrid as me? He will be happy here. Lord knows you love it enough.

"Abuelita will make up some tale. He will not grow up knowing he is the bastard son of a pirate and a whore."

This seemed to exhaust her, and she rolled her head away and closed her eyes. "It is the best way, Mary, dear, depend upon it."

Mary held the baby tight and felt tears in her eyes and she knew that Anne was right.

Chapter 28

Soon after, Abuelita De Jesús came and took the baby from Mary and gave him to a wet nurse, and Mary saw him again only a few times. It was better that way, she knew, because her sense of loss was only increased with each moment she held the child.

With that warm bundle in her arms, looking up at her as she looked down at him, she was carried back to the Three Trade Horses and she was there in front of the huge fireplace that threw orange light and warmth over the room and she was holding a baby—her and Frederick's baby—and Frederick had his arms around her waist and was looking down at their baby, over her shoulder, and smiling that beautiful smile of his.

But that never was, and it never could be now, and Mary could not endure the thought of it. She yielded the child up to Abuelita and did not ask to see him again.

Mary could not fathom Anne's complete lack of interest in the baby. She did not hate Annie for it, or lose respect for her, or feel jealousy. She just could not understand, and she did not ask Annie to explain because she doubted that Annie could.

Anne was asleep and Mary realized that she was very hungry. She wandered out of the room in search of food. She ambled down along the edge of the courtyard, seeing nothing. At the front door she stopped. The bodies of the soldiers were gone, the blood cleaned up. There was nothing but the shattered tile left to mark what had happened there. Mary looked out the door. The body of the officer was gone as well, the dark patch of blood covered over with fresh sand.

Mary had no notion of who had disposed of the bodies or how. She did not ask.

Anne Bonny's convalescence lasted for one night. She was up early the next morning, buoyant and cheerful, and Mary might have thought that she had been drinking at that early hour if she had not been so clear eyed. Having some semblance of her former body back, and the dread of pending childbirth behind her, seemed to lift Annie extremely.

"Now that I am able, Mary, I will cheerfully help you with your housekeeping. Sweep, cook, beat shirts with a bloody rock, whatever you might wish." Anne was perched on the edge of Mary's bed, and Mary, still half-asleep, could only grunt in reply. It was quite the opposite of the natural order of things.

"And when we are done with that," Anne continued, "I think we should look to our weapons. It is in the articles we signed, you will recall. I grieve to think of the state of our blades in this horrid climate, not to mention our firelocks. We must be ready for when the others return."

Again Mary grunted. But she knew Anne was right. Soon they would be in the sweet trade again. She threw off her blankets, pushed her fantasies aside, and climbed out of bed.

For another week they carried on with their routine, helping out with the housekeeping, eating, sleeping, strolling in the evenings. Anne became more animated with each passing day, discussing future plans, places where the *Pretty Anne* might cruise, things that they might do with their growing fortune.

Mary was polite, and listened, but did not add much.

And then, on the morning that Anne's son turned eight days old, on the morning that Anne first said, "Damn it, it is high time that Jack returned," in a tone that was at once hopeful and edged with growing concern, one of the fishing boats pulled back to the beach with the news that Calico Juan's sloop had been seen in the offing.

Anne and Mary hurried down to the beach. From the surf line they looked out over the water. That familiar topsail was just visible past the low-lying islands around the entrance to the harbor at Caibarién.

Anne turned and looked at Mary with the most genuine look of pleasure she had worn in some time. "Oh, body of me, Mary, I have never been so happy to see anything in my life!"

Mary nodded, but she did not smile. "Yes indeed, Annie, dear. It is time for us to quit this place."

They walked back up to the De Jesús home and Mary went into her room and with great sadness she took off her soft cotton dress and once again pulled on her wool shirt, slop trousers, red waistcoat, and blue jacket.

But she had not lied to Anne. She was happy to see the sloop, ready to leave that town. She had been playing at the quiet life, but it was not really hers. The peace, the near bliss, she had found in Caibarién was not real. It was an illusion. Mary Read had had a surfeit of ephemeral happiness and she wanted no more.

It was time once more to go to sea.

The *Pretty Anne* rounded up into the wind and the anchor was let go and it plunged down through the clear water. Jack Rackam stood at his quarterdeck rail, his best sword at his hip, his fine clothing hanging a bit loose on him. He had not been eating well.

He felt a vague dread that seemed to center in his stomach, but he could not attribute it to his being reunited with Anne. That was a part of it, to be sure, wondering how he would be greeted, wondering if Anne had fared well, if she had had a difficult birth, facing the silent censure of that bitch Read—Lord knew what they had been up to, what unnatural things she had been filling Anne's head with—but that was only a part of it.

The dread, the hard thing in his stomach, was not a passing fancy. It had settled in, like an unwelcome guest who would not leave. It was all his fears, wound up so tight that they became something solid and took up residency in his guts.

It was the poor hunting they had found, the few pathetic fishing boats they had robbed, the potential discontent of the men who might turn him out, like he did old Charles Vane. It was the certainty of the noose if they were caught, with him having accepted the Governor's pardon and then gone out on the account once more. It was the possibility of disgrace and the possibility of piling the sloop up on the rocks and the yellow jack and the thousand things that plagued a man such as he.

It was the *Pretty Anne*. She was growing increasingly decrepit, beyond what the pirates were able to repair in their secluded coves on their sparsely inhabited islands. They would have to get another ship, but that meant his finding one and then successfully capturing it.

It was the *Guarda del Costa,* the Spanish guard ships that patrolled the Cuban coast. The Pretty Annes' depredations had not been grand, but neither had they gone unnoticed. Jack had no doubt that they were being hunted; the Dons were keeping a damned sharp eye out for him.

Damn Dons, goddamn Dons and their damned guard ships . . . Of all the world of enemies he faced, it was the Spaniards he feared the most.

If the English, his countrymen, caught him, they would hang him for piracy. While he was not enthusiastic about that possibility, it still was preferable to the Dons, who would draw and quarter him, disembowel him, burn him at the stake, impale him so that he would take days to die. When he thought of it, it made the hard thing in his stomach turn over, made his insides feel less than solid, so he tried not to think on it, but he could not help it.

"Anchor's holding, Captain," said Richard Corner, lumbering aft, and then, a second later, "Are you well, Jack, my dear?"

"Yes. Why would you ask such a thing?" Jack snapped.

Corner shrugged. "You looked like you was not well."

"I've a world on my shoulders, you know. I'll warrant

you don't appreciate what it is like, to have command such as I do."

Corner nodded. He was a big dog. Kick him, pat him, it made little difference. "Shall I get the boat over, then?"

"Aye, get the boat over."

Jack wondered if other captains felt these fears. Old Charles Vane, who always seemed so cool, did he have that hard thing in his gut? It was difficult to believe. And if not, did that mean that he, Calico Jack Rackam, did not have the stuff of which captains are made? That possibility frightened him most of all.

Ten minutes later, Jack, in the stern sheets of the boat, hand resting on the tiller, was rowed ashore, into the bosom of the enthusiastic crowd on the beach, and that gave his sagging confidence a bit of a prop.

The bow ran up on the sand and the men of Caibarién grabbed on to the gunnels and pulled the boat up onto the sand. Jack stood and lifted a small chest of money and handed it down. It was for all of the village, he explained to the grinning men, and though it cut much deeper into his personal fortune than his previous gifts had, still he could not let the people of the town think that he was any less successful now than he had been in years past. His sense of himself would not allow it.

He hopped down into the sand, pleased by his welcome but nervous still because he had yet to see Anne. And then, like a ship parting the seas, Abuelita De Jesús pushed through the crowd, Anne on her arm—a smiling, lovely Anne in her European dress, a relieved, beaming Anne, Anne with arms wide, happy to see him, and for a moment Jack felt a reprieve from all the anxiety as he took her in his arms and hugged her to the cheering of the crowd.

They made their farewells to the De Jesúses and the others, gave their thanks all around, collected up Anne's things and Mary's as well, and within the hour they were back aboard the *Pretty Anne* and under way.

The lovely little town of Caibarién was just disappearing around the headland when it occurred to Jack that he had never asked after the baby. He opened his mouth, even

uttered the beginning of a word, and then thought better of
it. If Anne had not mentioned it, no reason that he should.
Best not to stir all that up.

At least, he hoped that that was the best course of action.
He was not sure. He felt the thing in his stomach turn over
again.

They stood on for another mile or so and then the wind,
which had been steady, began to come in puffs, a sure sign
that it soon would fail altogether.

Anne had shed her fancy silk dress and once again was
wearing her big wool shirt and her loose-fitting slops with
the wide leather belt and sheath knife around her waist, a
red cloth bound around her head. She was barefoot and she
delighted at the smooth, warm planks underfoot once more.
She loved the familiar motion of the sloop.

"Let us come to an anchor, yonder," Jack said, pointing
over the starboard side. A half mile away was the mainland
of Cuba. At the place where Jack pointed, a small island
stood just off the coast, no more than two hundred yards
at the farthest, a green hump of jungle-covered land with a
shallow channel between it and the big island.

Thomas Quick, at the helm, pushed the tiller over. Anne
sprung to her feet, whipped the mainsheet off the cleat to
which it was made fast, let the rough line run through her
palms. Her hands had grown soft again during her time
ashore, and the rope burned her and the tiny sharp bits of
manila left splinters where the sheet passed, but Anne did
not mind. It was time to get her hands tough again.

They ran down toward the channel that passed between
the small island and Cuba proper, sometimes bobbing in
the swell as the wind failed, sometimes shooting ahead in
a burst of speed when they caught a puff. The water grew
more shallow and light in color as they closed with the
land, the seas more choppy.

At last they were in the mouth of the channel, tucked in
between the island and the mainland. On either hand, the

shorelines were a thick tangle of mangrove, impenetrable, impossible to determine where the water left off and the shore began, a dark and wild place. Jack ordered the sloop to luff up and the anchor let go. The *Pretty Anne* was as hidden from view as she could get.

The anchor plunged into the clear water and took firm hold of the sandy bottom. The sails came down on a run and were hurriedly stowed. The breaker of rum came up on deck, and the portable stove and the unhappy goat they had purchased in Caibarién, and soon a grand bacchanal was under way, with the sky growing dark and the evening warm and the sloop gently rocking in the swell.

Anne drank her share of rum—no insignificant amount— and dined on goat and enjoyed the rough companionship of her tribe. It was a relief to be back, to no longer have to play the lady, to give not a cuss for manners or decorum. The pirates did not take offense at much, and on those rare occasions when offense was given, it was settled ashore with swords and pistols. It was all very simple and direct and Anne loved it.

She was glad to be back with Calico Jack, glad to have his company, his fawning attention, as annoying as he was being that moment. He was ready to dive below for a flourish, she could tell, and it was irritating him that she wished to stay on deck and enjoy the company of the others.

She ignored him and his ill-disguised peevishness, and continued her banter with Dicky Corner and George Fetherston and Mary Read and Noah Harwood and her fellow rogues.

Anne Bonny had gone to sea so that she might be with Jack, but it was more than that now. She was more than Jack's woman. She was a part of the crew, an equal to any in their company, and she was starting to resent Jack's assumption that she was there as his plaything.

At last the men began to drift away and find places to sleep, or to change from a sitting position to one that was prone or supine. Mary had lain on her back on the main hatch, enjoying the stars, and now she was breathing soft and regularly.

Anne stood and stretched. "What, ho, Jack? Are we for bed?"

Jack, who had been leaning against the bulwark with arms folded, straightened and said, "I reckon," though he was annoyed, and Anne wondered if he still wished to make the beast with two backs. Either way, she would be content.

Jack picked up the lantern that was sitting on the hatch and they stepped aft and climbed down the narrow scuttle to the tiny great cabin. Anne stepped aside for Jack, stretched her arms, and said, "Oh, I am exhausted."

Jack came down behind her, hung the lantern on a hook driven into an overhead beam, then put his hands gently on Anne's waist and turned her around until she was facing him. For a second she was looking up into his eyes, and then he pulled her toward him and kissed her.

Anne was ready for a rough kiss, a coarse embrace, the kind of lovemaking that was as much an expression of anger as love, but it was not there. Jack's lips on hers were tender, and passionate and exploring and forgiving, but more than anything they were desperate for her.

She was surprised, but his kiss made her own passion flare like an ember in tinder and she wrapped her arms around his neck and pulled him into herself and for long moments they stood, devouring each other.

Anne felt Jack's hands moving down her back, over her bottom and down her thighs. He took hold and lifted and Anne lifted her legs and wrapped them around Jack's waist and he was holding her like that, and she was wrapped completely around him, arms and legs, and their lips never came apart.

Jack carried her across the cabin, moving with precision, avoiding the hundred obstacles there, and Anne felt as if she were clinging to a rock, so strong were Jack's arms, so steady was he on his feet.

He laid her down on the cushion on top of the after locker and with a swift motion shed his coat and his waistcoat as Anne lay on her back and watched him. He moved like a dancer or an expert swordsman, not a wasted motion, his allure undeniable, and Anne felt herself growing hot.

He came down on top of her, resting on his elbows, kissing her mouth, running his lips over her neck and pulling her shirt aside and kissing her shoulders. He took little bites of her neck and with his tongue he tickled her behind her earlobe and she gasped—she could not contain herself—and wrapped her arms around him and pulled him tight. If Jack sometimes did not seem so sure of himself on the quarterdeck, in these maneuvers he was absolutely composed of confidence and he had no equal.

Anne felt her desire and her love and her relief all building in equal measure. It was so good to be back aboard, to have her Calico Jack back, have things the way they had been. Cuba, the baby, it was just an interruption, and it had changed nothing, and Anne felt her trepidation melt away.

Jack ran his lips down her neck and over her chest. Anne felt his fingers curling around the edge of her shirt and then he pulled and the fabric parted and Anne felt the cool evening air and Jack's warm mouth on her breasts and her hard nipples.

She moved under him and savored the sensuous pressure of his body on hers. And then she half sat up and gently pushed Jack off and he let her. She stood and pulled her tattered shirt off and let it fall and undid her slop trousers and let them fall. For a second she stood there, running her hands over herself, watching Jack as he watched her.

Then she kneeled before him and unbuttoned his shirt and ran her lips and hands over his strong chest, his flat stomach. She pushed the shirt off his shoulders, worked the buttons on his breeches, and peeled those and his socks off in one practiced motion. She took his hard cock in her mouth, reveled in his manly smell, enjoyed the way that Jack writhed and groaned with the pleasure of it.

At last he eased her back onto the cushion and entered her and they fell into the familiar rhythm of their lovemaking.

It was when they coupled like that, with a motion so perfect that it did not seem possible that they could be two separate people, it was then that Anne was certain that she and Calico Jack were together through some force greater than simple coincidence. It was too perfect to be chance, the way they gave such pleasure to each other, the way that together they came to their gasping, teeth-clenching climax, trying to mute the screams that threatened to burst out of them, their bodies seeming to compact and then explode out like hand grenadoes.

And then lying together, their skin slick where it was pressed together, breathing hard in a kind of numb rapture.

It was in that blissful situation that Anne fell asleep in Jack's arms. At some point in the night she was aware of him pulling a blanket over them to defend against the night air that was cool on their naked skin, but other than that she slept, deep and luxurious.

It was bright daylight when she woke and she was aware of some commotion on deck. She sat up and listened and it seemed that whatever was happening had been happening for some time.

The scuttle overhead opened and Jack, in clothes hastily pulled on, came below.

"Jack, my dear, whatever is it?"

"It is the Dons. The damned, goddamned *Guarda del Costa*," he said, and in the morning light Anne thought he looked very pale.

Chapter 29

FROM THE MASTHEAD, THE SPANIARD WAS CLEARLY VISible, at least through a telescope. She was hull-down, running west along the coast under easy sail. She was ship rigged—three masts, square sails on all masts—though she was not a large vessel. What the British would call a sloop-of-war. Perhaps eighteen great guns, nine- or twelve-pounders. Not huge, but vastly superior to the *Pretty Anne*. She seemed in no great hurry.

"Could we not run for it? Sure we could sail away from that beastly thing?" Anne asked. She and Mary were in their favorite spot, up on the crosstrees, enjoying their rare privacy.

"Beastly she may be, but she would run us down," Mary said. "The speed of a vessel has much to do with her length, you know. And see here, she sails in company with another."

Mary had just seen the second vessel. She was off the Spaniard's lee quarter, and the guard ship hid her from the *Pretty Anne*'s view, until that moment when the guard ship sagged off to leeward, exposing the other ship.

"Deck, there!" Mary called out.

"Aye, aloft!"

"There's another there as well, off the *Guarda del Costa*'s lee quarter. Looks to be a sloop. Could be a prize, can't tell."

How that news was greeted on deck, Mary could not tell either. She and Anne turned their attention back to their approaching enemy.

"You said yourself that she is not a man-of-war of any great size," Anne continued, "and they are only Dons, for the love of God. I don't see why we do not attack them and take their ship. This sloop is half-rotten, we need a new one."

Mary shook her head. "She may not be of a great size, my dear, and they may be but Dons, but they are too much for us."

"Are you afraid?"

"No, but neither am I a fool." Mary paused for a moment and then added, "I would be afraid, were we to attack them."

"Well, I am not afraid, nor am I a fool. I reckon I am just too brave, is all."

Mary smiled at her friend. "You would be surprised at what close cousins bravery and foolishness be."

"Humph," Anne said, and said no more.

The two women watched the slow approach of the Spaniards for ten minutes more and then returned to the deck.

They slid down the backstay and right into the midst of a hot debate on the best course of action.

"Damn them, the damned bloody Dons!" George Fetherston was ranting. "Ain't but a sloop, and them just Dons, I say we are for them!" He shouted the last words in such a way as to bring a cheer from the men, but they remained silent and stared at him.

"There, do you see?" Anne said to Mary in a soft voice. "I am not the only one who is for attacking."

"Yes, Annie, but Fetherston is a fucking lunatic. I would expect better from you."

And then Richard Corner stood and said, "What ho, Jack? You are captain here, what say you?"

"What? Well, see here now, you know . . ." Jack was pacing. His sword was out and he was casually swinging it, using it as a walking stick in a most dramatic fashion. He stretched and yawned in a great display of disinterest.

Calico Jack was afraid. Mary recognized the signs, she had seen it often enough. She looked around at the others to see if they, too, could see how the captain's guts were churning, but she saw no sign of it. Perhaps these wild men had not witnessed as much fear as she had. She kept her mouth shut.

"Well, this is a hell of a spot, you know." Jack was still temporizing. "And seeing as how we are not in a fight, I am not, as it were, in sole command, so I would leave it to you gentlemen—" he bowed an elegant bow that brought a few smiles "—to decide on the course of our action."

"They've bloody got us now, was we to show ourselves," offered Noah Harwood, a simple statement of fact. "I reckon we should tow the sloop into the channel best as we can, see if these bastards don't sail on past and never discover we're here."

This at last met with murmured consent, and Mary added her sounds of affirmation to the others. It was the only course that made sense.

"Are we agreed then?" Jack asked brightly. He seemed buoyed now that a decision had been rendered. Mary suspected that he was relieved that the others had not voted to attack, but she was loath even to think it. Cowardice was the most heinous of things; she could not accuse anyone of it, not even in her thoughts alone, without genuine and irrefutable proof. She would not brand Jack a coward.

Being afraid was not cowardice; Mary understood that. Everyone was afraid, save for madmen like Fetherston and dumb beasts like Corner. It was what you did with the fear, how you used it, that would make a man a hero or a coward. She wondered what the bold Calico Jack would do if the iron really started to fly.

But Jack was giving orders now and his old aplomb had returned. He slid his sword back into his sheath and said, "Let us have the longboat over the side with the five-inch cable to the bitts. I reckon that will do it."

The men moved fast, despite the hard night of drinking they had had, despite the still air and the sweltering heat and the bugs from the close-by swamps.

They swayed the longboat over the side and attached to the samson post in its bow the cable, a hemp rope five inches in diameter and nearly two hundred yards long, the lightest of the cables.

With the windlass they hauled up the anchor by which they were attached to the bottom, their hands sweating and slick on the oiled handspikes they used to turn the big winch. It took half an hour and then the anchor was up and hanging from the cathead and Mary and ten of the others took their place in the longboat, the long oars held straight up like columns in a Greek temple.

"Very well," said Dicky Corner, standing in the stern sheets and holding the tiller. "Ship oars! Give way, all!"

The oars came down and the boat crew pulled and fathom by fathom they hauled the cable out, rowing farther up the narrow channel that ran between the island and the mainland. The water grew more still, the air more close and oppressive, and the men and Mary rowed on.

More than ever before Mary wished she could strip off her shirt and her waistcoat, but in that heat she knew that her shirt was soaked clean through, and without the waistcoat, the wet and clinging fabric would reveal more than she wished revealed.

They pulled for one hundred feet and then the strain came on the heavy rope, and the *Pretty Anne,* which had begun to drift with the gentle current, fell into line with the boat. Twenty feet astern of the boat, the cable rose out of the water and ran in a great curved line to the *Pretty Anne*'s bow.

For a moment they seemed to be stopped. Mary glanced at the shoreline as she leaned into the oar, grunting with the effort, sweat running unimpeded down her face. They were pulling hard, but they were going nowhere, held back by the weight of the sloop.

Oars up, lean forward, oars down, blades biting into the water as they put their backs into it, and this time there was some movement, a grudging forward motion as the boat began to pull the sloop behind.

Blades up, dripping water, lean forward, blades down, pull, inch by inch the boat made forward progress, pull by pull their speed increased as the sloop built her own momentum. The thick jungle crawled by as the sweating crew of the longboat pulled the *Pretty Anne* farther up the channel, to a place where she might be hidden from sight of the passing *Guarda del Costa.*

Dicky Corner looked over the side, down through the clear water. He turned and hailed the sloop. "That's it, lads! You may come to an anchor here!"

The channel was no more than five feet deep beyond that point, and the *Pretty Anne* needed nine feet at least to move. They had pulled themselves up into a dead end, and if they were seen, then they were trapped. They had gambled everything on the Spaniards' inattentiveness.

They rowed the longboat to the edge of the mangrove swamp and with their cutlasses they hacked away what foliage they could and brought it back to the sloop. The branches were hoisted aloft and lashed to the topmast and the yard to further disguise the sloop, and then there was no more that they could do. They were hidden as well as they could be, and now it was only a matter of waiting.

The beaker of rum made another appearance. "Need something to pass the bloody time, till this damned Spaniard sails us by," Fetherston announced as he plunged his tin cup into the little barrel, and the others concurred as they did likewise.

The afternoon floated on, a ship at her anchor under the weight of the tropical heat, the heavy liquid air that made the sweat run unchecked down faces and arms and backs, just from the effort of being alive. Each breath seemed inadequate, as if there was too much water in the air, as if they were drowning by degrees.

None of this was helped by the rum, but they drank anyway.

Tucked in as they were behind the island, there was no more than a narrow strip of open ocean visible to them from the deck. In hour-long shifts they stood watch at the masthead, monitoring the slow progress of the *Guarda del Costa* and calling the dull and repetitive reports down to the others. "Standing on . . . no change of course . . . Oh, they've set their spritsail topsail now! That second one's sagging off to leeward . . ." And so it went.

The sun moved off to the west and the long shadows of the mangroves reached across the channel and wrapped themselves around the *Pretty Anne.* The shade brought a certain relief—from the relentless sun and from the discomforting sensation of being exposed. They were not in the bright light now, but lurking in the shadows, an altogether more secure place to be.

John Howell, who had the watch aloft, came riding down the backstay and stepped onto the quarterdeck rail. "Reckon that Don will be in sight from deck here directly," he said.

The mood on deck had been subdued but jovial, as if they were sitting in an agreeable tavern waiting for a storm to pass. They had talked quietly among themselves, laughing softly, going about what business they had in an unhurried manner. Not so tense that it was like holding their breath, but rather as if they were trying to be unobtrusive, as if moving fast might attract the Spaniards' attention.

All that changed with Howell's quiet announcement. In

the next minute, or the next, the *Guarda del Costa* would cross the mouth of the channel in which they were hidden, perhaps a mile away. Now, for the first time since they had spotted the Spaniards, the *Pretty Anne* would be exposed to the enemy's sight, from waterline to masthead.

Everyone on deck fell silent, and they all gravitated toward the bow, which was pointing toward the open ocean. They climbed up on the rails and up in the shrouds and they looked out from their shadowy place, out toward the brilliant blue and flashing white of the sea. Nobody spoke. Now they were holding their breath.

They were not at the bow for above a minute when the *Guarda del Costa*'s spritsail and spritsail topsail, two little squares of white against the blue, appeared around the corner of the island, and then, inch by inch, the rest of the ship revealed itself as she passed by that unremarkable spot of coast, patrolling in her unhurried manner. She was a bit more than a mile away. She looked lovely in the late afternoon sun.

In her wake, trailing like a stubborn child, came the sloop that Mary had first seen from aloft. She looked very like the *Pretty Anne*.

Corner had the telescope to his eye, and after the pirates had watched the *Guarda del Costa* for some minutes he said—it was no more than a whisper—"I sees eight gunports." Heads nodded at this news, but still no one spoke.

"Sloop's got Spanish colors over English," Corner announced next. That meant she was the guard ship's prize, an English sloop that had unwisely wandered too close to the Cuban coast and had been snatched up by the *Guarda del Costa*.

Mary felt sorry for those poor souls on the sloop. It would go hard on them. But her sorrow was the kind that she had felt looking at the battlefield dead—sorrow mixed with relief that it was they and not she. She knew that the others felt the same, save perhaps for Fetherston, who seemed too wild to think on another's distress, or that mean little bastard Billy Bartlett, who gave not a cuss for any person other than himself.

The guard ship sailed on. She was nearly across the mouth of the channel, her bowsprit just becoming lost from sight around the western headland with never a change in direction, and that brought a general easing of tension on the deck. Mary could see heads nodding, the first glimmers of smiles on the men's faces. Jack Rackam seemed to be moving toward a quiet euphoria.

And then Corner said, "She's hauling her wind," and all that good humor was crushed under the weight of those quiet words.

Heads snapped up, men stood more erect, craning their necks out to sea. The *Guarda del Costa* was wearing ship, turning from her present course until her bow was pointing almost directly at the *Pretty Anne*. The pirates waited for her to keep turning, to spin around through 270 degrees, to sail off toward the northeast on some unknown mission. But she did not.

Instead she settled on this new course, her sails hauled over on a larboard tack, her bowsprit pointing like an accusing finger right at the *Pretty Anne*.

The Spaniards had seen them. They knew what the hidden sloop was about. They were coming now to pry them out of their hiding place like pulling a rotten tooth from a patient strapped to a chair.

"Come up here, then, and kiss my arse!" Fetherston roared at the *Guarda del Costa*.

"We're dead men now, and that's a fact," said Billy Bartlett. "You done for us, Rackam, you and your little doxy."

Calico Jack jumped down from the rail. He landed on the deck and raced below with never a word.

Chapter 30

TEN MINUTES LATER, JACK RACKAM, COMING BACK ON
deck, paused at the scuttle, took a deep breath, and then
stepped out into the open. He had two braces of pistols on
ribbons around his neck, his best fighting sword on his hip.
He was wearing his white calico coat with the little roses,
the most audacious of his clothing.

"All right, lads, now I am ready to meet these bastards
proper!" he shouted, waving his sword, and he saw the
looks of approval, blessed, blessed approval, on their faces.

The taste of vomit was still sharp and bitter in his mouth,
and his throat burned from puking. He had made it to the
great cabin, had thrown up into one of his shirts and then
disposed of the shirt out the great cabin window, lowering
it to the water so it would not make a splash.

He was frightened beyond reason by the Spaniards, and
just as frightened that his men would discover him. The
fear made him feel brittle, like he was frozen, like he might
shatter, but he was hiding it well. He could see that.

He snatched up a cup, filled it with rum, took a deep
drink. The rough liquor felt good going down and Jack
hoped it would bolster his faltering resolve and cover the
smell of the vomit on his breath.

"Well, now, Captain," Dicky Corner called out, "I reckon
we're into it now, and so you may pass orders as you will."

"Of course, damned bloody Dons," Jack said, and could
think of nothing else. He was expending such effort just
holding his fear in check that it seemed too much by half
to have to think of a plan as well. "Well, to arms, lads! Let
us clear for action!" *Yes, yes, there we go . . . clear for action, of course . . . and what else?*

"A spring, too, let us rig a spring so we might turn the

sloop around and give these bastards their due!"

The men hurried off to carry those orders out, clearing away their few inadequate guns and rigging a spring—a rope running from their anchor cable to the stern of the *Pretty Anne* that, when hauled upon, would turn the sloop so that she could present her broadside to the attacking Spaniard. For all the good it would do. The *Pretty Anne* had four four-pounder guns per side. The Spaniard had twice that number, and they would be twice as big.

But it was something for the men to do, and if they were busy, then they would not bother Jack for more orders, and they would not see that the fox was once again gnawing at his guts and that he would puke again if there was anything left for him to puke.

With the men working as they were, Jack had the luxury of a few moments alone with his thoughts, and that gave him some relief. The wind might come offshore, he realized, and blow the Dons out to sea. A storm could come up and then the guard ship would not care to remain on a lee shore.

He was grasping at every good thing he could think of, like a drowning man clutching at little bits of wreckage. But grasp as he might, he knew there was not much there and he knew that he was going down.

Anne Bonny, standing on the quarterdeck rail, watched the first plume of smoke burst from the *Guarda del Costa*'s side, near the bow. It was lovely, lit up orange in the evening light. And less than a second after the smoke came the flat *pow* of the gun and the crash of foliage as the round shot plowed into the vegetation on the shore close by the *Pretty Anne,* and then the derisive howling of the pirates.

They were all pretty well drunk, having turned to the rum and brandy with gusto once the guns were loaded and the spring rigged. They took up on the spring, swung the sloop broadside to the channel so that her guns would bear on the Spaniard, and, one gun at a time, they were taking aim and firing and cheering their own efforts.

None of them thought the guns would have much effect. It was just something to do, a way to amuse themselves before the Spaniards battered them into a wreck and then captured whoever might survive.

Another gun from the Spaniard and this time the ball screamed across the deck and shattered the boom in a great spray of splinters and the pirates screamed and jeered and waved their swords and pistols. Anne loved their spirit and she shouted and cursed along with them. It was unlikely they would live another twenty-four hours, but they would not go quietly.

The *Guarda del Costa* closed to within a quarter mile, close enough that their shot hit as often as it missed, but then the wind began to fail them. The Spaniards put a boat over the side, towed their ship in toward the land, but the light was going, too. It was a race to see if the Spaniards could get to a place where they might batter the *Pretty Anne* to splinters while there was still light enough to do it.

The sloop that was with them, the unfortunate English sloop, had disappeared east around the island. No doubt the guard ship's captain did not care to risk injury to his valuable prize.

Another shot from the Spaniard and the *Pretty Anne* jarred underfoot and then Fetherston fired off one of the four-pounders and the world was lost in the great rush of noise and smoke. It was exhilarating. There was no other word for it.

Anne thought back to the night when she had married James Bonny, the delicious taste of danger and excitement and abandon. Or walking brazenly into the Ship Tavern. Or humping Jack while her husband was watching. This was like those moments, only many, many times more.

She savored the insane thrill of it all, understood now what went on in George Fetherston's mind. She thought it would be all right if she died that night, because she did not know if she could tolerate even one mundane second again, after this crystal intensity of emotion.

She looked up at Jack, who was standing on the rail,

watching the Spaniard, and she could tell that he was not enjoying this fatal circumstance as she was.

Poor, dear Jack, Anne thought, *so much on his mind. It's easy for us to love this so, without the weight of responsibility.*

She reached over and ran her hand up his calf and he jerked in surprise, scowled down at her, and she smiled up at him.

"Never you fear, Jack, my love, we shall do for these bastards yet!" she shouted up at him. It was in the spirit of the thing, to make such bold and improbable predictions, but Jack just grunted and turned back to watching the enemy's inexorable approach.

"Jack, we shall have their ship. What say you?" Anne called, and when Jack did not respond she said, "Jack, do you attend?"

Jack scowled down at her again. "Yes, yes, goddamn it, I bloody heard you!" he hissed in a voice that startled Anne.

"Jack." Anne spoke as soft as she could and still be heard over the noise. "Whatever is the matter?"

"The matter?" Jack gave a humorless laugh. "We are about to be captured by the Dons, you stupid, mindless bitch! Or do you not realize that?"

Anne stepped back. She could not have been more shocked if Jack had slapped her. Suddenly all of the chaos of the battle was lost to her. She could no longer hear the cannon, the shouting, the beating of blades on the rail, the distant sound of the Spaniard's guns. She could hear nothing but those words—*stupid, mindless bitch*—and she heard them over and over again.

A minute before, her life had been reduced to the purest simplicity, a fight to the death; nothing could be more clear and unequivocal, and she loved it.

Now all that was gone. Now the world that she had embraced and come to love did not seem quite real, as if she suddenly realized that all along she had been watching a play. Now she suspected that she did not understand a thing.

Mary stood on the main hatch, just behind the guns, and handed out cartridges of gunpowder to the gunners and cheered and howled with the men because she understood the value of enthusiasm and unity. She handled the cartridges because it was helpful and because as long as she was doing it, then none of the others—such as Harwood with his lit pipe clenched in his teeth, or Fetherston, who was repeatedly snapping the flint of his unloaded pistol, to what end Mary did not know—none of them could blow the *Pretty Anne* to eternity before the Spaniards had their chance.

"Powder monkey! Here!" John Howell shouted from the aftermost gun. Mary slipped the tight-filled canvas bag from the leather cylinder and tossed it gently to him.

The evening was settling down on them, the flashes from their guns and the *Guarda del Costa* growing brighter in the failing light. The Spaniards had lost this evening's race. They would not be able to work themselves into a position to devastate the *Pretty Anne* before the darkness deprived them of a target. The pirates had a nine-hour reprieve, and then at dawn they would be slaughtered.

The others drifted away from the great guns as the Spaniard ceased firing. Without the flash of their cannon, the enemy was all but lost in the gloom. The rum and brandy flowed, the shouting and cursing did not let off, but now they were just waiting. One more night and then the end.

They were giving up. Mary had seen it before. It was not a sullen and despondent kind of surrender, it was the fatalistic acceptance of the inevitable by bold men who always knew they would die a violent death, and here it was.

But Mary was not ready for that, nor did she subscribe to their philosophy of a short life but a merry one. She was trained to combat, and surrender did not come naturally. She wanted to fight back in a meaningful way.

Oh, Lord, what shall we do?

The men were wallowing in their debauchery. Calico

Jack Rackam was paralyzed—dare she say with fear?—and could no more lead the men than he could defeat the Spaniards single-handed. She had been watching him on and off through the evening, chewing on the end of his mustache, fiddling with his sword and his clothing, saying little. She saw the weak smile, the pathetic attempts at cheering with the men.

Jack was useless, the others were drunk. They were trapped under the Spaniards' heavy guns. It was the wheat field all over again, and the French artillery and the officers blown from their mounts. If they were to be saved, then Mary knew she would have to do it, because she was the only one still thinking.

What, what, what . . .

They could not remain where they were. Even as night fell they could see the Spaniards moving their ship with their anchors, working the guard ship into a position to pound the English pirates to kindling.

Very well, we must leave. We cannot get through the mangrove swamp, so we must leave by sea. For that we need a ship of some sort. The Pretty Anne *is lost, and we cannot take the Spaniard, so what then . . . ?*

"Corner!" she called to the quartermaster, who was holding the breaker of rum in his arms and pouring the last of its contents into his cup and over the deck and hatch. "A word, pray!"

Corner tossed the empty breaker over the side, picked up his cup, and staggered over on uncertain legs. "Aye, Read? Here, a toast to you, sir!" Corner grinned a big dumb grin and quaffed his rum.

"Corner, see here, if you would live to see another night, I have had a thought as to how it might be done. It is our last shift."

"Eh?" said Corner, but Mary could see that she had his attention.

"That sloop, the prize, the one that was under the *Guarda del Costa*'s quarter, they sent her off, and I reckon she is anchored on the other side of this island. It is the only thing that makes sense. The Dons will not see her as they warp into the channel.

"What say we take to the boat, make our way down the channel and around the island the back way. We can fall on the sloop with cold steel and have her and be gone, leave only this crazy old hull for the Dons to fire into, come morning. The *Guarda del Costa* will never see us, the island will be betwixt us."

Corner was nodding as his listened, and it took a moment for Mary's idea to work its way through the fog of rum, but as it penetrated, so his grin grew wider. "Ha ha, goddamn your eyes, Read, this is a fine thing! But why do you not tell it to Captain Jack?"

"I think the captain has little regard for me, and fear he would not listen to any plan of mine," Mary said, and that was true enough. At the same time, she did not think Jack had wits enough left to see the sense in what she was saying, nor courage enough to see it through.

"Pray, you tell it to him," Mary added, "and see he puts it into execution."

"Aye, that I will, Read, you whore's son!" He wheeled around, roared, "Jack, my dear, a word with you, sir!"

Corner pulled Jack aside, talked into his ear, and Mary watched the play of emotions across Jack's face: doubt, understanding, fear, resolve. He nodded, swallowed, cleared his throat, then stood up on the main hatch.

"Listen here, you men! Here is our main chance! We might live yet, if you'll listen to me!" he shouted, and the men gathered around.

The Pretty Annes were fourteen in all, and they just managed to fit in the longboat. Every space was taken up, so that the people at the oars had barely room enough to work them, and the gunnel of the boat was a mere nine inches above the water, amidships.

Mary was at her oar, holding it straight up, waiting for the order to ship oars. In the stern sheets sat Calico Jack and beside him, Anne Bonny, tight-lipped, looking away. Something had happened, Mary could see that, but she did not know what it might be.

"Ship oars," Jack said, in a raspy whisper, and Mary lowered her oar down, adjusting it so that the cloth bound around the loom fell between the thole pins. The cloth would prevent the oar from creaking as they rowed. Silence, silence, and cold steel was the order of the night.

"Give way!"

Mary pulled easy on the oar, felt the familiar resistance of the blade in the water and the motion of the boat as it gathered way. Up in the bow, Dicky Corner felt ahead with a long stick, poking at the sandy bottom in an effort to feel their way through the bars and shallows. It was a very dark night, no moon, and the stars afforded them just the barest visibility.

"A little to port, methinks, Jack," Corner whispered, and Jack nudged the tiller and the boat moved down that dark avenue of a channel, with the looming shapes of mangroves passing on either side.

For an hour they crept along in that black void, with only a wide strip of stars overhead, visible through the break in the jungle between mainland and island. Three times they ran the bow into a sandbar, once so hard that they had to tumble out of the boat into the waist-high water to pull it free.

That was when Mary was most frightened, standing in that black water, warm as blood, wondering what unseen things were circling her legs, finding their way into her loose-fitting trousers. It was a terrific relief for her to pull herself dripping over the gunnel and take her place again on the thwart.

At last the motion of the boat changed from the smooth, millpond water of the channel to a more pronounced pitching and rocking, and then they were bobbing in the swells of open water. Mary swiveled her head, looked forward as best she could. The black corridor of the channel had opened up to a great canopy of stars, clear down to the horizon, and one bright white light that could not be a star but had to be an anchor light on the prize sloop.

Jack put the helm over and pointed the longboat on a course directly for the light and it was lost from Mary's sight.

Mary could see grim faces now, grim and determined. This was the last ditch for them, the forlorn hope, perhaps the final gambit of their lives. If this game did not go their way, then it was execution, Spanish style, for the lot of them. Silently they pulled for the sloop.

Five minutes, and Mary looked again and now they were coming up with their intended victim. Out of the night a surprised voice called out, something in Spanish that Mary did not catch. The voice called again and this time Jack called back in his own easy Spanish and there was nothing more from the prize.

"Toss oars . . ." Jack hissed, and the oars came up and suddenly they were alongside the sloop. Corner grabbed on to the chains with the boathook and then they were up and over the side, moving by tacit consent, with never a word spoken.

Mary leapt up, stepped up on the thwart and onto the boarding step on the sloop's side. She felt taut and charged, she felt ready, all potential, like a loaded gun. She leapt up the three steps and onto the sloop's deck, her cutlass in her right hand, pistol in her left, as more of them swarmed out behind her.

To her left she saw the startled face of a Spanish sailor, wearing bits of what might have been an officer's uniform, a young man, nineteen at most, a midshipman, Mary reckoned. The glow from the anchor light fell on his startled face and his mouth flew open to shout, but Mary raised her pistol and pointed it at his forehead, five inches from the muzzle, and she said, "Shhhh," and the officer closed his mouth.

The rest of the Pretty Annes swarmed over the sloop and down below and a minute later three confused, partially clad Spanish sailors had joined their single officer in the bows, and that was all there was of the sloop's defense.

The vessel was theirs, with not a shot fired, not a single noise louder than a footfall.

The men, Calico Jack's men, slapped him on the back and grinned and praised his bold plan and wished him joy of his victory, and Jack smiled in return and thanked them. Mary watched this and she smiled because she found it genuinely amusing, but beyond that she did not care. She did not want congratulations or credit. She only wanted to live.

"Let us slip the cable then and go," Jack said once the adulation had died down some. A few of the men went forward, pushing the terrified former crew of the sloop out of the way as they pulled the loops of anchor cable off the bits. Others cast off the lines holding the jib and the mainsail in place and they hoisted those sails up until they were set and flapping gently in the light ocean breeze.

Jack had a hold of the tiller. "Let the cable go!" he called forward, and Harwood took off the last turns and the heavy rope snaked out of the hawsehole and disappeared into the sea.

The sloop, freed from the anchor's hold on the bottom, began to buck in the waves. The bow turned slowly and the sails grew quiet as they filled with wind.

It was like a magical thing, order from chaos, as the irregular motion of the drifting vessel, the clattering and banging of the disorganized sails and rigging, became the steady, silent, deliberate rhythm of a vessel under way. Experienced hands trimmed the sails until they were providing the maximum thrust and the sloop heeled further and the gurgling of the water along her side rose in pitch.

In the glow of the anchor light Mary could see great, wide grins of triumph, of delight, of utter relief. They might have been prepared to die, but they still preferred to live, and now there was every chance that they would, and aboard a new vessel taken from the Spaniards in a bold and audacious stroke.

Fetherston took down the anchor light and blew out the flame and the sloop made the best of her way toward the east, plowing a wake through the dark sea, leaving the un-suspecting *Guarda del Costa* astern.

On the afterdeck, Jack Rackam still held the tiller, his eyes, through long habit, moving from the sails up to the stars and then forward, beyond the bow. They moved from one to the other to the other in a steady sequence, which he kept up without ever thinking about it.

He found the North Star and lined it up with one of the sloop's backstays and in that way held the vessel on a steady course, even though he could not see the compass. He did not even know if there was one aboard.

He took a deep breath and let it out because he knew that that was what people did when they were relaxing, but it did nothing for him.

I took the sloop, I took the goddamned sloop, stole it right out from under the Dons' noses, the bastards, he thought, because he reckoned that thinking such a thing would help him enjoy his triumph, but it did not.

Before, when he had come up from the great cabin, dressed up in his finest, weapons at the ready, pretending that that was why he had gone below, and not just to puke in private, he had felt brittle, like a china figurine.

Now he was that same thing still, that same fragile thing, only he had been dropped from a great height. He was shattered, broken into a thousand pieces.

He had said something to Anne, back then, back during the nightmare in the channel with the Dons coming for them, but he could not recall what. Whatever it was, she seemed to be disgusted with him.

The others, however, had congratulated him on his victory. He had lived, he had won, he had not been discovered for the coward that he knew himself to be. Before, that had always been enough. Before, if he had those things, he could find some joy in his life.

But not this time. The terror he had experienced back in the channel, when he knew that the Dons would take him, that he could not escape, that terror had become a part of him. He could not shake it, could not talk himself out of it.

The others might look at him and see a whole man, but he himself knew that he was only tiny fragments, somehow held together, but only just. He did not know if he would ever be whole again, and that made him more anxious still.

Mary slept and then she woke before dawn and stretched and looked around and recalled where she was. She pulled herself to her feet and scratched distractedly at her stomach.

Anne was awake, standing in the bow, staring off toward the slight gray band of light in the east, just the hint of sunrise. Mary walked over to her. They were alone there.

"Bonny, what say you? You appear low this morning."

"Hmm? Oh, good morning to you. I have been thinking."

"Indeed?" Mary said, but Anne ignored her.

"I have been thinking about Jack. Sometimes I do not know who he is."

"How is that?"

"Oh, Lord, I do not know. He takes the weight of his responsibilities so hard. It distracts him, sometimes to the point where he cannot think, or so it seems."

It is called "panicking," my dear, Mary thought, but all she said was "Hmm . . ." in a thoughtful tone.

"I thought . . . oh, I swear . . ." She looked away again, sorting her thoughts out, shaking her head slightly as she did. "I might have thought the very worst of him, were it not for this bold thing that he has done, taking this sloop from right under those damnable Spaniards' noses!"

"Bold indeed, and well done. He has saved us all."

"But still . . ." Anne turned back at Mary, and there was a searching look in her eyes. "Back in the channel, when it seemed all was lost . . . Jack seemed . . ."

"See here, you cannot necessarily know the measure of a man by the way he acts in a fight. I have seen the most useless creatures become heroes, and the ones you might think would stand the boldest cower away. It is against the nature of things, battles and such. There is no way to know how one might react, or, indeed, what is in a man's heart."

"So what think you of Jack?"

Mary shrugged. "I do not know what is inside him. I know only that he was captain, and he led us in this bold thing and we have won. Beyond that I cannot say."

Anne gave Mary a weak smile. "I reckon you are right, that one cannot know anything, beyond what one sees," she said. "And you are one to know. I will not even tell you what thoughts I had."

The sky was growing lighter and they could now see all the way to a watery horizon. Off the starboard rail, the mainland of Cuba, and behind them, directly behind, and a good eight nautical miles, the island behind which they had tried to hide. The *Guarda del Costa* was nowhere in sight.

Mary and Anne stood for a moment, enjoying the morning quiet. And then, far off and muted, came the sound of gunfire. Heads snapped around, ears cocked, listening. The sound came from astern, from the place they had left. It was the *Guarda del Costa,* opening up on the abandoned sloop *Pretty Anne.*

The cannonade was unrelenting, and soon a billow of gunsmoke could be seen rising up above the little island astern. The pirates smiled, shook their heads, spit on the deck in derision. But they did not cheer, did not congratulate themselves or throw insults at the Spaniards. It had been too close for that.

In the next hour they put another four miles between themselves and the guard ship, and in all that time the gunfire did not cease, only grew less audible as the distance opened up.

They hove to long enough to hustle their Spanish prisoners into the longboat in which they had attacked the sloop. It was in poor shape, as indeed all of the former *Pretty Anne* had been, but it would serve to get them safe ashore.

Ten minutes later they were under way again, and still the gunfire did not let up, or even slacken.

"They are damned earnest, ain't they?" Fetherston offered, and no one laughed, but several nodded their heads in agreement.

Then from the forward scuttle came the voice of Thomas Earl. "Halloa, there, lads, see what I have here!" he shouted, and out of the scuttle stepped a man of middling age, gray and thinning hair that was wild on his head, his clothes in great disarray and filthy, and behind him, two more men and then Earl, herding them along. "See here, Jack!" Earl called aft. "These here is the rightful owners of the sloop, and don't you have some explaining to do!"

Jack stood and ambled forward and Mary saw he was the confident, swaggering Jack whom she had first seen aboard the captive *Hoorn*. He stepped up to the older man, bowed an elegant bow. "And who might I have the pleasure of addressing?" he asked.

"I am James Larson and I am owner and master of this vessel. We was taken by the Dons four days back. I don't know who you are, or how you come to have her now, but I am right grateful to be free of them Spaniard bastards."

"As well you should be, sir. I, sir, am John Rackam. Calico Jack Rackam. You have heard of me?"

"No."

"Well, you bloody have now. And you may be sorry to learn, sir, that this sloop is no more yours now than it was when the Dons had her. For the price of rescuing you I shall keep her for my own use. You may be glad at least that you will not be burned at the stake as a heretic."

Larson regarded Jack for a moment and then glanced around at the rough men in his company. He had the look of a seaman, and as such he was able to see right off how things lay.

"Pirates. Bloody pirates," he said. "Just my bleeding luck. Well, I wish you joy of your capture, sir, and I will be grateful if you could put us ashore in the first place that don't answer to the pope."

"Perhaps I will," said Jack, "and perhaps I will not."

All this Mary watched from the bow, but her attention was not on the interplay between Calico Jack and James

Larson. Rather, she was watching one of the two men behind Larson, presumably the former crew of the sloop.

The young man—he looked to be somewhere in his twenties—was frightened, but standing straight, head up and defiant, pushing his fear down by force of will. He hair was curly and almost black and tumbled over his shoulders. His chin was strong and covered with several days growth of beard, his features finely chiseled, almost feminine in their precision.

He wore the clothing typical of a deckhand on a small vessel, the wide slops, the loose shirt, the neckerchief bound around his throat. In his arms he held, most incongruously, a violin, which he seemed to shield as a mother would a child.

He was, if not the exact image of Frederick Heesch, then something very close. And it was not his looks alone, but something in his bearing, the pride and resolve to not be afraid, that damned violin.

Mary shook her head, pulled her eyes away, looked over the side, toward Cuba, toward the horizon, toward anything but that man. She did not want to look on him because when she did she could see her past and her future, all at once.

Oh God, Jack, put him ashore, she thought. *Please Lord, Jack, do not make that one sail with us.*

BOOK III

A TRYAL OF PIRATES

Chapter 31

WHEN AT LAST THE BAILIFF RETURNED TO THE HOLDING cell to tell the men on trial for their lives that His Excellency the President, Sir Nicholas Lawes, and the Honorable Commissioners had rendered their verdict, he found John Rackam still sitting on the stone bench, back against the whitewashed bricks, staring straight ahead.

The bailiff saw a pensive and serene Calico Jack.

What he could not see was that Jack was no longer afraid.

He had gone beyond fear. The fear had finally consumed everything that was inside him, there was nothing left, and like a fire that incinerates all the flammable material within its reach and then goes out, so Jack's terror had faded to a cold nothing, a charred black spot.

The bailiff held up a list, one of his interminable lists, and called, "The following prisoners will proceed with escort to the courthouse: John Rackam, George Fetherston, Richard Corner, John Davies, John Howell, Patrick Carty, Thomas Earl, James Dobbin, and Noah Harwood."

Those men stood in a jangling chorus of manacles and leg irons and Jack stood as well, though it took an extraordinary effort. He would have been pleased to just sit on that bench, unmoving, until he died. But Sir Nicholas, he knew, would not allow that.

He glanced over at Jacob Wells and those others, standing at the far end of the holding cell, trying to distance themselves as much as they could from the genuine pirates, those bound for the gallows. Jack thought for a moment that he would march back into the courthouse and tell old Lawes that they had joined in with the pirates as willingly as ever did the most despicable rogue. He would do it just for spite, just to bring them along to hell with him, but even as he thought it he knew he did not have the will or the energy.

At the door to the holding cell stood the merciless bailiff and four armed soldiers. Through the door Jack could see the audience and standers-by, who had withdrawn from the courthouse for the Commissioners to render a verdict, now filing back in. They had been disappointed in their desire to see the women pirates stand their trial, but at least they would have the chance to watch the men's faces as they were sentenced to death.

Finally the last of the crowd shuffled by and Jack and the others were led back into the huge courtroom and once more set at the bar.

Sir Nicholas made them stand and wait for a few minutes as he shuffled papers and mumbled to the bailiff and generally let the tension build, as one will do who understands the mechanics of drama. At last he looked up, his face like a sunburned bulldog, scowled down at the men at the bar, and said, "This court, having maturely and deliberately considered all the evidence which has been given against the prisoners—"

Jack felt a spark of hope, a little orange glow where the charred stuff was stirred, but then it went out because he knew it was foolish.

"—have unanimously found you all guilty of piracy, robbery, and felony charged against you in the third and fourth article of the above-said articles which have been exhibited against you. Have any of you anything to say or offer why sentence of death should not be passed upon you, for these said offenses?"

Why should he not be killed? The reasons flowed from Jack's mind. How could this body, this physical thing that had been Jack Rackam, that had given pleasure to himself and to so many women, how could this thing that was he be put to death, be killed, be strung up until it was just a lifeless nothing? It was absurd, it could not be done. It was an unimaginable waste.

But it would be done, and Jack knew it, and he said nothing.

The others were silent as well, for the most part, save for a few desultory mutters of "We're not guilty, m'lord, we swears it," which did nothing at all to aid their circumstance.

"Very well," said Sir Nicholas, when he had listened to all the halfhearted protests he was willing to hear. "You, John Rackam, George Fetherston, Richard Corner, John Davies, John Howell, Patrick Carty, Thomas Earl, James Dobbin, and Noah Harwood, are to go from hence to the place from whence you came, and from thence to the place of execution, where you shall severally be hanged by the neck till you are severally dead. And God of His infinite mercy be merciful on every one of your souls."

Lawes issued that last order to God in the same disinterested and mechanical manner with which he had ordered the men's death, and then he rapped his bench with his mallet.

And then Jack heard his own voice speak. It sounded very far away, and he seemed to have no knowledge of what he would say.

"My Lord?"

Lawes scowled down. "Sentence has been passed. It is too late now for further argument."

"My Lord, might I request that, before I am hung, I be allowed to say my farewells to Anne Bonny, to whom I am in spirit betrothed."

Lawes continued to scowl as he considered that. "This court does not consider a betrothal in spirit to be anything more than adultery and fornication, which it is. But yes, I will allow this. Bailiff, you will see that the condemned, before going to the place of execution, is allowed to speak one last time to the prisoner Bonny."

"Yes, my Lord."

The condemned . . . Jack thought. *Yes, that is me. The condemned. And such was I from the day I was born.*

At five o'clock the jailor brought Mary and Anne's supper—boiled meat of some sort, bread, small beer—pretty unappetizing fare, but by the standards of shipboard, not so bad, and Anne and Mary took it without complaint.

"What of the trial? Is it done with?" Mary asked. There was anxiety in her tone, but of course, there would be, and the jailor was a kind man.

"Aye, done and gone. Would you know the outcome?"

"I have no doubt of the outcome," said Anne from her cell across the alleyway. "They did not need that great farce of a trial to sentence them to hang, but I reckon Nicholas bloody Lawes will sleep better if he knows he done it the way the King wishes. Very well then, for the sake of formality, what was the verdict?"

"Guilty, Annie. Each and every one of them, severally guilty."

"Well," said Anne, "we need no ghost come from the grave to tell us this."

"What of those other rogues?" Mary asked, and her tone was a reasonable approximation of disinterest. "That Wells and Montgomery and them? They were not at the bar with Jack Rackam and the others."

"No, they was tried separate, and I do not know why. But they was all found to have been forced into piracy, and so was set free. Them Frenchmen what gave testimony, they both swore those fellows was forced into it."

Mary nodded, but inside she felt herself floating, her spirit lifting off. Jacob would not hang! It was the most she could hope for, indeed it was all she could hope for, and it had come to pass and so the rest of it, what would happen to her, did not matter.

She knew that she and Anne would hang. They would be charged with the same articles as were Rackam and his crew, and condemned by the same witnesses. But Jacob would not. She could die if she knew she had not sentenced Jacob to death as well.

All of this joyful song she kept inside her and betrayed none of it to the jailor, who, if he became suspicious that Mary had some special feelings for the young man, might feel compelled to report the same, kind man though he was, and Jacob would find himself once more under the angry stare of Sir Nicholas Lawes.

So instead she took a bite of bread, chewed it, and said, "Well, I'll warrant them for drowning, since they wasn't born to be hanged."

Jacob Wells, clutching his fiddle and standing up bold to Calico Jack. Mary had pulled her eyes from him and wished that Jack would set the young man ashore. She did not want him aboard, because in that first glance she could see how things would go, could see it with the startling clarity that one gets looking through tropical water down many fathoms to the bottom.

She did not need the complications, the heartbreak. She had run away to the Caribbean to escape that.

Jack was in fine, strutting form, safe as they were with the *Guarda del Costa* miles to leeward. He was leaning on his sword, making Larson, the former owner of the sloop, answer questions for the pirates' amusement. It was nearly as good as any such performance he had given, but he had been drinking, more than was his custom, and it somewhat dulled his delivery, though the Pretty Annes saw nothing amiss.

"Do you, sir, not wish to be a freeman and lord, such as we here are?" he asked, and when Larson said, "I am a free man without being a pirate as well," his answer brought jeers and howls and laughter from the gathered men, as, indeed, any answer would have.

They laughed at Larson and they mocked him, but in the end he won their respect because he showed no fear. He was bold and defiant and that was worthy of admiration among the Brethren of the Coast.

When Jack was done with him, he moved on to the young man with the fiddle, as Mary knew he would.

"What ho? What have we here? A musician? Play us a tune, then."

"I am no great artist with this," the man said, his voice clear and strong.

"No? But you hold it like a mother holds her babe, which ain't what I would expect from one who does not know the use of an instrument. Play."

The young man put the violin under his chin. His eyes were fixed on Jack's, holding them firm. He raised the bow and drew it across the strings in something like a melody, but with enough screeching and squealing to make the hair on the back of Mary's neck stand up, and set the others shouting and hissing.

Jack lifted the sword, held it under the man's chin so that the wicked point was just pricking his skin.

"Play good," Jack said.

For a full measure they stood, regarding each other, and then the dark-haired man applied the bow again, moving it fast and smooth, and the sound that came from the instrument was the sweetest that Mary had ever heard.

He played on, a tune that was at once lively and melancholy. Fore and aft the pirates fell silent as they listened and the young man closed his eyes and looked as if he had no notion of where he was, or that he was playing under duress.

He played beautifully, passionately. It was a form of defiance, showing all of them that he was not too afraid to perform with such grace. He was saying, *Sod the lot of you, you cannot do this.*

Mary shook her head. *You bloody fool,* she thought. *You have just sealed your fate.*

With a grand flourish the young man brought the piece to a close. He lowered the bow and the violin and looked Jack in the eye once more, as if to say, *There. Now what say you?*

There was a second of silence on deck and then the pirates burst out into cheers and applause. Jack smiled wide, stepped up to the young man, clapped him on the back, and said, "Excellently well done! What is your name, lad?"

"Jacob Wells."

"Well, Jacob Wells, we have need of a skilled fellow

like you, can spin a merry tune such as that! How would you care to join with our company of gentlemen adventurers?"

"I would not. I'll have no truck with piracy."

This bold statement brought more howls and jeers. Over the others Jack said, "Well, my dear, the thing of it is, we'll not give you the choice. Willing or no, you are a pirate now, lad! And God in His infinite mercy be merciful on your soul!"

At this the others cheered and crowded around Jacob Wells and slapped him on the back and plied him with rum, which he drank after sufficient coercion.

Mary shook her head, looked beyond the bow toward the island of Cuba to starboard and the open ocean beyond the larboard rail.

She was happy that Jack had made Wells join them, and she was angry and she was miserable and she was delighted. It was all mixed up in her and she did not know what she was beyond very, very uncertain.

The new *Pretty Anne* stood north and east, leaving Cuba below the horizon as quickly as she could, making for the relative safety of open water. They sailed on in that manner for all of the next day, then came about and made their way southeast, finally running down the windward passage between Cuba's easternmost end and the northwestern tip of Hispaniola.

It was not long before the pirates realized how fine a bargain they had made. The sloop they now manned was newly built and fully provisioned, her sails crisp and white and not hanging in big, baggy pockets, her bilge clean and sweet smelling.

It was a further delight to realize that not only had they stolen the Spaniards' valuable prize, and left a near worthless one in its place, but that the Spaniards had beaten the only prize left to them to kindling before they knew it.

A fortnight after their escape from the *Guarda del Costa*

they raised the island of Jamaica. They skirted the northern shore and stood in to Dry Harbor Bay, and there they put Captain James Larson ashore, but kept on board Thomas Montgomery, who proved to be a skilled carpenter, and Jacob Wells, who was their delight.

Jacob was an adequate sailor, but his skill with the violin was astounding. At dinnertime every afternoon he was made to play for an hour, and again during the dog watches, often for two hours straight.

He seemed never to repeat a tune. Mary could not tell if he was making the melodies up as he went, or if he had in his head a great repertoire of music. He played hard and tirelessly, he played because he loved it and because he could lose himself in the music and forget his circumstance, he played as a matter of defiance, just as he had first played for Jack.

And despite his oft-expressed dislike of the pirates, the pirates came to like him very much, because he was a good-natured fellow, and a fine musician and a tolerable sailor.

"You love him, do you not?" Anne said one morning, high aloft, and it startled Mary.

"Who?" Mary asked, flushing, since she had at that moment been staring down at Jacob Wells, who was standing in the bows and sewing a patch in his second best shirt.

" 'Who'!" Anne laughed. "La, Mary, do you think I am blind?"

"If you mean Wells, well, he is a handsome lad, with much to recommend him, but as for love, I think not."

"A short life and a merry one, dear. I do not know how long we can go like this. You must take what you wish and take it quick. I would never warrant you for being afraid, but in this I think you are."

"Afraid? Of what?" Mary asked, but of course, she knew full well. She was surprised that Anne understood what was in her, but then she had learned before that Anne was a woman of more insight than one might guess. Mary was not pleased to hear that insight given voice.

"You are afraid to love him."

"Perhaps, I'll grant you, there is something in what you

say . . ." It was all very complicated, and all jumbled together in Mary's head, all of the implications of her feelings. "But we are not exactly in a private drawing room
here. I am still playing the man and would not care to see
what these rogues would do if the truth were revealed. How
would I tell Jacob and be sure he would not tell the others?"

At that Anne laughed, to Mary's annoyance. "Forgive
me, Mary, dear, but that is a weak excuse. You revealed
yourself to Frederick in the midst of the army, revealed
yourself to me and your secret has been held. I am sure,
with some thought, you could manage the same with Jacob."

Mary nodded. Anne was right, of course. Keeping her
sex a secret was the least of it.

"You are afraid to be hurt again," Anne continued, "such
as you were with Frederick. I can understand that. But if
this all ends and the two of you are parted, you will never
have the chance again. Given a choice, would you prefer
to have never known Frederick, to have never had what
you had with him?"

Mary thought about that as she stared out at the horizon.
She had always told herself that it would have been better
if she and Frederick had never met, never fallen in love,
never married. Better that she should never have known
what happiness was, so that she would not know later what
she had lost.

But she knew that that was not true. Better to have had
that bright moment of joy, better to have known Frederick
and loved him and lost him than to never have had that
honor.

And then something else that Anne had said called for
her attention. "What do you mean, you do not know how
long we can go on like this?"

Anne frowned, shrugged, looked out to sea. "I feel sometimes that it is all coming to an end. They are rounding up
the pirates and hanging them by the score. We have taken
nothing worth the taking in . . . nothing since we have re-
joined the ship, and they took little while we were in Cuba.
Fishing boats . . ."

Anne paused and then turned and looked Mary in the eye. "Jack is shattered, Mary, my dear. I cannot guess what happened to him back there, with the *Guarda del Costa* and such, but he has not been the same man since. Only once since then has he lain with me, and it was a poor attempt at best. Have you not seen how nervous he seems? How much more he drinks?"

Mary nodded. "I have. And I have seen it before, I daresay, in other men. A person can take but so much, so much fear, so much worry, so much responsibility. With no respite, anyone will collapse under the weight of it, in the end."

"I fear that has happened to my Jack. And if he is not able to command, then we are done for, in the sweet trade. There is no other. Dicky Corner may be a great brute in a fight, but he is no leader."

"No, he is not."

They were silent for a moment and then Anne said, brighter, "So, my dear, if you will not squander your opportunity, I suggest that you make love to this handsome young man, with ever as much passion as I made love to you. And let us hope, with happier results."

Chapter 32

THAT EVENING, AS THE *PRETTY ANNE* PROWLED ALONG the north coast of Jamaica, Mary listened to the wistful strains of some tune that flowed like magic from Jacob's violin, watched him as he played as if in a trance.

His eyes were closed and his mouth was set in a bit of a frown, giving his otherwise boyish face a stern look. His bowing arm moved with a motion that hardly seemed human, more like a sapling swaying in the wind, or water tumbling over rocks.

His long fingers crawled over the neck of the instrument—Mary could not pull her eyes from those fingers. His body had none of the soft, awkward quality of one who had spent his life in conservatories and drawing rooms. He was lean and well formed. The muscles in his arms stood out as he worked his bow and produced those lovely airs.

Mary glanced fore and aft, saw with some amusement the hairy, beastly pirates who were quietly listening to the delicate melody, some looking as if they might weep.

She thought of Annie's words, about making love to Jacob, about how all this might end.

That talk frightened her. It echoed a sort of nebulous dread of pending disaster that had overcome her now and again. Nothing that she could examine, it was not so definite as that. Just a sense of the end coming closer.

Hardly bloody surprising, she though. Piracy was not a trade that offered much longevity. Killed in battle, or by disease, or drowned or hung, a pirate's life might not always be merry, but it was generally short.

Then I shall not tarry a moment more, Mary decided. *Into the breach and all that.*

She stood as Jacob finished up his evening performance, and as the others drifted away she approached him and leaned against the bulwark. "That bit you played, next to the last, that was by that fellow Bach, was it not?"

Jacob looked up, surprised. "Yes indeed. I did not know you were so learned about music."

Mary shrugged. "I have picked up a bit, here and there." In fact, she knew nothing about music, save for marches and camp songs and that one piece that Jacob had played, which she had heard when a traveling musician played it at the Three Trade Horses, and it had so delighted the audience that he was made to play it three more times. "But tell me, how does one so talented come to be a pirate?"

"I was forced. You know that."

"I know. I am fooling with you. But how did you come to be sailing aboard this sloop?"

Jacob wrapped his violin in a cloth and placed it gently in a wooden box that Montgomery had been ordered to run up for him, the pirates being now as anxious as he to preserve the instrument. "We lived in Bath. My father was a tutor of music and dance. A few years ago he decided to move us all to Jamaica. He reckoned on grand opportunities there, but soon after we arrived he and my mother and sister took sick with the yellow jack and died.

"I was quite destitute and could not make a living with my playing, and then Captain Larson was good enough to take me in and offer to teach me the sailor's trade. He is a kind man and we are very close, though he acted as if he hardly knew me whilst he was aboard. I think he reckoned it would go hard on me, was these . . . fellows to think I was close with the captain."

"Mmm," Mary said. *You have seen you own share of pain,* she thought. It showed in his eyes. That was part of what drew her to him, she realized.

"Will you follow the sea, still?" Mary asked.

"I do not know. I reckon now I shall be hung for a pirate before I ever get the chance."

Mary laughed at that. "I do not think your time in the sweet trade will be very long lasted. I do not reckon mine will be."

Jacob glanced around, clearly unsure if such a discussion would be tolerated by the others, but Mary looked unconcerned, so he spoke. "Are you forced to this? Do you not wish to be . . . on the account, as these rogues are wont to say?"

"Oh, I entered into this trade of my own free will, I will confess to that. Mine has been a rambling life. Soldier, man-of-war's man. I have been such as one would call a pirate for near two years now and I have come to see the folly of it. It is not the life for me, and as soon as I get the chance I will go ashore and foreswear it."

"Honestly?"

"Honestly."

Honestly? Perhaps. Or perhaps I say that so that you will not find me despicable.

Mary did not know. To have again what she and Frederick had, there was nothing she would not foreswear. But she would not trade this carefree life in the West Indies for the misery of Europe, the frigid hell of sailing the North Sea.

She would give up the sweet trade for something better, but right then she could not picture what that might be.

Jacob Wells seemed much relieved to have a sympathetic friend aboard the *Pretty Anne*. After their discussion at the rail that evening, he made an effort to stick close to Mary, which did not displease her.

Soon she invited him to join her mess, the four-man groups into which the crew was divided for purposes of cooking and eating. It was one of the most intimate divisions on shipboard, and one's messmates were considered to be of higher priority even than one's other watchmates or crewmates.

This invitation Jacob gladly accepted, and soon he found himself taking his meals with Mary and Fetherston and Thomas Earl, and slowly, day by day, he grew more comfortable in that rough company.

But still Jacob did not alter a bit in his opposition to piracy, and Mary, who felt ambiguous at best on the subject, did not waver in her assurance that she, too, had no taste for the sweet trade.

"I have a thought," Mary said one evening, "to make some small fortune on the account, and then perhaps set up an inn. Perhaps in Freetown, or Kingston. Barbados. Someplace in the West Indies. I'll not go back to that cursed Europe."

Jacob nodded. "As hard as my lot has been here, I feel the same. The water, the jungles, the warm trade winds ... there is nothing can compare to the West Indies. I reckon to spend my days here as well."

They stood for a moment, close, in companionable silence. "Michael," Jacob said at last, "here is a silly question ... or perhaps it is not ... but there is the one fellow, with the reddish hair? Bonny?"

"Yes?"

"Well, no one has said as much to me, but ... is that not a woman?"

"Yes, she is indeed a woman."

There was a moment of silence as Jacob digested that. "Is that not passing strange, a woman dressed in men's clothing and sailing as a pirate?"

"You would be surprised, Jacob, dear. But yes, it ain't usual. Anne, that is her name, she and Calico Jack are lovers. Have been these past two years or more."

Jacob nodded and again they fell into silence. At last he spoke again, hesitatingly. "Michael, may I . . . Could I ask you . . ."

"Yes?"

"I . . . Lord, I should never ask such a thing, but I feel, somehow, because you have been so kind to me, that I might . . ."

Mary felt a flush of fear, embarrassment, anxiety. *Has he bloody guessed the truth of me?* There was still none aboard but Jack and Anne who knew her true sex. Mary was still not certain how the news would be received, if she dared let her shipmates know.

"What is it?"

"Well, you are not so big a fellow, and I would reckon you are not even as old as me. Are you . . . are you not afraid, in such company as we sail?"

Mary smiled, mostly from relief. She had not yet even decided if Jacob was to know the truth, or if she could trust him, and she did not want him smoking it on his own.

"At first, perhaps," she said. "I was sailing aboard a Dutch merchantman that was taken by this lot; that is when I joined them. It was a damned frightening sight, I'll tell you, seeing the likes of Fetherston and Corner coming over the rail. And Jack with his strutting about like he is deciding whether or not you shall live.

"But for all his peacock's ways, Jack is merciful. He does not kill for the pleasure of it, and I would not have joined him if he did. Yes, these fellows can be frightening, but they are all great republicans. If you obey the rules, then you will get along fine. Hell, you are messing with Fetherston, and he has not knocked you on the head yet, has he?"

"No."

"Just keep away from that little bastard Billy Bartlett. He is the meanest of the lot, and the only one will do you harm for his own amusement."

Jacob nodded, and looked somewhat mollified. "I am no great fighter, I'll own that."

"I had a notion that was so."

Aft and below in the tiny great cabin, which was an altogether finer dwelling than the cabin aboard their former sloop, Anne Bonny was waiting on Calico Jack.

She lay back, propped up on her elbows on the cushion on top of the after lockers. Her hair was loose and hanging in all its thick, reddish blond beauty over her shoulders and down her back. Her shirt was partway unbuttoned, revealing the alluring tops of her round breasts. Her belt was off, and she was barefoot, and the top buttons of her trousers were undone.

Jack was drunk.

"Ah, Annie, dear, you are a one to set a man's heart to pounding!" he said. He took an uncertain step toward her, and then steadied himself on the table and raised the bottle of brandy to his lips and drank.

"That was my hope, Jack, dear," she said. "Now, pray, put down the bottle and come and attend to me."

Jack nodded, but he did not look his old cocksure self. He wedged the bottle in place between two cushions, stumbled over to where Anne lay. He pulled off his coat and tossed it aside and lay down on top of her, kissing her, exploring her mouth with his tongue.

Anne closed her eyes, tried to enjoy herself, tried to summon up her former passion. Jack's mouth tasted of brandy and rum and the smoke from his pipe and some other vague memories.

His mouth had always tasted that way, of course, given the amount of drinking and smoking that was part of the pirates' normal day.

Anne had loved that once, the foreign, dangerous quality. It was the taste of Port Royal and Nassau and Madagascar, all those wicked places.

But now there was something decayed about it, something miserable and desperate, and as Jack fumbled clumsily with Anne's shirt, squeezing her breasts overly hard, it just made the whole thing worse.

Anne ran her hands through his hair, stared up at the deckhead above, and missed the beautiful, attentive lover with whom she had run away.

Jack pulled her shirt open, popping the buttons off. It was not the first time he had done that, but for the first time Anne thought, *Now I shall have to sew the damned things on again . . .*

He ran his mouth over her breasts, handling her roughly, but it was not the alluring, desperate, panting rough play they had once enjoyed. It was just rough.

Anne moved under him, made a sighing sound as his tongue ran over her nipple, but she did not really mean it. Jack was breathing hard and sweating and once his hand slipped off the cushion and he fell on top of her, and then pulled her hair as he set his hand back on the locker.

Ten minutes of that awkward, irritating play and Jack sat up, closed his eyes, threw his head back. He looked as if he might cry.

"Annie, my love, it is no use. Do you see? I am unmanned, I cannot make love to you."

Anne looked at him. Once she would have been angry. She could picture Anne Bonny of a year before flying at him, furious that he should not be able to perform. She would have seen it as a personal affront. Putting hands on her fine body should be enough to send any man into a frenzy of desire.

"Come, Jack, my dear, let me hold you." She reached out her arms and he lay down in them and she hugged him as he rested his face against her chest. She could feel his tears on her naked flesh.

Oh, Jack, Jack, my love. Is it all over? And what will we do now, my dear? Wherever can we go?

Chapter 33

THEY SPENT SOME TIME IN THE SPRING OF 1720 TUCKED away in a small harbor on the northern coast of Jamaica. Some luck had finally come their way in the matter of prizes, and they went to that hidden place to celebrate, as the buccaneers were wont to do, riding at anchor so that there was not even the concern of keeping a vessel at sea to interfere with their revelries.

For the rest of the spring they continued to hunt the seas between Jamaica and Cuba. They took what vessels they could, but they were small-time prizes, for the most part merchant sloops and fishing boats smaller and poorer than the pirates themselves. The great days of buccaneering on the Spanish Main, the days of the noble Spanish bullion fleets, the armies of freebooters, the Drakes, the De Graafs, the Morgans, were gone.

Jack was not doing well. Mary could see that. He was drinking more than she had ever seen. He was quiet, morose, and spent more and more time below. She had tried to broach the subject with Anne, but Anne was not of a mind to discuss it, so Mary let it be.

At the same time, Mary's feelings for Jacob Wells—soft spoken, gentle, yet quick-witted, firm in his opinions and masterful with his violin—had grown deeper and more complicated. They were dear friends, which was the most they could be, with Jacob believing as he did that Mary was a man.

Mary showed him the ways of arms, and how to display the proper ferocity when boarding a prize, and how to play the pirate so he would not seem too ill suited for his role. And Jacob, while never embracing the pirates' ways, came at least to find his situation tolerable, and at times, though he would not say as much, enjoyable.

"Come, Mary, dear," Anne asked, after a few weeks of this, "will you not let the poor fellow know?"

They were sitting way out on the bowsprit, in the late evening, while behind them the bulk of the *Pretty Anne* plowed her way along, and on deck Jacob gave his evening performance to an appreciative crew.

Mary, for all of her passion for Jacob and the pleasure she took from his company, would not allow that affection to come between her and Anne. She loved Anne. Sometimes she thought that she loved Anne more than she could any man, because there was between them none of the complications that come between a man and a woman.

"Yes," Mary said, "I think I shall give him a hint."

"A hint?"

"I will tease the poor fellow. For my own amusement."

"You are a wicked villain, if ever I saw one." Anne was quiet for a moment, and then in a different tone said, "You told me once of the terror you felt in revealing yourself to Frederick. Do you not feel that now?"

Mary thought about that. "No, I do not," she said at last. "I do not know why. Perhaps because I do not feel so desperate here, in the West Indies, as I did in Flanders. Perhaps this life, the sweet trade, has made it so I cannot take anything too serious." She smiled at Anne. "Perhaps because I know that even if Jacob did reject me, I should still have you."

Anne smiled as well. "That you would, my dear. Blood sisters, do you recall?"

And so there was a certain playfulness, a certain light-heartedness in Mary when she told Jacob to accompany her down below and help her rearrange some cables. She felt none of the panic she had with Frederick in the tent when, in the sweltering heat of the cable tier, she unbuttoned her red waistcoat and then, in a convincing accident, tore her shirt and let the rent hang open just long enough for Jacob to get a glimpse, to draw in his breath with a startled gasp, before she closed it up again.

She turned and met the confused, openmouthed face of Jacob Wells with an expression of innocence, then buttoned her waistcoat and announced they were done.

"But hold a moment . . ." Jacob stammered, grabbing her arm.

"Yes?" asked Mary, as if nothing out of the ordinary had occurred. Jacob, she could see, was not entirely certain of what he had seen in the dim light of the cable tier. No doubt it would seem more reasonable to him that he was mistaken than that Michael Read should be a woman.

Finally he seemed to lose the courage to ask so outrageous a question as he had been considering. He let go of her arm, muttered something Mary could not hear.

They went topside, into the brilliant sun and the cooling trade wind, and drank their fill of water. Mary could feel Jacob's eyes on her, could see he was again on the edge of saying something, but again he did not.

For two more days he did not, though Mary could tell that he was not easy in his mind.

Finally he stepped up to her, an hour or so after his evening concert, after he had poured some Dutch courage down his throat, and said, "Michael, might I have a word with you? Below, perhaps?"

Mary followed him below and forward, up near the bows, in the quiet place where the spare sails were stowed. He stopped, turned to her, and blurted out, "Michael, we are friends, and you will forgive me a question that seems too insane to even think on, but . . . goddamn my eyes . . . are you a woman?"

Mary held his stare for a moment, and then she smiled and said, "Yes, Jacob. Yes, I am."

Jacob sat down heavily on the pile of canvas behind him, his eyes never leaving Mary's. For a long time neither of them said a word, and Mary could not help but think back to a time, eight years ago—it seemed like eighty—and a similar scene in a tent in Flanders.

Similar, and yet so very different. Her love for Jacob was real, as real as had her love for Frederick been. She wanted him to love her, and she knew that she would be unhappy if he did not.

But still, the fear was not there, the desperation. Perhaps it was the Caribbean, perhaps it was Anne. Perhaps it was that she was beyond caring. In any event, she did not feel, as she had with Frederick, that her entire life hung on the decision that Jacob would make.

And then he stood and put his arms around her and pulled her toward him, kissed her, gently, sweetly on the lips. She put her arms around his neck, ran fingers through his hair, and recalled how wonderful it was to be held and kissed by a man whom she loved.

June was hot and dry in the Caribbean, with regular, violent thunderstorms in the late afternoons that forced the Pretty Annes to take in sail and allowed them, for twenty minutes, to enjoy a reviving shower of fresh water before the storm moved on and the sun came out again.

Anne made Mary recount to her in every detail the mounting romance that she was enjoying with Jacob Wells. She insisted that Mary tell her everything about their stolen moments forward in the sail locker, the feel of his strong fingers on her face, her neck, running through her hair, the gentle confidence that he showed with her.

Mary did not ask, but she wondered if Anne was not taking a vicarious pleasure in her and Jacob's romance. Jack, often drunk, occasionally belligerent, did not seem up to his old, flamboyant, romantic self.

"Well, Mary," Anne said in a conspiratorial whisper, even though they were up aloft and alone, as was their habit, "I could arrange for you and your Jacob to have the great cabin for an hour or so, and quite alone, if you would have such conversation with him."

"Ah, no, my dear, thank you. I am quite satisfied with our little play among the sails."

"But I'll warrant your Jacob is not. Will you not lie with him?"

Mary sighed. "I do not know. I had long ago resolved never to lie with a man without the benefit of marriage. And so I have been with but one man, and he my husband."

"Just one man? La, Mary, what have you been doing all your life?"

"Well, you know what I have not been doing."

"Indeed. But pray consider, there is little chance for marriage out here, and preachers are not so easy come by in our trade."

"I'll warrant that's so."

They were quiet for a moment, and then Anne began to laugh.

"Something amuses you?" Mary asked.

"You do, you and your morality. You would be a pirate, rob innocent merchants, kill them if they resist. Take the King's pardon and then spit on it, fight those in legal authority if they came to arrest you, yet you will not lie with the man you love because it is a sin?"

"You make a point, my dear. Though just because I am a wicked sinner on the one hand does not justify my being a wicked sinner on the other."

They continued to prowl the north coast of Jamaica, and over the course of a week they sighted but two sail, and those quickly disappeared over the horizon. Near the end of that week, with tempers and liquor growing short, and the sun brutal just eighteen degrees north of the equator, Noah Harwood aloft called down a sail, fine on the starboard bow and hull-down, but not so great a distance off.

With hardly a word spoken, the Pretty Annes spread all the sail they could, including the skyscrapers and the ringtail, and gave chase. They closed quickly—the chase, which they could see was a fishing boat of no great size, could not manage a third of the *Pretty Anne*'s speed.

On the *Pretty Anne*'s larboard side, the green and mountainous island of Jamaica, to starboard, the open ocean, and just ahead, the fishing boat, crossing from right to left in front of them, desperately clawing its way toward the island, toward what refuge they might find there.

The pirates fired a bow gun, but the boat did not slow. They hoisted the black flag with the death's head and crossed cutlasses, the flag of Calico Jack Rackam, and the crew of the fishing boat began to throw overboard whatever they could to lighten their craft.

The mood aboard the *Pretty Anne* was dark and volatile. They had not taken anything of genuine value in weeks. They were all but out of liquor. The sloop was leaking, weed covered below the waterline. The bilges stunk. Jack was drunk and had been for some time.

"Keep a care of yourself, Jacob," Mary said, soft, standing beside him at the fife rail and watching the fishing boat make her desperate sprint for the island. "These rogues are much out of humor and they will be looking for a chance to vent their spleens. I reckon it will go hard on these unhappy sods." She nodded toward the distant boat.

"I reckon," said Jacob, shaking his head. "Sorry bastards, and them just trying to make a poor living."

"In any event, you must not be at the fore of this attack, lest you be thought of as one of the pirates here. But neither must you hang back, for if any of our company think you a coward, it will go very hard on you. Do you understand?"

"Yes. But the one would seem to make the other impossible."

"Tricky. Not impossible. There are some in the sweet trade would murder any who could speak against them, but we are not like that. We will rob these unfortunates, but we will not kill them, and that means they might someday depose against you at trial. You must not let them think you were at the forefront of the attack."

"But what of you? I have as much care of you as you of me. What will save you from their bearing witness against you?"

"Annie and I are well protected. Any witness might testify to two young men joining in the attack, but those two young men will not be aboard if we are captured. Just too unhappy women, taken aboard a pirate ship against their will. As long as none whom we attack recognize us for what we are, then we are safe."

Jacob nodded, but he did not look certain. "Better that we should foreswear this life, and soon."

"I agree, my dear. We must only wait our chance."

Anne Bonny stood on the quarterdeck, aft, near the taffrail. She was dressed out in her long blue coat, her slop trousers, her brace of pistols around her neck, her sword heavy on her hip. Her head was bound in a red handkerchief, her thick hair tied back with a bit of tarred marlin.

Ten feet in front of her stood Calico Jack. He was watching the not-so-distant prize which was about to disappear around some headland and into an unseen harbor, and she was watching him.

He was a pitiful sight. He was losing weight, and his clothes hung loose on him, and they were wrinkled because as often as not he passed out wearing them. His hair, of which he had once been so inordinately proud—more so than Anne had ever been of her own—was now tangled and knotted and hanging in disarray.

He held his sword in his right hand, one of the last bottles of brandy in his left. With his hands full he looked that much more awkward on those occasions when the sloop rolled and he had to grab on to something to steady himself, a move that would not have been necessary had he been sober. Anne closed her eyes, shook her head.

Jack had not even attempted to make love to her after his last failed effort, despite her assurances that it was all right, that he was hardly unmanned by a onetime failure. He would hear none of it. He drank, became more withdrawn, muttered that the crew were plotting against him, that there were none he could trust. He made dark comments about Mary Read, but would not elaborate.

Anne's emotions boxed the compass, like an unsteady breeze, veering from pity to anger, from disgust to guilt. It occurred to her that she might be in part to blame for Jack's downfall, that perhaps she had expected too much of him.

She tried to think back to the old days in Nassau, when she and Jack had first become lovers, first gone on the account. Had it been her idea? Had Jack wanted to turn pirate again, or had she coerced him? It seemed a hundred years before, and she could not recall with any kind of clarity.

The *Pretty Anne* followed the fishing boat around the headland, and behind the jungle-covered point of land, tipped with its strip of white sand, they saw a small half-moon harbor, more like an indentation in the coast. There was nothing onshore but a sandy beach, and beyond that, thick jungle. The fishing boat was just coming to an anchor, the four men aboard desperately trying to get their small yawl boat over the side.

Forward, Richard Corner shot off one of the guns and the ball smashed the fishing boat's short bowsprit. The Pretty Annes shouted and waved their weapons. It was not the lively vaporing of the pirates eager for a fight. There was a different quality to the thing. Uglier. Anne could feel it. There was real anger there, and whatever the source, it was directed at this fishing boat which had foolishly fled from them.

The fishermen had no more than a minute to get their boat in the water and make their escape, and that was not enough time. The *Pretty Anne* slammed into their side, Fetherston at the tiller making no effort to soften the blow, and the screaming pirates leapt onto the fishing boat's deck, pistols firing, slashing at whatever they could, despite the entire lack of resistance.

The fight was over in less than a minute. One of the fishing boat's crew lay dead, his head half shot off, the others up in the bows, but Jack was not done with them. He raised his pistol, aimed at the one who seemed to be the captain, screamed, "Run, will you? Run, you goddamned sneaking puppy? You'll not strike to the flag of Calico Jack Rackam?"

There was a high-pitched quality to his voice, a nearly hysterical tone, and he shouted, "Goddamn your eyes!" and fired the gun and missed the cowering, unarmed man at whom he aimed.

Anne spit on the deck. Jack was putting on a pathetic, stupid, cowardly display. She wanted to slap him, to push him over the side.

"Jack," she shouted. "Jack, leave them be and take joy in what you have captured."

Jack turned, squinted at her. She could see the gun trembling in his hand, like a leaf in a breeze.

"Look, Jack, dear, you have made a prodigious haul. As grand as any you have taken in the past month, you wicked rogue. See here . . . fishing nets, empty barrels, some rotten canvas . . . oh, look here . . ." She kicked over a bucket of bait, festering, stinking fish guts, that spilled over the deck in a slimy, gelatinous pile. "See what you have here, Jack Rackam, you fearsome villain."

"Goddamn you!" Jack held his sword up, pointed the tip at her. He was ten feet away, but she could see that rage in his eyes and she did not care. "Goddamn you, you bloody whore! You mock me? What would you have me do, you bitch? Any of you, what would you have me do?"

There was silence on deck, silence that was more than the mere absence of noise. The seconds went by, one, two, three.

"I would have you play the man, Jack," Anne said soft.

"Would you? You little tart, were you a man, I would run you through!"

"Do not let my sex stop you from trying, Jack," said Anne, and she pulled her sword from her shoulder belt and held it ready. She had learned a great deal about blade work in her time on the account. She did not think that Jack, drunk and furious, could best her.

For another long measure they glared at one another, swords drawn, and then Jack said, "I'll not have it added to my sins that I killed a woman," and he slid his sword back into its scabbard.

Anne continued to glare at him, toyed with the idea of making him fight her. At a certain point he would have to accept the challenge, and then lose to her, and let his men turn on him. Or he would have to refuse until it was clear that he was afraid, and again the wolf pack would fall on him and tear him apart.

Anne was disgusted with him, furious with him, but she did not hate him, not to that degree. She remained silent, then pulled her eyes from Jack.

The others fell to tearing the fishing boat apart.

Anne slid her sword back into its scabbard, turned to help the others in their looting.

Mary Read, with arms folded, leaning on the boat's rail, watched the confrontation and wondered how it would play out. She was not happy with Anne, pushing Jack thus. Jack was teetering and Mary wondered if this would be the nudge that sent him plummeting. If he fought Anne, and lost, as Mary guessed he would, that certainly would be the end for him.

And then what? Had Anne thought this through? But Anne let it go in the end.

Mary straightened up as Anne slid her sword back into its scabbard, unfolded her arms, realized how tensed she had been. The others were tearing up the hatches, plundering the cabin, ripping into the fishing boat as much to release their own smoldering anger as out of any hope of finding something really worth the taking.

Good, Mary thought. *Let them get it out on these poor sods.* If the Pretty Annes did not find some outlet for this rage, then they would turn on one another.

She stepped forward along the side deck. From the bow Jacob was coming aft, toward her. Standing on the main hatch, Billy Bartlett was drinking deep from a bottle of wine he had found someplace.

Mary stopped and gasped. It was as if the veil over the future had been pulled back to reveal the next minute, and the next. She could see what was about to happen. She opened her mouth to warn Jacob, but before a sound could come out, his heel came down in the spilled fish guts on the deck. His foot shot out from under him and he fell and he shouted, "Son of a bitch!" and then he fell against Billy Bartlett, who spilled the wine over the front of his shirt and down his trousers.

"Bastard!" Billy shouted, and he kicked Jacob even before Jacob had pulled himself up from the hatch on which he fell. "Push me, you whoreson? And call me 'son of a bitch'?"

"It was an accident," said Jacob, leaping to his feet. "My words were not for you."

"Now you think me a fool? That I do not know what I saw? Eh, you goddamned clumsy bastard?"

"It was an accident, Bartlett." Mary stepped forward and Bartlett shifted his rat gaze on her.

"Oh, will you defend your boy, then, Read?"

Mary shut her mouth, folded her arms, realized she had made a grave mistake. Now Bartlett saw an even better opportunity for mischief, and he would not suffer it to pass.

"You, you little trained monkey." He pointed a finger at Jacob. "I'll have satisfaction of you, do you hear? At noon on the morrow, on yonder beach, we shall settle this with sword and pistol. Unless you will not play the man?"

Jacob was no coward, Mary knew that, and his hateful glare did not waver as he accepted Bartlett's challenge.

"Aye, I'll meet you, you blackhearted bastard," Jacob said.

Not that he had much choice. Forced into their company or no, the pirates would not allow a man to back down from such a challenge. To do so would be an act of unforgivable cowardice. Any man who did such a thing would be marooned, left on some desolate spit of land with the clothes on his back and a little jug of water and a pistol for when the water ran out and the thirst was more than he could bear.

Better that he should die from a quick bullet or sword thrust on the beach, die like a man under the eyes of the watching crew.

Bartlett turned to Mary, and he gave her just a hint of a smile, a flash of triumph. Her and Jacob's friendship was

no secret. Bartlett knew that with one pistol shot he could
inflict misery on two people. Then he ambled forward to
join in the looting there.

Mary felt dizzy. The sun seemed overhot.

She had seen Billy Bartlett in action many times. He had
no training with sword or pistol, but he was wiry and fast
and he had some natural ability. More, to be certain, than
the musician Jacob Wells.

Jacob would not back down, he would not die a coward's
death. He would meet Billy on the beach and fight him and
die like a man. But what was that? He would still be dead.
In all her time in the company of men, Mary had tried to
understand the distinction that some men made between the
two, but she never did, not really.

The men she knew, combat soldiers, men who lived with
death, understood that the distinction was meaningless.
They, like her, had learned that dead was dead, and it hardly mattered how it had come about.

And so Mary understood that on the morrow, not long
after noon, on the beach yonder, she would, for the second
time, witness the death of a man she loved.

Chapter 34

THE PRIZE, AS IT TURNED OUT, WAS ENGAGED NOT ONLY
in fishing but in small-time island trading. As a result she
had on board not just those items that Anne had cataloged
for Jack's benefit, but also two moderate-sized breakers of
rum and a couple of goats. That, and the fact that they were
now anchored in a pleasant and decently sheltered harbor,
was reason enough for a grand bacchanal.

The pirates abandoned their ship and moved the feast to
the wide, sandy beach. The three living prisoners were allowed to bury their shipmate with whatever ceremony they

wished, and when he was interred they were made to
butcher and cook the two goats over a fire the pirates had
built in the sand.

Soon the air was filled with the smell of burning wood
and roasting goat and rum and the sounds of freebooters
who were, for the moment, satisfied with their lot. Even
Jack seemed to unwind, just a bit. Mary saw him laughing
with the others on a few occasions as he stumbled around
in the sand.

Mary sat by herself, off near the edge of the jungle,
brooding, as evening swept over the beach. Her mind
moved from one plan to another: Put something—what?—
in Jacob's drink so that he would be too sick to fight. Steal
one of the boats and make their escape, take Jacob and
disappear up the trail that they had discovered through the
jungle, near where the pirates had made their fire. But
where did the trail lead?

Anne sat with her for some time, suggested that a solution might be negotiated. The pirates, after all, did not care
to have their musician skewered by a little rat like Bartlett.
But in the end Mary rejected the suggestions. She did not
think the others would acquiesce. She knew that Jacob was
too proud to let her try.

No, it was all foolishness. They could not escape their
fate, which was set for them at noon the following day.

Mary took a sip of her rum. *Goddamn Billy Bartlett, the
little whoreson villain, the bastard* . . . She had seen a lot
of what men could be in her wandering life, and still she
was amazed at the depth of his viciousness. She had never
understood the reason for indulging in cruelty just for the
pleasure of it, though she had seen it often enough.

Would one not prefer friendship to hatred? she wondered.

And then it came to her, and she smiled at first and then
she laughed out loud, and shook her head to think so obvious a solution should elude her, even as she was thinking
about such nonsense as running off into the jungle or taking
a boat for the open sea.

Mary got to her feet, picked up her tin cup of rum, and

walked toward the fire. She was not so steady, and the soft sand made it worse. Jacob was playing his violin. He had been put to it for hours now, despite his being slated for a duel the next day. Such things as fights to the death were common enough among the pirates that they did not merit special consideration.

Billy Bartlett was off a ways from the others, sitting in the sand with his knees drawn up to his chest. His fellow pirates were not pleased that he would be killing their musician on the morrow, and they let him know, but there was no more they could do about it. The articles they had signed were absolute law, and they could not make an exception just because a fellow could play a sweet air.

Mary ambled over to where Bartlett sat.

"Here, now, Billy, how do you do?" she asked.

Bartlett looked up at her through narrow eyes, wary and suspicious. "What of it?"

"I just ask how it goes with you, Billy. I'm a shipmate, ain't I?"

"Aye . . ." said Billy, alert and nervous, like a deer in a clearing. Some others of the tribe had noticed Mary approaching Billy and were watching their exchange with interest, which was as Mary had hoped.

"Well, then. I just come over to have a drink with my shipmate," said Mary, raising her cup.

"Sod off."

"What say you? You'll not drink with me?"

"Sod off, I said," Billy spat at her. He clearly did not know what she was about, but he would have none of it.

"Sod off? You tell me to sod off, you little bastard? You whoreson, am I to suffer such an insult from you?" Mary kicked sand on him, right in his face, and Billy leapt to his feet, spitting and rubbing his eyes.

Mary threw her cup at him and the rum splashed over his shirt. "I'll not keep company with any man will not raise a glass with me. And no one tells Michael Read to sod off, you little rat. I'll have your apology, now."

All eyes were on them. Some had stood up; those close by were backing away. Jacob had stopped playing and the only sound was the crackling fire and Bartlett's fast breath. "You'll get no apology from me," he said.

"Then I'll have satisfaction for your insults. On this beach, tomorrow, at ten in the morning time," Mary said.

"Aye, I'll meet you, and glad of it," Billy hissed. He paused, and Mary could see on his face the moment that her trick dawned on him. He opened his mouth to protest, but it was too late. The meeting was set, and any attempt on his part to change it would look like equivocation, and that was not acceptable in a duel.

"Good," Mary said, and now it was her turn to give him the flash of triumph before she turned and walked away.

The pirates had an innate sense for theater, whether they realized it or not. They loved a show, and there was no show like a duel, with the stakes as high as they could be. It was the Roman games, writ small, perhaps, but with much less disinterest among the spectators. These were not anonymous gladiators or criminals doing battle. These were their shipmates, their brethren, and when it was over one of them would be dead.

And so it was with that heightened sense of anticipation that the Pretty Annes began to assemble high up on the beach as the hour of ten o'clock approached.

Jacob stood off to the side, silent. He did not try to dissuade Mary from what she was about to do. He had already tried that, spent hours pleading with her, looking for some way out, begging her to let him fight Bartlett first. But she continued to refuse, and finally he gave up.

Anne was at her side. "Mary, dear, I am certain there is some way we can avoid this. Let us have a vote, among the men, on the matter. They will vote that Bartlett has gone too far in this."

Mary shook her head. It was a pointless gambit Anne was suggesting, and they both knew it. "There is nothing for it."

Anne took up Mary's hands in hers, met her eyes. Someone would be dead within the hour, and there was every chance it would be Mary. "Godspeed, Mary, my dear."

"Godspeed."

And then Mary squeezed Anne's hands and let them drop. No time for morbid good-byes; she had a fight to fight and win.

Mary stepped into the circle formed by the watching men. She shed her coat and took great pains to drape it carefully over a low bush so that Bartlett would understand she had every intention of donning it again. She pulled her sword and took a few practice lunges, stretched her arms and legs. She had abstained from drink after her challenge was made, and her head felt clear and her body strong and limber.

Richard Corner came lumbering up from the boat. As he was quartermaster, the affair was his to run. "Gather round, you two, over here," he called, and Mary and Billy Bartlett stepped over to him.

"Pistols at ten paces. Turn and fire on my word. If both of you misses, then cold steel. Agreed?"

"Aye," said Mary.

"Aye," said Billy. Mary had hoped to see some fear, or some wavering in his confidence, but there was none that she could detect.

"Good. Here." Corner handed them each a pistol. They each examined the weapon, snapped the flint down on the frizzen to check the trail of sparks it produced, then each in turn loaded his or her own gun.

"Ready?" Corner asked, and both nodded.

"Billy, you stand here." Corner positioned Billy Bartlett with his back to Mary. Then he paced out ten paces, which was a much greater distance than it would have been if they were Mary's paces, and said, "And, Michael, you are here." He took Mary's shoulders in his big hands and positioned her with her back toward Billy Bartlett.

Mary held the pistol up so the flintlock was right by her face. With her back to the others she could see nothing but a virgin strip of sand, curving away to the edge of the half-moon bay, and the lovely blue and white surf and the green jungle bunched up near the beach. She thought of her body being lowered into a hole in that white sand. It was paradise, and that made it all the more strange to think that she might be dead in just a minute or so.

How odd, if it were to end here . . . Mary thought. After all of the many strange turns, for her life to end on this beach, by a pirate's bullet.

And then, perhaps not so odd . . . She thought back to the many, many strange circumstances in her life, the many times she had found herself in situations that seemed entirely unlikely. If an angel had appeared to her then and said, "Mary, you will die on a beach in Jamaica in a duel with a pirate," she reckoned she would have shrugged and thought, *That is not so great a surprise.*

"Get ready, then," Dicky Corner called out, and Mary pulled herself from her reverie. She felt herself tense, felt the little sparks shooting out along her fingers and arms and legs. It was a familiar feeling—the moment before a bayonet charge, or a cavalry attack, or leaping onto the deck of an intended victim.

"Set . . ."

Either she would be dead or Bartlett would be in the next few minutes. Better that she should die than see Jacob murdered. She was taking the easy way out. In either event she would not see her lover killed.

"Turn and fire!"

Mary came around, bringing the pistol level, holding it at arm's length, looking over the barrel at Bartlett, who seemed an impossible distance away.

A blast of smoke from Billy's pistol and Mary squeezed her trigger, though she was not quite ready, and she thought, *Damn it!*

The pistol jumped in her hand and the buzz of Billy's shot screamed in her ear and Billy was lost in the burst of smoke.

And then it cleared and she was still standing and Billy was still standing and neither of them was hit.

Mary tossed her pistol into the sand and drew her sword and Billy did the same. This was the moment of clarity that

Mary loved and dreaded, when everything that she was was concentrated on the task at hand. It was a sensation like no other, and it could not happen unless one's life was in the balance.

She closed quickly with Bartlett, stopped just short of fighting distance and circled, looking at his eyes, his stance, the way he held his sword. There were openings that she could exploit, openings that a more expert swordsman would not have left, but Mary waited. She knew enough about blade work to wait.

But Billy did not. With a sound like a grunt and a shout he lunged, taking an awkward step to close the distance, and Mary beat his blade away easily, but before she could counter he was beyond the reach of her arm.

Fast little bastard . . . she thought. That was no surprise, she had guessed he would be, but he was even faster than she had supposed.

She continued to circle. The sand made the movement hard and tiring, but it was tiring for Billy as well as her.

Mary kept her defense in the sixth position, giving Billy no opening, not attacking, not stepping back, just circling. She could see that Billy was getting confused and frustrated and that was good. He lunged again, more awkward, and Mary got a piece of his shirt before he was able to leap back, and this time Mary followed him, lunging as he was off balance, opening a small wound in his shoulder as Bartlett stepped back fast, a few awkward steps.

The pirates where cheering, Mary realized. She had entirely forgotten about those men sitting in a line in the sand, watching the fight. Her eyes were entirely on Bartlett and she did not see them and had not even heard them until they registered their approval of her thrust.

Mary lowered her sword, beckoned to Bartlett, a gesture designed to provoke him with its cockiness, and it worked. Bartlett snarled at her, took a few steps forward, and this time Mary attacked first, beating his blade aside, lunging hard and driving the point into Bartlett's side as he twisted to avoid her onrush. He yelled in pain, jumped back again.

He was bleeding now from two places, breathing hard, furious.

The pirates roared.

Mary was breathing hard as well and her legs felt rubbery and she knew they would have to end this. If they grew too weary for swords, if it devolved to knives, then Billy's superior strength of arm would give him the advantage and she would lose. Time to end it.

Mary gulped air. "Come along . . . you little prancing dance master . . . let me stick you again . . ."

"Son of a bitch!" Bartlett roared, and Mary recognized the moment when anger trampled subtlety and caution underfoot.

Bartlett took two quick steps and they clashed blades, thrust and parry, counter, parry, thrust. Bartlett knocked Mary's blade aside and rushed her, charging flat out, but Mary snapped her blade back, backhand, knocking Bartlett's aside with a smack. Billy Bartlett ran right onto the point of her sword with all the momentum he had thrown into his final assault.

Mary's blade ripped through him and she saw the bloody, gleaming point over his shoulder as it came out his back.

Blood erupted from his mouth, his eyes went wide and he fell toward her and she was all but holding him up with her sword.

Their eyes met and Bartlett reached out at her, reached for her neck. As his last act on earth he would try and strangle her.

Clawlike, his hand went for her, but she shied away and his fingers missed her throat and came down her neck. He grabbed the collar of her shirt and his fingers hooked there as he fell. Mary tried to push him away, but his weight was on her and he was going down and she could not get out from under.

She stepped back, let go of her sword, grunting as she shoved the dying Bartlett aside, but his fingers were clenched on the fabric of her shirt.

Down he went, into a dark spot of his own blood, down,

in a chorus of cheers from the watching pirates and tearing and rending cloth as Mary's shirt and waistcoat tore, down into the sand.

And then he was still, his face pressed into the sand, and above him, Mary stood, shocked and horrified, covered in his blood, her shirt and waistcoat torn open before the silent and stunned pirate horde.

Chapter 35

MARY GATHERED UP THE TORN REMNANTS OF HER shirt, turned, and fled. Her feet found the trail that cut into the jungle and she ran along it, blindly, not looking or thinking. Just running.

She was exposed, stripped naked and held up to scrutiny, and she could no longer deny who she was, not to the pirates, not to herself.

She wept as she ran. Wept with the humiliation of the thing, with fear of what trouble her exposure would bring, wept for Frederick and for the fact that she was still dressing like a man and for all the sorrow in her. She ran and she wept for herself.

At last she stopped as the trail widened out at a big pool of water and overhead a gap in the canopy of trees over the pool let the sunlight pour down into the forest. She stopped and breathed hard and looked at the dried tracks around the pool, the marks where barrels had been rolled that way. This was why the trail was there, she realized. Local fisherman and coastal traders must use this place to water their vessels.

Two hundred yards from the beach the trail ended at that spring-fed pool. She and Jacob would not have made it very far if they had tried to run that way.

Mary sat down on a big, warm rock and put her head in

her hands. She was a broken vessel and the tears poured out of her. She knew better than think that life was in any way just, but she did not understand why it had to be so damned, damned unjust to her, and the frustration sometimes was overwhelming.

She did not know why she had been forced to squander her life, living it in disguise, denying who she was. She did not know why her single moment of happiness had been so summarily snuffed out.

Rarely did Mary open that door of her life, the one that shut up all the grief, and look inside, but now that she had she could not pull her eyes away, and she cried harder still.

There were soft footfalls on the trail and Mary looked up. Anne was there, and behind her, Jacob. She turned away from them, sunk her face in her hands again. She wanted to be alone and she wanted them there, all at the same time.

She heard footsteps coming up to her and then felt Anne's hand on her shoulder, just resting there, and for a long time neither of them said anything. At length Anne spoke. "That was one surprised damn bunch of pirates you left on the beach, dear."

Mary smiled despite herself, choked back a sob. "What do they say? Will they maroon me now?"

"No, no, I do not believe so. They have always esteemed you one of their own, you know. And I think they feel that anyone drives a bloody great sword through Billy Bartlett has done them a good turn."

Mary nodded because she did not trust herself to speak. Anne gave her shoulder a squeeze and said, "I am going to return to the beach now. I do believe your Jacob has something he wishes to say."

Mary reached up and put her hand on Anne's, then turned and looked up into her friend's face. She wanted to tell Anne to stay, that it was her company that she craved just then, but she knew, as did Anne, that she and Jacob needed this moment together. Again Mary smiled through the tears and Anne smiled back and then she was gone.

Jacob approached her, tentatively, unsure. Mary gathered

her rent shirt together and sniffled and met his eyes. He stopped and knelt down in front of her and reached up and took her hands and still they did not speak.

Mary looked at her hands in Jacob's. They were covered with blood, Billy Bartlett's blood, as was her shirt and her chest, and it felt sticky and repulsive.

Jacob let go of Mary's hands and stood and with never a word he pulled off his own shirt and plunged it into the pool, then pulled it dripping from the water and wrung it out. He knelt before Mary once more and gently opened up her shirt and began to clean the blood from her.

The wet cloth felt cool and sensual against her skin, and Jacob's touch was light and sure as he gently ran the shirt over her stomach, her chest, her breasts. Mary closed her eyes and let the luxurious sensations wash over her.

When he was done Jacob rinsed the shirt in the pool and then laid it on a rock to dry in the sun. His body was tanned from his time at sea, and lean and hard, the muscles on his arms rippling as he moved with his quiet elegance. He had the build of a hardworking sailorman and the touch and the sensitivity of a musician.

He knelt before her once more, and they were eye to eye, and he ran his hands under her shirt and around the naked skin of her waist and pulled her toward him, just a bit.

Jacob lowered his head and then looked up again and at last he spoke. "No one has ever done for me what you did, not man nor woman. And in defense of me you have been thus exposed. If Anne is wrong, and the pirates fall on you, then we shall die together."

Mary bit her lip to hold back the tears and ran her fingers through Jacob's hair and nodded. They would die together. Jacob would have been less of a man, and she could not have loved him as she did, if he had felt otherwise.

Jacob stood and he eased Mary to her feet and pulled her close to him. Her shirt fell open and her naked skin pressed against his. Her head swam with the sensation of it. Jacob's big hands slid around her back and up her shoulders and he pressed her closer still and their mouths came together in a desperate and hungry kiss.

They stood there for some time, kissing in that way. In Mary's head, images of Frederick and the big fireplace in their bedchamber swirled together with Jacob and the tropical island on which they stood until it was all a great amalgam of tender sensuousness, like a warm bath into which she was slipping, deeper and deeper.

Jacob ran his hand down her back, down her thigh, and in one easy motion he picked her up and held her in his arms.

"Oh!" Mary gave a little shout of surprise and resisted the urge to regain her feet. She could not recall the last time she had been held in a man's arms, completely supported. It was wonderful and frightening all at once, to be so cradled and so vulnerable. For so long had she affected a man's swaggering confidence and relied on none but herself that it seemed unnatural to be carried in that way.

But she ran her hands through Jacob's hair and they kissed again, him holding her in his strong arms as if she weighed nothing, and soon Mary was delighting in it. She felt a part of him, like she was curled up inside him, like she could let go and he would protect her. It was an alien and wonderful feeling.

He carried her away from the pool to a place where the foot-tall grass marked the outer edge of the encroaching jungle, and laid her down easily, then lay down beside her. He ran his lips over her neck and behind her ears and she closed her eyes and let the sensation consume her. His long fingers played over her stomach and caressed her breasts and she gave a little moan, quite involuntarily.

"Oh, Jacob, oh, my dear Jacob . . ." Mary took his hand in hers, brought it to her lips and kissed his fingers. Jacob sat back and their eyes met.

"What is it, my love?"

"I have been with but one man before, and he my husband. And never did I wish to have such conversation without I was married."

"Oh, my dear. I would plight my troth to you this very second, was there a minister here. I would wait for all my life, did I think we could get safe to a church and be married in that way, but I fear that will never be done. We are outlaws now, you know, and I think we will never be safe in such a place."

"In truth, you are right."

For a long moment Jacob just looked at Mary, then he ran his finger along the edge of her face and her jaw. "It is funny, you know. I thought you a man for so long. But now I see you are not only a woman, but a very beautiful one at that."

"I wish you could see me in silk and womanly clothes."

"I would like that of all things."

They fell silent again, and then Mary said, "You would plight your troth to me? Now?"

"This very instant. But as we cannot, then I shall love you as a brother, or in what way you would have me."

Mary ran her hand over Jacob's face. His two-day growth of beard was coarse, though it made little impression on her calloused hands. She noticed for the first time the prefect line that the edge of his whiskers made across his smooth cheek, the tiny wrinkles that radiated out from his eyes, his dark blue eyes, the color of deep water. She wondered if she was half as beautiful a woman as he was a man.

"Very well, then, Jacob. I will hold you to your word, and let you plight your troth to me, this instant." She smiled at him, his confusion. "Do you, Jacob Wells, take this woman, Mary Read, for your wife, for richer, for poorer, in sickness and in health, till death do you part?"

"I do." Jacob stroked her cheek with his crooked finger. "Do you, Mary Read," he said, "take this man, Jacob Wells, for husband, for richer, for poorer, in sickness and in health, till death do you part?"

"I do. You may kiss the bride."

Jacob leaned down and gently pressed his lips against Mary's and they kissed, a long, luxurious kiss. Then Jacob propped himself up and looked down at her again.

"There, now," Mary said, and her voice was little more than a whisper. "I will consider us to be man and wife, in my eyes and in yours and I pray in the eyes of God."

"I love you very much, Goodwife Wells."

"And I love you, my husband."

Jacob leaned over her once more and kissed her, more passionately this time, and Mary wrapped her arms around him and kissed him back. Their tongues explored one another's mouths and then Jacob ran his lips over her neck once more, and over her chest and her breasts.

Mary let her head loll back and she sighed and shifted and felt the passion building within her. Jacob was breathing harder as he covered her with little kisses and Mary arched her back and thought the sensation was too much to bear.

With his famous dexterity Jacob undid her belt and the buttons of her breeches. He got to his knees and slid her breeches down, and his own as well, and Mary found herself naked, lying in the grass, a most unusual situation.

It was so odd for her to be naked in any event, having become so practiced in hiding her sex, that she involuntarily recoiled from such exposure. And to be naked there, in the open, in the grass with Jacob . . . The sensations were a blur. She could not think and she did not want to.

Jacob lay down again, half on top of her, and continued to kiss her all over and his sure fingers ran over her body, just barely touching her, exploring her, playing her as if he were playing his violin. She felt goose bumps rise at his touch, felt her nipples get so hard they hurt.

"Oh . . . Jacob . . ." Mary said, catching herself an instant before she said "Frederick." "Oh, I want you, now . . ."

She pulled him on top of her and braced because it had been a very long time and she knew it would hurt like it had the first time. But Jacob was no overeager lover, and he seemed to sense her reticence, and he moved very slow, easing himself in with just the gentlest of motion.

Mary wrapped her legs around his thin waist and clenched her teeth and shut her eyes hard and felt herself consumed by Jacob, Jacob on top of her, Jacob pressing her down, Jacob inside her.

He moved slowly, letting the rhythm build, always aware of her, never doing anything that might cause her pain. And

for Mary it was pure joy, the feeling of all their naked flesh
pressed together and Jacob moving inside her, filling her
up. It was like being held in Jacob's arms, but many, many
times more.

Slowly, slowly the motion built until Jacob was moving
easily inside her. She dug her heels into him and ran her
feet up and down his strong back and gasped with pleasure
and then they were both stifling shouts as their ecstacy
peaked, perfectly together.

They lay for a long time like that, intertwined, aware
only of each other's subsiding breath and the warm sun on
them and the sound of the birds and the water bubbling up
from the spring. It was so perfect that Mary wanted to lie
like that forever, she wanted to die right there, just let the
life seep gently away, like water from a cracked cup, so
that her last moment on earth would be that perfect moment, and she would not have to go back to the beach and
face whatever it was she had to face there.

At last Jacob rolled over on his side and they were side
by side in the grass and naked and looking up at the sky.
The sun had moved quite a bit since the last time that Mary
had looked and she knew it was time to go. Time to face
life again. Time to see what new misery was to be her lot.

She rolled on her side and kissed Jacob's chest and
smiled at him and then they both stood and pulled on their
clothes. Jacob gave Mary his shirt, now quite dry, and she
gratefully pulled it on. Then they made their way back
down the trail.

The smell of fire and roasting pig and the sounds of the
freebooters' ongoing bacchanal greeted them long before
the trail opened out into the wide sandy beach. They
stepped from the shade of the forest and crossed to the fire.
Mary's heart was beating fast; she could feel her muscles
tense and the sweat on her palms and she could sense that
Jacob was tight as well. She could not recall ever being so
unsure of the situation into which she was marching.

One by one the pirates fell silent and all eyes turned
toward them as they approached. Mary searched the band
of men, seeking Anne out. She was on the other side of the

fire, sitting cross-legged in the sand. Their eyes met and Anne did not speak, but gave a nod of her head, a barely perceptible motion that spoke volumes to Mary. It was the all clear, the assurance that they would not have to fight their former shipmates for their lives. Mary felt the tension ease, just a bit.

She stopped, arms folded, and looked from one man to the next, daring anyone to speak. If Anne had misjudged the thing, she was ready for a fight, ready to go to pistols or cold steel if need be. She had been defending herself through force of arms all her life, she was perfectly ready to do so now.

George Fetherston's voice boomed out and made Mary jump. "Well, 'Michael,' what the hell should we call you now?"

Mary held his eyes. She did not smile. "Mary. Mary Read."

"Ah, ha, ha! Do you hear that, Corner, you great dancing master!" Fetherston roared. "It was a 'Mary' near done for you, took off part of your ear! Ha, ha! And we thought our Annie the toughest bitch in the West Indies!"

"All right," Noah Harwood yelled, "any other of you sons of whores are women, let us know now!"

The others laughed and then turned back to what they were doing and no more was ever said. Mary and Jacob took their place by the fire, ate their share of the wild pig that Thomas Earl had shot, and then lent a hand with loading everything back into the boat.

Near the edge of the jungle Mary could see the fresh-turned earth where they had buried Billy Bartlett. She thought of his body, some feet down there, already moldering away.

He is gone now, with never a trace, Mary thought. *So why had he ever lived? Why was such a thing as Billy Bartlett ever created?*

She did not know, and she did not ponder long on it. The pirates pushed the boat into the surf and tumbled in and pulled back toward the *Pretty Anne.*

She did not know why any of them was alive. She knew

only that she was, for the time being, and she once again had the chance to find some real peace and even happiness.

If it was not too late, she and Jacob might quit the pirates, scrape up the money to open an inn or a tavern or some such. Perhaps Anne might join them, when she was finally sick to death of Calico Jack.

Perhaps they would, if it was not too late.

The pirates under Calico Jack Rackam continued on in their hunting, wandering from Jamaica to Hispaniola, taking what they could. Jack was still drinking, still wallowing in his misery, but in the rough democracy of the pirates it did not matter so very much.

Mary found this both surprising and intriguing. In her experience, a failure of leadership meant that everything below would fall apart in turn. But not so with the pirates. The crew as a body voted on their actions, discussed their plans, and Jack's faltering leadership had little effect.

It was only when they were in a fight that he became the undisputed master, and since in the past months they had fought with nothing more substantial then small trading sloops and fishing vessels, there was not that much required of him then, either.

So Jack managed to hold himself together, and they soldiered on.

With Mary's secret now revealed, neither she nor Anne felt the need to continue on in their disguises. When the pirates happened to take a sloop that had aboard a few bolts of fine white holland, the women took it for themselves and ran up simple dresses. These they wore as a matter of course, to the delight of themselves and the men aboard the sloop.

When the *Pretty Anne* cleared for action, the women shed their dresses and kitted themselves in their men's clothing, their blue jackets and long trousers, with handkerchiefs bound around their heads.

They continued on, but the hunting was poor and the *Pretty Anne* was a weary vessel, leaking, rotten, stinking of all the filth that had accumulated in her hold. The men were tired, worn down by two years of near constant cruising.

They talked of Nassau. No one knew where the idea had come from, it just seemed to appear like a spirit among them, but once there it would not leave. They talked about the King's pardon, abandoning the sweet trade, setting up taverns, all of the dreams embraced by broken sailormen in all the seaport towns of the world.

It was talk that Mary liked to hear, and she even dared hope that this was their moment, the chance to give up the life on the account, to settle down; her, Jacob, Anne.

The more the pirates talked about Nassau, the more it appeared to them as some mythical place, some El Dorado where, if they could only reach it, they would find peace and joy, rivers running with rum, women desperate to bed them, filthy and vermin-ridden though they might be.

So they turned the sloop northeast and made for that place. It was a decision arrived at by tacit agreement, with never a formal discussion or vote, but it was a decision that sat well with all of them. And on the morning when the rising sun revealed the green crooked line of the island of New Providence rising up from the sea, the excitement and relief on board were palpable.

Mary stood on the heel of the bowsprit and watched the land as it seemed to rise from the sea. Unlike the other *Pretty Annes*, she had never been to Nassau, that fabled pirate haven. She knew that the others were expecting a grand welcome, a boisterous homecoming, the prodigal buccaneers returning.

She wondered if the others realized, as she did, that things might well have changed after two years of Woodes Rogers's governorship. She wondered if the others were too swept up in their romantic vision of this pirates' paradise to understand that they might all of them be people out of time, that the world might have moved on and left buccaneers such as them behind.

Chapter 36

IT TOOK THEM THE REST OF THE DAY TO CLOSE WITH the island. The sun was hanging just above the hilly country inland as the *Pretty Anne* rounded the easternmost point and stood into the familiar channel that ran between New Providence and Hog Island.

The men lined the rails, pointing to this and that, commenting on what was new since last they came, what had remained unchanged. There was more shipping, and more of it looked of a reputable nature, and that was certainly a new thing. The fort in which Woodes Rogers had first made his home was much improved, and looked like a genuine defensive structure ringed with a high wood palisade, and not an abandoned ruin.

Jack stood on the quarterdeck, let the relief bathe him like the last rays of the sun. He had considered the possibility that there would be no welcome for him, that he might be a wanted man, but somehow he could not imagine it was so. Nassau had always been his haven, the place where he was the celebrated Calico Jack, and he could not think that the presence of one new Governor could change that.

They dropped the hook a cable length from the dock and took the longboat ashore. The dock to which they tied was not the same half-rotten structure from which they had embarked to steal the sloop *Nathaniel James*. Rather it was new built of substantial timbers, decked over with two-inch planks, as solid as a stone quay. They climbed up the ladder that ran into the water, stood silent for a moment, looking over their town in the golden light of evening.

It was not the Nassau they remembered, not entirely. Some of the old buildings still stood, but they were surrounded now by new construction; private homes and stores, taverns, ordinaries, chandlers, merchants. Nassau had grown in their absence, grown, apparently, into a legitimate town.

"Come, lads!" Jack said, loud and bold, breaking the quiet moment. "Let us off to the Ship, our old meeting place, and see what news is there!"

They walked together, a happy band of brothers, along the dock and then onto the dusty street. People stood in doorways and watched them pass, leaned out of windows to see the new arrivals. Jack waited for a hail, a hearty cheer of "Calico Jack!" or a wave from some familiar figure, but there was nothing. Only the muted sounds of a small Caribbean town at dusk, and the call of birds, and their own feet on the road.

They came at last to the Ship Tavern, and to Jack's relief, it still stood, and looked much as it had the last time he had seen it. It would have been too much to bear, had it been otherwise. If the Ship had been gone, then Calico Jack would have understood there was no place left for him.

He pushed the door boldly open, just as he had the time he first met Anne. He paused, but there was no cry from within, no warm greetings. He walked into the low, dim tavern room and the others followed.

There were people there, sitting at the familiar tables, but none whom Jack recognized. He stepped up to the bar, his shipmates around him. The publican was tapping a keg, but he stopped, looked up, squinted at the men.

"Jack? Calico Jack Rackam?" he asked.

"It is me!" Jack said, loud, spread his arms. "Calico Jack, come back!"

The publican smiled a weak sort of smile, held out his hand. "We had heard you was shipwrecked, down around Cuba," he said.

"Shipwrecked? Never in life. Come now, rum, rum all around!"

The publican began to produce bottles and glasses and the men began to pour and drink, but they did so in silence, and Jack wondered where all the raucousness was, the roaring good humor of the pirates, the musicians and the pretty whores and the unchecked debauchery.

They drank and talked amongst themselves and pried from the publican all the news of what had taken place over the past year and a half, since they had slipped the cable aboard the *Nathaniel James* and drifted silently out of the harbor.

They talked for ten minutes or so, learned of the great changes that had taken place in Nassau, the way that Governor Rogers had bent the people there to his will through tireless cajoling and hanging, inducement and exile.

The door opened behind them, the cool air swirling away the pipe smoke and fetid smell of the men. Jack turned and the others turned. A figure stood in the door, the dark shape of a man, and Jack felt a sudden flush of panic, an irrational fear, like he was watching the angel of death come near.

Then the figure stepped toward them and Jack smiled and laughed. "Ben Hornigold! Goddamn my eyes, it is old Ben!"

Hornigold came up to Jack and took his outstretched hand, but he looked more serious than delighted.

"Ben, damn you!" Jack continued. He ran his eyes over Hornigold's rich coat and waistcoat, the glint of silver buckles on his shoes, the dull gleam of his gold-headed walking stick. Hornigold had not pissed his riches away as most pirates would.

"You have prospered, Ben, I see. Up to old tricks, I should think? On the account?"

Ben Hornigold shook his big head. "No, Jack, none of that." He paused, looked around at the gathered men, nearly all of whom he knew, and with many of whom he had once sailed. "George, Richard, Noah," he greeted them with a nod and they muttered their greeting back.

Ben's eyes turned to Anne Bonny, standing at Jack's side. "Ah, Annie, you have returned," he said. "You've become damned well known around here."

His gaze moved past Anne. "And this must be Mary Read. Oh, don't look so surprised. Tales have spread, you know. Such a one as you cannot be kept secret long."

This talk was making Jack more and more uncomfortable. It was not the greeting or the banter he would have expected from his old friend. "Come, Ben," he said, hoping to liven the increasingly funereal atmosphere in the tavern, "will you have a drink with us?"

"No, Jack. I think not."

"Then what is it you want of us? Why have you come here?"

"The question, my dear boy, is more why have *you* come? For what reason have you returned to Nassau?"

Jack looked uncomfortably around, looking for some support from his fellows. "We had thought to accept the King's pardon."

Again Ben Hornigold shook his head. He frowned and his heavy jowls gave him a bulldog look. "You are far too late for that, Jack, dear. There's no pardon for you."

Jack said nothing. There was nothing to say. He did not trust himself to speak.

"This ain't the place it once was, Jack. And the sweet trade ain't what it was. Things have changed. I'm no longer on the account. I hold a command from the Governor now."

It took a moment for the words to register, but when they did Jack jerked upright, took a step back; his hand reached for the grip of his sword. "What say you? Are you here to arrest us?"

"No, no." Ben held up his hands. "Word was sent to me as soon as you landed, but I have not seen fit to inform the Governor. I take no small risk in keeping you a secret, you may be certain."

There was an uncomfortable silence. Someone poured more rum into a glass, thumped the bottle back down on the table. Ben Hornigold continued. "We were friends once, Jack. And I know you for a decent man, not one that kills and maims for the pleasure of it. That's why I come here. To warn you. There's no place for you here, and Rogers will hang you, hang the lot of you, if you stay. That goes for Annie and Mary as well."

Hornigold looked around at the stunned faces. Then he turned and walked back toward the door. He paused and turned back and for a moment Jack thought he might say, "Of course . . ." and offer some means to their salvation, but instead he said, "Get back aboard your sloop, Jack. The lot of you. Get back aboard and sail away and don't come back. I won't be able to pretend I didn't see you a second time." And then he stepped out into the night and was gone.

For a long time no one said anything, or if they did, Jack did not hear them. He was floating away, disconnected, like a feather lifted on a breeze. Nassau, his home, the one solid thing left to him, was gone, and all of the fantasies he had entertained were gone with it.

And then someone said, "We had best get out of here," and then the others were moving, and Jack, with never a thought, followed along.

They hid out in the wild country west of town, near the beach, and decided what they would do. They could not stay. They could not sail the *Pretty Anne*—she was too far gone to be of service anymore.

The next evening they stole a sloop, the *William,* belonging to John Hamon, in much the same manner as they had the *Nathaniel James.* They drifted unseen out of the harbor and they were off to sea again.

Mary Read stood at the rail in the waist, watched New Providence fade in the distance. She had arrived with the vague hope that her life would take a turn onto a better path, and left two days later with things much worse than they had been.

They knew who she was. The word had filtered out somehow, traveled over the great network of people who plied their trade on the waters of the Caribbean, reached to the office of Woodes Rogers. Her name, even her sex, was known. She could not hope to retire in anonymity now. She could no longer dream of settling on some island in the West Indies, her and Jacob and Anne, and living as civilized people do. She was branded in the hand, as much as if a hot iron had been put to her flesh.

She had tried to get Jacob to abandon her, to stay on New Providence. She had argued that he was as yet unknown, that he could melt into the population and never be known for a pirate.

He had stated simply that she was his wife, that he had not plighted his troth lightly, that he would not leave her. Mary was furious and relieved, frightened and bolstered by his bold act.

For a month the new *Pretty Anne* again prowled the Jamaican coast, taking fishing boats, canoes, pettiaugers, a few island traders. They met with no vessels more substantial than that. Nor would they have been able to effect much if they had—they were only ten in number now, and their sloop would not have been able to run down much larger prey.

In September they sailed from Jamaica and made their way to the French part of Hispaniola, but the taking was not much better there. They went ashore and stole some cattle, and pressed into service two Frenchmen named Peter Cornelian and John Besneck, who were hunting wild hogs.

Soon after they had the good fortune to take two sloops whose cargo proved to be of some worth. Not a fortune, to be sure, but better than the holds full of fish that had been their lot.

"Jacob," Mary asked, as the Pretty Annes looted the second of the sloops, anchored in a small bay on Île à Vache, "do you speak French at all?"

"Yes, a bit."

"Well then, here is what you must do. You must speak with those two there—" she nodded toward the two Frenchmen, sulking in the bow "—and tell them that you, too, were forced to sail with us. Tell them it is best if they try to get along, as you do, that is the way to not get your throat cut. Tell them you are looking for the main chance to escape us and that you will help them escape as well."

"But, Michael, I am not even sure that is true any longer."

"I do not care if it is true. Speak as if it is. Now go and

tell those Frenchies what I have said to you, and make them understand you do this against your will."

Jacob looked at her, a protest forming on his lips. She glared at him, gave him a look that she had learned from more commanding officers than she could recall, and he shrugged and ambled off forward, to speak with Cornelian and Besneck.

After some weeks in Hispaniola they sailed again for Jamaica with the Frenchmen still aboard. Jacob became friendly with them, on Mary's insistence, assuring them in his halting French that they were all in the same predicament, that he was feigning cooperation to save his life, and that they should do the same.

Mary did not explain her intentions to Jacob. She did not mention her growing sense of finality, her feeling that their luck—in her mind she saw it as the sand in a half-hour glass—was running out. She did not tell him that his conversations with the Frenchmen were in fact the foundation of a legal defense.

On the north side of Jamaica, in Ocho Rios Bay, a bit more than twenty miles west of Port Maria, the *Pretty Anne* came gliding into that curved harbor, almost upright in the light breeze, moving silently, save for the little ripping sound along her hull.

Near the middle of the bay, a big oceangoing canoe was waiting as they closed, like a deer driven until it has collapsed with exhaustion. The canoe was around thirty feet long, loaded to the gunnels, two native paddlers at either end, a white person amidships.

The *Pretty Anne* had come around the point and come upon the canoe making its way from one shore to the other. The people in the boat had tried to run from the pirates, paddling furiously, but with five knots of breeze off her quarter pushing the pirate sloop along, it was futile. One shot from the *Pretty Anne*'s forwardmost gun dissuaded the canoe from further attempts at escape. The paddles came in; the three persons aboard awaited their fate.

The pirates lined the rail, laughing and speculating as to what the canoe was carrying. There was no great excitement aboard—it took more than a canoe to inspire shouting and banging and firing pistols—but the mood was good.

Anne and Mary were forward, standing on the bowsprit on either side of the forestay and each holding it for balance, and talking softly as the sloop ran down on the open boat. With the *Pretty Anne* going in for an attack, even as lopsided an attack as this, they had changed into their male attire, their long coats and trousers and handkerchiefs around their heads. Anne wore a cocked hat, pushed down over her hair.

"We have been too long on this shore," Mary said. "There can be no doubt that the Governor here has had an earful of complaints about us. Soon he will have to send someone to run us to ground, and it will not be hard to find a vessel that can overwhelm our company. We are but fourteen now, if you count the Frenchmen and Jacob. But the Frenchmen will not fight for us, and I will not suffer Jacob to."

"What would you have us do?"

Mary shrugged. "Return to Hispaniola for a time? Make for the Leeward Islands or the coast of America. The Carolinas, the Chesapeake. Quit the sweet trade."

Anne nodded. "You would like to quit this life?"

"Oh, Annie, dear, I do not know. Had I the money to set up in something, I think I should quit this very moment. Do you not get the sense of our time running out?"

" 'At my back I always hear, time's winged chariot hurrying near . . .' "

"What is that?"

"Oh, just some bit of a silly poem, which was writ to rob some poor girl of her maidenhead, which I reckon is why most men write poems. But I am not so certain that I see the end, as you do."

"I do not think that poor Jack can go on much longer," Mary said.

Anne was silent for a moment, staring hard at the canoe,

one hundred yards off. "Humph," she said at last, and then, "Where would we go? What would we do?"

"I do not know. We would need to go somewhere out of our knowledge. The colony of Rhode Island, perhaps? Or Barbados. Of those we have robbed, there are none could come against us, as I think none have seen us for women."

"There are the Frenchmen."

"Yes. I wish that Jack would put them ashore in some place where they could make their way, but where they might never be found out by the officers of any court of law. The luck of our disguise cannot hold out forever."

"Let me think on this, my dear," Anne said. "It seems I have been my whole life in the sweet trade. I do not know what else I might do." She turned to Mary and smiled. "It is the only thing I have ever found to which I am so well suited."

And then, silent, the *Pretty Anne* glided up beside the canoe, rounded up into the wind, and hands at the fife rail let the halyards go and the sails came down. Harwood and Dobbin tossed lines to the native boatmen and obediently they tied the canoe to the sloop, as if this meeting had been carefully planned. Men who worked on the water in the West Indies understood the benefits of cooperating with pirates.

Amidships, the third person sat prim and stoic. She was an Englishwoman, with a silk dress and a big straw hat and a face full of resignation.

"Come up here, come up here and have a wet with us!" Jack roared down at the people in the canoe. The natives scrambled up the side and showed no hesitation in accepting the proffered bottles. The woman did not move.

"Come on, dear, get your arse up here!" Jack roared, and that sentiment was echoed among the others. The woman looked up with scorn. She was of middling age, not unattractive, but tanned, as women were wont to get in the West Indies.

"Corner, see a bosun's chair rigged for m'lady!" Jack called, and then the woman stood and without a word she climbed up the boarding steps and onto the deck. The pirates grabbed her arms, looked her up and down with hungry, wolf eyes.

Mary and Anne climbed down from the bowsprit, ambled aft. Mary could see the fear in the woman's eyes, but she held her lips firm and her jaw set and displayed more courage than a lot of men whom Mary had seen in similarly dire circumstances.

"Over here, sweetheart!" Corner said, and reached down with his big hand and squeezed her ass, and the woman spun around and slapped him, hard, with a loud, smacking sound, but the blow made little impression on the big man. He laughed out loud, as did the others, then he pushed her back against the fife rail and ignored her.

In the canoe the Pretty Annes were pulling off tarpaulins to reveal quantities of fresh food—bread and cured hams and smoked meat, beef and fish freshly put down in barrels—and wine and brandy in bottles and breakers. This sparked even greater enthusiasm among the men, and soon the woman found herself quite alone at the fife rail.

Mary, fifteen feet away, was looking her over and her thoughts were meandering off. *What is the difference between you and me?* she thought. *Why do you have fine silks, and me a sailor's kit? What quirks of fate have put you there and me here?*

And then, as if she had heard Mary's silent query, the woman turned her head and looked right at Mary. Their eyes met and for a moment they stood, staring at one another. And then Mary saw the woman's eyes open wider, saw them flash down the length of Mary's body, and then over to Anne, and then just as fast she looked away.

"Goddamn it!" Mary said.

"What?" Anne asked.

"That bitch has smoked us. She knows us for what we are."

"How do you know?"

"I could see it in her eyes. Damn it all! Now she will come against us, for sure." *Of course another woman would see through this thin disguise!* Mary thought, and cursed herself for not having realized as much, and kept from her sight. It would take no great art for this woman to realize that the two women pirates had to be Anne Bonny and Mary Read, whose fame had spread as far as Nassau and God knew where else.

"Jack!" Anne shouted. Her sword was in her hand and she was pointing it toward the woman prisoner. "Jack!"

"What? What is it?" Jack called back. He had cut a slice off of one of the hams and was eating it off the tip of his dagger.

"We must kill that one. She has smoked us, Jack."

That brought about an uncomfortable silence, and glances back and forth among the men. The cold-blooded murder of a woman was not to their liking.

Oh, God, could I live with her blood on my hands? Will Annie and I hang if we do not do this thing?

"I will do it myself, Jack," Anne said, "if none of you are man enough for such work."

There was no one aboard who doubted Anne's sincerity, though their faces registered some surprise at her shocking ruthlessness.

She is doing this for me, Mary realized. She thought back on their conversation of just a few moments before. Anne was not concerned about someone deposing against them; she had all but said as much.

She would do murder for my sake. Mary took a step forward, ready to put a stop to this. She could not let Anne commit murder, certainly not in her defense. She would hang before she would be a party to such a vicious thing.

But before she could speak, Dicky Corner said, "I reckon this should go to a vote, such a thing. Who here would see the prisoner dead?"

There was no show of hands, never a sound from any of them. *If Billy Bartlett was here, he would have cut her throat with pleasure,* Mary thought. *Now I am sorry I skewered that little bastard . . .*

"How many, then, would suffer her to live?" Again there were no hands, just a muffled chorus of "aye"s. The Pretty Annes had no stomach for killing in that fashion.

"I'm sorry, Bonny," said Corner, "but we'll not do such a thing."

Anne made a disgusted sound, threw her sword into the scuppers, and stamped away, climbing out onto the bowsprit, her back to the others.

Ten minutes later the canoe was empty of everything that the pirates wanted, which was practically everything it had been carrying, and the native boatmen were sent back aboard, having enjoyed their stay with the pirates.

The woman, still frightened, still determined, climbed down after them. She could hardly believe that she was still alive, and unmolested—Mary could see it in her face. She did not say a word, did not look up, kept her eyes well away from Mary and Anne. She knew there was still time for her fortune to change.

Five days later, as Anne Bonny drew a deep breath and pulled the unconscious Jack away from the cabin door, where he had passed out and was obstructing the way, as Mary and Jacob, curled in their nest among the spare sails forward, talked in the low tones of lovers, as Richard Corner and George Fetherston took the five-pound top maul and smashed in the head of the penultimate breaker of brandy liberated from the canoe to get at the last, recalcitrant inches at the bottom, they were, all of the pirates aboard the *Pretty Anne,* at that moment, the topic of conversation at the highest levels of colonial government in Jamaica, though of course, they could not have known it.

Behind a great, cluttered desk sat His Excellency, Governor Archibald Hamilton, Captain General and Governor in Chief in and over His Majesty's island of Jamaica and the territories thereon depending in America, Chancellor and Vice Admiral of the same. At the sound of his secretary's knock and quiet entrance he looked up from the interminable official document that he was struggling to read.

The Governor's office in the government building in St. Jago de la Vega was a vast, cavernous room, and it took the secretary a few seconds to make his way from the door to the desk.

"Yes?"

"Captain Jonathan Barnet to see you, Your Excellency," the secretary reported.

"Yes, good, pray send him in."

"Very good, Your Excellency." The secretary walked back over the great expanse of tiled floor. He opened the huge door, said, "His Excellency will see you now," and beckoned to the unseen man.

Hamilton stood as Barnet stepped in with the crisp stride of a naval officer, which he was not. Barnet was a merchant captain and sometimes privateer. Five years before, Hamilton had granted him a commission for the suppression of pirates, and the man had managed to suppress a few in that time. He was tough and fearless in the naval line. Hamilton had always figured him for a frustrated captain of a man-of-war.

"Good of you to attend on such short notice, Captain," Hamilton said, shaking Barnet's calloused hand.

"Not at all, Your Excellency, not at all."

"Pray, sir, have a seat. A glass of wine with you?"

"I should be delighted."

Hamilton rang the little bell on his desk and instructed the servant who appeared to hurry along for the Madeira, then he turned to Barnet. "You know this John Rackam, and his little band of rogues?"

"I have heard of him. He is making something of a pest of himself around the island, robbing fishing boats and the like. I had heard he was off to Hispaniola."

"He is back, I believe. I have here . . ." Hamilton shuffled around his desk. By the time he found the document to which he had alluded, the wine was brought in, poured, and Barnet had enjoyed several sips.

"Ah, here. This is a proclamation from Rogers over on New Providence. Says, 'Whereas John Rackam, George Fetherston, John Davis,' et cetera, et cetera, 'and two women, by name Anne Fulford, alias Bonny, and Mary Read did on the twenty-second of August . . .'

"In any event, they stole a sloop from New Providence belonging to someone from whom a sloop should not be stolen. Yesterday I received a report from a very distraught woman from Ocho Rios, Dorothy Thomas. Do you know her?"

"I do not."

"Good woman. Her husband has a small plantation out there, and he has the ear of some damned influential men. In any event, she was taken in a canoe by some villains and they had in their company two women, dressed as men. It must be Rackam; any other would be too great a coincidence."

"I would reckon so. Was Mrs. Thomas molested in any way?"

"She says that the women were for running her through, but the men would not allow it. She says she was unharmed."

"This is all quite against the nature of things."

"Might you be in a position to go after this Rackam and bring him in?"

"How many are in his company?"

"Mrs. Thomas told me not above a dozen, or fifteen."

"My sloop is readied for a trading voyage to the South Keys, in Cuba, but it would be no great hardship for me to ship extra men and go in pursuit of Rackam on the way. With a good company aboard there should be no difficulty in taking twelve or fifteen of the villains."

"Excellent, sir, excellent. Mrs. Thomas said they was bound west from Ocho Rios Bay, and that five days ago."

"Then west it is for me." Barnet stood. He was an active man, eager to get under way.

"You will sail soon, Captain?"

"I can hope to sail on the next tide. There can be not a moment wasted when hunting these rogues."

"No indeed, sir. I wish you Godspeed."

They shook again and Captain Jonathan Barnet took his leave, his heels making clicking sounds on the tile as he strode out. He walked with the stride of a man to whom the very idea of failure had never occurred.

Chapter 37

THE PRETTY ANNES COULD FEEL FORTUNE TURNING IN their favor.

The booty from the canoe had set them up: good food and lots of it, liquor meant for the gentry, not the rough fare that was generally their lot. The food and drink put the edge back on, and so they were on their mettle when Thomas Spenlow's schooner hove into sight.

The *Pretty Anne* was sailing west with the wind behind her. Spenlow's schooner was tacking out to sea, working her way off the Jamaican coast, which was little more than a dark green line on the horizon. The pirates were flying a British merchant's ensign, and sloops such as she being so ubiquitous in the West Indies, Spenlow thought nothing at all was amiss until the buccaneers fired into her with small arms, and ran aloft the black flag with its skull and crossed swords.

The *Pretty Anne* came alongside in a great flurry of flogging canvas and the enthusiastic pirates leapt across onto her decks, shoving the crew—now their prisoners—up into the bows, and began their preliminary exploration of the schooner.

This was what Anne loved best; it was the golden moment in the pirates' trade, when their feet first hit a foreign deck and a prize was theirs and there was still the anticipation of what they might find belowdecks.

Try as she might to shake romantic notions—and Anne Bonny knew better than most the reality of the sweet trade—she could not help but think of the massive, lumbering Spanish treasure galleons and the ships of the Great Mogul of India, the great buccaneer fleets that had roamed the Spanish Main and had sacked great Spanish cities of gold. It made the fishing boats and canoes that were their lot seem all that much more pathetic.

But this was different. This was a schooner, a vessel that was bigger than the *Pretty Anne* and might well have in her hold something more valuable than rotten nets and fish guts.

Perhaps they would take and arm her, entice some of her men to join with them. Use the schooner to take yet a bigger vessel and move on up until they might rival the exploits of Blackbeard or Ben Hornigold.

"There we go, lads! Rip into her, let's see what we have!"

Anne looked up as Jack, bottle and sword in hand, directed the men in the removal of the tarpaulins over the main hatch. He was smiling wide and Anne recognized the cocky swagger in his walk. Jack was brimming with pride, acting like he had taken the entire plate fleet.

There was Dicky Corner, strong and dumb as the ax he was using to smash in the hatch. George Fetherston, laughing at something, the perpetual joke in his head. Here were the bastard children of Drake and Hawkins and De Graaf, who had lost their way.

Anne felt her enthusiasm melt. *Bloody pathetic. Perhaps Mary is right.*

They plundered the hold and found fifty rolls of tobacco and nine bags of pimento, which was not a bad take at all, even if it was not Spanish gold. They spent most of the day there, the two vessels tied together, the pirates eating and drinking whatever they could find, the prisoners up in the bow, terrified, then curious, and finally bored.

As evening came on they put four of the six prisoners, including Thomas Spenlow, the master, aboard the *Pretty Anne* and left the rest aboard the schooner. Then the *Pretty Anne* and her prize filed away, still running west, pirate and victim keeping company through the night.

Fetherston had command of the prize, with three of his shipmates and the prisoners to work the vessel. On and off through the dark hours his booming voice would come across the water, belting out some snatch of a song or yelling some non sequitur at which he would then laugh out loud.

All the next day they continued west, running along the north shore of Jamaica, always with some relatively sober hand aloft, searching for the next bit of prey that might be swept up into their net.

"Now see here, Mary, dear," said Anne as they ate their dinner on the main hatch. They were wearing their holland dresses. The cloth was cool and comfortable after their burdensome wool and canvas sailor's rigs. The sun and the trade winds made for a most agreeable climate. "We have a bit of a squadron now, do you see? Two vessels, and when we have company enough to man them properly, then we shall be a formidable enemy of mankind."

Mary nodded. "You are right. We have doubled the strength of our fleet."

They were silent for a moment as they ate, and then Anne said, "You still think we are too long on this coast?"

"Yes."

Darkness came with never a sail sighted, and still they continued on, moving farther offshore to reduce the risk of sailing coastwise at night. Late in the forenoon watch the following day they rounded the headland that made up the eastern end of Dry Harbor and there saw two sloops riding at anchor. Calico Jack ordered the *Pretty Anne* hove to.

"Captain Spenlow, lay aft, sir!" Jack bellowed from the quarterdeck, and Spenlow, who spent most of his time in the bow, as far from Jack as he could get, reluctantly stood and moved aft with his odd shuffling gait.

"Yonder I see two birds in the bush, sir, so I have no further need of my bird in the hand! Fly away, little birdie!" The Pretty Annes were enjoying the show.

"What mean you?"

"I mean, you may go. Corner, pray get the boat alongside and carry Master Spenlow and his men back to the schooner. And relieve Fetherston of his command."

Fifteen minutes later Fetherston and his men were back aboard the *Pretty Anne* and Spenlow and his men were back aboard their schooner and setting all the sail they could, as swiftly as they could, and sailing a course as directly away from the pirates as the wind would allow.

In the course of that fifteen minutes the pirates had cleared the sloop away for a fight, brought weapons on deck, and loaded the great guns and ran them out. They backed the headsails and the *Pretty Anne* gathered way and the black flag snapped out at her masthead. The *Pretty Anne* rounded the point, tacked, and stood into Dry Harbor.

When the forwardmost gun would bear, Harwood touched it off, blasting round shot and grape at the anchored sloops. They could see clearly the panic on board the anchored vessels as their people fell over one another to flee, tumbling into their boats and pulling for the dubious safety of the shore, followed by the pirates' derisive laughter and curses and small-arms fire.

The *Pretty Anne* rounded up and dropped anchor beside the larger of the two sloops, both of which they now considered to be theirs. The mood was high and jovial. No more fishing boats; they had managed one decent prize after another. They certainly harbored no ill will to the men forming up on the beach in some version of a line of defense.

"Halloa!" Fetherston shouted, and his huge voice came back in the form of an echo which delighted him. "We are English pirates, but you need not be afraid! We desire you to come aboard us!"

There was a moment of silence, once the echo had faded, and no response from the men on the beach. Then Fetherston added, "Pray, do not make us come to you!"

That seemed to move the men on the beach. They pushed their boats back into the water and climbed in and slowly pulled for the *Pretty Anne*. Alongside, one by one, like men heading for their own executions, they climbed up the side.

But the pirates were in far too jovial a mood to begin executing anyone, and instead they welcomed the men aboard with grand bonhomie, slapping their backs and handing them bottles of rum and wine which two days before had been the property of Thomas Spenlow.

"Welcome aboard the *Pretty Anne* sloop," said Jack,

bowing deep. "I am Calico Jack Rackam. Delighted to make your acquaintance."

The men from the sloops, not certain how to react, gave weak smiles, nodded their heads, made noises that sounded like greetings.

Anne Bonny, watching the show, did not know how to react either. Calico Jack was in rare form. His spirits were up, he was less drunk than he had been in a long time. Their little string of successes seemed to have done much to bring him back to being the man she had fallen for on New Providence.

And yet, there was something out of place. He was not Calico Jack, not entirely. He seemed more like someone doing an impersonation of the old John Rackam, someone who had the act almost perfect, but was missing a certain undefinable element, so that the impression was not quite right.

Oh, I am a deep cove, Anne thought. *What is this nonsense?*

But still she could not shake the feeling. Try as she might to assure herself that nothing had changed, that things would get better from here, she could not quite believe it. If Jack was just playing at being the old, bold Jack Rackam, then she knew that she, too, was just playing at her former self, just pretending to harbor the same reckless optimism that drove the newly wedded Anne Bonny to Nassau and into Jack's bed.

"Such fine vessels you have here," Jack was saying now, parading before the men from the beach, who did not even know if they were guests or prisoners. "Pray, which of you gentlemen are the masters?"

"I'm Thomas Dillon, and I'm master of the *Sarah,* which is the sloop just alongside here. T'other sloop's the *Mary.*"

"Ah! And who might be the master of the *Mary?*"

A pause, then one of the men, who was wearing a long blue coat as the only distinction between himself and the other deckhands, said, "I am. John Spears."

"You?" Jack turned on him. "You seemed damned backwards in speaking, John Spears. Are you reluctant to tell us what we ask?"

"No," said the man, reluctantly.

"I should hope not, and we such great friends and all. Will you not drink with us?"

"Aye. I will."

" 'Aye' indeed. Then drink, man, drink!" Jack pointed to the rum bottle that Spears held in his hand, a bottle he had reluctantly taken from Fetherston after coming aboard. Spears hesitated, looking around at the others.

"I said drink."

John Spears raised the bottle to his lips and began to drink, to the cheering of the pirates. Two big swallows and he lowered the bottle and Jack held his sword under the man's chin and said, "Drink!"

Spears tilted the bottle up again and Jack stepped forward and grabbed it and held it so the man could not lower it from his mouth.

"Drink! Drink, goddamn your eyes!"

With eyes wide, choking, gasping, spilling rum down his shirt and coat, Spears quaffed the bottle of rum, and when it was gone, half down his throat, half on his clothes, he staggered back, gasping and retching.

"Don't you puke on my deck!" Jack shouted, holding the sword level with the man, and seemingly by sheer will Spears kept the rum down, leaning back against the rail and swallowing air.

When that fun was played out, Jack turned back to Thomas Dillon. "You are to be commended, sir, on keeping so fine a sloop. And I will do you the honor, the great honor, of choosing your vessel as my prize. Do you think that an honor, sir?"

Dillon looked around at the grinning pirates and nodded his head. "An honor," he agreed.

For the rest of the afternoon the crews of the two sloops were made to unload all of the cargo of any value from the hold of the *Mary* and stow it down aboard the *Sarah,* which Jack had decided to take for their own. Once again the pirates enjoyed the kind of day that made piracy so attractive to seafaring men: lazing away under the tropical sun, eating and drinking their fill, while other men worked at transferring booty to their newly acquired vessel.

With the sun an hour or so from setting, the Pretty Annes won their anchor, and Fetherston and his crew aboard the *Sarah* did the same, and together they stood out of Dry Harbor and made for the open sea. Once clear of the dangers of the shore, they turned and again ran west before the unfailing trade winds.

Soon after sunrise on the following day the pirates reached the end of the island, the westernmost point of Jamaica, a headland called Negril Point, a green hump of land, and beyond that, only open water.

The *Pretty Anne,* with her prize on her leeward quarter, rounded Negril Point and stood into the little sheltered place there, surprising the crew of a small pettiauger who took to their boat pulled ashore, then fled into the jungle to escape what they rightly presumed to be pirates.

The two sloops came up into the wind and dropped their anchors, and not long after, the pettiauger's crew reappeared on the beach, curiosity having apparently got the better of them.

Fetherston called to them. "Halloa! We are Englishmen and we would desire you come aboard and drink a bowl of punch with us!"

There seemed to be some conferring among the men on the beach, but they made no reply. "I shall go get these fellows and have them drink with us!" Fetherston announced, and he and several others climbed down into the sloop's canoe, which had been pulled alongside, and in it they rowed to shore. Ten minutes later they returned with the pettiauger's crew.

There were nine men from the pettiauger, big bearded men, with cutlasses and muskets, and they looked as near to pirates as men might look without actually being on the account. They had bought the pettiauger, to go a-turtling, they explained, and were grateful for the pirates' hospitality, as their own liquor was all out.

"Come below, then, come below!" Jack roared, and he

led the nine men, along with the Pretty Annes, down the scuttle. A minute later, the once-crowded deck was all but deserted, and in the wake of the raucous insanity, only Anne and Mary and Jacob were left behind.

It was a lovely evening, warm and still, with the island itself shielding the bay from the steady trade winds that swept Jamaica along her whole length, east to west. The sloop hung at the end of her gently curving anchor rode, riding over the low humps of the waves that worked their way around the point and rolled in from the sea.

To the east, directly astern of them, the island loomed up and up, tier upon tier of thick jungle climbing away from the white beach to reach its pinnacle somewhere in the wild interior.

The sloop's jib boom pointed west, toward the lovely sunset building over the straight line of the horizon. The thin sea haze was lit up pink and orange and red as the sun moved toward the edge of the world, the edge that was visible from the sloop's deck.

Negril Point, like a stubby finger, pointed toward the Spanish Main, as if to say, *There, there the great riches of empire once were found, but now they are gone.* Beyond that western horizon lay Grand Cayman, Little Cayman, the Yucatán peninsula of Mexico. But from the deck of the sloop there was nothing to see but water ahead, and beach and jungle behind.

The shadows were long. The sloop's forestay made a bold line down the center of the foredeck. Mary was sitting on the bulwark, one hand on the shrouds, staring forward at the lovely yellows and oranges in the sunset.

Jacob was stretched out on the main hatch.

Against the base of the single mast, Anne Bonny reclined, a pistol in her hand. She pulled back the cock, pulled the trigger, watched the shower of sparks fall to the deck and then blink out. Then she pulled out powder and shot and loaded the weapon.

She and Mary were still dressed out in men's clothing.

From down below, muffled by the deck and the scuttle, the sounds of building riot, the cadence of men yelling, laughing, singing, though those on deck could not make out the words.

"Very well, Mary," Anne said, getting to her feet, "where would we go?"

"Pardon?"

"If we were to give up the sweet trade, where would we go? What would we do?"

"In my life I have known only soldiering, sailing, piracy, and innkeeping. Of those, I should say innkeeping was the best of the lot. We've had a bit of luck, as of late. Perhaps our share of what we have taken would buy us a little inn. Say in Charles Town or Norfolk."

Anne smiled. "Not Charles Town, dear. There is no welcome for me there."

"Yes, of course. How could I have forgotten? Very well, then, perhaps Newport, in the colony of Rhode Island. A liberal place, as I hear it, where the people are not given to much inquiry as to the source of another's fortune."

"Too bloody cold," Jacob offered.

Mary nodded. "You are right. Too bloody cold."

From down below, a burst of laughter, a shout. Something crashed into something else and then there was a pistol shot. The three on deck froze, listened, waited for the sounds of an all-out brawl, in which case they would have felt obligated to dive below and join in. But the gunshot was followed by more wild laughter, more shouting. Mary shook her head.

Anne began to prowl the deck, back and forth. Even without asking, Mary knew the thoughts rolling around in her head. They had not known each other so very long, she and Anne, but it had been an intense time, decades of living crammed into the past year.

Anne was not one to worry about the future. She had never felt the need to seriously consider what course she might take, or the consequences of her decisions, and now that she had to consider such things, she did not know how.

Sometimes Mary thought she knew Anne better than Anne knew herself.

Back and forth she paced and Mary loved to watch her. She was such a beautiful woman. There was such strength and grace in her stride. It was catlike. There was no other way to describe it, no other simile that so perfectly described Anne Bonny in motion. Catlike. Mary did not think that Anne could make an awkward motion if she tried.

The rough men's clothes did not disguise her beauty, her perfect face, her thick reddish blond hair tumbling down her back, her lithe body. It was no wonder, Mary thought, that men had died for her. Mary knew that she would die for Anne as well, if it came to that.

It is time to set this girl on the right path, Mary thought.

Jack was lost to them; he would not come back. Mary had seen it before. There was only so much that a man could endure, even a brave man, which Jack was not. Like a sail, there was a limit to the pressure under which a man could hold together, and when that limit was exceeded, he blew apart. The encounter with the *Guarda del Costa* had been Jack's fatal gust and it had torn him to ribbons.

If Anne did not come to understand these things, then Jack would bring her down with him.

Mary had held her tongue in this matter, recalling how little Anne appreciated her unsolicited advice. But time was short. *I must speak to her, whether she wishes to hear it or no.*

Thus resolved, Mary hopped down from the bulwark and opened her mouth to speak, but before she could say a word, Anne cried, "Damn me!" and raced for the bow, her eyes fixed over the starboard side.

"What, Annie? Whatever is it?"

"Ship!" Anne cried, pointing toward the hulking Negril Point, and Mary followed her finger. A mile away, coming around the point, the bowsprit and headsails of a sloop, her canvas washed with orange in the setting sun.

"Damn it!" Mary cried, and she felt a surge of panic, an unpleasant sensation. *I have gone and frightened myself, with all my talk of being too long here,* she thought, but she could not shake the feeling. She raced aft, threw open the little doors to the scuttle. The noise of the frolicking men and the smell of rum and tobacco smoke swept over her.

"Ship! A ship! Turn out! Turn out!" she cried, and her words managed to cut through the din and the noise fell off and the men came staggering up from below.

Drinking was as much a part of the pirates' life as ships and gunpowder. Mary had seen each of the Pretty Annes drunk before, she had been drunk herself with them, many times, but now they were more far gone than she had ever seen. The turtle fishermen were a rough lot, and Mary guessed there was some sense of pride and competition driving them all, to see who could consume the most rum and brandy. Mary had seen such things often enough in the company of men. It was not a lovely thing to look on.

"There is a ship, standing in around Negril Point, and I think we might look to our guns," Mary said.

"Ah, damn them, damn their eyes!" roared Fetherston, tripping on a ringbolt and falling to the deck in a great flurry of coats and weapons.

"Come then, let us clear away the guns!" Jack roared, infused with the courage he had found in his rum bottle. "Annie, Annie, fetch us up some powder, you little powder monkey!"

The men fell clumsily on the guns and Mary opened up the powder chest and extracted a canvas cartridge since she could see that Anne, who did not appreciate Jack's remarks, was not about to do so. She handed the gunpowder to Harwood, who stuffed it down the forwardmost gun, and fortunately no one asked for more, as she was not about to start handing out gunpowder in quantity to that crowd.

The sloop had rounded the point by then, carried on the trade winds that were blocked from the *Pretty Anne* by the island, and was closing boldly, and Mary did not think that a hopeful sign.

"Stand clear, stand clear!" Harwood yelled, and the men who were crowding the rail and shouting at the sloop moved out of the way of the gun. Harwood touched the match to the touchhole and the gun went off with a great roar and the flames from the muzzle looked impressive indeed in the failing light.

The echoes from the gun had not yet died away when the sloop put up her helm and tacked away, turning her stern to the pirate and beating back the way she had come. This brought a chorus of jeers and curses and threats from the drunken horde, who continued to shout until the sloop was lost from sight behind Negril Point.

"Down below, lads, and back to it! Let us toast our bold victory!" Fetherston shouted, and once again the lot of them, pirates and turtlers, filed down below to continue with their grand frolic.

Five minutes later it was quiet again on deck, and from below, the renewed sounds of the bacchanal, and it seemed to Mary as if the whole thing had never taken place—the sloop, the gun—as if it had all been a dream.

I could wish for happier dreams, she thought as she resumed watching Anne and Anne resumed pacing, back and forth, her caged-tiger walk.

Captain Paul Bonevie was relieved to see Negril Point come between his sloop and the one that had just fired on him. His was not a large vessel, nor heavily armed or manned. He was not in a position to fight pirates.

He stood on, close hauled, beating west against the trade winds. Four miles away, directly to windward, was the sloop with whom they had been sailing in company, a sloop commanded by Jonathan Barnet, who Bonevie knew would be most interested indeed in what had just transpired.

It took the vessels and hour to converge and then Bonevie hove to and Barnet did the same and Bonevie hailed Barnet over the water.

"I have just come up with two sloops, at anchor beyond Negril Point! One fired upon me, but they did not give chase or seem to haul their anchor cable aboard!"

Barnet climbed up onto the sloop's rail, one hand on the shrouds. "How many aboard her?"

"I could not say for certain. Twenty, perhaps. Not much above that."

"It might well be this Rackam! I would suggest you stay to weather of us, and we will see to him!"

"Aye, that I will! And good fortune to you!" Bonevie called back.

Barnet was confident, but Barnet had close to fifty men with him. They were all crowded on the weather deck, well armed and eager for a fight.

Bonevie thought of that gun blasting in the twilight, heard the dull echoes of the laughing and cursing that had come on the wake of the gunfire. A bizarre, unnatural sound, the laughter of the damned, gobbling up their last moments of earthly pleasure.

Chapter 38

IT WAS FULL DARK, AND THE WARMTH WAS GOING OUT of the deck planks. Anne could feel the coolness of the wood, though her once delicate feet were now so calloused that she could easily climb barefoot up the thin, rough manila ratlines that ran like a rope ladder to the masthead.

She paced, back and forth; she could not seem to stop herself. Sometimes she let her mind linger on the sensuous feeling of motion, of leg muscles rippling under her slop trousers, the tightness in her forearm as her hand gripped the hilt of her sword. Sometimes she let herself think on the beauty of the night, with the rising moon making blue shadows on the deck.

Sometimes she spoke with Mary and tried to work up the courage to ask Mary for help. *Tell me what to do, where we should go, do not let me make a fool of myself,* she wanted to say, but she could not, not yet, not even to Mary.

Then every few minutes she would go forward, climb up on the base of the bowsprit, strain to see past Negril Point, to see if there was an enemy coming in from the sea, some overwhelming force that would make all of her thoughts and worries of the future moot.

She tried not listening to the raging sound of the men coming from below, but she could not ignore it. It seemed sometimes the deck might burst from the pressure of the noise filling the hold.

Then the after scuttle opened and the noise spilled out and Anne looked aft. Jack was making his way with some difficulty onto the deck. "Hey, there, boy! We'll have some music below!" he shouted.

No one on deck moved or spoke. Jack took an uncertain step forward. "I said we'll have some music, boy!"

Jacob got to his feet. "I'll not play to that crowd."

"What? I am ordering you to play! Will you defy me?"

"I said only that I will not play to that mob."

"You pup!" Jack roared. "Oh, will you have your little doxy run me through, like she done Bartlett? Or will I kill you both, right now?"

Now Mary was on her feet and Anne took a step closer—like players arranging themselves for the final scene, the resolution of all the tension that had been building, act upon act.

Mary would not suffer much of Jack's threats or abuse, and Jacob had been long enough among them that he would not either. Jack could hardly stand, he was in no position to fight, but the spirits that robbed him of his ability only augmented his ardor.

"Jack," Anne started, swallowing her disgust, hoping she sounded reasonable. "Pray, my love . . ." But Jack seemed to have forgotten the fight already.

"What ho? What ho?" he cried, staring out past the starboard bow and staggering toward the rail. "Is this dog back again?"

Anne turned and looked in the direction that Jack was pointing. A sloop, standing in around the headland, her sails dull gray in the moonlight, a silent specter looming in the dark.

"Back for more of our metal, are you?" Jack shouted, but Anne was not so certain. The cut of the jib, the length of the mainsail's foot . . . Anne had learned a few things about sailing ships in her time on the account.

"Jack, I do not think this the same sloop as the last," she said.

"Anne's right," Mary concurred, but Jack said, "Bah, you bloody doxies, what in hell does Betty know about such things?" He staggered back to the scuttle, shouted down into the din, "Come up, lads, come up! They have come back for more, the sorry dogs!"

One by one the pirates and the turtlers came back on deck and their condition was worse than before. Those whose stability was not what they might wish sat on the deck and the others staggered to the rail.

"Your eyes are all out from the rum, Jack Rackam," said Corner. "This is never the same sloop as that what we drove away. She is half again as big, and she is for us, I'll warrant."

Bloody horse's arse, Anne thought. Had she not told him it was a different sloop? But she was too furious, too disgusted, to take any pleasure from her being right. She did not mention it to Jack. She did not think he would recall their conversation of two minutes before.

"I say, let us quit this place!" shouted Noah Harwood, and that met with a chorus of "Aye!" and a gang of men staggered forward and with much difficulty began to haul the anchor in, hand over hand, while others went clumsily about setting the mainsail and the jib.

Anne went aft and grabbed up the tiller because no one had thought to man it. A moment later Mary joined her. She had two pistols jammed in her belt and two more hanging from a ribbon around her neck. Another pair dangled from a ribbon she held in her hand.

With never a word she looped the ribbon over Anne's neck, like she was presenting her with a knighthood. The guns thumped against Anne's stomach as she moved the tiller, and the ribbon pressed into her breasts with the weight of the weapons.

The *Pretty Anne*'s bow began to turn, slowly, the stars moving lazily past as the anchor came free from the bottom. At the same instant, Anne and Mary turned and looked for the approaching sloop.

"She carries the wind with her around the point, and we have all but naught," Mary said. The strange sloop's sails were filled, not billowing out, but full enough, and she was making way through the water, while the *Pretty Anne* was doing little more than wallowing, catching only the lightest puffs of air off the land.

"Damn it, damn it," Anne said. She was not accustomed to feeling afraid, had never experienced any real sense of dread, but she was getting it now. "What sloop do you think this is?"

"I have no notion. But see how she comes for us. I think they know what we are, and are seeking us out, and that means they must reckon they can take us."

Anne nodded, bit her lower lip, and pushed the tiller over as the *Pretty Anne* caught a puff and heeled a bit to larboard.

As soon as you think you have pushed your luck too far, you know that you have, she thought. It was a lesson she had learned long ago. And, like so many important things that she had learned, a lesson that she always chose to ignore.

"Come along, come along, load the bloody gun!" Jack roared as his drunken men stumbled and cursed and wrestled with the cannon as they tried to load it. One might have thought the cannon a living thing, something that was consciously trying to resist them, for all the difficulty they were having.

"Come along!"

Jack felt like two men. There was Calico Jack Rackam, ready for a fight. That man was a shell, filled with rum;

rum was the blood that animated him. And inside that shell, way inside, utterly hidden, the tiny little cowering John Rackam who wanted only to crawl back below and curl up in a ball and hide and hope that it would stop, all of it.

He threw a filthy oath at the approaching sloop and took another long pull from his bottle. He had to keep the life-blood flowing. If the shell collapsed, then there would be nothing left, nothing but the little cowering figure inside.

"Stand clear, stand clear, you bastards!" roared Harwood, and the others scattered and he touched off the gun, which fired with an impressive roar and blast of flame on the moonlit night.

The sloop rocked with the recoil and the sails fluttered and filled and the *Pretty Anne* gathered a little way. Then the sails fell limp and flogged as the puff deserted them, and the approaching sloop, which still held a bit of the ocean breeze, drew closer still.

"Oh, damn them, damn their eyes!" Jack roared. He felt the shell collapsing inward. He took another drink, but it did not seem to help. They had fired into these people and still they came on, and that could only mean they were ready for a fight and reckoned they could win.

Oh, damn it, damn it all! Panic was setting in, even with all the rum in his belly.

Wait, wait . . . Jack flailed around for a reason to hope. *I got us free of the damned* Guarda del Costa, *did I not?*

But of course, he had not. That had been Corner's plan. He had been ready to roll over and die. And if Corner or some other man of the crew did not think of something now, then they would all die, be it tonight under the sword, or in a month at the end of a rope. This was it.

Someone bloody think of something!

The two sloops, the *Pretty Anne* and this black and gray specter, continued their macabre drifting chase in the light winds behind Negril Point. Jack had no notion of how long it was, or what had happened, really, but it seemed to take an extraordinarily long time. He could no longer hold the shell together. It was collapsing in on him, and soon there would be nothing of it left.

The others were screaming and cursing at the approaching vessel, but all the sound seemed to blend together. And then a voice, not from the *Pretty Anne* but from the other, which was no more than one hundred yards off, called, "What sloop is that?"

George Fetherston leapt up onto the rail, shouted back, "John Rackam, from Cuba!" And Jaek though he might puke. *You stupid bastard, don't give them my name!* he wanted to shout, but he kept his mouth shut.

Fetherston jumped down from the rail, grabbed up a swivel gun and a slow match, and pointed it toward the sloop.

"Strike!" came the voice again. "Strike to the King of England's colors!"

"We'll strike no strikes!" Fetherston roared, and touched off the swivel gun, blasting its load uselessly at their enemy.

Then the voice called, "Fire!" and the dark exploded with the blast of five cannon and countless small arms, big and little flashes of fire, the boom and crack of great guns and small. The shot tore up the air around them, screaming and buzzing and smashing into the hull and tearing up rigging.

A cannonball struck the main boom square and shattered it. The heavy spar fell in two pieces to the deck and tore the mainsail from foot to head and ended for the *Pretty Anne* any hope of sailing out of danger.

"Goddamn them! Goddamn them!" Jack cried, and this time he made no effort to keep the despair from his voice. The shell of Calico Jack was gone now, and he was only the little thing inside, and he cursed this sloop that had come up with them and he hated it for exposing him and for taking away what little he still had and for the fact that it would soon take even his life.

"Goddamn them all!" he shouted, and threw his sword onto the deck and staggered aft. He would go below, he would sit and drink and wait for them to come. He did not have anything left inside him with which he might try and save his life, and even if he did, it would have been pointless. It was over.

Goddamn them all. He staggered below.

John Rackam from Cuba. Captain Jonathan Barnet stood on the rail of his sloop. He was leaning forward, like a dog straining at a leash. He could not help himself. Some unarticulated part of his mind believed that standing straight would slow his vessel's progress.

The sloop with which they were closing was a ghost, no more, dimly seen in the moonlight, the suggestion of a hull floating on the bay, the shadowy outline of mast and rigging.

Jack Rackam! The villain had the audacity to shout out his name! Rackam was no Blackbeard; his capture would not bring Barnet the glory that Maynard had enjoyed. Still, here was the nuisance that the Governor had sent him to eradicate, and eradicate he would.

"Strike!" Barnet shouted. "Strike to the King of England's colors!"

"We'll strike no strikes!" Rackam shouted back.

Then, across the water, barely heard on that still night, just audible over the ripple of water that passed down the sides of the sloop, the familiar hiss of powder in the touchhole of a gun, and before Barnet could say a thing the single cannon roared out, a brilliant flash that stayed on Barnet's eyes long after it was gone. The round shot screamed past, punched a hole in the mainsail, and flew off into the night.

It was like aqua vitae to a midwife. Barnet felt his excitement swell.

"Fire!"

Barnet's men responded, five cannon to the pirates' one, and small-arms fire as well, a hail of iron in response to this Rackam's audacity. He could hear wood shattering and he strained to see what they had hit, but with the dark and his eyes ruined by the muzzle flashes, he could see little. It did not matter. He was hot and his men were hot and they were ready to be at them.

Mary watched, incredulous, as Jack abandoned the deck. If he had fled below in terror, she might have understood, but he did not. He just left, as if his work there were done.

She was about to make some comment on this when Fetherston shouted, "There now! Brother Jack has the idea! Damn them all, I am with him! Will we let these bastards stop our revels?"

And with that Fetherston stumbled after Jack, and behind him, the other Pretty Annes made for the scuttle.

"What are you about?" Mary screamed. This was not possible; they could not be leaving the deck at such a time. "They will be on us directly. Where do you think you are going?"

"Ah, damn their eyes, Mary, dear!" Fetherston shouted. "Come below and drink with us!"

"Get back here, you bastards! You blackhearted, cowardly sons of bitches!" Mary screamed, but she was yelling at their backs and one by one they made their way below and then once again it was just Mary and Anne and Jacob, and the sloop, fifty yards away, drifting down on them.

"Goddamn them!" Anne shouted. She looked around, as if searching for the cause of this incredible behavior. Mary could see that she was frantic, desperate, confused. "What are they about?"

From the sloop, an order was shouted, as clear as if it were given aboard the *Pretty Anne*. "Boarders, stand ready!"

Mary felt panic, and rage at being thus abandoned. She raced back to the scuttle, threw the door open, and shouted below. "Get up on deck, you cowardly dogs! They are near upon us, get up here and fight like men!"

She pulled a pistol from her belt, fired it down into the hold, but in the quiet as the gunshot faded she could hear nothing of her shipmates but some low talk and the thump of bottles and clattering of tin cups.

Mary flung the pistol below. "Goddamn their black hearts!" She turned to Anne, who was staring wide-eyed at her.

"They are gone. It is you and me, Annie, my dear. We are the only here who will fight like men."

"I am with you," Jacob said, but Mary had already decided that he would not fight. She would not let him.

"No, Jacob. Go below."

"I will not."

"There is still a chance that you can prove you sailed against your will, but not if you are on deck, fighting, when they come for us. Go."

"I will not."

Mary pulled another pistol, pulled back the cock, pointed it at Jacob's head. "Go!" She could see the end of the muzzle shake, could feel the tears in her eyes. "Go!"

"No. You would not shoot me."

"I bloody well will shoot you! I'll blow your damned head off before I will see you hang! I'll kill you this instant, damn your eyes, and myself as well before I let these dogs take us!" The tears were flooding now, running unchecked down her face.

"Please, Jacob, I beg of you, do not make me do this thing."

There was a moment of silence, and then Jacob said, "I will always love you, Goodwife Wells." He backed away, and then turned and disappeared down the scuttle.

And then it was only Mary and Anne, alone on the sloop's deck, and the night was quiet save for the lap of the water and the ominous sound of many, many men gathering to board them, the click of flintlocks going to half cock, the clash of cutlasses banging on bulwark as the boarders prepared for their leap.

Fifteen yards away and the women were looking right at this ghostly sight, bearing down on them. A strange quiet hung like mist around them. Side by side they stood, their shoulders pressing against one another.

Mary reached out with her hand, found Annie's and gave it a squeeze.

Anne turned and they looked at one another, hand in hand, and Mary thought, *Blood sisters,* and she knew that Anne was thinking it as well.

Barnet pulled his eyes from the anchored vessel long enough to check on the readiness of his own men. They were crowded at the rail, stomping like racehorses at the starting line, wielding pistols, cutlasses, swords, dirks, axes. They were grim faced, but they were eager and ready, like him. There was glory to be had tonight, and possibly riches as well, and those things were powerful motivators.

Barnet looked back at the sloop. Twenty yards away and they were closing fast with the few knots they were making through the water. Details of the enemy were coming visible now: the sweep of the rail, the few guns, the boom sagging in the middle and the sail spilling in an unholy bundle off the spar.

That must have been the shattered wood, Barnet thought. He took a fresh grip on his sword. Ten yards and he could see everything on deck, quite clearly now. It was just as he had imagined, save for the men.

"Where the bloody hell are they?" A voice from the waist of his own vessel, as if the fellow were reading the text of Barnet's own thoughts. *Where were they?* There were only two men on deck that he could see.

"Watch for a trap, lads!" he called out. "Watch the scuttles and behind the bulwarks!"

Barnet had a sudden flash of apprehension, a sensation approaching fear. Where were they all? What surprise did these rogues have in store? What were they about? For a wild instant he thought of hauling his wind, standing off, blasting them with cannon fire.

Too late! Too late! Five yards, they could not turn now. Barnet stared at the two figures facing them, shoulder to shoulder. Young men and clean shaven, standing bold and ready.

And two women, by name Anne Fulford, alias Bonny, and Mary Read . . . Barnet recalled what the Governor had read to him and his mouth fell open because it was suddenly clear that these were the two facing him, the women. Anne Bonny and Mary Read.

He opened his mouth to shout an order, an admonition to take them alive, to go easy, that these were women and were to be treated as such, and then the two vessels struck.

Mary released Anne's hand, jerked a pistol from her belt. The sloop, this enemy, hit their ship with an impact that jarred the *Pretty Anne* and made the women stagger.

"Bastards!" Mary screamed, and she fired the gun into the mass of men as they broke over the rail and crashed down onto the deck. She flung the gun away, snatched up two more that hung from ribbons, and Anne did the same and they fired, four guns at once, and it did not slow the rush for an instant.

They dropped the guns and pulled their swords, in perfect synchronization. Pistols went off, lead balls plucked at Mary's clothes, she felt a grazing wound on her leg. Then, together, Mary Read and Anne Bonny charged.

Headlong into the press of men, screaming like demons, sweeping great arcs with their blades, striking their tormenters down as they came, Anne and Mary plunged into the fight.

It was the maddest thing that Mary had every seen, and she had seen some madness in her day. Faces loomed up around them, men shouting, weapons flashing, and she and Anne hacked away, slashing at whatever was before them.

Mary could feel the blood running under her clothes from a dozen wounds, but she could not feel the wounds themselves and she fought on. Already her throat ached with screaming.

"Watch the scuttles! Watch for the others!" she heard someone shout, and in another circumstance she might have smiled. How could these men guess that she and Anne were all there was, all who were willing to stand the deck and fight?

Arms enveloped her and she put her shoulder into the

man's chest and heaved him back, half turned. Anne was surrounded; hands reached up behind her, swords flashed like a school of fish.

"Anne!"

But before Anne could react, before Mary could move to protect her, she felt an arm around her neck, hands on her arms, and suddenly she could not work her sword. More hands grabbed her, and then more, like devils snatching her up and dragging her down into hell.

She felt the weight of the men on her, hands holding her like she was bound with rope. She could not see Anne through the press of men who were falling on her. Fleeting images of faces and hands and shirts and feet, the smell of stale sweat and rum on breath.

"Stand to the scuttles and hatches! Keep a look!" There was that voice again, still convinced this was a trap, still sure that it could not be only these two women standing in defense of their vessel.

Down, down to the deck, Mary felt herself pressed, first to her knees, then on her side, hands grabbing her everywhere, and she could not move. She had meant to die fighting, but now she realized that she might not.

She cursed, kicked, and twisted, but she could not break free of the hands. She struggled until she had no strength left and then she just stopped and closed here eyes.

"Down below! You lot, down the forward hatch. The rest follow me! Have a care!" Mary listened with eyes still closed as the boarders prepared to search the vessel for the others. She listened to the sound of the scuttle doors thrown open, of footsteps rushing below. She could hear shouts of surprise, roaring, drunken curses from her own shipmates, harsh orders, the sounds of submission. She heard not one gunshot or clash of steel, not one note of even token resistance.

Up from below, feet on the ladder and on the deck, and Mary heard someone say, "They was all bloody below, and drunk as lords. Not a one but these bloody sluts would stand and fight!"

The hands that held her pinned now rolled Mary over on

her stomach and pulled her arms behind her. She felt thin rope cutting into her wrists as she was bound and she thought, *Please, oh please, kill me now,* but she knew that it would not be that simple, not that clean and quick.

Chapter 39

JOHN RACKAM SAT IN HIS PRISON CELL. IT WAS THE place from whence he had come, and from thence he would be taken to the place of his execution where he would be hanged by the neck until he was dead.

He sat perfectly still, his eyes staring straight ahead. The words ran around and around. *Hanged by the neck until I am dead. Hanged by the neck until I am dead. Until I am dead.* Sometimes the idea seemed as real and immediate as a gushing wound, and sometimes it did not seem to make sense.

Bells rang outside and they made him jump a little, made his stomach do a twisting thing. Yesterday the trial had ended. Today they would hang him. Extraordinary, how time could creep so slowly by, and at the very same instant, fly away.

Will they hang my body up in chains? he wondered. That thought had not occurred to him, but of course, they would. They would debase his beautiful body by hanging it from a gibbet, so that all could see the fate that awaited pirates.

He looked down at himself, pictured this body, this fine body, which had given so much pleasure to so many women, hanging from chains, bloated, putrid, being picked at by birds. The flesh would turn black and then slough off until there was only the ragged clothing, his beloved white calico coat and breeches, flapping in tatters, and inside the clothes, the bones of Calico Jack. Jack had seen enough bodies hung in chains to know what he soon would be.

The thought made him want to puke, but he had eaten nothing in days and there was nothing for his stomach to throw up. He swallowed hard, tried to think on something else.

At the far end of the cellblock a key rattled in the door and Jack jerked up and did not move beyond that. He could not move, he could only sit and wait. The sensation was perfectly the same as that moment, his last moment as a free prince, down in the *Pretty Anne*'s hold, when he heard the scuttle open, heard the sounds of his enemy coming for him.

He had gone below because the fight was out of him and there was no reason at all for him to be on deck. There was nothing he could do there. The others could call him a coward, they could maroon him, they could do as they wished; he was done and so he just went below.

And to his surprise, the rest followed him and took up where they had left off in their celebrations, as if there were not another ship around for a thousand miles.

The others—Fetherston, Corner, Harwood, the turtlers—had continued the revelry in earnest, drinking hard, shouting at one another, and only their tendency to speak of the end of things, toasting the short life but a merry one, gave any indication that they were in any way aware of their fate.

But not Jack. He knew what was coming, he knew how pathetic it was that he was cowering below while overhead, Anne Bonny and Mary Read stood the deck alone in the face of their enemy.

That was the difference between Jack and the others in the hold, and Jack alone knew it. He would not fight because he was a coward, and they would not fight because they were so utterly without fear that they did not care. He knew how pathetic it was, but there was not one damned thing he could do.

And so he sat, just stared straight ahead and listened to the sound of the two sloops as they hit, the feet rushing overhead, the pistol shots, the shouting, the clash of steel. He could not believe how long the fight lasted—it was only two women, for the love of God! But they must have fought like wildcats, because it was some moments before it was quiet again.

And then, like the key in the prison door, the scuttle opened and the armed men poured down into the *Pretty Anne*'s hold and there was Jack and there were the others and they were too drunk or too frightened to fight, and so they surrendered. They cursed and they spat, but they surrendered like children, and the men who had taken them could only exclaim in amazement that of all those aboard, it was only the two women who had fought at all.

And so Jack knew that for all the fantasies he had, sitting in his cell, about escape, all his dreams about fighting his way out of prison, about pulling some clever ruse to gain his freedom, he would, in truth, march placidly to the gallows, do as he was told, and hang by the neck until he was dead.

The door opened at the far end of the cellblock and footsteps echoed around the stone building and from the other cells the Pretty Annes hooted and jeered, but Jack sat silent.

The footsteps stopped outside his cell and he looked up at the unsympathetic face of Chief Justice William Nedham, and behind him, the jailor and the bailiff and Mr. Norris, the Register.

It is time . . . Jack thought, but he could not reckon why Nedham was there. Once Lawes had passed his judgment, the Chief Justice's job was over. It was in the hangman's hands now.

The jailor opened the cell and Nedham swept in and said, "John Rackam, I wish to ask you a few questions this morning."

Jack just looked at him and nodded. Norris came in behind the Chief Justice and sat himself on the bench opposite Jack. He had a writing tablet and a pen and ink bottle, which he arranged beside him.

Nedham spoke again. "I would you would depose to us all that you know of the willing involvement of one Anne Bonny, alias Bonn, in any of the piracies, felonies, and robberies committed on the high seas of which you and the others were lately convicted."

He stopped, as if no more needed to be said, but Jack did not quite understand. *Alias Bonn?*

"Annie . . . ?" he said, weakly. *Oh, he wants me to say that Annie is guilty as well!* "Annie? No, I know not of her willing involvement. She was in love with me, do you see? Poor, silly girl, and see what has come of it . . ."

Nedham scowled at him, but Jack did not care. He would say no more on that subject.

"Very well, then. What know you of the willing involvement of one Mary Read in any of the piracies, felonies, and robberies committed on the high seas of which you and the others were lately convicted?"

"Mary Read . . ." He had not thought of her as he sat here, awaiting his fate. Mary Read. Damn her. How much of this was her fault? What if she had not come between him and Annie, what might have happened then? How might his fate have been different? He had often wondered what unnatural things she had led Anne to, during their long stay in Cuba.

"Mary Read . . . well, let me see, now. Sure, she came aboard us, in the guise of a young man. One day I do recall falling into a conversation with her. I did not then know her sex, you see . . ."

Jack sat more upright, warming to his story. "I asked her what pleasure she could have, being concerned in such an enterprise, where her life was continually in danger from fire or sword. I told her she must be sure of a bad death if she should be taken alive.

"But bold as brass she said to me, she answered that as to hanging, she thought it no great hardship, for, were it not for that, every cowardly fellow would turn pirate and so infest the seas, that men of courage must starve."

Nedham turned to look at Norris and Norris looked up from his frenetic writing and raised his eyebrows at this. And Jack, who did recall a conversation somewhat along those lines, was pleased to see that he was giving the Chief Justice what he desired.

"Mary Read said this to you?" Nedham asked.

"Yes, Your Honor. And she said that if it was put to the choice of the pirates, they would not have the punishment be less than death, the fear of which kept some dastardly rogues honest. She said that many of those who are now cheating the widows and orphans, and oppressing their poor neighbors who have no money to obtain justice, would then rob at sea, and the oceans would be crowded with rogues, like the land, and no merchant would venture out, so that the trade, in a little time, would not be worth the following."

Jack shut his mouth, afraid that he had already said too much, that he had dulled his credibility with too many words. But the Chief Justice did not seem to think so. He nodded to Norris and Norris blotted the deposition and presented it to Jack to sign.

Jack looked at all the neat letters scrawled across the page. He guessed that they represented the story he had just told, but of course, he did not know. He could not read.

Norris held the pen out for him. Jack looked up at him, then down at the pen, and then took the quill in uncertain fingers. He could never get the feel for holding a pen correctly. He saw Norris and Nedham exchange glances, and then Norris pointed to a spot at the bottom of the page and said, in a most condescending tone, "Your mark there will suffice."

Jack felt himself flush, humiliated by his illiteracy, full of guilt for what he had just done. *Well, the bitch said words to that effect,* he thought, *and she was as willing a pirate as ever sailed, damn her eyes.* He scrawled a shaky X where Norris had indicated.

"Good," said Nedham. He took the deposition from Jack's hands and breezed out of the cell, saying, "Jailor, you may bring the condemned to the women's cell and then deliver him unto the sheriff." The Chief Justice was done with John Rackam.

Oh, God, is this it? Jack thought. *Was that my final moment in my cell, given over to deposing against Mary bloody Read?*

The jailor came in and Jack quietly suffered him to put the manacles on his wrists and lead him out of the cell.

The portly jailor led the way, and behind him followed Jack, and behind Jack two armed soldiers. They walked down the length of the prison building and from various cells the others called out to him, saying, "There you go, Jack, lad! A short life and a merry one!" and "We'll see you in hell, Calico Jack! Spare a drink for us!" but Jack kept his eyes on the floor five feet ahead and said nothing.

They stepped through the door at the far end that opened into the big stucco room with the polished tiles. Jack was used to turning to the left to go to the courtroom, but this time the jailor led him across the room to the door opposite, and when he opened it Jack saw that it led to yet another long row of cells.

This would be the cellblock where the women were held, this whole part of the prison for two dangerous women. Without a word the jailor headed down the alley between the cells and Jack followed quietly behind.

Now Jack's stomach was turning and he knew that if he had eaten anything at all, he would be vomiting freely. He was more afraid than he had been at any time since Barnet had turned them over to the militia guard in Davis's Cove and they had been marched to Spanish Town jail.

He had not spoken to Anne in weeks, and then just a fleeting word or two as they were led from one place or another. He had not really spoken to her since their capture. She had not spoken to him at all.

Oh, God, I am to die today, Annie. Won't you send me to my death with a kind word? Jack could hardly remember his mother. He had only vague, shadowy images of comfort and love. That was what he wanted.

At last the jailor stopped and turned and Jack knew that Anne must be in that cell and he was very afraid. He glanced to his right, to the cell across from Anne. Mary Read was sitting there, sitting on the stone bench, one foot propped up and her arms folded on top of her knee. Their eyes met and Jack looked away quick, and hoped that his face did not flush red, though it felt as if it had.

He looked to his left. Anne was there, standing, her hands gripping the bars that held her in. Jack's eyes lingered on those hands, those long, delicate fingers. Such delicate reeds, he had loved to kiss them.

Jack's eyes traveled up to Anne's face. Her lips were pressed tight together and there was fury in her eyes and it made Jack's stomach twist again. That was not the face he hoped would send him off to eternity.

"Annie . . ." he said; it was barely a whisper. "Annie, my love, I go off to die . . ."

He paused and there was silence and he looked into her eyes. He wanted to hug her, to lie down with her, to rest his face on her breasts and weep, to cry out all his sorrow and let his tears melt into the coarse fabric of her prison dress. He wanted comfort; for once in his miserable life he wanted tenderness and understanding. But there were the bars between them, and there was Annie's expression, which was harder still, and more unyielding.

"Annie . . . ?"

"Well, Jack," said Anne, and her voice was hoarse and there was no tenderness there, "I am sorry to see you here, but if you had fought like a man, you need not hang like a dog."

It was quiet again and they looked in one another's eyes. Then Anne let go of the bars and turned her back on him and walked to the far end of the cell and that was the end of it.

Jack stared at her back. *Say something, say bloody something!* But he could think of nothing to say, could think of nothing that he might do, so he just stood there until the jailor took him gently by the arm and led him away.

He was led out of the building to the parade ground on the south end. He blinked hard in the brilliant sunlight and the tears streamed down his face. In the open air he could see how utterly filthy he was, his clothing torn and stained, his hands black with dirt, and his face, he imagined, was just as bad. Was it any wonder he was so quickly condemned?

On the parade ground stood an open wagon, and in the

wagon sat George Fetherston, Richard Corner, John Davies, and John Howell, the men who would join Jack that day. Flanking the wagon, a detail of horse guard sat on top of restless mounts, their helmets and pikes flashing in the sun.

With some difficulty, Jack, his hands still manacled, climbed into the wagon and took a place on the bench next to John Davies. The teamster made a sound and the wagon lurched and rolled forward and the horse guard was under way as well and the little parade moved along toward Gallows Point.

They rumbled down cobbled streets and the wagon made a terrible clatter and shook the men in the back. They were silent, save for George Fetherston, who roared out at the crowds who lined the street to watch them pass, cursing at them and cheering them, to the watchers' delight. He belted out song as they rolled along, managing to outdo the iron-rimmed wheels in volume.

"My name is Captain Kidd, who has sailed,
My name is Captain Kidd, who has sailed,
My name is Captain Kidd;
What the laws did still forbid,
Unluckily I did while I sailed,"

And then Fetherston sang the chorus as well:

"While I sailed!"

The horse guard kept their eyes ahead and made no attempt to shut him up. There was not much you could do to threaten a man who was scheduled to die within the hour.

Jack watched the whitewashed buildings, the cobbled street, the crowds, all receding as they rolled along, and he thought it was like his life, just flowing past, and somewhere up ahead, where he could not see it, the end.

Everything looked sharper, more colorful, and there was a weird, slow quality, very like a dream. He was not afraid, really, and that surprised him.

Jack recalled that in England when he was a boy there

would on occasion come a freezing rain, and when it was done everything would be coated in a thick layer of ice, down to the most delicate tree branches, everything encased in this clear, deep layer.

That was how he felt. Like he was coated in ice, like there was a thick layer surrounding him that dulled what he should feel sharply. How else to explain the fact that he was not afraid? He would be dead, and soon, and yet there was just an odd sort of feeling about it. A little disturbing, a little unreal, but not frightening, really.

1 George Fetherston continued to sing:

"From Newgate now in carts we must go!
From Newgate now in carts we must go!
From Newgate now in carts,
With sad and heavy hearts,
To have out due deserts we must go!"

Then the wagon came to a halt and Jack's stomach sank, but still he did not feel the panic that he had always thought would attend this event. He was less afraid now than he had been when they sighted the *Guarda del Costa,* much less afraid, though his demise was much more certain.

Odd, he thought.

There were soldiers there and none too gently they pulled the condemned men from the cart and marched them toward the gallows. Jack could see it now, just a simple wooden frame, ten feet high, with a noose hanging from the crossbeam, and gathered around, a hundred or so people who had turned out to watch the spectacle.

The soldiers pushed the condemned men off to one side, flanking them with muskets ready while the manacles were struck from their hands. The teamster who had driven the cart to Gallows Point now backed it up to the wooden frame where it might be used as a platform from which the condemned were pushed, and he soon had the cart in position, so practiced were he and his horse in that evolution.

There was a great deal of sound—the creaking of the cart, the chatter of the crowd, Fetherston's ramblings, the wind blowing through the high palms—but it was all one in Jack's ears, all one big buzzing sound of the living world, and he knew soon it would be lost to him.

He wondered for the first time what might become of him when he was dead. Not his body, but him, whatever it was that was John Rackam. He wondered if perhaps the preachers had been right all along, if that should give him pause. But still he felt ice cased and he could not muster the energy to care.

More hands grabbed his arms, men on either side, and through no will of his own he was propelled toward the cart and then up on the cart where the hangman stood waiting for him.

The hangman turned him around so that he was looking out over the heads of the watching crowd, and shuffled him forward to the very edge of the cart. Jack saw the hangman's hands take up the noose and saw it pass over his head and felt the rough manila rope around his neck, felt it scrape his skin as the executioner pulled the noose taught.

Someone was saying something in an official monotone, his sentence of death, no doubt, but it was only part of the big sound and was no more distinguishable as words than the wind in the trees.

Jack looked out past the shoreline and the sandy spit of land, out toward the ocean, the great, rolling, flashing blue ocean, his home for most of his adult life.

What a strange, strange thing this is . . . he thought. *How very odd to die.*

He had not been a bad sailor, not at all. Perhaps if he had stayed an honest seaman and not gone on the account, then things might have ended up differently for him. But that had not happened, and here he was.

I am not afraid, he thought, and the realization startled him. Here he was, at the profound moment, the bitter end of his life, and he was not afraid. It gave him a surge of pride and happiness, a glimpse of redemption for all of the self-loathing with which he had flailed himself for all of his cowardice over the years. He felt warm and light.

I am not afraid. Wouldn't Annie be proud of me now?

He felt a hand on his back, pushing into the small of his back, and then a hard shove and his feet came off the edge of the cart. He saw his beloved ocean swimming in front of his eyes, felt himself falling down, down, felt the rough noose come tight around his neck, a fraction of a second's constriction, and then he was dead.

Chapter 40

JOHN RACKAM'S BODY HAD BEEN HANGING IN CHAINS from a gibbet on Plumb Point for eleven days before the trial of Anne Bonny and Mary Read commenced.

"That was not kind of you, sending Jack to his death thus," Mary had said as the jailor led the broken man away.

"It would have been quite beyond my poor powers to hide my disgust with that man," Anne said, and they spoke no more on the subject.

When the jailor told them how Jack had gone boldly to the gallows, with never a sign of fear, Anne could say only, "I would he had fought for his life with half the boldness that he gave it up."

Then on Monday morning, November 28, the seventh year of the reign of King George of England, the jailor and the bailiff and the soldiers came for them, and once more they were marched into a crowded courtroom, where hundreds of spectators jammed shoulder to shoulder to hear their sordid story.

It was not so very different from the last time they had been in that room. The Commissioners were all there, the same men who had sent the other Pretty Annes to hang, and Mary did not think they would be any more disposed to mercy when it came to considering their fate. There was Mr. Norris, the Register, and the Chief Justice, William Nedham, who was too busy with his papers to look up, the only man in the room not staring at them as they made their entrance, heads up, eyes ahead.

They took their place at the bar and Sir Nicholas Lawes swept in, red faced, white wigged, jowly, and lugubrious, and the trial commenced in the usual, plodding manner. Norris took his place in front of Lawes's grand bench and read the articles against them.

". . . did piratically, feloniously, and in a hostile manner, attack, engage, and take several certain fishing boats . . ."

Bloody pathetic, Mary thought.

". . . and then and there, piratically and feloniously, did steal, take, and carry away the fish and fishing tackle to the value of ten pounds of current money of Jamaica and the goods and chattels of the aforesaid fishermen . . ."

How humiliating, to hang for such a thing!

At last Norris got to the second article, which covered the two sloops they had plundered in Hispaniola, and the third, which was Spenlow's schooner, and the fourth, which was the taking of Dillon's sloop, the *Mary,* which, with its apparel and tackling, was valued at three hundred pounds, and by that point it did not sound so bad.

Three hundred pounds . . . as if we might have seen but a fraction of that . . . Mary found her mind wandering off, thinking of the use to which she would have put three hundred pounds.

Then Norris was done with the articles and he turned to them and said, "What have you to say? Are you guilty of the piracies, robberies, and felonies, or any of them, in the said articles mentioned, which have now been read unto you? Or not guilty?"

"Not guilty," said Anne.

"Not guilty," said Mary. It was silly, but what else was there to say?

Then the Register called the first witness, and Mary was not pleased to see the woman from the canoe step forward and take her oath.

"I knew we should have run this one through," Anne whispered.

"We shall see many today we would have done well to run through," Mary replied.

The woman, who gave her name as Dorothy Thomas, took the stand and described to an enthralled courtroom how she had been stopped by Rackam's sloop and how the two women now at the bar were then on board.

She described how they wore men's jackets and long trousers and handkerchiefs around their heads, how they each had a machete and pistol in their hands. Her voice quavered as she described how Anne and Mary had cursed and sworn at the men to kill her to prevent her coming against them.

"What was the reason," Norris asked, "for your knowing and believing them to be women?"

"Why, by the largeness of their breasts," Dorothy Thomas replied.

It did not get any better from there. Thomas Spenlow was called next and he gave much the same blunt testimony that had helped send the others to the gallows, adding only that in all the time he had been forced to keep company with the pirates, the women had been there as well, and they did not appear to do a thing against their will.

After Spenlow, the Frenchmen were called, Peter Cornelian and John Besneck, speaking through an interpreter, and theirs was the most damning, the most provocative of all. They told how in the weeks they had been forced into involuntary servitude aboard the *Pretty Anne* they had witnessed Anne and Mary fully a part of the pirate tribe, the two women doing the same work as any of the men.

"They were very active on board and willing to do anything," said Simon Clarke, the interpreter. He paused, listened to Besneck's rapid words, then continued. "Anne Bonny, one of the prisoners at the bar, handed gunpowder to the men. When they saw any vessel, gave chase or attacked, they wore men's clothes, and at other times they wore women's."

"Mr. Clarke, pray ask the witnesses if the prisoners at the bar appeared to be kept or detained by force," Norris said.

Clarke translated the words. The Frenchmen shook their heads.

"Non," said Cornelian. Clarke did not bother to translate.

But Mary could not hate the Frenchmen for their testimony because, in faith, it was the truth. What was more, it was their word that had led to Jacob's release, and she did not think she could hope for more than that.

When all of the depositions were done, Sir Nicholas asked Anne and Mary if they had any witnesses of their own to call, or if they would question any of the witnesses already deposed.

"We have no witnesses, Your Honor, nor any questions to ask," Mary said.

The bailiff escorted them from the courtroom and placed them in a small cell and they could hear the sound of the standers-by leaving the chambers so that the verdict could be discussed behind closed doors.

"I fear we are done for, Mary, my dear," said Anne. "What Barnet's men with all their swords and guns could not achieve will now be done by these fat men in silly wigs."

"I would that Barnet had given us a clean death. Fighting, that is how we should have died. The Lord knows we tried hard enough to bring it about."

"But now we shall have ample time to think of some clever thing to say before we hang, some stirring final word from the gallows. That way we shall be long remembered in history."

Mary smiled. "I do not think histories are written about such as us. Poor doxies who rob fishing boats. Camp followers who dress against their sex."

"Lord, you are a sorry one today. One would think you had been sentenced to death, when in fact it will not be for another half an hour, at least."

It was in fact forty-five minutes before the doors were opened again, the great crowd of standers-by allowed to jostle back into position to see the famous women pirates, and Anne Bonny and Mary Read released from the holding cell and once again escorted into the courtroom.

They were stood at the bar, their manacled hands held before them. Mary stole a sideways glance at Anne. She was standing straight like a mast, her head slightly back, her eyes fixed in front, her face set. Her long, thick, red-blond hair was tied back with a piece of spun yarn and there were still a few bits of straw stuck there.

Anne's rough dress was tight around her breasts as her hands against her stomach pulled the cloth tight. She was still beautiful. Mary realized that she was seeing Anne, proud and defiant, in exactly the way she would look as they put the noose around her neck.

Sir Nicholas took his place, cleared his throat, looked down at the women, and Mary was surprised to see that his look was not entirely without sympathy, his voice not as cold as it had been.

"Anne Bonny and Mary Read, this court has unanimously found you both guilty of the piracies, robberies, and felonies charged against you in the third and fourth articles of the articles which have been exhibited against you. Have either of you anything to say or offer why sentence of death should not be passed upon you for your said offenses?"

"No, Your Honor," said Anne.

"No, Your Honor," said Mary.

"Very well," said Lawes, with more emotion than Mary had yet heard from him, and it occurred to her that there might have been some hope of finding mitigating circumstances, some thought of letting them go, but in the face of the witness's testimony that was not going to happen.

"You, Mary Read, and Anne Bonny, alias Bonn," Lawes said, lapsing now into his official tone, "are to go from hence to the place from whence you came, and from thence to the place of execution, where you shall be severally hanged by the neck till you are severally dead. And God of His infinite mercy be merciful to both of your souls."

He banged his gavel down. Mary looked at Anne, and Anne gave her a conspiratorial cock of the eyebrow.

"Your Honor?" Mary said, and Lawes, surprised, looked up.

"Yes, what is it?"

"If it please Your Honor, we would ask that there be a stay of our execution."

"What? On what basis?"

"We plead our bellies, Your Honor."

"Your . . . bellies?"

"Yes, Your Honor," said Mary. "We are both of us quick with child."

Chapter 41

MARY READ WAS NOT MUCH GIVEN TO DRAMATICS, BUT she had to admit to some small delight with the effect that this last statement had had.

It was met at first with silence, absolute silence throughout the courtroom. And then, all at once, as if they had been cued by a stage manager, the standers-by all began to talk at once and the Commissioners exclaimed in surprise and Chief Justice Nedham and Register Norris both began to shout, "Your Honor? Your Honor?"

Anne was smiling a hint of a smile, but Mary looked straight ahead with her parade rest attitude, betraying no emotion.

It was not for dramatic effect that they saved this news until the end. They had discussed at length the moment that it might be revealed, had decided that there would be no reason to mention their being with child at all unless they were condemned to die. And so they kept their secret, right up to the moment when Lawes had ordered them hanged.

Lawes pounded the desk with his gavel, bellowed for silence, and slowly, slowly, the courtroom settled down from their shock and listened close for what now must be a prurient tale indeed.

"You are both of you quick with child?" Lawes asked.

"Yes, Your Honor," Anne and Mary said together.

Further silence as Lawes arranged some papers on his desk. "Anne Bonny, who is the father of the child you allege to carry?"

"He is John Rackam of Cuba. If you wish to ask him the truth of that, you may find him at Plumb Point, I believe."

This brought a tittering from the standers-by, from those who dared laugh, and a pounding of the gavel from Sir Nicholas. "You will keep a civil tongue in your head or it will go hard on you," Lawes warned. "Mary Read, who is the father of your child?"

"I would decline to say, Your Honor."

This brought a louder buzz still from the audience and more pounding from Lawes. "If you will not say, then we must assume that he is not one of these rogues that was hanged. There should be no reason to not name him, unless you are afraid he might be taken up for a pirate."

"I will say only, Your Honor, that my husband was an honest man, with no inclination to such practices, and that we had both resolved to leave the pirates at the first opportunity and apply ourselves to an honest livelihood."

"Your husband? You mean to say you and this unnamed man are legally wedded?"

"We had no church wedding, Your Honor," Mary said. "We would have, sure, had we the chance, but such fine things are not to be enjoyed by the likes of us. I looked upon our marriage as a marriage in conscience, as good and true as any done by a minister, and so yes, I will call this fellow husband."

"Neither this court not the civilized world recognizes such a thing as a marriage of conscience. There is no difference to be made between your action and that of any adulterer and fornicator."

Mary stood stiff and met Sir Nicholas's eyes. She wanted the judge, and the world, to understand what was in her heart. It was a point of pride with her. Her marriage to Jacob Wells was as true a thing to her as anything in her life.

"I have never committed adultery or fornication with any

man," she said, and her voice was even and strong, "and I condemn any court that will say otherwise."

There was a long silence; even the standers-by held their tongues as Mary Read and Sir Nicholas Lawes looked one another in the eye. And in the strange atmosphere of that silence Mary seemed to feel some sympathy from the red-faced judge.

And then he nodded and his wig flopped a bit, back and forth, and he pounded the desk with his gavel.

"Very well," Lawes growled, "I will order that the condemned persons be taken from hence to whence they came and there an examination shall be performed by a qualified doctor of physic. And if it is found that Anne Bonny and Mary Read are in fact quick with child, as they so claim, then their executions shall be stayed until after the time of their laying in. Bailiff, pray, remove the prisoners."

Anne and Mary were taken back to their cells, and soon after a doctor arrived to carry out the orders of the court. The women submitted themselves to his gruff and humiliating examination, and when it was over he said only, "Congratulations. You are both to bear the bastard children of pirates. May God have mercy on your souls," and he went off to report his findings to Sir Nicholas Lawes.

And so the guilty lives of Anne Bonny and Mary Read were extended, by court order, in consideration of the innocent lives they carried in their bellies.

The months dragged by in weary sameness, the one thing that Anne Bonny could not stand, and the passing of time was marked only by the changes in the sun's angle as it streamed through the bars of her cell, and by her ever-increasing girth.

She hated being pregnant. She grew more awkward by the day, more achy and unable to move, and she hated that. Her fine, feline body was gone, taken over by some alien thing, and she wanted it to end. Even the realization that she was bound to hang once the baby was born did not make her want to extend her pregnancy by a moment more.

"Do you not loathe this being with child?" she asked Mary. It was a fine winter day, still some months from the time of her lying in, and she and Mary were taking their exercise on the parade ground, walking back and forth under the less than watchful eye of a guard, who leaned against the building in the shade.

"No, in truth, I do not," Mary said. By their best guess, Anne was two months further along than Mary, but still Mary's belly was showing to great effect. "I find there is something wondrous about having a baby growing in me. Jacob's baby," she added, softly.

"Humph. For all your soldiering and rough and ready life, Mary, dear, you are far more womanly that I. I have always thought so. But just wait until you are as far along as I am, and then you will not be so happy about this."

"Perhaps not," Mary said, and they walked a few more turns, up and down.

"No," said Anne, as if their conversation had not paused, "you will love it all the more, when your belly is as great as mine. Do you think on hanging at all?"

"I think of it. I think if it was not for the baby, I would not have so much care about it. I have lived with death for so very long that my own seems no great hardship. But it grieves me, Annie, it grieves me deep, to think on my little baby who will never have mother or father, who will grow up in circumstances that I cannot guess. It makes me very sad to think of leaving this child, and this child will never know what he or she is."

"Humph," said Anne. "Well, as for me, this is not the first child I leave behind, as you well know. And still I think that a child is better off with anyone but me for mother."

"You are too hard on yourself, Annie, too hard by half."

In that way they took the air on the parade ground every afternoon, and sometimes they even spoke of the chance for escape. But bored as the guards might be, the women knew that in their condition they could not fight and they could not outrun anyone, and they would not be so nimble in their flight. Nor was there much place to hide, not when nearly all of St. Jago de la Vega had attended their trial and knew their faces well.

And so they left off any discussion of escape, and with it any hope.

The rainy months came and the women were not able to walk in the open air and Anne grew to hate her confinement more and more. "You are a wild animal, dear, and you do not take well to a cage," Mary said one morning, and Anne only grunted, though she knew that Mary had hit it just right.

And then May, and the weather grew warm and Anne's water broke. There in her cell, on a pile of straw, with Mary and the midwife in attendance, Anne's labor began. It was a sensation she remembered well from Cuba, the clenching contractions, the great release as they passed, the horrible anticipation as they came on again, faster and faster.

And once more she was profoundly grateful that she had Mary there with her, holding her hand, mopping her forehead. The midwife was a kind woman, her fat face lined from decades of worrying over birthing babies, and she knew her business, but still there was no one on earth who could give Anne support and comfort the way Mary could.

For three hours Anne labored in her cell, and then the insatiable urge to push, the stretching, the agony, and then the great rush of relief as the baby was born; a baby girl, healthy, pink, and bawling.

Anne collapsed back on the straw, gulped air, let the feeling of being done wash over her. She cocked her head, watched Mary clean the baby some and swaddle it tight in clean linen that the midwife had brought. Then Mary brought the baby over to her, held it up for Anne to see the little face, then set her to nursing at Anne's breast.

Anne looked away, tried to ignore the child. Confusion, uncertainty, conflicting emotions, these were not things that Anne was used to and she did not like them. For her, the path had always been clear. She had always understood what she wanted and she had taken it and that was all there was.

But near the end, with Jack, she had been unsure. And now she was unsure again.

La, what am I on about? she thought. *It is the gallows for me; there is not one damned thing I need think on now.*

Then, despite herself, Anne looked down at the baby and stroked her cheek as she nursed. There was something appealing about her, wrinkled and pink and alien as she was. Anne had to admit it to herself.

"What is to happen to the child?" she asked the midwife.

"In a few days I reckon it will be taken to the orphanage," the midwife said in a brusque tone meant to cover her discomfort.

"A few days . . ." Anne said, soft. "Well, I reckon I can play at being a mother for a few days, if it will keep the hangman away."

For the next two days Anne did her best to mother the child, nursing her when she was hungry and sleeping with her on her straw bed for hour after hour, and she felt her affection for the baby grow, despite all her assumptions about herself. And suddenly the thought of hanging seemed a dreadful thing.

Still, after seven months of thinking on it, she was ready to face her death, as ready as anyone might be, and so it came as a great shock when the jailor announced a reprieve of her sentence, staying her execution for another week.

There was no explanation for it; the jailor could not tell her why it had been issued, only that it had. And so Anne braced herself for one more week of life.

On the morning of the seventh day of her reprieve, ten days after the birth of Jack and Anne's baby, Anne Bonny woke to the sound of the prison door being opened. She sat upright and listened. For seven months their routine had hardly varied by a minute, day in and day out, and so she knew that this was not normal.

They are coming for my baby, she thought, and she was startled to find herself in a panic. She picked up the sleeping child, held it close, and moved warily to the front of the cell.

Across from her she could see Mary, just a hump of

blankets, still sleeping, which was also unusual. Mary was the early riser. Anne would have expected the sound of the prison door opening, the footsteps approaching, to have woken Mary as it did her.

Anne took a step back, instinctively, to protect her baby, hugged the child tighter, tried to see down the alleyway between the cells.

Then the jailor was there, his round familiar face, the most familiar face in Anne's life now, save for Mary's. And behind him, a big man in fine clothing, his walking stick clicking on the stone floor. A familiar man, but in the dim light and against the backdrop of the prison it took Anne a moment to recognize him.

"Daddy?"

"Annie, oh, Annie!" Big Bill Cormac took a step toward the bars of the cell and Anne took a step back. She saw him as she had last seen him, red faced, raging, physically shoving her and James Bonny from his house. Vindictive man, what was he doing here? Suddenly she was furious.

"Have you come to see me hang, Father? Come to make certain they finish off your slut daughter, wipe out any disgrace to the family name? As if you were not disgrace enough." She spit the words.

William Cormac looked as if he had been struck. He stopped short in his approach, all but staggered back. "Annie, no . . . dear God, no. I have come to take you home."

Anne's eyes narrowed. There was no vindictiveness in her father's tone, no hatred or disgust. She could hear only love and worry. She was Bill Cormac's little girl, just as the baby she held in her arms was hers. Two weeks before she would not have understood this, but now she did.

"Home . . . ?"

"Yes, Annie, my dear." William Cormac took a tentative step forward, afraid of his daughter's reaction, and then, when she did not move or speak, he took another and held the bars of her cell in his big hands.

"You are too late, Father. I am condemned to die for my crimes. It will be any day now."

Bill Cormac shook his head. "No, Annie. I have friends

here in Jamaica, men with whom I do business. Very powerful men. I have arranged it so that you are to be released into my custody. I will take you home. You and your baby."

Anne felt dizzy, confused. How could things change around so fast? How could this be possible? She looked at the jailor, whom she knew and trusted more than her own father, an imploring look, and he said, "It is the truth, Annie. I have my orders to release you into his custody."

Anne shook her head, slowly. It was too much, too hard to change directions that quickly. But there it was, and there was no reason to believe that it was not true.

"But not without Mary," Anne said.

"Pardon?"

"I will not leave without Mary. She must be released as well, or I cannot go."

Bill Cormac glanced over at the jailor, uncertain. He did not look pleased. "Annie, my dear, it took no end of pleading and no small fortune to get you released. I do not see how they will be inclined to release this other one."

" 'This other one' is Mary Read and she is my sister, as much as ever woman had a sister, and I will not leave her behind." Digging in her heels, standing fast with absolute resolve, this at last was a sensation that was familiar to Anne Bonny.

And she was resolved, absolutely. She and Mary would sail to Charles Town, or they would march to the gallows, but whatever they did, they would do it together.

From the moment that Sir Nicholas had intoned those words—*you shall be severally hanged by the neck till you are severally dead*—Mary Read had felt depression and desperation coming over her like rising water, rising infinitesimally slow, a fraction of an inch per day. As the months passed, as the gallows grew nearer, she could not keep her dark thoughts at bay.

She had not lied to Anne; her own life meant little to

her. She would have marched to the gallows as boldly as ever did any man, but for the life inside her.

A baby! A baby had always meant to her a home, a woman's life, something to love without condition or deception, and something that would love her back, just as much.

If she had a baby, then she would never again dress as a man. She would make her way and she would provide for her baby because she would have to, and with her strength of arm and mind she knew they would be all right. If she could not have Frederick, or Jacob, then she could have her baby and together they would face the wicked world.

Anne's baby had been born and Mary had held it and it had given her just the briefest taste of what it would be like to hold her own baby in her arms, to nourish it with her body. It was a lovely feeling, like stepping from a night of freezing rain into a warm kitchen with fire blazing, it was a love so profound that it could only happen between mother and child, that sacred bond.

But instead they would take her child away. She would give birth and her child would be taken from her arms and carried off to some place, where, she knew not. She would stand on the gallows, the rope around her neck, and in her mind she would see nothing but her baby; cold, frightened, alone, crying for its mother, but its mother would never come.

She would go to her death knowing her baby was out there and beyond her protection and she felt sick with the thought of it.

For months that fear had built and weighed on her, though she tried to be brave and cheerful, for Anne's sake if nothing else. Then Annie had had her baby, and Mary had held the innocent little thing and it brought home again the reality of her own situation. She was filled with sorrow, brimming over with it, and it was nearly impossible for her to hide it.

And then on the morning that Big Bill Cormac came to take Annie home, Mary woke in the predawn hours, freezing, trembling with the cold. She struggled to pull the blankets more completely over her, to bury herself in their warmth, but still she shivered, and the beads of sweat stood out on her head and she felt as if she might fall down, even though she was lying on her bed of straw.

She came in and out of consciousness in those hours, and once she was able to sit up and see if something had happened, if some strange quirk of the weather had plunged the island of Jamaica into a preternatural freeze. But the sunlight streamed in through the bars, as it always did, and Anne was moving around and nothing seemed any different than it had been for the past eight months.

Mary pushed herself under the blankets again, huddled her arms against herself, clenched her teeth to keep them from chattering. *Oh, no, dear God, is this it?* she thought.

Later that morning she heard the prison door open, heard footsteps and then voices. They moved through her head like a dream, just sounds without any meaning. She was drenched in sweat, but she did not dare move, because every time she did, the chill ran right through and then the shivering would start, with its attendant misery.

Time did not seem to pass in its normal way, but later she heard her cell door open and heard Anne's voice, which was cheerful and odd. "Mary, dear, stir yourself! This could be the day of our salvation."

With some difficulty Mary rolled herself onto her back. She could hear her breath coming, shallow and fast, and she clenched her teeth again because they were chattering against the awful cold. She opened her eyes.

Anne was kneeling over her. She looked worried, terribly worried, and Mary could not recall having ever seen Anne look that way.

Behind her, near the door of the cell, Mary could see the kind jailor and a big man whom she did not recognize. She heard the jailor gasp.

"Mary, my dear," Anne whispered. "My father has come. He is going to take us out of this place."

Mary nodded and smiled as best as she could. "God bless you, Annie . . ." she said, and her voice was hoarse. "You will have another chance. Rogues . . . like us . . . do not often get a second chance."

"We, Mary dear. We will have a second chance."

Mary shook her head. "No. No. I am done for. The fever . . . Go. Go now."

Tears were coming down Anne's cheeks, running in two perfect wet lines down her fine skin. "No, Mary, I will not leave you . . ." she said, but Mary could hear the conviction going from her voice.

"You must. You have a baby now, and she needs her mother."

"Mary. Her name will be Mary."

Mary tried to smile, hoped that she had managed at least to convey the intent. "Then I shall live on. Go now, Annie. Go back to your home."

Anne took Mary's hand in hers, and Mary thought her hands felt so warm against her own cold flesh. Anne was sobbing, Mary realized. She had never seen that before. "God bless you, Mary. God bless you, my sister . . ."

"God bless you, sister Anne. Go and live for us both."

And then, exhausted, Mary closed her eyes, and when she opened them again, it was dark, and Anne was gone.

Time held no sort of logic for Mary. She lay in the straw in a misery of cold and sweat, sometimes conscious, sometimes not, sometimes tortured by weird and undulating dreams. At times she would wake and it would be daytime and at times it would be night, and she had no notion of its passing from one to the other.

Once she woke to find the jailor standing over her, a worried look on his face, and beside him, kneeling down and holding her wrist, the doctor who had once confirmed her pregnancy.

She looked at the doctor, who looked off into the middle distance and shook his head. He laid her wrist down on the straw and stood.

"Jail fever," he said to the jailor as if she were not there. "It will not be much longer."

Mary woke later and he was gone and she could not tell if he had really been there at all. It was daytime, and the beam of solid light was coming in through the bars and it looked warm, but she was very cold and very, very sad that she would die and never hold her own baby in her arms.

And then, as if she had stepped into another room, her teeth stopped chattering and she felt warm all over.

Not warm like she was standing in front of a fire and being warmed from the outside, but rather warm from within, like the fire was inside her, not burning her, just warming her and making her comfortable and happy.

She opened her eyes and smiled and looked up at the whitewashed ceiling of her cell. The sun had to be close to setting. It was growing dark in there, around the edges of her vision.

Then, along with the warmth, Mary was filled with a great happiness, a joy that started in her heart and radiated outward.

All along she had grieved at the thought of being separated from her baby, but now she understood that that was not going to happen. A good and just God would not allow her and her baby to be separated, would not allow their family—her and Frederick and their baby—to be pulled apart.

It was Frederick's child she held in her womb. The realization came like a flash of lightning. It had to be. Who else was there who could create life within her?

Their family.

And now they were all going to be together, all the disparate parts of their family joined again, the way it was supposed to be. It was a wondrous thing, and it made her profoundly happy.

Mary looked down at her swollen belly and her child who resided there. She put her hands on her baby and she smiled and in a whisper she said, "I'll take you away now, my little one. I'll take you away to a better place. I'll take you with me."

Historical Note

THE STORY OF ANNE BONNY, MARY READ, AND CALICO Jack Rackam is true. This book could not have been written otherwise; as it is, the coincidences and extraordinary events that make up their lives are quite incredible. If this story were pure fiction, it would be too much to believe.

In his *General History of the Robberies and Murders of the Most Notorious Pirates,* published in 1724, Captain Charles Johnson admits that

> the odd incidents of their rambling lives are such, that some may be tempted to think the whole story no better than a novel or romance, but since it is supported by many thousand witnesses . . . the truth of it can be no more contested, than that there are such men in the world, as Roberts and Blackbeard, who were pirates.

It is a tricky thing, writing a novel based on the lives of real people, and the end result is, invariably, an odd amalgam of history and fiction, not entirely one or the other.

Regarding the writing of history, the philosopher and historian R. G. Collingwood, in his book *The Idea of History,* says,

> . . . [I]n addition to selecting from among his authorities' statements those which he regards as important, the historian must in two ways go beyond what his authorities tell him. The one is the critical way . . . the other is the constructive way. I described constructive history as interpolating, between the statements borrowed from our authorities, other statements implied by them. Thus our authorities tell us that on

Caesar was in Rome and on a later day in Gaul; they tell us nothing of his journey from one place to the other, but we interpolate this with a perfectly good conscience.

Thus a history, and likewise a novel based on historical fact, is constructed from the writer's imagination of what took place, what Collingwood would call "a web of imaginative construction stretched between certain fixed points provided by the statements of the authorities."

The place where the novel differs from the straight history is in the extent to which the "web of imaginative construction" is indeed imagined, or made up, if you will. The historian will tell you that Caesar traveled to Gaul. The novelist will tell you what he (most likely) ate, drank, thought, and felt along the way.

Anne Bonny and Mary Read are the most well documented of all female pirates, but that is not saying much. The authorities, or sources of information about them, are few. In fact, there are only three of any genuine importance.

One of these is a proclamation for the arrest of Jack Rackam and crew for the theft of the sloop *William* out of Nassau Harbor on the 22nd of August, 1720. The published proclamation, issued by Governor Woodes Rogers, goes into much greater detail in describing the sloop than it does the pirates, who are merely mentioned by name.

What is of particular interest to the historian is that the proclamation includes ". . . two women, Anne Fulford, alias Bonny & Mary Read . . ." Here we find one of the only firm dates for the whereabouts of Jack, Mary, and Anne.

But more than that, the proclamation is singular proof that by that date it was well known that the two women were sailing with Jack Rackam and engaging in piracy. There has been much debate among historians as to whether the crew of Rackam's ship was aware of the women's gender, especially Mary's. Perhaps early on they were not. But clearly if Woodes Rogers knew their secret, then it is a safe bet that by that date others did as well, especially the women's fellow crew members.

The second source for their lives is the transcript of the trial of Jack Rackam, et al., and that of Anne Bonny and Mary Read (tried separately), and of the unfortunate turtle hunters who were taken up with Rackam and his band when Barnet captured them. The trial transcripts are fascinating documents, and arguably the only genuine primary sources, that is, the only actual eyewitness accounts by people who we can be reasonably certain saw Anne, Mary, and Jack in action.

In those pages are firsthand accounts of the women's participation in piracy, their being "both very profligate, cursing and swearing much, and very ready and willing to do any thing on board."

There are the words of Dorothy Thomas, who told the court,

> . . . the two women, prisoners at the bar, were on board the said sloop, and wore men's jackets and long trousers, and handkerchiefs tied around their heads, and that each of them had a machete and pistol in their hands, and cursed and swore at the men to murther [*sic*] the deponent; and they should kill her, to prevent her coming against them . . .

Thomas is the only documented person to recognize Anne and Mary for women when they were dressed as men. There is also the testimony of the Frenchmen who saw Anne and Mary dress as men for a fight and as women other times.

This documentation is in many ways the most interesting and compelling as it is the most indisputably authentic. In this novel, all of the astoundingly dull official court language, as well as the names of the officials involved and much of the proceedings and exchanges reproduced in this book, were taken directly from the trial transcripts.

Unfortunately, the transcripts cover only the very end of Anne and Mary's piratical career, no more than three months. For the rest we must look to the third and most important source, *A General History of the Robberies and Murders of the Most Notorious Pirates.*

A General History, a meticulous documentation of the lives of a number of pirates, was published in 1724 and was an instant hit. The book is credited to a Captain Charles Johnson, though many believe that Johnson was actually a nom de plume for the famous novelist Daniel Defoe. Whoever the author was, he knew pirates, and since the book's publication there has been much evidence to corroborate the authenticity of Johnson's work. *A General History* is the foundation for most of our current knowledge about the early-eighteenth-century buccaneers.

The childhoods and early lives of Mary and Anne are taken from *A General History.* It is certainly true that the accuracy of Johnson's account becomes more suspect the further back he goes. It is likely that Johnson (or Defoe) spoke to people with first or secondhand knowledge of the women's pirate activity, and certainly witnessed their trial or read the transcripts. In regards to their childhoods, however, he was in all likelihood simply repeating common tales. But true or not, it is all we have.

One of the frustrating aspects of *A General History* is that Johnson does not integrate the stories of Jack, Mary, and Anne, but tells them in separate chapters and seems to purposely avoid any overlap. Thus in the chapter on Mary Read, when discussing her going to sea again after her husband's death, he will say, "It happened that this Ship was taken by *English* Pyrates, and *Mary Read* was the only *English* Person on board, they kept her amongst them . . ." without ever saying if the pirate was Rackam. In the chapter concerning Jack he does not mention the women at all until the very end, so that he can give the story a sensational twist, with two of the pirates pleading their bellies.

The result of this is that it is very difficult to piece together a time line for the three: when they met and what parts of their stories happened before or after they were all together. Some historians, for instance, would argue that Anne went to Cuba and had her first baby before she met Mary. But I can find no evidence one way or the other, and so I went with what was best from a fiction standpoint, and put the women there together.

(Incidentally, the scene with the Cuban soldiers coming to arrest the pirates, and Mary's subsequent dispatching of them, is the only major incident in the book that I boldly and shamelessly fabricated. Nothing like it ever happened.)

Just as the sources described above are used to assemble the facts of our pirates' lives, they are also used to divine a sense of their personalities. Some readers already familiar with Anne, Mary, and Jack may well disagree with my characterization, and they are certainly welcome to do so. The personalities I have imbued these people with, however, are not purely my imagination, but based on evidence in their stories.

Jack sailed as quartermaster to Charles Vane, as vicious and effective a pirate as ever lived. By the end of his career, Jack was in command of a tiny crew taking fishing boats and the like, pretty small beer for any self-respecting buccaneer. Johnson tells us that when Barnet came for them, Jack and the others were below and would not come out and fight. Only Anne and Mary held their ground.

Johnson also tells us (though there is nothing in the trial transcript to verify this) that the most damning evidence against Mary came from Rackam's deposition against her. In the parlance of the gangster movies, he ratted her out. These are all clues that lead us to an educated guess about Jack's character.

Likewise with Anne, who ran away from a life of wealth with the penniless James Bonny. Johnson describes Anne as a woman "not altogether so reserved in Point of Chastity," who sailed as a pirate and stood and faced all of Barnet's men when the others had fled below. Her vicious parting line to Jack, "I am sorry to see you here, but if you had fought like a man, you need not hang like a dog," comes from Johnson.

A General History also gives us insights into Mary's character, the most telling perhaps being her riding out with her (unnamed) tentmate, whom she loved, to keep him from harm in battle, and her fighting a duel to protect her (also unnamed) lover when she sailed aboard Jack's ship. Mary's feelings about her marriage in conscience, and her never having committed adultery, are also from *A General History.*

The place where Calico Jack Rackam was hanged is known today as "Rackam's Cay." Mary Read died of fever in prison in the spring of 1721. It is not known for certain what became of Anne, but the general consensus is that she was paroled thanks to the influence of her father and returned to Charleston, South Carolina, where she lived the rest of her days in obscurity.

There are no major events in *The Sweet Trade* (save the aforementioned scene with the Cuban soldiers) that are not based on some primary source. For those who would like to examine the roots of this story, there are several editions of Johnson's *A General History of the Pirates* (as it is generally called) that are currently in print and easily had. Some of these list Johnson as the author, some Defoe.

On the pages of *A General History* the reader will see the bare bones of the story, the "certain fixed points" which I have used as a skeleton for this book. With this outline I have done what the novelist can do and the historian cannot, fictionalized the historical events and, I hope, come somewhat close to the truth of these three remarkable people.